"I opened up my new copy of *Hunter Brown and the Consuming Fire,* not knowing what to expect from this sequel to *The Secret of the Shadow*. From the first page I realized I was in the grip of another irresistible, fast-paced tale of adventure and lessons learned. Characters, both new and familiar, inspiring and despicable, populate this story of a chosen few who must execute a sacred duty assigned by the Author himself. Twists, turns, terror and comic moments will enthrall readers of any age. Definitely addicting!"

Susanne Greenman, middle school educator

"Easily enjoyed by all ages. The way the Miller brothers continue to create a unique transport into another world and weave the truths of God throughout its pages really makes this second book in their Hunter Brown series spellbinding. However, it should come with a warning label: May Cause Sleeplessness. It was hard to read just a little bit at a time. Even reading it to my grandchildren before bed was difficult as they always wanted just one more chapter and I would easily agree with them. Just one question, though: How long before the next book comes out?"

Barbara Tillery - grandmother and chaplain's wife

"Some books you just read. Other books make you jump in the story and live it. The Miller Brothers have this kind of gift; they make their stories so real you feel the swoosh of the blade and the clang of the hammer, a little too close for comfort. But you also feel the presence of Light—strong enough to pierce every shadow—a fire blazing with deep truth."

"Bongo Rod" Butler, The Coconut Hut Radio Show

"We were so excited to read *Hunter Brown and the Consuming Fire*, we felt like we were in the story too! We were hooked after the very first page!"

Micah and Tabitha Bertrand, ages 10 and 8

"My family, from youngest to oldest, enjoys reading each book the Miller Brothers have written. Each one is filled with descriptive language and wonderful lessons. The Codebearers Series is a well loved favorite in my house!"

Michelle Bertrand - mother of Micah & Tabitha

"It is unique to find a book that both my son and I enjoy equally. Rarer still is one that takes us on our own journey from fun to faith as when we follow Hunter and his friends on their adventures. These books are so thrilling that my son won't stop reading them, and so intriguing that they cause him to ask questions about the role of faith in his own life. Best of all, the excitement over Hunter's adventures leaves my son dreaming of not only the next Codebearer book, but of the book *he* may write someday. Thanks, Miller Brothers, for a book that helps my son love reading so much he wants to write!"

Susan Foucher, pastor's wife and mother of two

"This book had me hooked from page one, kept me flying through the pages and left me begging for more. There is no doubt about it, the Miller Brothers have mastered the art of storytelling. This is more than a youth fiction book—it's a story for all ages."

Scott Kaste, father of four fans of the Miller Bros
and president of CrossStaff Publishers

"Excitement leaps off the pages! This book was so much fun, even my dad liked it!"

Hayden Dobyns, age 11

"Me too!"

Bryce Dobyns, age 9 (Hayden's brother)

Dear Friend,

As you may recall, my first adventure in Solandria concluded with the scattering of my friends (the Codebearer Resistance), my failure to destroy the Shadow lord, Venator, and ultimately, in my unfortunate death through the uniting of the Bloodstone halves. In other words I pretty much made a mess of things but hey, at least I recovered the Bloodstone.

Before I died Ariad came to my rescue and fulfilled the Bloodstone curse. Even though I still died, I believe he saved me from a fate worse than death itself.

Thank goodness, the Author chose to rewrite me. He promised to give me a new story and returned me to the City of Destiny in the realm of the Veil. I returned to my life as it was before and waited expectantly for another adventure to find me.

For three months I waited but still the Author was silent. It was the silence before a terrible storm, one that would change the story of Solandria and the Veil FOREVER.

Hunter Brown

THE CODEBEARERS SERIES™

THE MILLER BROTHERS

Warner Press™

CONNECT • EQUIP • INSPIRE

Dedicated to

Our Faithful Readers

YOUR WORDS OF ENCOURAGEMENT
HAVE BEEN A FLINT OF INSPIRATION.
MAY THE WORDS OF THIS BOOK
SPARK A FLAME
IN YOU.

This is the second book in The Codebearers Series™. The characters and events in this book are fictional, and any similarity to actual persons or events is coincidental.

The Codebearers Series™ 2: *Hunter Brown and the Consuming Fire*

Published by Warner Press, Inc, Anderson, IN 46012
Warner Press and "WP" logo is a trademark of Warner Press, Inc

ISBN-13: 978-1-59317-357-9

Editors: Karen Rhodes, Robin Fogle, Arthur Kelly
Creative Director: Curtis D. Corzine

Library of Congress Cataloging-in-Publication Data

Miller, Christopher, 1976-
Hunter Brown and the consuming fire / The Miller Brothers. -- 1st ed.
p. cm. -- (The Codebearers series ; 2)
Summary: Armed with his Veritas sword and following the words of the Author, Hunter returns to Solandria where, together with new friends Trista, Rob, and Boojum, he races to save Hope and bolster the Resistance before the brutal Xaul can reach her.
ISBN 978-1-59317-357-9 (alk. paper)
[1. Magic--Fiction. 2. Friendship--Fiction. 3. Space and time--Fiction. 4. Books and reading--Fiction. 5. Adventure and adventurers--Fiction.] I. Miller, Allan, 1978- II. Title.
PZ7.M61255Htx 2009
[Fic]--dc22

2009021968

Printed in Canada
2009 – First Edition

www.warnerpress.org

www.codebearers.com
The Codebearers Series™
Lumination Studios

ACKNOWLEDGEMENTS:

No story is ever written once. *Consuming Fire* has been no exception. From the first chapter to the last, (and all the rewrites in between), we have benefitted from an intrepid team of editors (at Warner Press) and encouragers (family, friends, colleagues, and faithful readers) who dared to take this journey with us. The book you are holding right now is a testament of their dedication to us, for which we are truly humbled.

To our families - When we set off on this journey you cheered us on. When we needed time to write you created space. When the road got longer than any of us imagined you stuck by us. In short, you believed in us and we know you still do. No amount of words could ever express our full gratitude as husbands, fathers, and sons.

To our "family" at Warner Press - You consistently went above and beyond your job descriptions to support us throughout. Thank you Regina, Karen, Robin, Curt, Mike, Gwynne and the rest of the team, for your shared vision, your excellence, and your hearts!

To the "real" Codebearers - It is always an honor to hear from readers who enjoyed our book, and an even greater honor to have them volunteer their time to help us. Wow! Special thanks to our Codebearers.com moderators: BladeBearer, Ricki, Mike and active Web site members agentmonkie17, Aatashan, Ashley, Aviad, Caption Thunder, Cypher, Disarray, Glory90210, Luke, redwallgirl, rosmist, shelly, The Jelf, TTUG, Zachary, zaylee, and Zeeb. You all have made the Codebearers.com Web site a great place to hang out.

To all of the faithful readers of The Codebearers Series, we mean every word of this book's dedication to you. ***You rock!***

Contents

Chapter I

Reforging the Sword

Like untamed fire the ghostly menace rushed across the rocky forest floor. For all his speed, the figure moved with surprising silence beneath the pale moonlight. Only the occasional crack of a twig underfoot or the gentle brush of his cloak against the underbrush betrayed his approach. To the untrained ear these sounds would simply be dismissed as the wind or the falling of autumn leaves. But no one was listening—no one would hear him coming. The thought emboldened his steps and he quickened his pace.

The forest thinned sharply as he neared a canyon's edge. The broad expanse between the figure and the far side of the gulf was easily fifty feet but he showed no sign of slowing at the sight of it. Every hurried footstep brought him closer to the deadly gap. At the last possible moment, the figure leaped recklessly out over the gulf and into the massive expanse between it. Crossing his arms over his chest, he allowed instincts to kick in.

Like a gymnast he executed his motions with precision. Spinning and twisting through the air, he flew an unnatural distance toward the far side of the canyon wall, landing squarely against its side with both feet. His head jolted instantly away as he readied his counter jump. In a glance, he targeted a small cave ledge eighty feet down and launched himself back out over the expanse a second time. As planned, he landed safely on the rocky ledge below.

Gathering himself from the masterful leap, he rose slowly, reaching his full seven-foot stature. His timing couldn't have been better. A small cadre of armed goblins hobbled its way down the narrow switchback trail that led to the ledge he now occupied. There were six, each of them dressed in modest armor, carrying crooked spears.

Obviously they were not expecting anyone, as their expressions ranged from confused to terrified. Raising their weapons, the six scurried over to guard the mouth of the cave from the unwelcome intruder.

To them, he was a giant—a ghostly sight dressed completely in white from head to toe. In stark contrast, his skin was as black as soot, which made his face appear invisible beneath the white hood. Only his gleaming silver eyes hovered there, floating brightly in the blackness. The thing that most marked his appearance, however, was a waist-wide belt and enormous stomach plate. It was embossed with the only splash of color on his otherwise monochromatic outfit, a crimson *X*.

"Who goes there!" the tallest of the guards commanded somewhat weakly. "This is a highly restricted area."

Paying no mind, the stranger began walking straight for the entrance of the cave. He continued steadily forward with carefully paced steps until he was within inches of their trembling spears.

The leader of the guard cut to the front of their formation and toughened his voice, "I'm warning you, stranger! No one can pass beyond this point. It is forbidden!"

Again there was no response. The man stood in place as stoic as ever, daring them to attack with his daunting silence. This angered the guard even more.

"What are you, deaf? Didn't you hear what I just said? Be gone or else…ack…" His tirade was cut dreadfully short as he grasped his neck in agony and keeled over. The others watched in disbelief as their leader writhed in pain from some unseen force. With a flash of movement the attacker vanished in the commotion.

"Stop…ack…him…!" were the final words that slipped past the dying guard's lips before his body fell limp. The remaining goblins turned around in terror, unsure of where the killer had gone or even how he had killed. High above, the white and black assailant hung unnoticed from the ceiling of the cave like a spider, watching the confusion unfold below.

"He…he's…vanished!" one said at last.

"It's a phantom…!" the fattest shrieked nervously, toying with a stone medallion that hung around his neck.

"No," the third scolded. "This one is real alright and he's here somewhere, I'm sure of it." Then he lowered his voice and commanded the troops in a half whisper. "Spread out and search the perimeter of the ledge. Gorgic, you stay to the center and remember, no matter what happens, protect the keystone."

Gorgic, by far the roundest goblin of the bunch, nodded anxiously above his double-chin, clutching the medallion tightly in his hand. His eyes darted left and right as the others dispersed to examine the ledge.

Cautiously, the four began inching their way out toward the edge of the precipice, searching for the invisible threat. Their plan was horribly flawed and unknowingly provided an advantage to their attacker who had dropped back to the floor unnoticed. He slipped into the shadow of the cave and removed four tiny black daggers from his belt pouch. With pinpoint accuracy the attacker hurled the daggers at his foes, killing all four in the process. Only Gorgic remained, still fidgeting with the medallion. Watching as his companions fell, the last goblin panicked and scurried back toward the cave entrance in hopes of finding shelter. It was the wrong move.

The mysterious assassin appeared out of the shadow of the cave like a ghost, blocking Gorgic's path. Sliding to a stop, the frightened goblin barely managed to hurl his spear at the man before slipping awkwardly onto his ample rump. In a shocking display of power, the intruder snatched the spear out of midair, only inches from his chest. Gorgic was stunned. Sitting up, Gorgic frantically scooted away from the man who now held his spear, turned against him.

"Stay away, Ph-ph-phantom!" the guard whimpered, trying his best to keep a safe distance from the ruthless attacker.

Without so much as a word the ghostly menace stepped forward. With each advance the guard was forced closer to the edge of the pit until at last he could move no further without falling. Glancing over his shoulder, he watched as a few stray pebbles slipped off the edge and dropped down into the blackness below. He was out of options.

"Wh-who are you?" Gorgic asked. "What do you want?"

When at last the stranger spoke, it was with a strained whispery voice that sounded only half alive. "I am Xaul. I want the keystone."

"K-k-keystone?" the goblin stammered. "What keys-s-stone?"

Xaul was in no mood for games.

"Listen, grub, I'll make this easy on you. Either give me the keystone medallion so you can live, or I will kill you and take it from you."

Sweat ran down Gorgic's brow as he pondered his choice. Neither option sounded entirely fair to the unlucky goblin, but he had sworn on his life as a Shadow guard that no one would take the keystone. It was his mortal duty to protect it. Even if he failed and lived, he would likely be killed at the hands of his own commanders. Or worse yet, he'd face a fate worse than death from the dread Lord Sceleris, the serpent master the Shadow served. No, for Gorgic, failure was not an option.

Suddenly an idea came to mind.

"If you come a step closer, I-I-I'll…I'll jump. Yes, that's what I'll do! Then you'll never get the keystone."

For a moment Xaul paused, taken aback by the goblin's bold plan. He needed the keystone; without it he would never pass the first gate. Gorgic swallowed hard and glanced over the edge again. His eyes were full of fear; he was bluffing. It was time to take action before Gorgic could convince himself to jump.

"Suit yourself!" Xaul scowled, jamming the spear forcefully into the ground between the goblin's legs. A small crack in the ledge began to grow on either side of the spear, accompanied by the dreadful sound of cracking clay and shifting stone. The ledge was crumbling. Within seconds the surface gave way beneath the goblin's weight and fell into the abyss.

Gorgic scrambled to save himself but there was nothing to hold onto. Xaul reached out and caught hold of the medallion flailing around Gorgic's neck. Dangling over the ledge, the fat goblin hung by his neck, choking from the keystone's leather cord. Gorgic clutched the cord in desperation to keep himself from falling and to relieve the tension that threatened to choke the life from him.

Xaul pulled him up until Gorgic was able to grab hold of the now shortened ledge. Then, pulling out a knife, Xaul severed the leather cord, retrieving the keystone for himself.

"You should have taken the first option!" Xaul exclaimed, glancing down at the struggling Gorgic who could barely hold his own weight. Turning on his heel, Xaul left the goblin dangling helplessly above the chasm and marched into the mouth of the cave. He needn't concern himself with killing this worthless grub. Gravity would soon take care of him.

The cavern was not terribly deep; Xaul reached its end within a few hundred feet. Nestled in the back wall was a narrow stone slab—a door. It bore no markings of consequence, no handle or doorknob. In fact, few would recognize it as a door at all. Xaul knew better—he had been here once before.

Gripping the keystone in his palm, Xaul held it out toward the door and pressed gently. Magically, the door repelled the keystone like a reverse magnet. Gliding the device around the outer edge of the door line, Xaul listened until a subtle *clunk* was heard. The door had unlocked.

Tucking the keystone into his belt, Xaul slammed his shoulder into the stone slab. The hinges were stiff with disuse, but after much effort the rock door finally groaned opened, revealing a long, dark, cobweb-laced tunnel on the other side. Shutting the door for safety, Xaul found himself concealed in a tunnel of blackness. His eyes adjusted quickly as his nocturnal vision kicked in. That was what made him an excellent assassin; he could see when others couldn't.

With careful movements he made his way through the maze of unmarked tunnels ahead, even though some were only slightly wider than footpaths carved between cold rock walls. Eventually, Xaul caught the distant sound of clanging metal—a hammer and anvil.

Compelled by the unsettling tone, Xaul approached, letting

the eerie notes guide him through the blackness. Soon, a flicker of firelight reflected off the far end of the tunnel walls ahead. As he neared, a peculiar vile-smelling odor filled the air. The ground and walls began to grow visibly blacker even as the light intensified.

The tunnel opened into a large circular room. The room itself was in a state of disarray. The walls were coated in thick black soot that gave off a horrible odor. Apart from the haphazardly organized spread of tools on a small wooden table, it was downright messy—the den of a blacksmith. Several crates full of wrought iron bars were scattered across the room, and a roaring fire pit commanded the majority of the far wall, billowing smoke up and out of the room through a hole in the ceiling. The only comforts in the room were a grimy chair, a basin of water and an overturned cot.

"Hello, Xaul," a low and rumbling voice beckoned from the center of the room. There, standing over an iron pedestal, was the forger himself—a hunch-backed troll well along in years, but still very strong. The troll's back was turned to the doorway but he had sensed Xaul's presence nonetheless. "I always knew you would come back! How long has it been, ten years?"

"Twelve," Xaul replied coldly.

"Yes, that seems about right," the old troll replied. Turning slowly to face his guest, the forger lowered his hammer. His face was worn and pale. "Please have a seat," he offered, motioning to the filthy chair. Xaul thought better of it and chose to remain standing.

"I didn't come to visit, Peralys," he stated matter-of-factly.

"No, I don't suppose you did—no one ever does, you know!" He sighed, wiping his sweaty brow with a soot-blackened rag that left a smudge on his already dirty face. "So then, what is it?"

"This," Xaul said proudly, removing the hilt of a sword from his belt. He held it out to Peralys, but the man didn't move.

"Bring it here," the forger instructed, extending his outstretched palm and staring blankly at Xaul. Only then did Xaul notice the old troll's eyes were clouded over—he was completely blind.

Moving closer, Xaul pressed the hilt into the troll's grip. The troll turned it over in his large wrinkled hands. Xaul watched as the troll's fingers examined each feature. The markings were simple, yet defined. The grip of the hilt was smooth and rounded, the guard slanted slightly upward. In the center of the guard near the top of the grip was a symbol: three intersecting *V's*—the Author's mark. Peralys recognized it instantly.

"A Veritas Sword? Where did you get this?"

Not interested in being questioned, Xaul changed the subject. "That doesn't matter. What matters is whether or not you can re-forge it to my will."

"Reforging a Veritas Sword?" Peralys grinned. "Well now, that would be a challenge. I can't say it has ever been done before."

"Don't lie to me, Peralys," Xaul growled, his tone telling of his lust for power.

Closing his blind eyes, the old troll contemplated the task. "Even if I were able to successfully reforge this weapon, it would still be useless to you. A Veritas Sword has a will of its own, a hidden power that the Codebearers claim comes from..."

"Yes, yes...the Code of Life, I know!" Xaul interrupted. "I don't need you to lecture me on the misguided beliefs of the fools. What I need to know is if you can remove its allegiance—make it listen to me."

Peralys opened his blind eyes at last and grinned. "I am sure of it!" He hobbled across the room to the fire pit and held the sword out over the flames. The weapon gleamed to life in the heat of the fire, revealing a blade, which was invisible before. The softening shape of the sword's hilt burned vibrant orange, the color of molten lava, and the forger moved the steaming weapon to the anvil.

Picking up his blackened hammer, Peralys began to pound out a rhythm on the glowing hilt. The steady, pulsing beat seemed to switch notes from time to time, as if the hammer itself were singing a slow and melancholy tune. But there was something else hidden within the song of the hammer, something strangely dark and terribly powerful.

Clang, clang, clang!

Xaul watched with anticipation as the once golden sword began to change in appearance. The metal slowly darkened and twisted beneath the beat of Peralys' hammer, until at last it was black and curved. After safely passing his hand over the hilt where the invisible blade should have been, he smiled and handed the newly forged sword to its new master.

Xaul took the now altered hilt of the Veritas Sword and swung it hard at the table beside him. Nothing happened.

Peralys laughed. "It is as I said, the sword has a will of its own. Perhaps with patience and training you will learn to…"

Whooosh!

The blade of the sword flashed to life in Xaul's hands as he severed the table in two. The shape of the blade was as dark as midnight, silhouetted only by a faint indigo hue that glowed around the space where the absent blade might be.

Peralys was shocked. "Impressive…"

"I'm a fast learner."

Peralys knew there was more to it than that but Xaul was not one to share. "Your passion for the Old Way burns in your heart, Xaul. Tell me, what do you hope to accomplish with the blade? It will not change what happened to your people."

Xaul tensed at the mention of the fate of his tribe. "No, but it can bring justice…and reclaim what was once foolishly lost. This sword can bring hope to my cause—a restoration promised long ago."

"The eternal flame," Peralys said with a smile."You seek to find the eternal flame?"

Xaul shifted in place, uneasy with the troll's knowledge of his people's beliefs. "Who told you about the flame?"

Peralys moved back toward the anvil and picked up his hammer once more. "You forget we were once allies. Our relationship wasn't always this way, you know—we used to be friends.

Xaul pondered Peralys' remarks in silence. Nodding his head, the troll turned away with a sigh.

"Yes, things are different now. I'm afraid your mission is impossible, Xaul; even the Shadow's most skilled seekers could not find the flame. It is a lost cause."

"But I am not Shadow…I am Xin."

"Yes," Peralys nodded, "and a proud race at that, the Xin. But you are the last of your kind—the age of the Xin is over. Enemies of the Shadow cannot hide forever. It is a wonder you have survived this long. Why don't you join us? There is strength in numbers, Xaul."

"My business is my own," Xaul said coldly, raising the darkened Veritas Sword once more. Peralys sensed Xaul's intention but did nothing to stop him.

"I see," the old troll said sadly, understanding his death was imminent. Before Xaul could strike him down, Peralys made one last request. "Tell me, if you are successful in finding the flame, whose sword will release it? To whom did it once belong?"

Xaul paused for a moment and answered with a low angry tone.

"His name was Caleb."

With a flash of indigo light Peralys fell to the ground, his hand still clutching his hammer—the very one that reforged the sword that killed him.

Part 1

Chapter 2

One of Those Days

"Hunter, you lazy bum, for the last time get up!" my sister's shrill voice called from outside my room. The flimsy wooden door that separated me from the hallway shook loudly as she pounded it to exaggerate her point.

"Mmmmmph," I groaned weakly, hoping to convince her I was awake. Surprisingly, it worked. The groan had just enough force in it to satisfy her demands and send her tromping down the hall to finish her own morning routine. It was the same drill every morning. She'd knock another three times before I *actually* had to be awake. Without opening my eyes, I rolled over for a few more precious minutes of sleep.

Summer break had ended too soon for my liking—two weeks ago to be exact—and my body still wasn't used to waking up so early.

Unfortunately, now that Mom had found a new job that required her to catch a carpool at o-dark-thirty every morning, my sister, Emily, was put in charge of getting us out the door on time, a task she seemed to relish. She took particular pleasure in bossing me around lately. One thing was clear—the older she got, the less I liked her. We used to get along fairly well, but the last few years had really changed things. She was definitely the last person I wanted waking me up.

For starters, she was one of those peppy morning people, highly energetic and incredibly annoying. She expected me to be the same, but we couldn't have been more different. She hardly ever set her alarm, often bragging about how her "internal clock" woke her up every day on time without fail. I, on the other hand…well, let's just say I was a ten-times-snooze-button kind of guy. It's not that I'm lazy or anything, just more of a night owl.

Emily absolutely excelled at school. It was her talent in life. So, while she effortlessly produced straight *A's* out of thin air, I struggled to maintain passing grades. I was determined to do better this year, if only for the sake of saying I tried. Honestly, for the first time in years I actually wanted to do well, but old habits die hard and I often found my mind drifting in class despite my best intentions.

As a sophomore, I was still trying to find my own stride. Being a prankster last year had upped my cool factor significantly, but it also had gotten me into a lot of trouble with Cranton, the school bully, not to mention the principal. Over the summer I decided to try and find better ways to gain attention. So far, I was not making any progress.

Blam, blam, blam!

The pounding on my bedroom door began again.

"You better not be asleep again," Emily scolded from the hallway.

"Okay, I'm up!" I groaned angrily, still rubbing the sleep from my eyes. I ran my fingers through my scraggly blond hair and let out a slow sigh.

"I'm not your alarm clock you know," Emily hollered back through the hollow door. I was too tired to respond.

"Are you sure you're up?" she asked.

"Yes!" I moaned. "Leave me alone!"

"Fine, get yourself to school then; I'm leaving! Just be sure to lock up before you go."

Glancing groggily at the alarm clock, I nearly fell out of my bed at what it read: 7:43! How could it be so late already? School started in a little over fifteen minutes and I was just getting up!

Wham!

The back door slammed as Emily left the house in a hurry. If I didn't catch up, I was going to miss my ride and end up being terribly late. There was no time to delay.

Quickly sniffing a pair of jeans from the floor, I threw them on and darted down the hall. With what little time I had, the shirt I'd slept in would have to do. Grabbing my backpack and stepping into my shoes, I launched myself through the back door, hoping to catch up with Emily before it was too late. I exited just in time to watch the taillights of her car disappear around the corner, taking my only hope of being on time with them.

I threw my bag down in disgust. How could she let me sleep in like that?

School wasn't that far away, but fifteen minutes was more than pushing it. To make matters worse, my first class was biology—Mr. Tanner's class. Tanner was anything but a pushover. He was an intensely drab person, passionate about rules and order—not the type of guy to cut me some slack for being a few minutes late.

I had no time to waste. I quickly located my skateboard and

rode off down the street, searching for every shortcut imaginable. There was little hope of arriving at school on time, but I had to try.

The crisp morning reminded me that change was already in the air. Fall was coming. It was usually my favorite time of year, but not this year. There was already enough change in my life to go around.

For starters, my own friends seemed a bit more distant lately. Stubbs had actually moved to a private school in another town, and Stretch, who used to be my closest friend, was finding other things to spend his time on. We still hung out on occasion, but it wasn't the same as before. What's worse is that even though we both had traveled through the Author's Writ together, his decision to exit through the green door had erased his memory of Solandria entirely. He remembered nothing that had happened in our previous adventure, which meant I was the only one who seemed to believe in the magic of the book and the powerful Author who wrote it.

Instead, Stretch had finally decided to start a chess club at Destiny High, which was a big step for him but took most of his free time and left little opportunity to hang out anymore.

Beyond my friend trouble, there had been plenty of change on the home front as well. Mom had recently decided it would be better for us to sell the house and move into a small apartment nearer her work. So, in addition to losing my friends, I would soon be losing my home and my memories of having grown up here.

Through all the changes, Hope's medallion, Dad's broken watch and the Author's Writ were the three items I treasured the most. They were all that remained from my previous adventure and my only hope of one day returning to Solandria. Sadly, the book no longer seemed to possess the magic it once held. I read passages from it every day, but try as I might I had not been able to see beyond the words as I had before.

In my mind it all seemed so real, but the topic of a parallel realm was a subject not easily discussed at home or with my friends. To put it bluntly, they all thought I was crazy. Then again, who wouldn't if you told them you had been to another realm that co-existed with our own where you fought off a dark enemy and were saved by an old man who claimed to be the son of the Author.

Riding down the final hill, I had a sudden feeling that I was being watched. I might have shaken it off except for the fact that it wasn't the first time I'd felt that way. The feeling came and went a lot lately. Once before, as I was walking home from school, I thought I spotted a flash of black following me from a distance but I never was able to figure out what it was. This time I glanced over my shoulder, but as expected, nobody was there.

I arrived at school as the annoying buzzer, generally referred to as the hall bell, sounded loudly—class was starting. Without hesitation, I chucked my skateboard carelessly into the bushes by the front steps and raced down the hallway in hopes of making it to my home room before Mr. Tanner marked me late. To the amazement of everyone in the classroom and myself, I barged through the door just as Mr. Tanner announced my name in dutiful monotone.

"Brown, Hunter?"

"Here!" I gasped, catching my breath in the doorway.

Mr. Tanner turned his head only slightly in my direction and frowned. His beady eyes looked tiny behind his horn-rimmed glasses—covered in part by the reflection of the fluorescent lights in his thick lenses. His silver hair was slicked back perfectly and a number two pencil was set over one ear. As always, he wore his signature black tie, which featured a DNA double helix in its design. A simple black sweater vest covered his pinstriped, short sleeve dress shirt. The outfit was practically his uniform, and I often wondered if he had any other choices in his wardrobe at all.

"Well, Mr. Brown, I'm glad to see you decided to join us," he observed as he checked my name off of his attendance chart with a hint of displeasure in his mechanical motions. "And just in time too, how…spontaneous of you." With that he glanced a second time at his watch and shook it rapidly as if wishing it were a few minutes slow. He clearly felt robbed of the pleasure of marking me tardy.

"Sorry sir, it won't happen again," I replied, gasping for breath and expecting that would be the end of it. But he wasn't quite finished.

"While you are *technically* on time, Mr. Brown, I would rather prefer that you adapt your routine so as NOT to test my patience by showing up at the last possible moment," he scolded.

"Yes sir," I answered as I began to make my way toward the back of the classroom.

"In fact, let this be a reminder to us all; the here and now is all we have. Let's make the most of it, shall we?"

Precisely as he finished, my foot caught the leg of a desk chair and I tumbled to the floor. The classroom erupted in a scattered round of chuckles. Mr. Tanner tried desperately to regain their attention and to continue the roll call. I took my seat at the back of the room and tried to blend in. Stretch sat in front as usual. He looked back and raised an eyebrow as if to ask what happened. I shrugged him off.

When at last the roll was complete, Mr. Tanner set his clipboard down, cleared his throat and began his lesson for the day. As he spoke, he paced back and forth in front of his neatly organized desk, with his hands tucked snuggly behind his back.

"Throughout history the outcome of world events has been decided in part by secret messages. Because of secrets that were kept, and those that were not, wars have been won, dictators have been overthrown and the future of our world has been determined. From the hieroglyphics of ancient times to our modern alphabet, codes have been used to communicate. Of course, whenever there is a secret code there is also the desire to solve it…to crack the code, and learn its secrets."

He picked up a copy of our textbook, *Biology and You,* and held it over his head.

"Now, you are probably wondering why we're talking about history in a biology class. Actually, you might be surprised to learn that secret messages are as much a part of biology as they are a part of history—only more so. In fact, scientists have discovered a secret code hidden deep within our very cells. We call it…the Code of Life."

My ears perked at the mention of the Code of Life. After all, the Code of Life was something I had been taught about in Solandria by Sam and the others. According to the Author's Writ, the Code of Life was the manuscript of all life, written by the Author himself. I suddenly found new interest in what Mr. Tanner was saying.

"The Code of Life, or DNA as we call it, is the data sequence that exists in every living thing known to man. Over time, it has evolved into a highly complex code, nearly seven billion characters long, which establishes everything from the number of hairs on your head to the specific genetic traits passed from one generation to another. And the most amazing part of all is that this code, this supercomputer of data inside of you, all happened by pure…unadulterated…chance."

He paused for dramatic effect, though his voice lacked the charisma to give such a pause much impact. He then launched into a lengthy discussion about how amazing it was that the genetic code was responsible for so many varied forms of life. Most everyone in class slumped back in their chairs, ignoring his teaching and trying to catch a few more minutes of sleep at the start of the day.

Throughout his discussion, I couldn't help but think about what I had learned about the Code of Life not so very long ago. A voice from the past echoed in my mind.

Nothing comes from nothing...Every detail, down ta the very cells inside yer body, is a result of the Author's handiwork.

"In conclusion," Tanner said at last, sparking movement in the class for the first time since he started, "when you consider how many things had to go just our way in order for life to exist, well... you should feel very privileged and inspired to take advantage of every moment." He snapped the textbook shut and added, "Any questions?"

I raised my hand before I could talk myself out of it.

"Yes, Mr. Brown, what is it?" he inquired.

"Are you saying that the Code of Life...I mean, our DNA... just formed out of nothing?"

"Well...not directly. I'm saying that over time what once was nothing became the most simple form of something and mutated through random selection and eons of time into the complex sequence of genetic codes we know today are capable of creating life."

"But all by accident, right?" I asked.

"Yes, if you want to look at it that way—a series of wonderfully grand accidents." A smile of satisfaction crossed Mr. Tanner's lips, and he began scanning the room for another question. I raised my hand again.

"Yes, Mr. Brown," he said dryly.

"But what if it wasn't random?" I asked. "Isn't it more likely that there is an Author of the Code?"

At this everyone still awake turned to look at me.

Mr. Tanner was not distracted, "Ah yes, the theory of the Invisible Hand, the Author of Life or the Grand Architect as some call it. Yes that idea has been batted around for ages…though I must say it has been abandoned now for hundreds of years. Modern science is able to fill in the gaps to the point where we don't require the presence of any mastermind orchestrating our development—just time and chance are sufficient."

"But that's impossible!" I challenged, surprised at myself for saying it.

"I beg your pardon!" Mr. Tanner said, confounded by what he considered to be my lack of respect for his teaching.

"No offense, Mr. Tanner, but how on earth can something so complex and well-organized just happen on its own—from nothing?"

"I've already told you; given a sufficient amount of time anything is possible," he claimed.

"Like this book?" I asked, holding up a copy of our biology book. "Did it just happen to pop into existence as well?"

Mr. Tanner folded his arms in front of him and raised one of his bushy eyebrows. I expected him to scold me for speaking out, but surprisingly he took a different approach.

"I assume you are going somewhere with this," Tanner prodded.

"Well, you said that our DNA code is over 7 billion characters long, right? That's more than all of the letters in all of the words in this book combined."

"Yes…and your point is?"

"It just seems that everything you said about the complexity of the Code of Life points to the fact that it was intentionally made to be this way and not just a product of chaos and chance. After all, if a simple book can't write itself, how can we be expected to believe that living cells could have?"

Mr. Tanner said nothing. His arms were crossed and he stared at me with unblinking thought.

"What if we're not here by accident? What if we're part of something bigger and deeper? What if our world…and our lives are a story written for us to discover? I think the Code of Life is evidence that we might be part of a greater plan; that there is an Author who intended for us to exist and has a purpose for us. Every day is another chapter—another adventure waiting to be lived."

There was a short silence, followed by an eruption of laughter from the students around me.

"Dude, that's the stupidest thing I've ever heard," Cranton the school bully scoffed at me from two desks forward. "If our lives are part of a story like you said, then what is the point of getting up in the morning?"

"No kidding," another piped in. "What a depressing thought!"

The laughter continued as I shrunk back into my chair. Stretch didn't even turn around—too embarrassed to acknowledge me. Finally it was Mr. Tanner who spoke out.

"Now, now class; we must respect everyone's opinion no matter how strange it may seem to us."

Buzzzzzzzzzzzz.

The bell couldn't have come at a better time. Mr. Tanner tried to keep our attention for one last announcement about the next day's homework, but it was too late. The moment the bell had buzzed, the entire classroom moved for the door. I ducked into the stream of students and escaped the classroom unnoticed.

No sooner had I placed a foot in the hallway than a sharp tug on my backpack pulled me aside. I spun around and found myself face to face with Stretch, my last best friend. He was not happy.

"Dude, what were you thinking in there?" he challenged, obviously annoyed at something I had said.

"What do you mean?" I asked.

"You know—all that talk about the Author and stuff in class. I thought we agreed we were going to forget about it."

"No, you decided to forget about it when you walked through the green door. I *never* agreed to forget," I said, setting the record straight.

"Enough with the green door thing already, okay? The point is you didn't have to bring it up in class."

"Well, I couldn't just sit there and let him lie about what I believe without…"

Stretch finished the sentence for me, "…without making us both look stupid! People are going to assume I believe what you do!" he said.

"So what if they do? I never knew you cared about what other people think," I said. Stretch looked visibly upset; something was bothering him.

"I don't! It's just that…Look, I'm glad you found something to believe in, Hunter, I really am…" he stopped himself from finishing the thought.

"But…" I prodded.

"But you know I don't believe in it like you do. Besides, we're in tenth grade now. You just can't go blurting out whatever you want. Nobody will take you seriously anymore."

"But you were there with me, Stretch; we both fell into the grave together. Don't you remember the Dispirits? Evan's sword? The disappearing bookshop?" I asked, still finding it hard to believe that he could remember nothing at all.

"Hunter, we've been over this before. I'm sure there is a logical explanation for everything that happened that night."

"Oh yeah? Like what?" I challenged.

"I don't know. Like somebody was getting even with us for

pranking him or her earlier in the year. Maybe they were trying to teach us a lesson or something."

I shook my head in disbelief.

"Like THAT explains it!"

"Just keep it to yourself, okay?" Stretch pleaded.

A loud clatter from across the hallway pulled our attention toward the trashcan that usually stood out slightly from the corner. The can had toppled to the floor from an apparent collision and was currently rolling away. A lanky kid I'd never seen before lay sprawled in the trail of trash left behind, in an embarrassing display of clumsiness. What happened next was both unfortunate and hilarious at the same time. The rolling can somehow managed to take a sharp turn and plowed directly into the back of Cranton's legs just as he was bending over the water fountain to get a drink.

"Somebody's gonna pay for this!" bellowed Cranton as he lifted his freshly drenched face from the stream of water.

The new kid picked himself up and began to apologize to everyone around him as he leaned over to pick up the trash. His skin was a soft java brown and he wore his hair in braided dreadlocks, which fell into his face from time to time. Unfortunately, being new to the school, he was also completely oblivious to the severity of the situation he had caused—any normal person would have been running for his life by now. Clearly, he had no clue who Cranton was or what he was capable of.

"You! Dweeb!" Cranton demanded, stomping over to where the boy stood. "Did you do this?" he asked pointing to his face.

"Oh, I'm sorry; was that my fault? I just…" the boy started, but didn't get to finish his statement. Everyone gasped as Cranton picked the kid up by his shirt and slammed his back into the lockers.

"What's yer name?" he growled at the boy, water still dripping off his eyebrows.

The boy, obviously in pain, tried his best to answer despite the fact he could hardly breathe, "R-R-Rob."

"Well, Rob. You think it's funny to get me wet, is that it?" Cranton asked, still holding Rob against the lockers.

"N-n-no, I just tripped on my laces, that's all. See?" Rob lifted his foot and pointed at his beat-up shoes. The laces had come undone and were hanging limply to one side.

"Well that's too bad. You got me wet, and now I'm going to return the favor. I think it's time for a Royal Flush!" he said with a smile.

The crowd around him started chanting their approval, "Swirly, swirly, swirly!" as Cranton and his pals grabbed Rob and started down the hall. Even Stretch joined in on the chant. I looked over at him in disbelief.

"Hey, it's not me this time," Stretch said, leaving me behind and following the crowd. "I gotta watch this!"

I couldn't help but feel a bit sorry for the kid. Even though we had never met, there was something about him that I liked right away. His eyes were expressive and honest. He acted like he didn't care what others thought about his level of "coolness." I could tell he was a genuinely nice guy right from the start—although a bit clumsy. Cranton was bad enough last year but this year he seemed determined to make life miserable for anyone who looked at him the wrong way. Poor Rob, he didn't deserve what was coming to him, but I wasn't about to step in. I already had a big enough target on my back; there was no need to attract Cranton's attention now.

Fortunately, a teacher happened to be walking by and intervened before Rob could be flushed by the mob. Grateful for the escape, Rob nervously gathered his things and did his best to disappear around the corner before the teacher left the area. In the rush, he absentmindedly dropped a paper. The light blue sheet was the same one plastered all over the hallways on every third locker—an invitation for all students to attend the Destiny Fair for free this Friday. The fair was an annual event the school promoted at the start of each school year.

I walked over, picked up the abandoned flyer and was about to toss it in the trash when a sketch on the top corner caught my eye. It was only a doodle, but the mark was unmistakable—three interlocking *V's*. It was the same mark I had come to know as the Author's Mark, the very one that adorned my medallion from Solandria. Was it possible that Rob knew about the Author as well? I stood there, staring at the design and trying to figure out what it meant.

"So, are you gonna go?" a cheery voice shook my focus away from the paper. It was Trista, my sister's new best friend.

She clutched her books tightly as she swayed back and forth. She hardly ever stood still—one of the most energetic and upbeat people I knew. With such a positive attitude, I figured her to be an odd match for my sister but somehow their friendship worked.

On her left wrist, she wore a collection of mismatched bracelets and bands, a fading fashion trend she was determined to revive. At the moment she was smacking a piece of gum—something she always seemed to have in her mouth. Her blonde hair was pulled back in a long ponytail with a dark streak up the left side. Her smile held two of the deepest dimples you'd ever see—the kind of smile that was hard not to like.

"Oh hi, Trista...uh...go where?" I asked.

"You know, the fair," she said, playfully grabbing the sheet out of my hand and holding it out in front of me. "Students are free tonight. You *are* going, right?"

"Oh, that...yeah. Stretch and I were planning on meeting up."

"Well, my dad's working there this year," she bragged. "I told your sister that he can totally hook us up with free tickets. Maybe you guys would want to hang out with us?"

"Hey, yeah, that'd be great," I replied.

The school bell buzzed again, interrupting our conversation.

"Gotta go. I'll see you tonight then," Trista said cheerfully before spinning on her heel and zipping away to class.

"Yeah, later," I nodded, watching her disappear into the crowd of people fighting to make it down the hall to their next classes. Turning back to my locker, I hurried to gather my books and shove them into my backpack. The hall had emptied fast. Lucky for me my next class was only two doors down. I would be right on…

BLAM!

My locker door swung shut, just missing my head as it flew by. A black shape lunged out from behind the locker door and plowed into me, slamming my body forcefully to the ground. The impact completely knocked the wind out of me. Before I could react, my bag had been stripped from my shoulder and the rapid sound of footfalls could be heard racing away down the hall.

Scrambling to my feet, I was just able to catch a glimpse of a black, fully-cloaked figure before it ducked around the corner with my backpack. It was the first time I had been this close, but I knew in an instant it was the stalker!

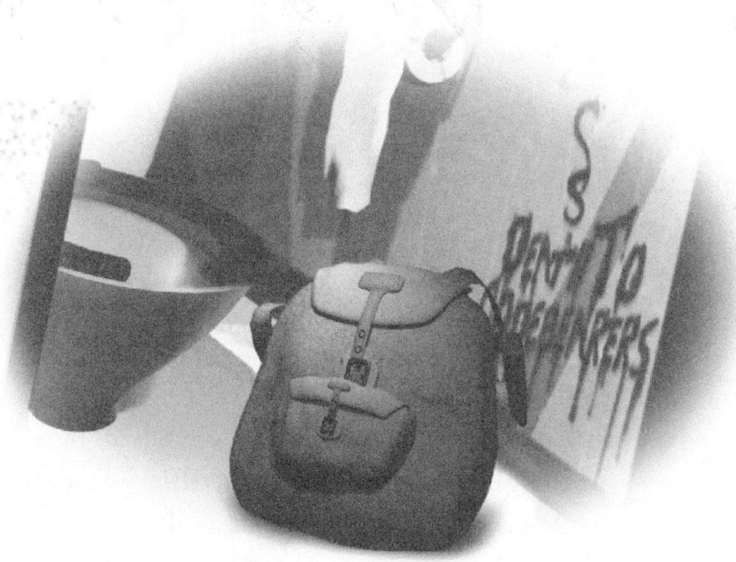

Chapter 3

The Shadow's Message

Without thinking twice, I took off in pursuit. Moments later I was staring down an empty side hall—the quick-footed thief had vanished! Or he would have if not for the sound of a familiar *creak* followed by a *slam.* My attacker's attempt to give me the slip had just been foiled by the men's bathroom door.

If not for the fact that this individual had shadowed me for weeks, I probably would have walked away. After all, it was just a backpack and there was little of value in it other than barely average grades. But instincts told me there was something more behind this stalker—he had been planning this for days. If I didn't confront him now, I might never get the chance. Besides, showing up to class without a bag or books would just mean more questions, and right now I needed answers. This mystery had to be solved.

I paused as I reached the bathroom door. Then, taking a deep breath I slowly pushed it open, being careful not to let the hinges squeak.

A collection of crumpled paper towels littered the orangey-brown tiled floor just inside. The unpleasant smell of musty porcelain filled the air. Quietly, I slipped inside. Taking cover behind the protective wall that kept the stalls and sink area out of sight, I listened carefully for any movement.

Drip, drip, drip.

One of the sinks had not been shut off completely and was allowing a drop of water to escape every other second. But I thought I could hear something else between the drips; quiet, slow and steady. I swallowed hard, finally recognizing the sound. It was breathing! I was definitely not alone. Easing my head out around the wall, I slowly scoped the scene.

The window was securely shut—there was no other way out. Wherever the thief was, he was hiding nearby.

Spotting a mop in the corner by the door, I quickly formed a plan. I'd just step out and give the coward a surprise attack of his own.

Putting on my bravest face, I did just that. My voice echoed off the tiled walls, "Hey, punk! Is this what you were looking for?" I brandished the mop as deftly as I would have a sword.

The lack of any response unnerved me a bit, but I tried again. "Playing hide-and-seek now? Aren't you a little old for that?"

This time, a response did come, but it wasn't a voice. The lights above the sink flickered and dimmed. Something seemed to be sapping the very energy from the room.

The door to the first stall squeaked slowly open, but there was nobody inside. There, on the floor beside the toilet, my backpack lay slumped open. Above it a message was written on the stall's wall in wet black ink, reminding me of the black blood that once ran through my veins in Solandria. The message was followed by a serpentine mark—the mark of the Shadow.

Death to Codebearers §

Any bravery I had mustered quickly gave way to a gripping fear. Clearly, my stalker had vicious intentions.

The mop clattered on the floor where I dropped it. Scooping up my bag, I turned on the spot and headed straight for the door. I pulled on the handle but the door wouldn't budge. I yanked harder but it still held firm, as if an invisible foe was holding it shut. My fear swelled to a new high with a sudden realization: this was no prank.

This was the work of the Shadow. They had come for me.

My plan seemed so foolish now in the face of this. I had walked into a trap! I had no weapon—no means of defending myself against the Shadow. My heart began to race at a near-panic pace, and my imagination ran wild with the possibilities of what kind of creature lay in wait for me.

The exit was sealed. I had no choice but to face my invisible threat. That is when a passage from the Author's Writ suddenly sprang to mind: "By his fear a man appoints his master." Those words rang true inside me, giving me courage. Though the odds were not in my favor, I could not let this enemy master me. I was a Codebearer! I served the Author!

Emboldened by this thought, I took up the mop once again. Gripping the wooden handle tightly in my sweaty palms, I knew there was little hope it would actually help, but at least I'd go out with a fight.

I resolutely made my way into the open again, every muscle tensed. Nothing moved. Scanning down the row of stalls, I took note of the handicap stall in the far corner. It was the only one that was shut. That was where the Shadow hid—behind that door. Even now I could hear its slow breathing coming from that corner. It was waiting, perhaps watching me from a crack.

If I had any hopes of surviving long, I would need to hit it fast and hard. I needed to gain some kind of advantage by creating surprise. I closed my eyes one last time, gritted my teeth and swallowed hard. Then, in a full-out charge at the stall, I aimed a flying kick at the door and screamed at the top of my lungs:

"I FEAR NO ONE BUT THE AUTHOR!"

The move was executed with precision, just like in the movies. The stall door exploded open with surprising force, and I jabbed the mop handle into the stall with a vengeance. What I found lurking behind the door was far worse than I ever possibly could have imagined. I was staring into the wide-eyed face of none other than Mr. Tanner.

He was seated comfortably on the toilet, reading a science magazine, wearing a pair of earphones and an expression that was priceless. Even though he did not yell, as many might have in that situation, I can honestly say it was the first time I had ever seen a look of shock on his face.

For one awkward moment we just stared at each other in silence. I dropped the mop, realizing I had just made one of the biggest mistakes of my life. He was the first to speak, his dry monotonous voice as calm and steady as ever.

"Well, Mr. Brown, we meet again!" He raised one thick eyebrow ever so slightly and I knew I was in deep...deep...trouble.

In no time at all, I was whisked to our new principal's office. "Sit," Principal Strickland said, pointing firmly at the hard wooden chair in front of his desk. I snapped into the cold seat as quickly as possible, not wanting more trouble than I was in already.

Strickland motioned for Mr. Tanner to close the door. The principal's office was frigid and very dark. The broad window that spread out behind the principal's desk was heavily shaded to block out all traces of sunlight. The only light that remained was from the glow of his oversized computer monitor, which cast a very unflattering hue onto Mr. Strickland's face.

I couldn't help but compare how much things had changed since Ms. Pickler had been principal. Even though I had tested her patience at times, she had always been somewhat reasonable. Firm, but fair. Strickland, on the other hand, seemed to relish his power as principal.

As for the room itself, I hardly recognized it now. Before, the walls were painted bright yellow and decorated with family photos and teaching certificates. Of course, that was before Ms. Pickler decided to retire over the summer, leaving Destiny Hills in the lurch and desperate for a new principal. Unfortunately for the students, Mr. Strickland had answered the call.

He had a very different approach, to say the least. Being an ex-military man, he kept things in order and had little sympathy for mistakes. His simple decor was much more formal and functional: large desk, white walls, green metal file cabinet, wooden chair and air conditioning…lots of air conditioning. The room was so cold I imagined it could easily serve as a refrigerator.

A long awkward silence passed as Strickland flipped through a folder marked "Brown, Hunter" that had somehow already found its way to his desk before I arrived. I thought it best to remain silent and so I waited. At last he broke the silence.

"Explain yourself" was all he said.

I launched into the story about my mysterious stalker and how I ended up in the bathroom, mistakenly shoving a mop into Tanner's stall.

"So you see, sir. It wasn't my fault at all; it was an accident."

"An accident? How curious. See, I've been informed that you

don't believe in accidents—that you had a problem with Mr. Tanner's teaching this morning. Am I to believe that as unlikely as it seems these two incidents have nothing to do with each other? Hmmmm?"

I gulped. "No sir, they don't."

"Outrageous," he said, leaving the word hanging in the air for a moment. "Let me remind you, Hunter, I've been a principal for fourteen years now. Just because I'm new to *this* school doesn't mean I'm new at this game."

"G-g-game?" I asked.

"Oh, don't play games with me. I know who you are, Hunter—the perpetual goof-off who seeks popularity from his peers by arranging pranks at the expense of others. It's pathetic really. In fact, based on your record, I'm surprised you've survived this long without a single suspension. Of course, there is always a first time for everyone."

"You're going to suspend me for this? But...I didn't do anything."

"Assaulting a teacher is a *very* serious matter, Mr. Brown. I can assure you I am well within my rights to suspend or expel you if I choose."

Obviously my reputation as a prankster in school last year had done damage to my credibility—a fact I was not proud of.

"But I'm telling the truth, I swear. I saw someone in the hall," I explained.

Strickland didn't wait to hear me finish; instead he exploded. "Listen here, *young* man!" Strickland yelled, putting extra emphasis on the word *young*. "I have no time for your childish games. Imaginary stalker or not, I run a tight ship and I expect everyone to follow my rules. I do not tolerate this kind of insolence in my school. Do you understand?"

Miserable, I nodded, giving up any hope of being understood.

"Good," he said, leaving a pause for thought. "Now for your discipline." He clasped his hands together in front of his lips to consider his verdict.

There was a sudden knock at the door and a flood of light burst into the dark room, breaking his concentration.

"A word, Mr. Strickland, if you please?" a woman's voice called from the doorway. I turned to see who it was but the light from the outer room only allowed a shadowy silhouette to appear. Her tone was firm but soothing.

"Who are you? Can't you see I'm busy?" he growled.

"It's about Hunter; it can't wait" came the reply.

Mr. Strickland scowled and rose from his chair, none too pleased that his session with me had been rudely interrupted. The two spoke in hushed tones outside the door for a minute.

A moment later Strickland returned. He was in a noticeably different mood, almost cheerful. I hardly recognized the man.

"I'm terribly sorry for the interruption; it couldn't be helped, I'm afraid," he said. Then he continued, "What were we talking about again?"

"My discipline," I answered sheepishly.

"Discipline? Why on earth would you need that? No, no…a boy like you just needs a little guidance from someone who can help you make good decisions. That's why I'm making a suggestion for you."

He scribbled something barely legible on an orange sheet of paper and slid it across his broad oak desk.

"Here you are. I really think you could benefit from a visit with the school counselor. She can do wonders, that woman. I'm sure you'll find her insight to be enlightening. Think you can handle it?"

"Sure," I said, eyeing him suspiciously. Since when did Strickland care about what I thought?

"All right then, off with you! Your friends will be wondering where you are by now," he said with a wink.

I embraced my freedom and bolted for the door as fast as I could. That room gave me the creeps and the chills. I couldn't wait to get out.

Entering the outer office, my pace only slowed long enough to take a quick look around for whoever had freed me from the discipline of Mr. Strickland.

The only person in sight was Ms. Trudy, Strickland's secretary, who was wearing earphones, humming a show tune and typing feverishly at her computer. She seemed completely oblivious to my presence as I exited the room. Not wanting to risk the chance of getting called back, I quickly ducked out into the hall and made my way to my next class.

Chapter 4

Sheppard the Shrink

The remainder of my school day flew by without incident. Rumors of what I had done to Mr. Tanner spread quickly. By lunch nearly everyone in school had heard one version or another of the story. To some I was the freak with the mop, to others a hero. I wanted to tell them the truth about what had happened, but I had to face the fact that nobody would believe me if I did. Besides, in the end I knew it didn't matter what I told them anyway. Now, I was more worried about what I would tell Mom.

Stopping by my locker to collect what I needed to take home with me, I found an official looking note stuck to my locker door. Printed across the top were the words, "From the Desk of Ms. Sheppard," with a campy image of our Destiny Destroyers' school mascot at the foot. The handwritten note in between read:

Hunter, I spoke with your mother earlier about this morning's inci-

dent. She agreed to allow you to attend an after-school counseling session. Please meet me down in counseling room, B-10. Ms. Sheppard

"You've got to be kidding me," I said aloud after reading the news. This day was going from bad to worse. Then again, it *was* the school counselor who bailed me out of Strickland's discipline. I at least owed her one for that.

Slinging my stuff back over my shoulder, I re-read the note.

B-10? Where was that supposed to be? Basement level?

As far as I knew, the school had never made use of the basement for anything but storage. But, when budgets get tight, pretty much anything goes, I figured. Taking the hall to the staircase I followed it down to the basement doors. I knew that in the past these doors were always locked, but today the *CUSTODIAL STAFF ONLY* emblazoned doors had been left ajar.

Even before entering, I could smell the distinct mixture of cleaning solvents, rubber and aged dust. I choked a bit on the smell as I peeked in, more uncertain than ever that I was even looking in the right place.

If you have ever been in a basement storage facility, then you know what I saw under the dim fluorescent lighting: rows and rows of shelving stacked high with equipment and supplies; plumbing pipes and air ducts running across the exposed ceiling; access to water heaters and air-conditioning systems. It looked like a high school basement, except for the plastering of "feel-good" inspirational posters framing one of the doors in the back wall. *B-10. Bingo!*

A poster taped to the door greeted me with the message, "Change can be beautiful!" and featured an oversized butterfly newly emerged from its cocoon as its spokes-bug.

Oh, spare me, I inwardly groaned. The cheery butterfly took a few raps between its eyes as I knocked on the door.

Knock, Knock, Knock.

No one answered, but the door did open slightly, giving me a peek at Ms. Sheppard's accommodations. The warmly lit room revealed walls painted in soft shades of green, which served as a backdrop to a series of gently curving, hand-painted messages on topics like "Respect," "Decisions" and "Trust Yourself."

"Hello... Ms. Sheppard?" I called tentatively into the office as I entered. Plush, padded carpet and a sweet, pleasant aroma were the first tips that this was no ordinary office. Whatever utilitarian function this room had served before was lost in the transformed tranquility that now occupied the space. Four overstuffed chairs and a pair of cubed end tables were arranged perfectly amidst a modest garden of potted plants, living quietly in the corners.

It was remarkable how much sunlight seemed to fill a room set partway underground. The overall effect was quite calming. Oddly, for being an office, there was not one filing cabinet, desk or even a stapler to be seen. Quite a stark contrast from Mr. Strickland's "strictly business" office.

My gaze landed on a silk cloth, partially covering a glass ball set in the center of one of the end tables. I figured it was a fish bowl though why it was covered I hadn't a clue. Curiosity got the best of me and I wandered over to take a closer look while waiting for Ms. Sheppard to appear.

A most unusual sound caught my ears as I neared the bowl. I heard a rumbling tone, like the purr of a cat. One thing was clear, whatever lay beneath the silk was no fish. I lifted the corner of the cover just enough to peek beneath it. The glass walls of the orb were thick and tinted, obscuring whatever hid inside. The purr grew louder as I gazed into the ball, straining my eyes to see through the darkness.

Nothing was there, but the sound continued. It was almost as if the ball itself was purring.

As I extended a finger to tap the side of the glass a startling pair of giant blue eyes suddenly opened before me, hovering within the darkened orb. I pulled my finger away in fright. The eyes were glowing with a light all their own, watching me as if they could see into my soul. All at once I wished they had never opened.

"Mine," a raspy whisper resounded in my ear. I had seen enough. Dropping the silk cloth over the orb, I turned to leave just as the door to the room shot open and a short woman stepped in boldly.

"Ah-ha! There you are," the woman said, startling me in the process. "I've been looking all over school for you. I thought you got lost so I stepped out to check upstairs. I'm so glad to see you made the effort to come."

She was a petite lady of Asian descent, smartly dressed in a professional skirt and blouse. Her straight black hair was loosely pulled back into a sort of low, twisted ponytail held in place by a set of ornamental sticks. The trendy look was completed by a pair of sophisticated, rectangular glasses tinted slightly pink.

"Hello, Hunter," she continued, turning to me in greeting and thrusting out her hand. "I'm Ms. Sheppard, the school counselor, but you can call me Connie."

"I'm Hunter," I replied a bit sheepishly as we shook hands, realizing she had already said my name. "Nice…uh…office you've got here."

"Office? Oh heavens, no. Wouldn't that be nice?" her light laughter filled the room. "I'd love to do away with my desk, believe me, but it tends to be a necessary evil for me to do my job properly." She held her hands out, "This room is our Serenity Center."

My blank stare prompted further explanation.

"It's sort of experimental right now, hence the odd location, but the concept is to have a room set up to provide reflection time for students I'm counseling—like an oasis. How often do we make poor decisions when we are under stress?" She smiled confidently in answer to the rhetorical question. "Please have a seat and we can get started." She closed the door and indicated for me to take my pick of the chairs.

As warm and inviting as the place seemed, I couldn't get over the feeling that I was still being watched from beneath the silk. As a result, I ended up picking the chair closest to the door. Ms. Sheppard took a seat somewhat opposite me, arranging a notebook and file folder on the end table next to her. Once everything was in order, she neatly crossed her legs, clasped her hands and began in a calm, steady manner.

"So, Hunter, I've been made aware that you had a bit of a rough morning today with Mr. Tanner. I would really like to hear your side of the story."

If I told the truth, my side of the story would make me sound like a lunatic. Nervous about how I should respond, I lowered my eyes and found myself staring at my shoes for answers.

"I... It's just complicated" was the best I could manage as an explanation, remembering how Strickland had responded to the truth.

Ms. Sheppard gave a knowing nod. "I understand, and when life gets complicated things get all out of whack, don't they?"

I nodded uncomfortably, choosing not to look up at her.

"Still that was no reason to attack Mr. Tanner," she scolded.

"It wasn't about Mr. Tanner," I clarified, looking up at her for the first time since we had met. "There was...someone else."

"Okay, can you give me a name?"

I shook my head. I could only imagine what kind of name a mysterious agent of the Shadow might have been given. I wasn't even about to bring up all of that with the counselor. Instead, I only shared the basics. "I thought it was someone else in the bathroom."

Putting down her pen, she looked me straight in the eye. "Hunter, let me remind you that this is a safe place to talk. What you say in here stays in here. It's just you and me. I've heard and seen a lot of things that are probably stranger than what you have to say."

"I doubt that," I replied, unconvinced that she could possibly understand.

"Fair enough," she conceded. "Then how about I go first?" She cleared her throat. "I believe there is more to our existence than meets the eye."

Something about the way she chose her words and her careful delivery of them struck a chord with me. Not willing to completely trust her yet on this subject, I pressed her further.

"Like what?"

"Like other forces at work in our world that we don't always see. I believe there is another realm of reality that many people never realize is there. How is that for crazy talk?"

"Well, it's certainly not going to make you very popular with most people," I quipped, thinking of how my biology class would have responded to her.

She laughed in agreement. "True, but being labeled a *shrink* doesn't do much for me either." I tried not to smile as she poked fun at herself. Taking a more serious tone, she followed up by saying, "So then, do you think *I'm* crazy?"

"Not really. There might be something to what you're saying." I was actually more intrigued than my casual response revealed.

"Good," she said, smiling sweetly and changing positions in her chair. "Then we're on the same page. So how about that crazy explanation of yours now? I'm listening."

"Alright," I nodded, feeling a little more at ease with how she might receive what I was about to share. After taking a deep breath, I began slowly describing the disturbing events involving my mysterious attacker. Ms. Sheppard didn't blink once, but continued to nod understandingly as she intermittently added notations to her paperwork whenever something piqued her interest. One thing led to another and, before I knew it, I had shared more about my experience in Solandria than ever before. After I had finished, she gave me a reassuring smile, "Now that wasn't so hard, was it?"

"I guess not." I let out a breath in relief. It actually felt good to have someone listen to my story, to all of it, and not doubt me for once.

"Tell me, Hunter, have any of these individuals—this Evan or the Codebearers—contacted you since you returned home?"

It was a simple enough question but the answer was hard to admit. "No... I haven't heard anything."

"I see," Ms. Sheppard's eyebrows raised as she scribbled another line down. "And has anyone *new* been in contact with you?"

Again I shook my head. "No. The cloaked stalker this morning was the first."

"Of course," she conceded, crossing out some of her notes. Satisfied with her work, Ms. Sheppard reestablished our eye contact. "For what it's worth, Hunter, I don't think you're crazy." Her sincerity was striking.

"That's a relief," I said, cracking a smile. At last I had found someone to talk to—someone who believed me.

"Actually, I'm quite impressed with what I've learned about you today. You are coping remarkably well!"

"Coping?" I wondered. "What do you mean, coping?"

"It's not easy for a young man to deal with the loss of a father, or an impending move for that matter. In all of your stories I am encouraged by how you seem to be engaging your inner struggles, not just simply ignoring them. This is a positive sign."

"*Stories*?" I snapped back in defense. "You think these are all just *stories* to me?"

Ms. Sheppard quickly qualified herself, "I believe you have developed an extraordinary gift, something called *second vision*—the ability to externalize your emotions in a way you can actually see."

"Second vision?" I asked.

Sheppard nodded back, but I wasn't buying it.

"Sounds like shrink code for nut case if you ask me!" I said in frustration, standing up to leave. "Why did I come here anyway? I should have known you'd be just like everyone else."

"Wait," Ms. Sheppard called, grabbing my sleeve before I could turn for the door. "Please let me explain."

"Why should I?" I challenged. "You think I'm just seeing things...some skewed version of reality."

"No, Hunter, just the opposite. I believe *second vision* allows your mind to see reality in its purest form—a world most people are unable to perceive. What you experience is real, Hunter—a world connected to your own, like two sides of the same page."

I had heard those words before in Solandria. Perhaps she wasn't as clueless as I had thought.

"The point is, when you go there and fight your enemies, you are accomplishing real objectives in your life. It's an amazing gift, Hunter, not something to be ashamed of."

"Then why does everyone treat me like it is?" I asked.

She motioned for me to sit again. I did, but I wasn't at all comfortable with the conversation.

"They don't understand how great you are," she said. "Normally, in cases like yours, the visions are not quite as defined. But there's something different about you, Hunter...something I can't quite put my finger on...."

Without explanation she reached over and quickly pulled the silk cloth off of the orb. Until that moment, I had practically forgotten it was there. My heartbeat quickened and I found myself gazing into the mysterious darkness beyond the glass ball. Ms. Sheppard's voice became little more than a murmur. Suddenly, the only thing that mattered to me was gazing into the orb and seeing the scarlet glow that began to grow in the center of it, moving and swirling in all directions like a small cloud of fluid. A strange sensation fell over me—a feeling of numbness and indifference. The fluid within the orb continued to swirl with life, then faded away once more into absolute emptiness and I felt as though the orb was calling me into itself.

All the while Ms. Sheppard's voice droned on and on, her words shifting in and out of my comprehension.

"...be careful who you trust...distortions of truth...only you can decide...there is no black...no white...only grey...only you..."

My vision blurred as I gazed into the blackness until at last an image took form. It was subtle at first but then became more defined. I could hardly believe what I was seeing, but there was no doubt about it; there before me was the face of Venator, my former enemy. His skull-mask fell down to reveal my own face behind it. Then I watched as his features changed before my eyes—his face bulging and shifting into something new—someone else.

"Don't you agree, Hunter?" Sheppard asked loudly, breaking my trance.

"Huh? I'm sorry; what were you saying?" I asked, shaking myself awake. She repeated the question as if nothing had happened. The silk cloth was back in its place exactly as I had left it, covering the ball.

"I was just pointing out that you need to realize you *do* have a choice in all of this. Your inner strength is what created this *magic* to begin with, not some book or Author. So use your power to better yourself as long as you need—just don't let it start controlling you. We wouldn't want any more bathroom barge-ins, would we?"

"No, I guess not," I said, still somewhat in a daze. I was unsure of what to believe about my so-called gift of second vision or Sheppard's ball for that matter. My head was foggy and unable to process what had just happened. All I wanted at this point was to go home and rest.

"Excellent!" She beamed proudly at my response and drew in a deep, satisfied breath. "Well, I think that gives you plenty to think about for today, don't you?"

"So…that's it?"

"Yes, for now," Ms. Sheppard efficiently gathered her papers and stood, inviting me to do the same. As she directed me out the door, she offered me one of her business cards.

"I'm *very* interested in hearing how things go for you. I trust that if anything new comes up—I mean anything or anyone—you will call. I want to help you sort through it."

I accepted the card, threw her a quick wave and hurried on my way.

As I walked home from school with my skateboard tucked tightly under my arm, a light rain plopped against my face. Considering how the day had turned out so far, I was in no rush to hurry it along. There was a lot to think about.

As I walked I tried to make sense of it.

Was everything I had experienced just a part of my "second vision" as Sheppard had suggested? Did I really just make it all up to cope with life? If they were real, why hadn't I heard anything from the Author or Evan or the others? And what of Sheppard's orb? Was I just imagining the image inside it or was what I had seen inside it real?

I became so lost in my train of thought that by the time I arrived home I couldn't recall which route I had taken to get there. I shuffled up the sidewalk past the weathered "For Sale" sign posted in our front yard. The flyer box was empty again, which meant we'd probably be expecting visitors within the week.

With Emily at track practice and Mom still an hour away, I knew I had plenty of time to stress over the details of what I was going to tell Mom about my actions today. Climbing the steps to the front door, I dug the house key from my pocket and reached for the doorknob.

Immediately, I knew something was wrong—the door was already cracked open.

Oh no! Did I forget to lock it in my rush out the door this morning? I thought to myself. I stepped into the house and realized that my little mistake had not gone unnoticed.

Our house had been ransacked!

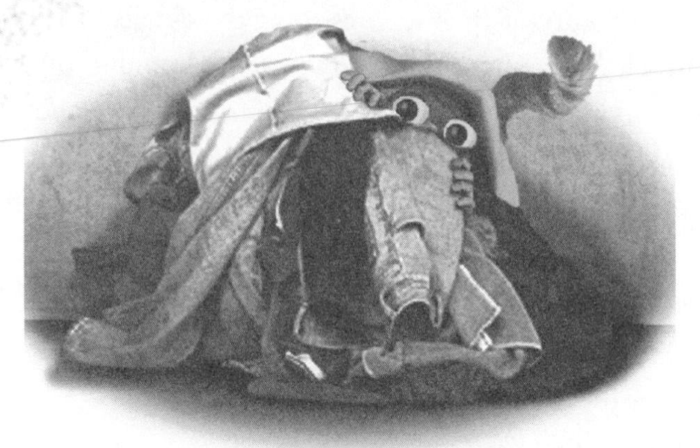

Chapter 5

A Guest Uninvited

All the blinds in the house had been pulled down and the lights turned off. A sickening feeling gripped my stomach as my eyes took in the grim scene. The coffee table in the living room was overturned and the corners of the couch cushions were shredded, spilling their fluffy innards all over the floor. The shelves of our entertainment center had been unceremoniously emptied, with books, DVDs and picture frames tossed carelessly about the room. It was probably much worse than I could see in the shadows.

I had just reached for the light switch when a loud crash from the kitchen stopped me dead in my tracks. I was not alone. Whoever had destroyed the house was still lurking nearby, rummaging through our things.

My first instinct was to run for help, but in our neighborhood it could be nearly thirty minutes by the time the cops arrived, and by then it would be too late. I had to have more to go on. I needed to catch a glimpse of the intruder so we had a chance at capturing him. Then, I could run.

Swallowing hard, I slipped into the hallway and pressed myself against the wall to listen. I heard pots and pans spill to the floor with a terrible clatter. *What a clumsy crook*, I thought to myself. *Then again, maybe it wasn't a thief.* The thought suddenly struck me that this might be the same shrouded stalker who had attacked me at school. He apparently had not found what he was looking for in my bag and now he was searching my house! This new revelation made the hairs on my neck stand on end.

Calm down, Hunter. Don't let your imagination get the best of you. He doesn't know you are here yet. Just one look, that's all you need, I reassured myself. Despite my pep talk, my imagination still ran wild with possibilities until a small squeaky voice shattered them all.

"Yum, yum," the voice said happily, amidst obnoxious smacking and crunching. From the sound of things, my uninvited guest had helped itself to a snack from our kitchen. Now, more curious than afraid, I turned the corner and entered the room.

A hazy white cloud billowed in the air like a dense fog. Apparently, one of the sounds I had heard earlier was Mom's porcelain container of flour, which had been smashed on the floor, spreading flour-dust throughout the room. A trail of three-toed footprints led through the powder to the far side of the center island where the munching sounds originated. From where I stood I couldn't actually see the other side, but I knew something was there. The pantry door was wide open and a variety of snack foods were being flung out in every direction, some landing near my feet.

"Come out of there!" I shouted, flicking the lights on, hoping to catch the thief red-handed.

Whatever it was let out a terrible scream and scurried away.

Before I could catch sight of the thief, the basement door shot open, followed by a painful tumbling down the stairs.

I made my way across the kitchen, carefully stepping around the mess of crackers, cereal and other snack foods the intruder had torn into. A cold draft blew up the stairwell as I stared into the darkness below. I grabbed the flashlight that we'd hung inside the door, switched it on and started my descent with cautious, creaking footsteps.

At first glance the dim basement appeared unoccupied, lit only by what little light spilled in through the small below-ground window cracked open above the dryer.

"I know you're down here!" I yelled. "Come out where I can see you!"

A scuffling sound seemed to come from behind one of the shelves. I targeted my flashlight in the general area and watched for movement in the shadows. Not finding anything, I continued down and clicked on the single pull-chain light.

The basement was an organized mess, a clutter of junk we had accumulated through the years. Piled high on several rows of slightly bowed shelves meant to hold half the weight we had put on them, was all our junk. It was here many of our childhood memories were stored. Boxes of sports cards, winter coats, toys we had outgrown, and of course, Emily's old trophies from past years in gymnastics, track and basketball. There were even a few choice items Dad had left behind, like his bowling balls, fishing rods and a pair of rubber boots still covered in mud. A pile of freshly folded laundry sat atop the dryer, pressed, folded and ready to be delivered to our rooms. Everything seemed to be okay.

A gurgle of water rushed out of the basement boiler and up into the pipes overhead. The sound startled me for a moment, but it stopped nearly as soon as it started and everything was quiet again.

That's when I heard something that didn't belong.

Shrump. Shrump. Shrump.

A dirty grinding sound seemed to be coming from behind one of the three rows of shelves. It was the kind of sound that made you grit your teeth and tighten your fists.

Shrump. Shrump. Shrump.

Stepping slowly forward, I peered down each aisle of shelves, hoping to find the source of the sound. The first aisle was empty; the second was occupied mainly by a large roll of spare carpet. The third and final row seemed empty as well until something short and square scooted out from beneath the utility sink and bumped into my foot.

It was a small box, turned upside down to cover whatever hid beneath. The box spun around and shuffled back toward one of the shelves, bumping into the side of it as well. What lay beneath was not nearly as threatening or large as I had once imagined.

Sh-rump. The box slid to a stop.

"Well then," I wondered aloud, "what do we have here?"

Bending low I grasped the box with one hand and lifted it gently, aiming the bright beam of the flashlight beneath it to reveal the intruder. A ghostly burst of black smoke rushed out into the room, followed by a horrible high-pitched shriek that chilled me to the bone.

"Ah-eeeeeeeee!"

The sound alone made my heart skip a beat and I stumbled back from the shock of it, nearly falling on my backside. The dreadfully angry racket, filled with terror and rage, seemed to circle the room with incredible speed. A powerful gust of wind blew past my face, shattering the light bulb in the socket. With the light gone, the room fell silent once more.

What was that? I wondered, suddenly very afraid of what I had just released. This was no ordinary creature.

I stood up and listened for any sound of life nearby. My heart drummed loudly in my ears, pacing off each second with its heavy beat. Just then, something cold touched the back of my neck, and my stomach dropped another inch.

"Stay back," I whirled around in fright, swinging the flashlight in self-defense. Nobody was there. The only thing moving in the darkness was the dancing chain of the ceiling light. I sighed in relief and caught the chain mid-cycle to stop its swinging.

With the light bulb shattered, all I had left was the light from my flashlight. I traced the bright beam anxiously across the wood ceiling overhead then down the walls and all around the room.

A clattering of aluminum cans in the corner directed my attention to the toppled recycle bag. Uncrushed cans were rolling every direction across the cement floor. I followed one of them with my light as it landed beside a ratty old blanket that was lumpy with movement.

"Hey, I know you're under there!" I shouted. My voice warbled nervously. I grabbed a shovel for protection with my free hand and added, "Whatever you are, come out now or I'll…I'll pound you flat!"

The lump stopped moving, but there was no response.

I balanced the flashlight on the edge of a shelf, carefully aiming its beam toward the blanket. Then, gripping the rough wooden handle of the shovel with both hands, I stepped forward to face the lump. As I approached the blanket, the thing moved again and started cooing softly. The sound was surprisingly friendly and cute—like a small helpless kitten.

"Sure…now you act nice!" I muttered to myself as I approached the blanket with shovel in hand. What kind of cold-hearted person could smash a purring kitten? Now, I had to see what hid beneath before I attacked it.

Thinking better of my "pounding" idea, I lowered the shovel and lifted the edge of the blanket with the tip. Another horrid blast of wind and black smoke blew past me as before. Only this time, the high-pitched squeal that came with it sounded closer to a word than a scream.

"Liiiiiiiiiiiiiiiiiiiiiie!" the invisible thing shrieked.

The flashlight fell to the floor, spinning in place and casting a dizzying array of shadows on the walls. I dropped the shovel and covered my ears at the sound. A second gust of wind passed overhead, blowing my hair back with its force. I ducked and covered my head in fright.

"Liiiiiiiiiiiiiiiiiiiight!" the scream wailed again.

This time I understood it.

"Light?" I said, eyeing the flashlight that was still spinning. Maybe this thing was afraid of the light. Of course, it all made sense now. That's why all of the blinds in the house had been pulled shut. I reached out and grabbed the spinning flashlight, putting a stop to the crazy display of light and shadow.

"Liiiiiiiiiiiiiiiiight!" the scream grew unbearably stronger.

I covered my ears in pain. As much as I wanted to keep the light on for protection, I couldn't possibly stand the sound much longer.

"Okay, I get it. You don't like light!" I screamed back.

I flicked the light off, but knew I had to come up with another plan quickly. Sitting alone in the dark was not an option either. Grabbing a dark sock out of the dirty clothes pile, I pulled it over the end of the flashlight to diffuse the beam to what seemed like a safe level. Perhaps the diminished light wouldn't be a problem. I flicked the flashlight back on, satisfied with my quick thinking.

"There…no more light…" I said aloud, wondering where the thing might pop up next. "You can come out now!"

I caught a brief flutter of motion out of the corner of my eye as the pile of laundry Mom had neatly folded toppled to the gritty cement floor.

Something moved beneath the heap of clothes.

Aiming the now dull light beam at the fallen pile, I watched with amazement as a small creature, not much bigger than a fat guinea pig, popped out from a T-shirt and peered at me with two enormous blue eyes shining in the darkness.

Those eyes. The eyes in the orb, I thought at first. But there was something different about these eyes…they didn't frighten me. For some reason, I felt at ease as I looked over the creature.

Amidst a frazzle of grey, fluffy hair was a round little blue face. Its gleaming eyes bulged out of its face like oversized orbs, gazing back at me with unblinking wonder. A long furry tail curled up behind it, making it look more like a monkey than a rodent—but definitely a cross between the two.

"Light gone?" it asked curiously in a weak voice.

"Uh…yeah…it's okay, see? I covered it!" I said, feeling more than a little awkward talking to a creature I had never seen before. It cocked its puffy head to one side and watched me with nervous anticipation of my next move.

"So you don't like light, huh?"

It shook its head and turned around to groom itself, tending to the singed hair that covered its body. From the looks of things, it had seen better days. Something had burned the little creature from head to toe, leaving patchy spots of missing fur all over its body. I began to wonder if it wasn't the light itself.

"Light bad!" it said, as if reading my thoughts.

"Listen, I'm sorry if I hurt you," I said, trying to sound as comforting as possible. "I had no idea the light was doing that."

My response seemed to calm the little thing for the moment.

The charred portions of its fur had already begun to miraculously heal and grow at a surprising rate. In no time at all it looked as if the creature had never been harmed.

"Wow, how did you do that?" I wondered.

The creature returned what looked like a smile and stood up on two feet, shaking the last edge of the shirt sleeve from its ear. Any reservations I had about the uninvited guest quickly vanished. All I could think about now was how charming it was. I reached down in hopes of petting the critter, but it scooted away and curled up into a perfect ball before I could touch it.

"Oh, it's okay, I'm not going to hurt you—I just want to feel your fur," I said gently, making a petting motion with my hand. It peeked out of its ball shape and trembled as I approached with a slower pace. When at last we touched, it relaxed and uncurled, cooing under the palm of my hand and leaning into each stroke I offered. Its fur was warm and soft, like the down of a bird.

"You're so soft, what are you anyway?" I wondered.

"Yor," it replied in a squeaky little voice.

"A yor, huh? I've never heard of a yor before; you must be from another realm," I reasoned. "Maybe from Solandria?" I stopped petting the thing for a moment, and it fell over into the laundry again.

"Are you from Solandria?" I asked.

"Yors, yours!" the creature repeated, this time pointing at me with one of its oversized five-fingered hands.

"Mine? Are you saying you are mine?"

It nodded enthusiastically, "Yours!"

"Oh no…no, no, no. There is no way on earth *that* is happening. I can't have pets."

To my surprise, the creature made the most pitiful face and burst into tears, sobbing much louder than its size should permit.

"Whoa, wait a second. It's not like I don't want you…it's just that I'm not allowed to have pets—at least not furry ones anyway. We had a bird once and Em has her fish, but Mom is allergic to animal hair and she'd freak if she found out I had a rodent in the house."

The little thing seemed only slightly comforted at my explanation. He dried his eyes with one of my socks and blew his nose into it. "Me yours," it insisted, "not Mom."

"Listen, I really wish I could," I admitted, trying to ignore the fact that my sock was now covered in fur ball slime. "It's kind of nice to have someone from Solandria to keep me company. I don't feel so…alone."

No sooner had I said this than the creature scurried up my leg like a monkey and perched on my shoulder, rubbing against my cheek. With each brush of his soft fur I began to think harder about how I could manage to keep him. I had always wanted a real pet and this thing was way cooler than a dog or a cat.

"Then again, maybe if I had somewhere to hide you," I thought aloud.

"Yes, me hide…no Mom see! Flee!" it said excitedly, disappearing in a puff of smoke.

"Hey where did you go?" I said, surprised at how quickly he had managed to disappear. In a matter of minutes he reappeared on my other shoulder.

"See? Flee!" he said with a smile and what looked like a bow.

I had to admit, it was pretty impressive.

"Awesome, this might actually work! If you stay out of sight when Mom's around, she would never have to know! Then you could be…"

"Yours!" it cheered, nodding emphatically.

Just then I remembered the mess we had left upstairs.

"Oh man, we've got to clean up, or she's bound to find out you're here. Come on!"

Chapter 6

How to Keep a Secret

Scrambling up the basement stairs, I arrived to face an even bigger mess than I'd remembered. The place could easily have been considered a disaster zone.

"You sure did make a mess of things for such a little guy!"

"Hungry," it replied, rubbing its tummy.

"Yeah, well hungry or not, if we don't get this place cleaned in fifteen minutes, Emily or Mom could be home and your chances of staying here will disappear quicker than you can."

I placed my new pet on the counter and set to work cleaning as quickly as possible—a task made more difficult with the lights off. There was no way to fix the shattered flour canister or couch cushions. I was going to have to think of something to cover up what really happened.

The little creature followed my every move, watching from his perch atop Emily's aquarium in the living room as I finished stacking the DVDs and books into separate piles to put them back up on the shelves.

"I don't know why I have to clean up *your* mess. You could help out, you know?"

"Hungry," it said again.

"I'll get you something to eat later; just hang in there. We're almost out of time."

Sure enough, just as I put the last of our DVDs back on the shelf, I heard Emily's car pulling into the driveway.

"Okay little fellow, it's time to hide!" I shouted.

"Mmph?" it said, with cheeks twice the size as normal. I then realized he was soaked.

"Hey, what's that you have in your mouth?"

It shrugged its shoulders, pretending not to know.

"Spit it out now!" I demanded.

The creature didn't budge. A car door slammed outside.

"Listen, spit out the fish now or I'm going to turn on the lights!"

At that he spewed Emily's prize fish onto the floor in a puddle of slime. The fish flopped helplessly around as I fumbled to recover and return it to the tank, a little worse for the wear.

"Man, how am I going to explain that?" I asked, looking at the fish's chomped up fins. There was no way it would survive the evening.

"Cat!" was the last thing the fur ball said before disappearing.

At that precise moment the front door jolted open and Emily came bouncing in, chatting away on her cell phone.

"I know...I can't believe it either. He's just like that Triss, totally unpredictable."

From the side of the conversation I could hear, I knew it was

Trista on the other end. They were probably talking about my crazy mop attack earlier today.

Within moments Emily spotted the couch and locked eyes with me, raising an eyebrow in shock at the scene.

"Hang on a second, Triss. I gotta call you back. Yeah, I will. Okay, later!" She snapped her flip-phone shut and gave me "the look."

"What happened here?" she asked, pointing at the couch.

With no better excuse, I decided to go with what the creature had said.

"A cat...was in the house....when I got home."

"A cat?" she folded her arms in disbelief.

"Yeah, a really ugly one, black and white...with a scar over one eye." I cringed—worried the scar thing was a bit over the top. "I scared it away when I got home but it had already ruined the couch."

"Seriously? Did you leave the door unlocked this morning?" she challenged, narrowing her eyes as if examining me.

"No...no, I locked it!"

"Then how did it get in here?"

"Uh, the basement...I think. The window was open a crack."

Emily softened a bit, swallowing the lie.

"Oh man, Mom is going to freak; you know how much she hates cats."

I nodded in agreement.

"Was it just the couch?" she asked, examining the disemboweled cushions.

I shook my head and looked down at the floor. "No, it tried to eat one of your fish too."

At this Emily's face sank. For the first time she actually looked concerned and not confrontational. "What? Which one?" She hurried over to the tank to see for herself.

"The blue one—your favorite!" I said, somewhat glad I was actually pulling this off. "I put it back in the tank but he looks pretty bad."

She whined about her fish for a moment more before noticing the shades were pulled shut.

"Ugh, it's so depressing in here; why do you have the blinds shut anyway?" She headed to the first window and started to pull it open. Even though he was invisible, I worried the creature might still be affected by the bright light and jumped to stop her.

"No…don't!" I yelled. She looked at me with one of those you-are-so-weird expressions. "Uh, I thought it might calm…the fish down," I lied again.

"Don't be silly," she said, flapping the first shade wide open before moving to the next. "Fish love light."

Surprisingly, there was no screaming. Apparently the light only hurt the little furry thing whenever it was visible. If that was the case, I couldn't help but wonder why he hadn't just disappeared in the basement—it would have saved me the trouble of hearing it scream.

"I can't believe it. You know what, I bet it's those new neighbors, the Fentons. They have a bunch of strays over there, and I swear I've seen them lurking around our house too. I'm totally going to call animal control…right after I call Trista and tell her about it."

Right in the middle of Emily's rant, Mom burst in through the back door and she sounded stressed. "Agh! I'm going to need both of your help, quickly! A buyer just called during my commute home and asked to see our house tonight. They'll be here in twenty minutes." She was about to set her coat on the couch when she saw the cushions. "What happened?"

Emily jumped in first and began to relay my entire cat explanation—only with much more dramatics. Mom was clearly upset by all of this account, but cut Emily off. "Okay! Okay. I'm going to have to hear the rest later. Right now, we just need to get this place cleaned up!"

Mom quickly gave out the orders. She would deal with the downstairs. Emily was charged with straightening up the bathrooms. *All* I needed to do was make sure my room was less of an eyesore than it usually was.

Ever since Emily had come home, I had been nervous to know where exactly the little home-wrecker had disappeared to. Not comfortable with making a scene calling out for it, I opted instead to snag a bag of cheese puffs from the pantry. Shaking the bag loudly as I walked, I attempted to lure him out with bait. He wasn't biting. Not until I stooped down to pick up my backpack from the foot of the entryway stairs did I notice a distinct trail of water drops leading up the steps.

By following his tracks, I discovered my little friend, resting comfortably in my room. The curtains were closed and he was digging through my drawers. The small lamp on my nightstand was turned to its dimmest setting, but he seemed to be okay with it.

"What are you doing?" I asked, looking at the growing pile of clothes being flung out of my dresser.

"Hungry!" the little thing said anxiously, chewing on a pair of my underwear.

"Yeah? Well, you can't eat those," I said, yanking them out of his mouth. "Here, try these..."

I emptied some of the cheese puffs onto the top of my desk. Like a trapeze artist, the big-eyed creature bounded off my dresser and across the bed to my desktop.

"Food?" it asked, poking the orange puffs with curiosity.

"Kind of—it's junk food since I don't have any pet food here yet. It should tide you over until I can get some real food tomorrow," I offered.

The little critter took a test bite and then started munching away happily on the rest as I began cleaning up my room. A couple armloads of clothing stuffed behind the folding closet doors, a few items kicked under the bed behind the blanket's edge and you wouldn't recognize the place. Okay, I know it was more like "relocating" the mess, but the end result looked good.

All that remained was the disaster on my desk. I brushed a landslide of papers and junk off the surface, into my lower desk drawer, trying not to disturb my roommate's dinner in the process. A soft light pulsed under one of the piles. Clearing the papers away, I unearthed the source—it was the Author's Writ.

The gold embossed design on the cover of the aged, leather, hardbound book was alive with light. In and of itself the glowing didn't surprise me; I was used to seeing the book come to life in this way each time I unlocked it. But, it had never reacted like this on its own before. No. Some other mystery was at work.

What did this mean? Could it be that the Author was trying to reach me? I held my breath.

Not even the abrupt ringing of the doorbell at that moment, or the swirl of commotion downstairs, announcing the buyer's arrival could pull me away from answering this call. Abandoning my room-cleaning mission, I quickly dropped into a chair and rummaged through my top desk drawer for the key—the golden key that the Author's son, Aviad, had given me months earlier at his mysterious bookstore. Curious to see what I was up to, my hungry little friend left his cheese puffs and hopped over onto my shoulder just as I pulled the key out.

Though it no longer hummed as it did in my first encounters, the key still gave a sharp tug as I set it into place in the lock. Gently, I twisted it and the faint glow on the book turned suddenly brilliant as the latch fell open.

With a tiny yelp, the light-averse creature retreated behind my back only to tentatively climb back up when the light safely faded away.

Opening to the first page, I held my breath as I watched with eager anticipation for words to appear. The effect on me never grew old, though they were the same words that always appeared at the beginning. I read them aloud for good measure:

Born into darkness,
deceived by the Lie,
a door has been opened,
through which you must die.
The world you now know
will soon be no more.
Your fading is certain;
your death will be sure.

They were grim words to those who read them for the first time, but they had become much more than words to me now. They were a constant reminder of my adventure to Solandria, of all that had happened. In a way they were part of my story, part of who I was, and for some reason I was grateful for them. Before I could turn the page, a new paragraph suddenly began to form below the first. A surge of wonder came over me as I read these new words for the first time:

The Way will guide you,
the Truth set you free,
a new Life is written
for those who believe.

Could it be true? I ran my fingers over the new ink that completed the passage and the Author's mark that appeared below it. The three interlocking *V's* in the mark were a symbol of hope and inspiration for the Codebearers.

"*Via, Veritas, Vita,*" I whispered in awe. "The way of truth and life."

Eager to see if more new passages might have appeared elsewhere, I took up the book and began flipping through the pages with great expectation. As it so happened, the book did have more to reveal—not *on* its pages, but rather *from* them.

Something slipped out of the book and fell to the floor. My furry guest was the first to react as soon as the object fell out of the Writ. Scurrying to the floor, he began poking curiously at a square carefully folded paper. I set the book down and retrieved the fallen piece before he could eat it. The tan paper felt thick and rough to the touch. *How could I have missed this before?*

Turning it over, I found a red wax seal holding it shut, the flattened lump pressed with a signet that mirrored the Author's triple-*V* mark. Yet, it was the flowing script inked just below the seal that nearly caused my chest to explode: *Hunter*.

My fingers trembled with excitement as I slid one under the seal and broke open the message bearing my name. Part of the broken seal fell to the floor, much to the delight of my pet. He gathered the wax crumbs and shoved them in his mouth before I could object. He swallowed the wax and looked up with eager eyes, expecting me to give him more.

"You're strange, you know that?" I said.

He made a funny sound and, sensing there were not going to be any more handouts, scooted back over to his collection of cheese puffs and began munching again.

I turned my attention to the letter. The creased paper

reluctantly opened up to reveal its contents.

Blank. There was nothing inside.

Perplexed, I turned the letter over to check that I hadn't missed something on the backside.

Who would bother to send a letter with nothing on it?

I laid it down on my desk and smoothed out the folds, looking for any clue. At my touch, a wisp of smoke rose up. Alarmed, I pulled my hand back and noticed a tiny scorched line had suddenly appeared on the page. The smoldering line evoked a faint ember from its center that began to spread the black mark outward. Afraid of losing my message and setting off the hall smoke detector, I quickly wet a finger and attempted to snuff it out.

Not only did the ember *not* go out, but thin flames leaped wildly up from it, propelled across the paper as if by an unfelt wind. I jumped to my feet, sending my chair to the floor and the furry critter scurrying for cover under the bed. Ribbons of flame instantly overran the paper. Just as quickly as they had charged to life, they retreated, reduced to flickering embers spread throughout the page. I gasped as I recognized the series of singed marks left in their wake. They were words!

Hear my request, oh Author of my days. Have not I stayed true to your words amidst the trials? Even now in my despair, I know you are at work…but I am growing weak.

If it had only been Sanctuary that fell to the enemy, that would have been tolerable—the Resistance could have stood. But the Shadow have not been satisfied with dismantling our refuge walls. The very leaders that once upheld your Truth have now been corrupted or killed. The truth is distorted in a web of lies. I fear that I may soon be the only one left.

Let not your silence divide us to ruin. Revive hope! Ignite our faith! Let not this great darkness consume us.

As in ages past, bring us true warriors to defend your Way. Assemble your chosen to carry your flame where I cannot.

In you, great Author, do I put my trust. For you will make a way when the time is right. Find me ever ready and vigilant.

~Petrov

The signature belonged to Petrov, the leading commander of the Codebearer Resistance in Solandria. I stood dumbfounded at all that I had just seen and read. Part of me felt a little embarrassed, like I had just read a page torn from someone else's diary. In Solandria, I had never heard Petrov speak in such a vulnerable way. He was the commander and carried himself just as you would expect of a man with such authority. But beyond feeling awkward, I mostly felt deep concern.

Had the Resistance really fallen so low?

If what Petrov said was true, and I had no doubt that it was, then the Codebearers were in serious jeopardy. I desperately wanted to return and help right then and there, to let Petrov know that another still would stand with him. But I knew there was no use trying to force it since the Author had called me out of the Veil and into Solandria before. For now, he had chosen to keep me here. For what purpose I wasn't exactly sure.

"Isn't there anything I can do?" I fretted aloud.

As if in answer, the parting words from Petrov's message came back to me, *Find me ever ready and vigilant.*

It didn't sound like much, but it was all I had to go on.

Voices and footsteps coming up the stairs snapped me back to the reality of the moment. I still had a desk to clean and a forbidden pet to hide before Mom and the buyers got to my room.

Lifting the blanket's edge, I called to the frightened critter, hoping to lure him into my bag with a cheese puff. He wasn't under there. Sitting up, I discovered he had already bravely ventured out and was inching his way up to the letter on my desk. Before I could catch him, he slapped a paw onto the paper and set off a surprising reaction. The paper instantly flared up into a raging fire. The terrified creature bolted away with an ear-piercing wail, an instant fur ball of fire.

Whatever my horrified mother expected to find on the other side of my door as she ran to my aid, she wasn't anywhere close to imagining what she found when she burst through the door.

Papers scattered, lamp shattered, curtains swayed, posters ripped and feathers floated around an avalanche of clothing streaming out from the cock-eyed closet doors, at the foot of which I was kneeling, hugging my backpack and panting for breath.

There was an awkward exchange as the prospective buyers quickly excused themselves from the house showing, promising to come back "at a better time" as they hurried down the stairs and out of our lives forever.

I nervously endured the ensuing silence as Mom shook her head, burying it in her hands. How was I going to explain this one? Instantly, the thought of how well the whole "cat in the house" thing had worked as a cover-up for my earlier mistakes came to mind. Maybe I could just work that a little more.

What was I thinking? The lie had gone too far. It had been a mistake in the first place. *Veritas*—truth; that was part of the creed I had given my life to as a Codebearer. I resolved that Mom would get the truth.

When her face finally emerged from behind her hands, I could see the tears welled in her eyes. "Hunter…" she spoke softly, "I… I'm worried about you." She let one of the tears fall before wiping it away. "First I get a call from your school this morning and then this, tonight…" her voice broke off into a stressed laugh. "Wow. I mean,

I know there have been a lot of changes in your life lately—my new job, Stubbs switching schools, selling the house…and I don't think any of us have really gotten over losing your dad either… but, this?" She motioned around at the unsightly scene and laughed again. Of all of us, things had been the toughest on Mom and I feared I had finally pushed her beyond the limits of sanity.

"Listen, Mom. I'm so sorry," I apologized sincerely, beginning to pick up pieces of the mess. "I can explain…"

"Explain!" she snapped sharply. "No, Hunter! There's no way you can explain this!"

"I know. It's my fault, I admit it, but the truth about today is that Solandria…"

Mom would not have any of it. She called off my attempt with her upheld hands, shaking her head. "Please, no! I can't take any of this talk tonight. I just don't have the patience."

Just like times before, Mom was shutting me out and I couldn't pretend it didn't hurt.

"Mom," Emily's voice called up the stairs. "It's getting late and I've got to leave to pick up Trista and the others now. They'll be waiting. I guess I'll be leaving without Hunter?" Her last comment was more a suggestion than a question.

Turning back to watch me continue my pitiful efforts at undoing the mess, Mom let out a sigh. "Listen, Hunter, my better judgment would tell me to keep you here, but I know that tonight was a big deal for you with Stretch and Stubbs. Cleaning this tonight isn't going to fix anything. You should go."

"Really?" I asked, dropping the pair of socks I'd been matching. I was completely shocked at her out-of-left-field verdict. Even though she was downstairs, I could still hear Emily huff her disapproval.

Mom nodded, rubbing at an obvious stress-headache as she

qualified, "Yes. But to be honest, I mostly just need peace and quiet more than anything else. All I'm good for right now is a quick shower and an early bedtime."

"Thanks, Mom," I replied, hurrying to grab my stuff. I didn't dare leave Emily waiting any longer than she had already.

Mom just waved it off as she shuffled down the hall calling back, "Yeah, well.... Don't think this gets you out of anything. Tomorrow you and I are going to have a serious talk."

CHAPTER 7

A DREADFUL DISAPPOINTMENT

The Destiny Fair was always a big deal. The sights, the sounds and the smells of the fairgrounds were too in-your-face to ignore. As a matter of fact, you could feel the excitement building from a mile away. I know this because that is precisely how far away we had to drive before Emily found a parking spot. Yup, there was no missing the fair—it was an electric event.

Once a year, for seventeen days and sixteen nights, the quiet northern valley of Destiny was turned inside-out into the brightest, loudest, assault-your-senses destination you could ever possibly dream up. People would travel from far and wide to take part in the annual traditions that made our fair one of the largest of its kind. It had all the charm of your typical county fair petting zoo and giant pumpkin-growing contests, paired with the sophistication of cutting-edge amusement park thrill rides. As we scurried toward the ticket booth, I found myself lagging behind the entourage of girls Emily had assembled to join her for the occasion. All the right girls had been gathered—planned weeks in advance, no doubt—in order to ensure her popularity at school was kept at a high level. We were still standing in line for admission and they were already discussing which boys they wanted to find first. Fun, fun, fun....ugh!

Don't get me wrong, normally being the only guy in a group of girls wasn't a bad gig, especially with the quality of girls Em had selected. In fact, if I worked it right it could be a real popularity booster, I supposed. The thought crossed my mind that I was passing up a golden opportunity—one most guys would die to be a part of. I quickly pushed the thought aside. I had other plans tonight. With my new pet hidden safely in my backpack, I was determined to prove to Stretch and Stubbs once and for all that Solandria was entirely real and not just some fantasy story I had dreamed up. The creature was all the proof I needed.

As we waited in line, I found my mind wandering back to the mysterious letter. Petrov's message sounded so desperate, so urgent. From what I could gather from the letter, things seemed to be getting worse in Solandria which only made me long to return all the more quickly. This was the first real bit of information I had received since my return. How could I ignore it? Then again, Petrov's message had said the Author would make a way when the time was right...so, maybe some good old-fashioned distraction was exactly what I needed to get my mind off things for the moment.

"Tickets, please," the attendant at the counter said in a decidedly bored voice. I flashed my school ID and she waved me through with free admission. The girls and I filed in through the Fountain Gate where Stretch and Stubbs had agreed to meet me. Now that I was inside, I scanned the crowds for any sign of the guys. From the looks of things, I was the first one to arrive.

"You sure you don't need someone to hang back until they come, *little* brother?" Emily chided me, half-asking and half-trying to make me look silly in front of her friends.

The courtyard clock indicated I was actually a few minutes early for once.

"Nah, you go on…I'll catch up later," I replied, trying to sound as cool as possible. It was exactly what she had hoped to hear. Without another word Emily whipped around and disappeared into the fair, taking her gaggle of girlfriends with her.

I walked the loop around the fenced fountain in hopes of spotting the guys. It would have been easier if there weren't as many people already swarming around. Bumping my way through the traffic, I staked out an open spot on the bench that ringed the fountain and climbed up. I could see the whole courtyard from here. The fountain cycled through its choreography; nearby a carousel glided to its tune and a juggling performer rocked back and forth on his unicycle while balancing a bowling pin on his chin to a barrage of corny music and lack-luster applause.

"Well, little guy," I said over my shoulder, "we're definitely the first ones here, that's for sure."

"Friends?" the creature said softly, peeking out of the pouch at the colorful displays that surrounded us. He shrunk back into the pack just as quickly, overwhelmed by the lights that flooded the scene.

"Yeah, I'm sure they'll be here. They're probably just running a little late."

The music blasting from the speakers of the stage performer suddenly took a decidedly ominous tone.

"And now, ladies and gentlemen, it's time for…" he paused for effect, allowing the perfectly timed audio track to deliver its setup before concluding his statement with a deep, goofy voice, "Flaming Death!"

A pre-recorded scream wailed, provoking nervous laughter among the crowd. With nothing better to do, I decided to stay put and watch his final routine. The daredevil juggling act concluded with the performer's pants catching fire and a pair of stage hands dousing him with fire extinguishers as he rolled on the floor. In the end, it turned out to be a gimmick as he removed his pants to reveal a large pair of polka dotted underwear beneath them. The crowd roared their approval and dispersed back into the flow of traffic.

With still no sign of either friend, I took another turn around the fountain, this time stopping to grab some of the free samples vendors were offering to each passerby. In no time at all I gathered a half-dozen energy bars from the Boojum health food company, a pack of dental gum and an impressive collection of sticker advertisements. My favorite was the "Sm-MOO-oooth!" cow sticker for Dandy Dairy Farms. That one went on my jacket sleeve.

When I had four stickers running down both sleeves from successive loops around the fountain, I finally resorted to dropping a quarter in one of the coin-operated BIGfoot massage chairs near the gate. I was getting bored.

Why couldn't my friends just be here when I needed them?

"Thirty-two minutes late and counting. Unbelievable!" I sighed out loud, as the vibrating foot massager came to a halt. I pulled out one of the Boojum All-Natural snack bars from the side pocket of my backpack and glanced over the label. The slogan on the front read, "Tastes so good, it can't be bad for you."

Yeah, right, I thought in disbelief.

I tore the end of the package open with my teeth and broke off a piece of the grainy goodness for my furry friend.

"Here ya go, little guy; I got you a snack," I said, tossing it into the bag.

There was a ferocious crackling and munching sound as the

creature tore into his new meal. Apparently, he liked Boojum a lot. I tossed in another piece, much to the satisfied moans and crunching of the hidden creature.

"Num, num, num!" it smacked happily, making so much noise it caught the attention of the plump man seated next to me. He turned and eyed my bag suspiciously. I smiled back and with a shrug of indifference took a bite myself in hopes of hiding the fact that there was something in my bag. The man stood up, raised an eyebrow and walked away, shaking his head.

The bar was everything I had imagined—crunchy, bitter and so *not* good! It tasted like edible cardboard with a few cranberries thrown in for good measure—definitely not my kind of snack. I was just about to spit the first bite onto the cement walkway when the vendor who had given it to me walked past. Not wanting to look like an idiot, I faked a smile and waved the bar at her as she glanced my way.

Unfortunately, she confused the gesture to mean I wanted more and ended up giving me another bag of bars on the spot. I forced myself to swallow what was in my mouth and thanked her as she walked away.

With a bad taste in my mouth and an equally foul mood, I shoved the remainder of the bar into the backpack.

"Here, eat this and keep quiet!" I whispered.

As I considered my options to redeem the night, a bank of payphones next to the restrooms caught my eye. That was just what I needed. I could ring Stubbs on his cell phone and find out what had been keeping them. Scooping up my bag, I walked over to the payphone. I emptied my pants pockets and was pleased to find I still had enough change to make the call. I lifted the receiver, dropped in the coins and dialed Stubbs' number from memory.

"C'mon, Stubbs, pick up!" I muttered as it rang.

Three rings later his voice mail answered. "Hello, it's me; you know what to do!" His simple recorded message ended with a short "beep." Since I'd already paid for the call, I decided leave a message.

"Hey, this is Hunter; I've been waiting by the fountain. Where are you guys? Hurry up!"

I slammed the phone down on the receiver in frustration. *It figures. The only time I need him to answer and he's not near his phone. You've got to be kidding me!*

I picked up the phone again and fished around in my coat pockets for any leftover change, despite the fact that I knew I was out of coins. Just then, my hand closed around something cold and familiar. I pulled out a gold pendant emblazoned with the Author's mark and let it dangle lightly from the chain in front of me. Hope's medallion.

In that moment, all the noise of the fairgrounds, even the dial tone in the phone, seemed to disappear under the sudden flood of emotions that filled me. Hope was my friend, the truest of friends. Even though her death had been my fault, she never blamed me for it. She accepted it as if it was meant to be. Hope had given me the medallion in Solandria just before she died, a gift to remind me that I was never alone.

Suddenly, a hand reached out of nowhere and snatched it from my grip. My stomach sank at the thought of losing my most prized possession. Dropping the phone, I turned to see who it was, ready to put up a fight. I was slightly relieved to find it was only Trista, my sister's new best friend.

"Oooo, where'd ya win this?" she asked, blowing a bubble with her gum as she spoke. "Mind if I try it on?"

Before I could say no she had pulled it over her head and adjusted the chain to fall beneath her hair, which wasn't pulled back in a ponytail as usual.

My muscles tensed at the sight of somebody else wearing the medallion. There was something wrong about it.

"So, how do I look?" she teased, striking a ridiculous pose.

"Annoying," I snapped, thrusting my palm out. "Now give it back!" I hoped I hadn't sounded as angry as I felt. Trista got the message and her once bubbly voice dropped to a lower tone.

"Ooookay, somebody's clearly not having a good time," she muttered in jest as she removed the necklace and placed it in my hand.

I slipped it back over my neck and tucked it safely under my shirt, feeling the urge to apologize for my attitude. "I'm sorry, it's not you, it's just that..."

"Fer-geda-bow-dit," she tossed back playfully, making a quick recovery and punching me gently on the shoulder. "I would have been royally irked too if my friends had bailed on me." Whipping out her raspberry-colored cell phone, Trista waved it at me with a pained expression on her face. "Got a message for ya. Stretch called!"

My stomach soured in anticipation of the worst. He had managed to avoid me at school today, and now he was ditching me again. I was beginning to get the idea we were no longer friends.

"Actually, he called your house earlier today, but your mom just found the voicemail. Bummer, huh?"

She explained that Stretch had caught the flu at school and couldn't make it to the fair tonight, and Stubbs couldn't come either because Stretch was his ride. I felt a little better knowing they hadn't intentionally ditched me, but the end result was the same.

"Great, I'm on my own," I sighed, contemplating what I would do for the rest of the night. "Thanks for the message anyway."

"Yeah, I'm sorry 'bout that," she said sympathetically.

I expected her to turn and head off, but she lingered a while, brushing her hair behind one ear. "Hey, listen, you know you could hang out with Em and the rest of us if you want."

If by "the rest of us" she meant their group of girlfriends, I wasn't all that interested. Then again, it beat being a loner.

"Sure," I shrugged and motioned for Trista to lead the way.

As we walked Trista asked, "So, where did you really get the necklace?"

The question made me tense. Until tonight, I had kept it mostly a secret. The only people I had shown it to were Stretch and Stubbs back when I first tried to prove that Solandria was real. That didn't help so I had been reluctant to show it to anyone ever since.

"Oh, it was just a gift…from a friend." I tried to say it in a way that would leave it at that.

"Some friend," she whistled. "What's her name?"

"Her name? I never said it was a girl," I said defensively.

Trista just gloated and gave me a light-hearted shove. "Puh-lease, like you needed to. I could tell by the way you were looking at it back there."

It was a lucky guess, but I had to admit she was right.

"Her name was Hope," I answered, quickly adding, "but it's not what you're thinking. It's mostly special because…of what it means."

"Really, so what does it mean?" she asked, blowing an oversized bubble with her gum and letting it pop. She sucked it back in before the slightest bit could stick to her face.

More than anything I wanted to speak up and tell her what I believed, but my knotted stomach was holding my tongue hostage. I was desperate to find any way to derail this train of conversation now that I knew my next stop was going to be "Loserville."

"It's a mark…er…a symbol from a book I found earlier this summer."

"You mean the Author's mark, right?" Trista's matter-of-fact response was not what I was expecting at all.

"How do you know about the Author's mark?" I ventured nervously, remembering the counselor's warning about toning things down.

"C'mon, you didn't think you were the only one, did you?" Trista said, casually pulling her hair back and sliding it into the rubber band she kept on her wrist.

"Well…yeah, actually," I said in disbelief. Now I could hardly contain my excitement. Finally, someone I could open up with and talk to honestly about Solandria. Emily was going to flip when she realized Trista believed in the Author's Writ too. "Oh man, this is awesome. You're a Codebearer?"

"Not really, I've just heard about it. At least, whatever I could understand from some of my little cousins. I recognized the symbol on your medallion right away. They have this book called the Author's Whit."

"You mean Writ," I corrected, suddenly feeling disappointed by my misunderstanding.

"Writ…right, whatever. Anyway, their family is really into the stories."

"They're *not* just stories," I said half-heartedly, recalling what Sheppard had said earlier.

"I know," she answered back, "there are riddles and symbols and stuff like that in there too. Don't get me wrong…from the little I've read it's all really mysterious and intriguing. But the way they talk about it, you'd think it was actually real…. Can you imagine believing in an unseen world of invisible beings?" Trista pressed further.

Before I had time to respond, there was a sudden rush of movement behind Trista. Out of the corner of my eye, I saw a horde of spindly black arms overhead, lunging down on top of us.

"Look out, Dispirits!" I wailed, launching myself out in a tackle and pulling her to the ground to escape the oncoming attack. We landed with a splash in a shallow puddle of rain-water on the cement walkway, followed by a dozen of our multi-armed assailants.

"What do you think you're doing?" Trista fumed, pushing me off of her in a state of confusion. A surprised group of onlookers gasped as I leaped to my feet with fists clinched tightly, ready to fight off my adversaries. You can imagine my embarrassment when I realized the "Dispirits" were nothing more than six-legged inflatable spiders, stacked in a tower that had just been inadvertently knocked over.

"Are you insane?" Trista demanded breathlessly as she picked herself up from the ground. "Balloon animals? You ruined my new skirt to save me from balloons? Ugh!" she fussed, picking up one shaped like a large hammer and whacking me over the head with it.

The gasps in the crowd turned quickly to chuckles. I would have apologized were it not for another commotion coming from the vendor's booth beside us.

"C'mon, kid! Can't you watch where you're goin'?" a tattooed vendor scolded, hovering over a boy in a camouflaged jacket who had also fallen to the ground. The vendor quickly nodded my direction and threw out an apology.

"Sorry 'bout that folks. This doofus here decided not to watch where he was running and plowed straight into this here display of fine merchandise!"

He pointed to a selection of cheap trinkets that were probably better described as "toilet paper on a stick." At least, that's what my dad used to call it. There was nothing fine about it. The clumsy kid who had caused the trouble stumbled as he tried to pick himself up, nearly knocking over another display in the process. Apparently he was the one responsible for knocking over the tower of cheap-o balloon toys that had buried us.

"I-I'm so sorry. It was an accident..." the boy stuttered nervously.

Grabbing him roughly by the collar, the worker shoved him over to where the bizarre assortment of product lay strewn about next to Trista and me.

"Save it, kid. Just pick up my stuff and get out of here before I charge you for it." The vendor turned his back and lumbered back to his post behind the small counter.

Not wanting to test the threat, the boy hastily set to work, but did a better job at dropping the products than he did at picking them up. As he pushed his black dreadlocks out of his eyes, I recognized his face immediately. It was the new kid from school.

"Rob, is that you?" I asked curiously.

He made no eye contact, only casting a brief glance at my face before returning to his task of cleaning up his mess. "Sorry, d-do I know you?" he questioned, looking nervously over his shoulder more than a few times. Something was bothering him.

"No, I guess not. I just recognized you from the hallway at school today. Weren't you the one who knocked...over the..."

"Yup, that was me alright," he said before I finished.

"Not your week, is it?" I pointed out.

Rob just shook his head and cast another look over his shoulder.

"You're telling me, I'm still running from that Cranton dude. He's determined to put me in the dunk tank since I didn't get wet at school. The guy is brutal."

"I know what you mean," I said.

By this time Trista had managed to figure out what had really happened and let my little "Dispirit attack" blunder go unpunished. She returned to my side and joined in helping pick up the balloon animals.

"Don't worry about Cranton," she answered nicely. "Guys like him eventually get what they deserve. I just hope I'm there when he does."

"Yeah well, I hope it happens sooner than later 'cause he's headed this way," I said, catching a glimpse of one of Cranton's Cobras pointing at us from his perch atop a bench.

"Over here," shouted the Cobra member. "It's the dork and he's with Hunter!"

"Good," Cranton growled. "We'll make it a double dunk!"

My stomach sank. After trying hard to stay out of Cranton's way this year, I figured I deserved a break from his harassment. Now, it looked like I was doomed to be a target once again.

"Leave 'em, we gotta get out of here," I shouted at Rob, who was still fumbling with a few plastic balloons. The three of us darted away, with Cranton and his pals hot on our trail.

Chapter 8

From Trouble to Terror

Dodging through the crowd, we made our way toward the far back corner of the fairgrounds, where the animal pins and farming exhibits were set up. Turning the corner, we ducked into the sheep barn and dove between a bail of hay and a dumpster. It was as good a place as any to hide…if you could get over the smell.

The place was noisier than I expected. The tin roof and walls echoed loudly with the buzz of a dozen giant fans that had been set up to circulate the stale stench of livestock. It was the perfect place to hide, though, providing an extra level of white noise to cover our heavy breathing. As long as we stayed out of sight, we had a good chance of making it without being discovered.

"Nice hiding place, Hunter," Trista quipped in a hushed tone. She pointed to the sign on the side of the dumpster that read Doo Doo Only. "You sure know how to show a girl a good time."

I had to admit, it was pretty tacky.

"I didn't hear you coming up with any better ideas," I whispered back. "Would you rather be soaking in the dunk tank?"

Trista rolled her eyes, "Whatever, I'm not the one they're after anyway; you two are, remember?"

I didn't want to argue with her about it, mostly because she was right. So I let her comment slide unanswered.

Just then, Cranton and his gang entered the barn.

"They gotta be in here somewhere," Cranton shouted, as he jumped up onto the hay pile to look around over the scene. "This place reeks of losers."

He was standing only a few feet away from Rob's head, but he was turned the other way and didn't seem to notice we were there. They looked around for a few minutes more while Cranton lit up a cigarette and watched it all.

"You sure they didn't go into the other barn?" one of his friends finally asked. "They aren't here!"

Cranton stood silent.

"You want to check out back?" one of them asked.

"Nah, the fair is boring anyway. Let's go do something a little more...*exciting*!" Cranton said, flicking the remainder of the cigarette to the ground behind him and right beside me. He hopped down from the hay bales and sauntered out the door with his gang in tow.

Even after they left, we didn't move, just in case it was a trick to get us to come out of our hiding place.

This was the first time I'd really had a chance to introduce myself to Rob. He was a scrawny kid, not much meat on the bones. He moved with an awkward gait that looked like an accident waiting to happen. From the looks of his clothes, his family was struggling to make ends meet. His shoes were well worn and spotted with holes, and his jeans had holes in them too, but not the cool kind you paid for. These jeans were out of style and likely handed down from someone else.

Despite his appearance, I really wanted to get to know him. After all, from what I could tell, Rob was the one who dropped the flyer with the Author's mark on it at school today. I wanted to find out for sure if it was him, but I needed an angle. I began to wonder how to approach him about it.

"So Rob…I don't think we've introduced ourselves. My name is Hunter, and this is…"

"Trista Golden," she said in a perky voice as she smacked her gum a little too loudly. I shot a worried look her way and put my finger to my lips.

"They could still be listening, you know," I said. She rolled her eyes and lowered her voice once more before continuing the introductions.

"I haven't seen you in any of our classes this year. Are you a freshman or something?" she asked.

"Yeah, something like that," he replied mysteriously, peeking over the hay bails, expecting to see Cranton pop in at any moment.

"What does that mean? You don't know what grade you're in?"

"Well, I'm only at school for a few classes," he answered. "I guess technically I'm a freshman, but the majority of my classes are more advanced. I'm homeschooled at the moment."

"Oh, smart guy, huh?" Trista said playfully.

"Not really, my dad's in the military so we move around a lot. That's why we started homeschooling. I like it though. It's easier to get ahead of the class when you don't goof around with your friends all the time."

"Like, I could never do that," Trista said. "I'm too much of a people person. Being cooped up at home all day would drive me crazy. No offense, but I like having friends."

Rob tried to shrug off the comment. "It's not as bad as you think."

A few moments of awkward silence passed as we waited for Cranton to reappear. There seemed to be nobody else in the barn but us and an animal keeper who was sitting in his overalls, reading a book near the entrance. When it seemed safe at last, Rob spoke up again.

"Listen, I should probably go. I don't want to get you into any more trouble than I already have."

He stood up and turned around, but before he could leave I spotted a glint of gold hanging from a leather clasp on his belt. I don't know why I hadn't noticed it before, but the form was unmistakable—the hilt of a sword.

"A Veritas Sword?" I blurted out before he could walk away.

Rob stopped dead in his tracks and turned slowly around, looking me straight in the face for the first time. A hint of confusion crossed his face.

"You know about the sword?" he questioned.

"Yeah, I have one too. Or at least I did before I…" I noticed Trista's curious gaze and decided to hold back a bit. "Before I lost mine."

Rob's eyes darted between me and Trista, trying to figure us out. "Where did you get it?" he asked.

This time there was no beating around the bush. I didn't care how weird it sounded to Trista; I needed a friend who understood what I had been through and Rob was my last best shot.

"Solandria," I answered. "I got it when I was called into the Author's Writ. I'm a Codebearer, Rob…at least I think I am."

Rob's stoic expression morphed into a wide goofy smile.

"Oh man, this is great! I thought I was the only one at school!"

"Me too," I said excitedly.

It was as if we were instant best friends. Rob and I started comparing stories about how we first found the Author's Writ and a little about our adventures. Before we could get too far, I sensed Trista growing more and more uncomfortable with the direction of the conversation. She was obviously the outsider, which was not her typical place.

"Whoa there, code buddies," she butted in at last. "It looks like Cranton's not coming, so unless you want to spend your evening at the Doo-Doo dumpster, why don't we get out of here and find the others?"

She grabbed my backpack and tossed it into my chest. I fumbled to grasp it before it fell to the floor. In all the commotion the creature inside let out a muffled yelp.

"What was that?" Trista said, glaring suspiciously at my backpack.

"What was what?" I replied, pretending I didn't notice the sound. The creature had been pretty quiet, but now began fidgeting and squirming uncontrollably inside. I clutched tightly to my pack in hopes of hiding the movements. Rob looked surprised to see the bag bulging and jerking in my arms, but it was Trista who wouldn't let it go.

"Your bag! It's moving all over the place; what's in there?"

I hadn't planned on showing the creature to anyone but the guys. The last thing I needed was someone blabbing about it to my sister or mother. My mind went to work, trying to create a viable excuse for the strange movement in my backpack. Unfortunately, the creature was not pleased that I was gripping it so tightly and started complaining by making a weird garbling sound.

"Well?" Trista prodded. "Are you going to tell us what that is or am I going to have to check for myself?"

There was no way around it; I would have to come clean.

"Okay, fine," I said, giving up at last. "Remember how Emily told you about the cat? You know, the one that destroyed our house this afternoon?"

"Yeah, so?" Trista said, her face plastered with a look of bewilderment.

"Well, it wasn't really a cat. It was something else. Something unlike any other animal I've ever seen. I think it's from another world."

"Get real," Trista replied.

"I'm serious," I said, "and I'll prove it, but you have to promise to never tell a soul. Not Emily, not my mom, not anyone... What you see is just between us three, understood?"

Rob and Trista agreed, their eyes widening as I set the backpack gently down on the ground between us.

"Just don't freak out or you might scare it!" I said as I slowly flipped open the main pouch of my backpack. "It's okay, little guy. You can come out now."

The creature's two furry paws were the first to emerge from the backpack, gripping the side and gradually raising its head out to look around. As soon as his large blue eyes glowed out from the bag, Trista gasped loudly. The creature startled and ducked back down into the bag.

"Trista," I scolded, expressing my disappointment.

"Oops, sorry," she said, covering her mouth with both hands. She leaned forward and peeked down into the bag. The furry creature slowly uncurled from a ball and looked back up at her.

"Oh my, it's adorable! What is it?" she asked.

"I told you I don't know. I found it in the kitchen, raiding our food. It seemed lost, so I decided to keep it as a pet."

Trista's dimpled smile seemed to soothe the creature's nervousness. It cooed gently, welcoming her touch as she reached out to pet its head.

"So you really don't know where it came from?" Rob asked suspiciously.

"No clue. When I got home earlier today, it was already there. Made a real mess of the place too."

Rob scratched his head and pondered this for awhile. Trista, on the other hand, fell immediately in love with it.

"Can I pick her up?" Trista asked, already reaching out before I could respond.

"Sure, you can pick *HIM* up!" I answered, making sure to add emphasis on my gender of choice.

She bent down and carefully lifted the furry creature out of the backpack, cradling it in her arms like a baby. It seemed content with her and snuggled tightly to her chest.

"What's her name?" Trista giggled, ignoring my previous comment and scratching it behind the ears.

"I haven't really thought of one yet, at least nothing that fits him. And stop calling it her; it's my pet and I say it's a boy, I think."

Trista rolled her eyes.

"Some pet. You haven't even named it yet." Trista turned to the creature and in her sweetest voice added, "We'll have to fix that won't we, little one? You're too cute to not have a name!"

"Hungry," it said abruptly. It was the first time Trista had heard it speak, and she nearly dropped the thing in response.

"It can…talk?" she said warily.

"Yeah, cool huh? And that's not even the half of it. He can disappear too! But he usually only does that when he's near a really bright light."

"Disappear?" Rob repeated, fascinated by the thing. "That's sweet! Are you sure you should keep it though? I mean, you hardly know anything about him. He could be dangerous."

"Relax," I said. "Does he look dangerous to you?"

"I guess not," Rob said in agreement, finally reaching out to pet the little critter. It cooed at Rob's touch and made him crack a smile. "I have to admit, he's pretty cool."

"Besides, if he starts to be trouble I can always get rid of him later."

"Hungry," it said again, this time a bit more forcefully. He scurried up Trista's arm and perched himself on her shoulder. He started picking at her hair in search of food.

"Hey, cut that out!" Trista said with a smile. "What do you feed her anyway?"

"*Him*," I stated firmly. "So far, *he'll* eat whatever I can find. It's practically the only way to keep him quiet."

"I'll bet it's still a baby," Trista expressed, pulling the creature's hands away from her hair once more. "My baby brother eats all of the time too. It's what they do."

"Yeah, well, he better get full soon or I won't have anything left to feed him," I said, digging through my pack for a snack. "Here, try these. He seemed to like them."

I tossed a snack bar her way, which she caught one handed. The furry creature scurried across the back of her neck to the shoulder closest to the treat.

"Boojum bars?" Trista asked with a smile, as she examined the packaging.

"Yeah, they're really nasty health bars," I said.

"I know what they are, and they're not nasty. They're my

favorite. *Taste so good they can't be bad,*" she said, singing the last line from the commercial jingle.

"Well, they *taste so bad, you can have them*!" I sang back in jest, proud of myself for coming up with it on the spot. Rob laughed at my joke. Trista stuck her tongue out at us and tore open the wrapper.

"Boojums!" the little creature shouted happily, when at last he saw what we were talking about.

"That's right," Trista chuckled, tickled that the creature liked her kind of food. "Hey, that's it! We should call her Boojum. What do you think?"

"I don't know," I shrugged, not wanting to admit that I kind of liked it.

"Please, please? I've never named a pet before," Trista begged, grabbing and squeezing my arm gently. Her green eyes sparkled with hopeful anticipation of my response. She had obviously perfected that look on her parents.

"Fine, but it's a he," I said forcefully.

Trista clapped excitedly at the name.

"Boojum it is then," Trista said, willing to trade choosing the gender for naming the creature. Boojum devoured the first health bar in no time at all, spilling crumbs all over his fur in the process. As he gnawed happily on the last bite of the crunchy snack, the lights overhead began to flicker.

At first, there was a slight popping sound, followed by a short burst of light before the lights finally went out entirely. The barn fell under a blanket of stale darkness and the fans wound to a dead stop. All was silent for a moment. Then the sheep started bleating and yanking on their tethers as if threatened by an unseen presence.

"Uh oh," Boojum moaned, folding his ears back to his head and clinging closer to Trista.

"Don't ya'll worry none, folks," a heavy southern voice from across the room hollered out. "We just blew a fuse er somethin'. But we'll have her back on quicker than you can spit and holler "Howdy."

Even in the dark, I could tell Rob was worried. Despite the reassurance of the voice, somehow he sensed there was more to the darkness than just a blown fuse. He fumbled for his Veritas Sword, his hands shaking with nervous energy as he pulled it out and held it in front of himself.

"Boys and their toys," Trista shook her head with a laugh. "Put it away. What do you think you're going to do with that silly thing anyway?"

A murmuring hum festered throughout the room, growing in volume and drowning out the troubled sheep. At first I thought it was just the sound of the fans turning back on, but when Rob pointed upward the true source of the sound was revealed.

We were not alone.

The metal rafters were loaded with a dozen or more of the strangest winged creatures I'd ever seen. They seemed to have no feet to speak of, just a long articulated tail they used to hang from the ceiling. The tip of the tail was armed with a barbed talon that even from this distance I perceived was as sharp as a razor. As we looked up, their long, vulture-like necks strained to watch us.

"Don't make any sudden moves," Rob said slowly, hoping Trista would listen for once. As usual, she didn't.

"Why? What are you so worked up about anyway?" she asked. "You aren't afraid of the dark are you?"

Rob shook his head and pointed up in the dark, pressing a finger to his lips.

"What? I don't see anything," Trista replied, not even bothering to whisper.

Just then, one of the hanging creatures swooped down toward

us, gliding on its leathery wings. Rob swung his invisible blade into the air, and it burned to life in a flash of orange light.

Boojum squealed at the sight of the bright sword-light and dove back into my backpack, pulling the top closed behind him. In the same instant, the flying creature was severed in two by Rob's sword. Half of the creature landed in the arms of Trista, who shrieked and immediately dropped the writhing part she held.

"Gross!" she yelled, trying desperately to shake the black ooze of blood from her hands. The severed half squirmed violently on the floor, flinging drops of blood every which way. A moment later it stopped moving and dissolved into wisps of black smoke. Trista just stared, looking wide-eyed at the spot on the ground where it had just disappeared. With the light of Rob's Veritas blade, she could now see what she hadn't seen before.

"What is that thing? Wh-wh-where did it come from?" Trista squealed. Nobody answered; there wasn't time to discuss it right now.

"We need to get out of here now!" I shouted.

"Yeah, about that" Rob answered with a groan, "I'm going to need a minute." After the first attack, he had somehow managed to lodge the Veritas Sword halfway down into the side of the Doo Doo dumpster and was trying desperately to yank it out.

Seizing their opportunity, the remainder of the flying serpents began to dive, first one then two at a time.

"Get down!" I shouted, pulling Trista with me as quickly as I could. She didn't complain as we collapsed to the floor, behind the hay bales. This time she knew the threat was real, but we were a moment too late. On their way down, a Treptor's single razor-sharp tail talon caught the back of my shoulder, ripping though my shirt and into my skin. I howled in pain.

Rob, who was still trying desperately to get his Veritas Sword unstuck, gave a final tug and fell back to the floor, landing beside us. Lying on his back, Rob waved the sword back and forth in the air above us, keeping the creatures at bay with its light. Only one of the creatures ventured too close. It was quickly whacked aside by the sword, its wings damaged in the scuffle.

"What are these things?" a terrified Trista asked again.

"They're Treptors," Rob explained. "More of a nuisance than anything, but larger flocks can be deadly."

"A nuisance? They're flat out freaky—that's what they are." Trista was obviously upset at what she was seeing.

"What are they doing here?" I asked.

"That's what I was wondering too," Rob said, still swinging his sword overhead. "The Shadow don't usually show themselves outside of the Veil."

"Do you two mind speaking English for a change? Not all of us know what your little code words mean," Trista asked, feeling a little put out. "What's the Veil?"

"Sorry, Trista," I explained, "the Veil is what people from Solandria call the world we live in. And the Shadow are...well, basically evil creatures like those things." I gripped my sore shoulder and glanced at Rob. The majority of the flock had given up its attack and perched themselves from the rafters once more, waiting for a better time. Only a handful continued to hover overhead, circling the room.

Rob lowered his Veritas Sword for a moment, setting the hilt against my wound. It healed quickly and the stinging subsided just in time for Rob to return his attention to the aggressive Treptors, who were still anxiously hovering above us.

"Make them go away...please!" Trista said anxiously.

"They only attack in confined spaces. If we can make it outside they'll probably leave us alone." Rob stated. "It won't be easy, but we'll have to make a dash for it. Get ready!"

Before another word was spoken, Rob jumped to his feet and sliced through another pair of the ugly creatures that were bearing quickly down upon us.

"Go! I've got you covered!" Rob shouted as the Treptors regrouped for another attack. "Run for the door…now!" he added with emphasis. As he spoke, he gestured with his glowing sword toward the exit, but the blade slipped from his grip and slid out the door. It was a heart-stopping sight. We were now unarmed and completely vulnerable beneath the Treptors' vicious gazes.

"Oops, that wasn't supposed to happen! My bad," Rob said, dumbfounded by his mistake.

"You think?" Trista remarked, looking whiter than a sheet.

One thing was becoming clear, if there was an award for mastering the art of clumsiness, Rob would easily have won it.

Recognizing their chance, the remaining Treptors reunited and poured down upon us like a mad rush of water. It was all we could do to keep our balance beneath the barrage of leathery wings.

"Whatever you do, don't stop!" I shouted, leading the charge to our escape. The others followed behind, headlong into the swarming horde of Treptors. Never before had twenty feet seemed so far. All the way the Treptors swooped and slashed at us, inflicting a few cuts across our backs. With arms flailing wildly overhead we pushed our way through the flurry of flying terrors and dove out the front door to safety.

"Hey, watch yourselves," a grumpy old man in an electric scooter frowned disapprovingly at us as we tumbled dramatically out of the barn, cutting in front of him and causing him to stop.

A nervous glance over my shoulder proved that Rob had been right. The Treptors were nowhere to be seen now, though their stinging cuts across our shoulders and backs still felt every bit real.

"They're gone…just like that?" Trista asked, her voice trembling.

"Yes, but we have to keep moving," Rob answered. "We're not safe yet."

"But you said they wouldn't follow us," said Trista, pointing at the seemingly empty barn behind.

"Treptors aren't the only Shadow we have to worry about," Rob said, still tense. "If there are Treptors here, I can only imagine what else might be lurking nearby."

Trista gulped, "You mean there are others?"

Rob and I both nodded.

Beep. Beep.

"Do you mind? Clear a path will ya, or I'll plow you over," the man on the scooter grumbled stubbornly, apparently unwilling to exert any energy on using his steering wheel to go around. We stepped aside and apologized, but it had little effect on his sour mood. "Darn kids think they own the place," he muttered and scooted away.

"Wait, where's Boojum? We can't leave him behind," Trista reminded us. The little guy had been hiding in my backpack ever since the first flash of Rob's sword.

"Forget Boojum; where's my sword?" asked Rob as he searched the ground frantically. "It should have been right here!"

A small flurry of motion directed my eyes over to where the old man on the scooter was honking at another hapless victim. There on the ground, just behind the scooter, was Boojum, with Rob's sword hilt tucked tightly under his arm.

Looking back towards me, Boojum simply waved and said, "Light bad," before catching a ride in the scooter's backseat basket as the old man zipped off through the parting crowd.

"Hey! Your little weasel's stealing my sword!" Rob fumed. "After him!"

Chapter 9

The Flying Gondola

We raced in pursuit, but the man on the scooter was quicker than one might expect. Being handicapped, he had the advantage of the crowd's pity. People seemed more willing to move out of his way than they were for us. Eventually the flow of fairgoers thinned enough so we could close the gap between us.

"Give me back my sword!" Rob shouted after Boojum.

"Nuh uh," Boojum said defiantly, gripping the sword tightly to his chest. "Light bad."

With that he hopped out of the basket and scurried up a ramp that led to the Sky Cars. It was the only ride on this side of the fairgrounds, and not really much of a ride at that. Its main purpose was to carry gondolas of spectators from one side of the fair to the other. There was no line—everyone else was saving his or her tickets for the thrill rides on the other side of the fair.

We wasted no time rushing up after him, but at the top of the ramp a broad man, as wide as he was tall, blocked our path.

"Tickets, please—four each for a round trip," he said, reaching out for the fare. We tried to explain but the man was not sympathetic to our plight.

"Look, if you wants on the ride, you have ta pay fer it. It's as simple as that."

Trista dug into her pocket and begrudgingly produced the twelve tickets required. He counted them and let us pass at last. By the time we reached the top of the ramp, Boojum had already snuck aboard an empty car, which was starting to slide up the cable and across the fairgrounds.

Another man, scrawny and gaunt, motioned for us to step forward to load up in the next car. Trista and I hopped into gondola seven, but Rob suddenly froze in place.

"What are you waiting for, Rob?" I asked.

He squirmed, unwilling to move past the yellow safety line that was painted on the ground.

"I was just thinking...maybe I ought to meet you guys on the other side," he suggested, his voice sounding a bit strange.

"Don't be stupid," Trista said in her usual blunt way. "It'll take you three times as long to get there. Boojum will be long gone by then."

"It's just that I'm afraid of heights, okay? They make my stomach sick," Rob confessed.

"So, ya goin' on or ain't ya, kid?" the slim man asked rather impatiently.

Rob didn't budge, still frozen with fear.

"Come on, Rob, we have to get that sword!" I encouraged him. "It's only five minutes across; it will be over before you know it."

The man who held our gondola door open added, "This here is

the safest ride in the park, son. Why, I've never lost a rider yet."

"Fine, I'll go, but don't say I didn't warn you," Rob said, stepping into the gondola against his better judgment. He sat down across from the two of us and scooted to the middle.

The door slammed shut and with the release of a lever the gondola swung forward, connected to the cable that stretched a hundred feet in the air. Rob shut his eyes tightly and gripped the metal railing that surrounded the compartment. With each sway of the cable car his fist tightened and he moaned weakly.

"Relax," Trista offered. "We're safe up here; nothing is going to happen."

"There's always a first time," Rob whined.

As we reached the highest point of the ride, there was a sudden jolt as the cable car stopped in place, swaying wildly back and forth from its previous momentum.

"Tell me we didn't just stop," Rob said, still unwilling to open his eyes.

"It's no big deal," said Trista. "I'm sure this happens all the time when they get backed up with passengers."

The fact that we hadn't seen any other passengers getting on with us crossed my mind, but I wasn't about to say it out loud. Glancing out over the fairgrounds, I spotted a series of phantom figures appearing on the sky cable tower ahead of us. They were not human. As they began to climb up the tower, I knew in an instant what they were—skinny bug-like creatures with six arms, a pair of long legs and bulging frog-like faces.

"Dispirits," I said, barely loud enough for the others to hear.

For the first time since he had set foot on the ride, Rob's eyes popped opened. He craned his neck slowly around to look where I was pointing. The shadowy creatures had reached the peak of the tower already and, using their six arms, had begun traversing along the cable toward our car.

"Great. Without my sword we're doomed," he moaned.

I started thinking of escape plans but nothing seemed to work. It was too high to jump (the fall would certainly kill us), and climbing out of the car seemed futile as well (by the time we made it to the cable the Dispirits would already be there). I had just about given up hope when a familiar voice called out from beneath my seat.

"Hungry," said Boojum, as he scratched at my backpack in search of a snack.

"Boojum? How did you get here?" I asked, surprised to see the creature in our gondola. "I thought you were over there in number six."

"Me flee, see?" said Boojum, disappearing and reappearing a few steps away.

Trista was delighted at the sight of the creature and snatched him up in her arms.

"What about my sword?" Rob asked, sounding sicker by the minute. We searched under the seat, but Boojum didn't have it with him.

"It must still be in the other gondola," I figured.

"Well, I can't fight with what I don't have," Rob pointed out.

"Maybe not, but there might be a way to get it back," I said, glancing down at Boojum. The plan was simple; we promised Boojum he could have a snack bar if he retrieved the sword from gondola six. With a little encouragement, he disappeared in puff of black smoke and returned a moment later with Rob's sword in hand.

"Good job, Boojum," Trista said, picking him up again and showering him with praise. In no time at all he was munching a Boojum bar, sitting contentedly on Trista's lap.

"Good job?" Rob groaned in response. "If he hadn't stolen my sword in the first place we'd be safe on the ground right now!"

"Well, if you hadn't scared him with it he wouldn't have run away," she replied.

"That still doesn't give him the right to run off with my sword."

"Then why don't you try holding onto it next time, instead of throwing it out the door."

Before I could break up the argument, a gruesome black arm shot through the top of the compartment, grasping for a victim. The Dispirits had found us.

Trista screamed at the sight, spooking Boojum back into my bag. I tossed the sword to Rob who ignited it on the spot and severed the arm from its shadowy host above. Two more arms reached down through the canopy like phantoms. Rob took care of them as well, then plunged the Veritas Sword up through the roof and into the Dispirit above.

The creature dissolved into a black inky mist and floated away into the night sky. We had no time to celebrate this minor victory. Two more Dispirits leapt off the cable and onto the car, one of them hanging from the side, thrusting its fanged face into the cabin with a loud hiss.

Rob jammed his sword into its mouth before it could release its long, stinging tongue. By now, the cable car was rocking violently back and forth from the commotion. It was enough to make even me sick. When the third Dispirit lowered its head through the roof and into the cable car, Rob lost all sense of reason.

"Taste this, bug brain," Rob said angrily, thrusting his lighted sword up through the roof once more, tearing a semicircular shape in the ceiling in the process. The Dispirit vanished with the touch of the blade, but apparently it was not all that was cut. For as Rob pulled his sword out once more, the cable car shifted and dropped, dangling at a steep angle from the cable.

The sudden shift caused everything in the cabin to slide to the right side of the car where the windows became gaping holes to certain death. All it took was for poor Rob to lose his footing and gravity handled the rest. He fell out of the window beside him, catching only his arms and elbows on the frame.

"Heeeelp!" he yelled in tearful desperation. "Don't let me fall!"

"Hang on, Rob. We'll get you back in," I shouted, grabbing his arm and pulling him back into momentary safety. Once his lower half was back inside the gondola he curled up on the floor and began to cry.

It was his worst nightmare come true.

A terrible, aching groan from above warned us that the worst was not over. It was the sound of sheet metal tearing. The Veritas Sword had severed the arm of the gondola and we were hanging from a very thin quarter inch of metal. A second later the quarter inch gave way and gondola seven plunged toward the ground.

The fall, a frantic, heart-pounding drop of sheer terror, blurred my vision and robbed all sense of time. My eyes slammed shut and my stomach tightened as the gondola plunged in a freefall. Clinging to the railing, I held tight with helpless desperation, bracing myself for the horrid end that waited below.

Then, unexpectedly, a powerful jolt shifted the gondola's momentum midair. All of a sudden, instead of plowing into the cement walkway we were being hoisted upward, like a yo-yo at the end of its rope. Once my stomach caught up with the rest of me, I opened my eyes to discover the three of us (and Boojum) soaring through the air—miraculously carried away from the fairgrounds by an invisible force.

Trista had buried her head in her arms and looked up for the first time. She wore an expression of stunned fright.

"What just happened?" Trista questioned, her voice quivering with emotion.

"I don't know; one moment we were falling to our death and the next..." I allowed my voice to trail off as we watched the fairground lights sparkling in the distance. The scene spoke for itself. Leaning lightly over the railing, I looked up only to find there appeared to be nothing around us or above us, just the gondola and the crisp night air.

"I think I'm going to be sick," moaned Rob. His tear-streaked face was a reminder to us all of just how close we had come to death. He bent over in pain, covering his mouth with one hand and his stomach with the other.

"This is impossible," Trista said, still in a daze. "We should be dead by now. Cable cars don't just fly off into the sky like this."

"Maybe not, but how else do you explain the view?" I asked.

Trista pondered this for a moment.

"We're probably in a coma of some kind, knocked unconscious by the collision. It happens all the time on TV."

"Look around you. Do you really think we're in a coma?" I asked. "We're all here together still, how can we be in a coma together? It doesn't make sense."

Trista looked baffled, but she quickly formed another idea.

"Well, there's only one way to find out for sure." Before I could object she reached over and pinched my arm, hard.

"Ouch," I yelped, rubbing the mark she had left. "What did you do that for?"

"To see if we're awake; now pinch me!"

"What? Why?"

"If you don't pinch me back, how will I know I'm not dreaming too? Come on, do it already!" she demanded.

I squeezed her gently on the arm just to amuse her.

"That was weak," she pointed out, rolling her eyes at me.

"Well, would you rather I maim you like that?" I said, pointing at the mark on my own arm.

"Oh puh-lease," Trista replied. "I hardly even touched you."

"Uh, guys," Rob interrupted, "I *really* don't feel good. I need to get down from here now."

"We're working on it, Rob!" Trista answered kindly as Rob curled up on his bench.

"How do we steer this thing?" Trista asked, trying to figure out what was happening.

"Craaaaa," a loud screech from outside the cable car caught us by surprise. Together, Trista and I leaned over the railing and looked up. There was a ghostly movement above the cable car, and a great whoosh of air like the flapping of invisible wings.

"Uh, I don't think we do!" I replied slowly, pointing to a pair of clawed feet that gripped the top of our ride.

Trista gasped at the sight.

"Feet? We're being carried away by giant feet? Now I know I'm dreaming!"

The two enormous bird-like feet clutched what remained of the severed gondola arm tightly in their grasp, but they themselves were not attached to anything, just floating through the air. I had seen this once before and turned quickly, scanning the space in front of us. Sure enough, floating out in the open, a huge yellow beak and a pair of glossy black eyes hovered in the otherwise empty sky.

"Faith?" I yelled out. "Is that you?"

"Craaaa," the invisible bird's voice squawked happily in response. Sudden warmth calmed my nerves as the majestic Thunderbird shimmered in the sky, making itself visible at last. She was an inspiring sight, her wings full of blue and gold.

Trista, on the other hand, looked as terrified as ever.

"What is that...that...thing?"

"She's not a thing, she's a Thunderbird. Her name's Faith, and she's come to help us."

Trista shot a puzzled look my direction, and I felt compelled to explain. I told of how Faith had rescued me from the Shadow creatures once before. At this, Trista seemed to accept that I knew what I was talking about; however, her reservations about Faith still remained. She still was unconvinced that we were safer in the talons of a giant bird than we were in the teetering cable car nearer to the ground.

We continued to climb upward, much to Rob's dismay. As we broke through the first layer of clouds, it seemed for a moment that we were already back in Solandria. The lower blanket of clouds stretched out to the horizon in front of us, while a darker, more sinister cloud covering the sky above us created a ceiling of sorts.

"Why does she have to fly so high? We must be thousands of feet in the air already," Trista asked.

Rob's face worsened at the thought, and he keeled over on the spot.

"Oh man, I think I'm gonna..."

"Oh no you don't, not in here!" Trista started, but it was too late. Rob threw up all over the cable car floor, barely missing her feet in the process.

"Ew, gross! You could have done that over the side, you know," she whined, holding her nose and turning her head away from the sight of Rob's vomit.

Rob looked up through watery eyes and shook his head, "Sorry, I told you I'm afraid of heights."

Trista dug through her purse and found a small bag of tissues, which she tossed at Rob. He wiped the edges of his mouth and thanked her for them.

"Well, that settles it," Trista said, still cupping her hand over her nose to avoid the smell. "This is the worst dream I've ever had. Wake me up when it's over."

"We're not dreaming," I added slowly, sensing there was something more at work. We're being called by the Author."

Rob shot a glance my direction. "That would explain the Dispirits and the Treptors," he said matter-of-factly.

I nodded.

"Let me get this straight. When the Author calls you, you get chased by weird creatures, nearly dropped to your death and carried off by a giant eagle into a storm?" Trista asked sarcastically.

"Well, sort of, but it's never the same as the time before," Rob explained warily. "Every time you go it's...well...different."

Boojum, who until that moment had been hiding in my backpack, overheard the discussion and butted in, "Go? Go? No no, don't go!" he said, his enormous eyes were wider than usual. "Bad things, danger!"

"What's he talking about? Go where?" Trista asked.

"To Solandria," I replied. No sooner had I said it, than a sharp bolt of lightning tore through the sky, followed instantly by a crash of thunder. It was as if the Author himself was adding the exclamation point to my statement.

Boojum shrieked at the flash of light and vanished in a puff of smoke.

"Hey, where did he go?" Trista wondered.

"Who cares," said Rob. "It's better that he stays out of our way anyhow!"

The clouds rumbled around us, followed by a heavy drenching rain. Another bolt of lightning flashed dangerously close to the cable car, passing by in a sharp angled slice. Faith dropped slightly at the sight and circled to the left, heading back toward the place it had nearly hit us. I realized then that this was no ordinary storm. All around us the clouds began to roll in a violent wave of fury. As Faith evened her approach, a gleaming sliver of light in the sky caught our attention. Only this time, it wasn't lightning.

Everyone was speechless as we flew toward the mysterious flickering white light. The closer we came, the more it seemed the bolt of lightning had actually ripped a small hole in the sky. The edges of the gap stretched and widened, ready to swallow us whole as we approached.

Trista gripped my arm and covered her eyes as we passed through the seam in the sky and into the blinding white light beyond it.

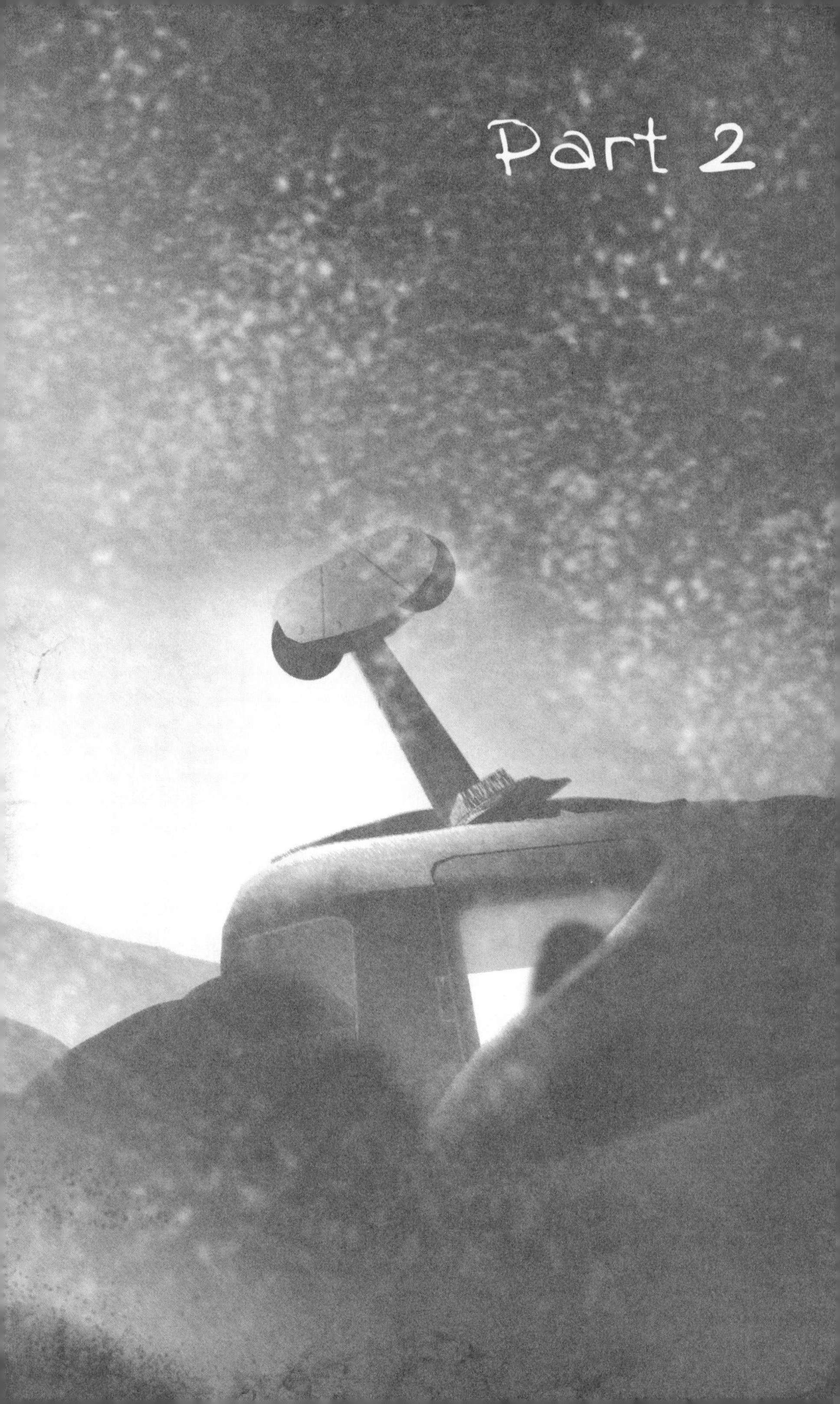

Part 2

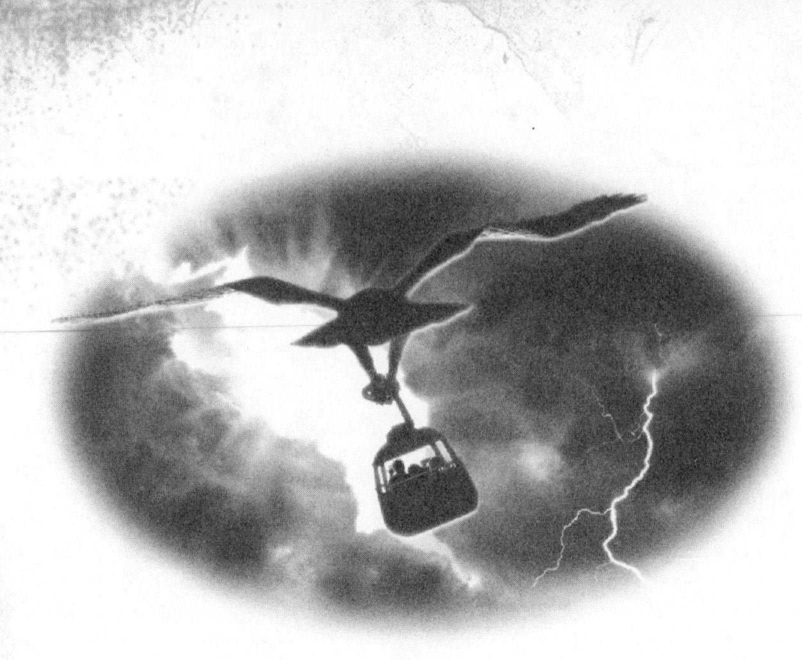

Chapter 10

Into the Thick of It

A deafening peal of thunder heralded our entrance into the new realm. The cable car started to shudder violently. My eyes shot open and I blinked against a barrage of tiny white lights streaking by. We appeared to be going twice as fast as before.

Suddenly, the rest of my senses kicked in. My skin tightened as it registered the icy wind. I gasped from the cold shock, nearly choking on the freezing air and… snow?

We had flown into a blizzard. Our gondola lurched suddenly as Faith struggled to fight through the violent wind.

"Where has she taken us?" Trista squealed, unwilling to open her eyes and gripping my arm even tighter.

"I don't know!" I yelled back over the howling wind.

I couldn't see anything but white. No matter the direction, wherever I looked the world was completely washed out. I was quickly losing my sense of direction. My only point of reference was what little of Faith's blurred form I could still make out through the pelting snow.

"Scrawwww!" she called and I caught one last glimpse of Faith before she completely vanished into the sea of white. At that same moment, the gondola's momentum shifted drastically, and I could finally say for certain which way was down again. For some reason, Faith had dropped us. We were falling!

"Brace yourself..." I began to yell, but it was too late.

Fwumpf!

Our freefall came to an abrupt and jarring end as the sky car cratered itself deep into a field of snow and stuck at an awkward angle. Gondola seven had been all but buried in the snow, leaving only the back half of our windows exposed. Above us, the howl of the blizzard raged on.

The three of us lay piled atop each other, buried in a heap of snow that had scooped in through the front window. With the gondola settled, we began untangling from each other.

"Agh! Get it off!" Rob protested, trying to shake some snow from his shoulders. "Cuh-cuh-cold! Ice down my back! Ice!"

Trista brushed the remaining snow from Rob's neck. "Chill. It's just a little snow."

"It's not the little bit that we should be worried about," I added, hugging my body tighter. "We're not going to last long in this weather. There must be a shelter nearby or something.... I'll have a look around."

I poked my head out of the window and realized immediately there was nothing to see and nowhere to go. The world was a blinding field of white. Venturing away from the gondola would likely end in getting lost. Our safest bet was to stay put and stick it out until the storm subsided.

"I don't get it! Why would Faith just drop us like that?" I wondered.

Already, I was losing feeling in my ears and nose from the numbing cold. It was only a matter of time before the elements claimed the rest of us. None of us were dressed for this kind of weather.

"Igloo!" Rob suddenly blurted out. Scooping up a handful of snow he began packing it into one of the window openings. "My dad taught me how to survive in severe weather. He learned from the military how to build igloos in the snow to trap in heat."

"Heat?" That was all Trista needed to hear. She immediately joined in with Rob and me as we walled off windows, completing our makeshift shelter.

It had been a great idea, except by the time we finished packing the snow by hand, our fingers were burning from the cold.

"F-f-funny. I d-d-don't feel warmer," Trista shivered as she tried to thaw her fingers with her breath.

"Huddle down on the f-f-floor," I directed. "We need to c-c-combine our body heat if we're going to make it th-th-through this."

Trista eyed the floor warily. It was still splattered with vomit, albeit frozen vomit. Reluctantly, she concluded survival was more important than personal hygiene and hunkered down next to us.

"S-s-so, what is this place?" Trista asked through chattering teeth.

"Probably the North Pole," I teased.

"Really?"

"Yeah, Trista," Rob smirked. "The Author c-c-called us out of the Veil to take us on a m-m-magical field trip to Santa's house."

Trista glared back. "Oh stop it! I'm not as clueless as you think I am. I *know* we're in S-s-solanchia."

"Solandria," Rob and I corrected her together.

"Whatever," she continued. "Where in Solandria…ex-x-actly? There must be a town nearby, right?" She looked expectantly at Rob and me, hoping one of us would know the answer.

"Beats me," I answered, shrugging my shoulders.

"C'mon, you r-r-really don't know w-w-where we are?" Trista pleaded.

I shook my head, "I've n-n-never been to this p-place before."

"Me either," Rob offered apologetically.

"Then… we're lost?" A look of panic came over her.

"Not if the Author called us here," I interjected. "He has a plan."

That idea didn't offer as much hope to Trista as it did to me. "Plan? For us to w-w-what? Just sit here and wait f-f-for a welcoming c-c-committee? We'll be kidsicles in twenty minutes."

When she put it that way, it sounded pretty bad.

Suddenly, Trista's face lit up. "Wait a m-m-minute! My ph-phone," Trista said excitedly, reaching for her back pocket to retrieve the raspberry-colored device. "We can call for help!"

Rob and I just looked at each other, neither of us able to decide who should explain the obvious hole in her logic. After pressing a few buttons and tapping the screen a few times, Trista finally tossed the phone aside with disgust. "Figures…no b-b-bars out here," she said with a scowl.

"Shhhh!" Rob hissed. "Did you hear that?"

"Hear w-what?" I strained to listen, but could only hear the wind whistling across the holes in our gondola's roof.

"I thought I heard crunching. Like s-s-something was moving around out there."

We all held our breath and tried to keep as still as our shaking bodies would allow. A minute passed—nothing stirred.

Rob shook it off. "Sorry. Guess I'm j-j-just hearing things."

Crumph... Crumph... Crumph... Crumph...

This time we all heard the sound. Something *was* out there.

Trista excitedly jumped to her feet and screamed out, "HEY! OVER HERE..."

I quickly pulled her down and covered her mouth with my hand, whispering harshly, "What are you thinking? We don't know what *that* is! For all we know, you just invited some wild beast over for dinner!"

She wriggled her head free of my hand and defiantly made a point of answering in a loud voice, "*Or*, I might have just found someone to save our skin!"

Crumph. Crumph. Crumph. CRUMPH. CRUMPH...

The muffled footsteps became much faster and louder. They were coming nearer; so close, in fact, that we could imagine the forceful weight behind them.

Trista gulped. She didn't look so sure of herself anymore, adding in a hushed voice this time, "Maybe a very *large* someone?"

CRUMPH. CRUMPH...CRUMPH!

Snow clumps shook loose from the inside of our handmade walls, crumbling onto our heads. This time, Rob didn't flinch when a piece melted down his back. No one dared to move.

A large, dark presence stomped across the roof of the gondola, blocking the light from the holes in the roof Rob had created with his sword during the Dispirit attack. The beastly creature sniffed forcefully through the holes, sending grunts and blasts of its warm breath down on us. It gave a hearty snort before withdrawing to let loose a deep, guttural howl.

I pressed Trista down low as Rob fumbled for his sword to defend us from the threat. Before he could get a hand on it, more earth-shaking footsteps barreled up, followed by an unexpected booming voice, "Ha ha! First ta find 'em!"

A second voice bellowed back from a distance, "Yah, sure ya would since ya done tied my snowshoes together, numb-brain!"

"Oo! Now there's a pretty face for a loser. Careful or it might freeze that way."

"Fine mum-talk comin' from an ol' ninny gabber like you. Quit yakin' and dig 'em out."

No sooner were the words spoken then a massive, furry arm blasted through the snow wall behind Rob and yanked him, collar-first out into the stormy white. An equally hairy face appeared at the hole, thundering, "Welcome ta Galacia!"

We were pulled from the gondola wreckage by the two burly men who had found us—brothers, as it turned out, by the names of Ven and Zven. Our "welcoming committee" piled us onto a sturdy sled where they sandwiched us between a dozen or so fur blankets to protect us from the elements. One of their shaggy snow beasts did the rest. Called "Scampas," the mammoth, white-furred creatures looked to be a cross between an oversized razorback pig and a wolf. They had sharp teeth that jutted out ferociously like tusks, and a pair of pointy horns protruding atop their head. Not the kind of animals you would ever want to cross paths with in the wild, but under the careful training of our rescuers these two were actually quite friendly and incredibly useful.

The sled moved quickly, pulling us to the safety of Ven and Zven's remarkable home. It was fashioned entirely from snow and ice, nestled up against a mountainside where we now sat in relative comfort on ice blocks draped with animal pelts. We were settled around a warm fire, donning borrowed coats and eating a hot stew before we knew it.

"So, don't cha believe none of my brother about being first ta find you," Ven added, waving a soup ladle at his brother. "'Twas really Godee, my Scampa, who nosed the lot of ya first."

"He was never part of the race," Zven barked back. "I won, and *you* know it!"

Trista bit her lip and tried to stifle a giggle behind her blanket. It was admittedly hard not to laugh at the ridiculous way the two grown men carried on.

They had introduced themselves as the Thordin brothers. Going on appearances you would think they were identical twins. Both were taller and wider than most men. Both spoke in the same loud, powerful voice—often at the same time. And both had bushy, reddish beards crowned by the thickest mustaches I'd ever seen. These dustbroom-sized features made it so that whenever they talked, you could hardly see their mouths move. For all their similarities, their only apparent distinction was that Zven, the younger of the two, was a stated quarter inch taller than Ven—a fact that was loudly contested by the latter.

"Ven, Zven," Trista cordially interrupted their dispute, "I never thanked you for saving us. I owe you my life!"

"Ah, the only one you be owing any life ta now, missy, would be the Author!" Ven replied, ladling some of the thick stew into a wooden mug.

"True, true," Zven nodded. "Were it not for him, we'd be livin' out here in the ice for no good reason."

"And...what would the *good* reason be?" I asked, curious to know why anyone would actually choose to endure such a harsh climate.

An authoritative male voice answered from behind me, "How about attending to the needs of a sickly, old friend like me?"

Ven and Sven immediately stood to honor their other guest. Following their example, I stood as well and turned to face him.

Making an entrance into the room from behind one of the

animal hide door flaps was a blonde-haired man with a well-trimmed goatee. Though he was wearing fur now, and not the armor I had always known him to wear before, I immediately recognized him.

"Petrov!" I blurted, forgetting any protocol and rushing over to hug him. The Commander of the Codebearer Resistance was somewhat surprised, but still graciously returned the embrace with one arm.

"It does my heart good to see you again, Hunter. Knowing my message got through means more than I can say."

Petrov looked over at Rob and Trista who were still standing by the fire. "Come. You must introduce us."

"Oh! Right. These are my friends," I began, "Trista, meet Commander Petrov."

Petrov nodded to her, "Trista, pleasure to meet you."

She smiled and did her best to curtsy, much to his amusement. "I take it this is your first time to Solandria," he chuckled.

Trista blushed, realizing her blunder, and remained uncommonly quiet.

Turning to Rob, Petrov added, "But not yours, if I'm not mistaken."

Rob looked amazed and sputtered, "Yes sir. I mean, no... That is, I've been here a few times before, for training mostly, at Sanctuary when I was younger. I'm just surprised you would remember me!"

"Oh! My apologies. I can't say my memory is *that* good. I only noticed that you carry a Veritas; what was your name again?" Petrov extended his left hand.

"Oh! Right. It's Bob, er...I mean, Rob, sir."

As they shook hands, I caught a glimpse of Petrov's right arm, which had been tucked beneath a thick cape until now. The bare arm was hanging limp in a loose sling; a good portion of the hand

and forearm were grossly discolored and scabbed.

"Your arm, what happened?" I exclaimed.

"It's a long story," he replied, "and one that will be told soon enough." He quickly pulled the cape back over the unsightly arm and then waved to the Thordins, announcing, "But first, we eat."

Ven and Zven heartily agreed to the idea and quickly portioned out stew. It was meaty, chewy and a bit burnt, but the flavor didn't matter all that much—it was *warm*! The meal finished quickly, as any normal attempt to engage in conversation at this temperature would have meant the difference between eating a hot meal and getting stuck with a stew-sicle to lick. The brothers were the first to finish, knowing this fact all too well.

"The meal was excellent as always, Thordins. Thank you," Petrov said as he handed his empty mug to Zven for washing.

"Now, before I tell you my story, I am eager to hear from you, Hunter."

His request had come mid-slurp for me. "Abowd whad?" I asked with a partially full mouth.

"About the night you disappeared. About what happened down in Venator's lair."

My expression, as I wiped a bit of stew from my mouth, must have been one of complete confusion. Up until now, I had always assumed that the accounts of my end would have been common knowledge to the Resistance, let alone its Commander.

Seeing my bewilderment, Petrov explained further, "You must understand, Hunter, we have had very little information to go on. The only survivor to have seen anything of what happened in there was Captain Faldyn. The last thing he reported seeing, as he stormed Venator's secret chamber, was the great serpent, Sceleris, being released from the Bloodstone you held. Faldyn fell unconscious soon after... and no one ever saw you or Venator again."

Across the firelight, I saw Rob and Trista exchange wide-eyed glances. Even the lumbering Thordins paused from their dinner cleanup. I could feel every eye trained on me, waiting to hear my explanation.

"Then I guess it's time I share the truth about who I was."

I went on to explain how Aviad had shown me the Bloodstone Prophecy, how he revealed that I was the chosen one that would bring an end to the curse. Never had I imagined what I was to discover when I finally faced the Shadow lord in battle. The truth was that I was Venator and Venator was me.

"Aw now!" Zven brashly interrupted at this point. "You're jus' pullin' our beards."

Ven gave his brother's beard a sharp tug and chided, "No, I am! Now mind yar manners, blubbermouth. Give the boy a chance to finish explainin' himself."

Petrov ignored the interruption, pressing me further, "If this connection existed between you and Venator, then how did you defeat him without..."

"Dying?" I finished the thought for him then shook my head. "At first, I thought I could—especially once I realized the stone's power for myself. It was more powerful than I had ever imagined. You see, Venator wasn't the only one carrying a piece of the Bloodstone. I had the other half hidden inside me all along—it was my heart. A heart of stone."

Trista gasped and there was a loud thump as Rob fell off his seat, having inched too close to the edge as each detail unfolded. Petrov, however, didn't flinch but continued staring deeply into the fire as I finished telling how the end came about.

I told how the idea of Aviad intentionally omitting the truth about my identity and my hidden power upset me, of how I let that thought poison my mind. *How could I trust that he had my best interests at heart? How would he and the Codebearers be any different than the Shadow? After all,* I had reasoned, *they both wanted a power that was rightfully mine to give or keep.* So I determined if I could hide Venator's half of the cursed stone to keep the two from ever joining, then I could prevent both the Shadow and the Codebearers from ever controlling me and avoid the promised curse the Author had prophesied.

"But I was wrong to think I could somehow outwit the Author," I concluded. "As soon as my hand touched the other half, the Bloodstone's power took over, fusing itself to me and releasing Sceleris. I completely lost control."

Trista piped in, "But how did you make it out alive?"

"That's just it. I didn't."

Ven leaned over to Zven and muttered, "I'm with ya now. He's definitely pullin' our beards."

Rob interjected, "Um, not to sound stupid, but if you died then why are you here now?"

Why was I here? I had not tired of asking myself that question. Not that I fully knew the answer, but each time I considered it I was reminded of the sacrifice that was made on my behalf.

"The Author saved me. Aviad came." I couldn't help but smile as I recalled the moment when he invaded time and space and met me in my most desperate time of need.

"Aviad?" Petrov murmured. "Tell me more. What did he do?" he asked excitedly.

"He gave me a choice to keep the Bloodstone halves and face the curse's end myself or..." I felt my throat tighten a bit and tried to swallow the rising emotion back down. "...or to give him the stone pieces—including my heart—and let him take the curse for me."

The whole room fell silent but for the crackling fire, as everyone considered the weight of that testimony.

"Then it's over!" Petrov suddenly proclaimed with amazement. "The Bloodstone Prophecy's curse is ended!"

"Aviad finished it himself?" Ven wondered solemnly. "That'd account for him being missin', now wouldn't it?"

"And for how aggressive the Shadow have been o'er the past three years since," Zven added. "Without the Bloodstone's power, they'd be grabbin' at all they could take before it all came crashing down 'round them."

"Hold it," I replied, trying to reconcile what I'd just heard. "Did you just say *years*? But I've only been gone for three months."

"No, Hunter. Ven's count is right," Petrov said. "You've been missing for just shy of three years here in Solandria."

I tried to make some sense of it, asking, "So, is it a month in the Veil is a year in Solandria?"

Ven cleared his throat and tried to explain, "That'd be simple enough, but...no. It's long been known that our times are not bound together in any partic'lar way. A year in Solandria can be a blink in the Veil..."

Zven butted in, "And a sneeze here could cover a lifetime fer ya Veil-folk."

Trista found the concept frightening, "You mean, I could be stuck here forever?"

"That's right, missy," Ven replied, then shrugged his shoulders.

Trista looked like she was about to faint again.

"Oh ho! Had you going there now, didn't we?" Zven finally said. "You don't have ta worry none about being lost here forever...why that's just nonsense. Never happened before."

Trista sighed and caught her breath for a moment. "Good."

"Ya, the longest anyone's been gone from the Veil was good ol' Eli and that was only fer like a thousand years or so..."

Trista didn't look impressed.

"Don't mind them," Petrov interrupted. "They're just having a bit of fun with you, I'm afraid. The Author always returns you where you most need to be. Your friends won't even notice you've been gone, right, Hunter?"

I nodded, reminding Trista I had been here before.

Taking charge of the conversation again, Petrov turned to me. "You had asked me earlier what happened to my arm. I believe now would be the appropriate time to share what has been happening here for these past three years. There is much to tell."

I listened intently as Petrov described how the Resistance completely routed the Shadow from the Shard of Inire, where Venator had ruled. The defeat of Venator, though riddled with mystery, had been a triumph for our small army. But the victory had not come without great price. Many good Codebearers had given their lives in that epic battle. As Petrov named some of the warriors who had fallen that day, I conjured up their faces, finally stopping on Hope—her head cradled in my hands as she died. I could feel it all over again; the pain of that loss still weighed heavy on me.

"It was my sword that killed her," I announced suddenly. Petrov stopped talking and waited for me to continue. "It was an accident. We were fighting Venator and..." I couldn't find words for the rest, looking away. "I just thought you should know that."

I didn't dare look at her, but I could tell that Trista was tearing up. She was certain to have put two and two together now to understand more fully why the medallion had been so special to me. As for the others, I had no way of knowing what they were thinking of me right now.

When he finally did speak again, Petrov remained remarkably calm. "Don't blame yourself, Hunter. The Author has a purpose in all things. Those who trust in him have only to wait—he will make all things known in time."

As it turned out, Hope had played a key role in what happened next for the Resistance. Petrov described how, after the doctors had identified the wound as one inflicted by a Veritas Sword, rumors and speculation began to fly about whose sword it had been and why. Though a few rumors involved me, the more popular ones implicated Faldyn in one way or another. The fact that he already had been at odds with the Council on other issues certainly had not helped quell the growing tension between them.

"What's more," Petrov explained, "when Faldyn first brought Hope to us she was still alive, though barely. Faldyn claimed he had already revived her once by using a concoction stolen from the Shadow and tried to persuade us to let him attempt more such treatments. While his intention was to help, this clearly went against the Code of Life, which teaches that the wounds of a Veritas Sword can only be healed by the Author. Faldyn was publicly rebuked for his part and only grew more bitter over time."

"Hope remained comatose and unresponsive for two months while cared for at one of our outposts on Inire. During that time, I took it upon myself to find a more suitable long-term caretaker on my home shard of Obduront and arranged for her transport."

"Is that where she is now?" I asked, eager to see her again, no matter her condition. "Could I visit her?"

Petrov's pained expression betrayed his answer before he even spoke a word. "No, Hunter. The ship never reached Obduront.... It was found later. All signs pointed toward a Shadow raiding party. One of the survivors claimed he saw Faldyn among the enemy. I'm sorry..."

I nodded somberly. Even though I had seen her die and had lived with that fact for months, it still felt like she had just died all over again. Some wounds never really heal, I guess.

"The death of a friend can make any of us question the Author's goodness, question his plan. Because of the more publicized nature of Hope's disappearance and Faldyn's betrayal, such questions became widespread among the Resistance. Soon Codebearers across the realm were questioning the Author's motives and more specifically Aviad's. He never contacted us again after Sanctuary fell.

With every passing month of silence, people began to wonder if he had truly been who he had claimed to be—the Author's son. Despite the Council's attempts to avert it, divisions quickly sprang up among the ranks. The Shadow have not wasted the opportunity. They have become stronger. Their attacks have become more frequent and bold. And perhaps even more concerning is the arrival of a new threat."

I noticed Ven and Zven shift uncomfortably in their seats. They obviously knew what was coming next and apparently were still troubled by it.

Petrov pulled back the cape from his right shoulder to expose the injured arm I had noted earlier. Trista quickly turned away, not wanting to see the extent of the damage, while Rob and I stared. We could see the clear mark of a gash on the bottom of his forearm. The cut itself, which was relatively shallow and not very long, didn't look all that remarkable. The severity of this wound was not in its depth or size, but in its effect. Surrounding the cut was what looked to be a very painful infection. Most, if not all, of Petrov's right forearm was colored a sickly greenish-yellow and pocked with scabs.

"I was on a mission to assemble the Council when a lone warrior attacked me," Petrov continued.

"Shadow?" I asked, trying to imagine what Shadow would have attacked on its own—they usually worked in groups.

"No," Petrov shook his head. "He was Xin."

"Xin?"

"They were a fiercely independent people who shared our belief in the Author, but not in all of his ways."

"What do you mean?"

"The Xin had long-held a belief in a supreme being, the Author of all who controls all things. They even declared the Shadow as a common enemy. In fact, much of their lore was rooted in fragments of the Author's Writ, but those truths became greatly distorted and twisted over the years. As a result, their understanding of the Author and his ways was steeped in superstition and rituals. Up until twenty years ago, they were extremely hostile to anyone who threatened their beliefs… namely the Codebearers."

"What happened twenty years ago?"

"Around that time a small band from the Resistance took up a risky mission to reach out to the Xin. Evan was among them. The Codebearers were immediately captured and should have been killed, but for some reason their chief, Xaunos, spared them, content to keep them in captivity. Over a period of forty days, he would pass by their cells every week to mock and test them. Throughout their captivity, the Codebearers remained true to the Author's ways and answered Xaunos in kind when he challenged them. On the fortieth day of their imprisonment, the great Xin leader, Xaunos, inexplicably broke down weeping and accepted the truth he had learned from his captives. That day, by decree of the chief, the entire people of Xin came under the teaching of the Code of Life and committed their allegiance to the Author and the Resistance. It was an incredible day!"

"So, the Xin are now allies?"

"Well, they were…and good ones at that. But sadly, that entire group was wiped out within a year's time. The Shadow, upon learning of their newfound allegiance, mounted a full-scale attack on them. As skilled as they were, the Xin warriors had never trained for what hit them that fateful day."

"So, if the Xin are extinct, where did this lone warrior that attacked you come from? And why would he attack you?"

"That still remains a mystery to me. But one thing I do know: the Author did not intend for me to die that day. Though I had been caught completely off guard, the Author allowed me to escape with only this small cut."

Trista, finally having braved a look at his arm, winced as she pointed out, "But usually a small cut doesn't do all that."

"That is another mystery; the Xin warrior carried what looked to be a Veritas Sword...only something was different about it. It was dark and twisted...altered in some way, possibly even poisoned. The wound I suffered in the attack began to grow quickly, killing more of my limb as it spread. Because of the rate at which it was spreading, I knew I couldn't expect to live longer than a few days, but I've lasted over a month now."

"How?"

"Well," beamed Ven, "so happens that Galacia has the perfect answer ta such things."

"The ice!" Zven piped in, stealing Ven's thunder. Noticing the glare he received from his brother, Zven shrugged, "What? Not like ya was the only one that knows."

"But I *was* the one tellin' first," Ven complained before reasserting himself. "What we mean is that the ice allows us to slow that poison from spreadin' farther, so long as we keep Petrov's arm rightly cold."

"Yes. And I'm indebted to the Thordins for setting up this remote camp. Their unique knowledge of surviving in such severe cold has allowed me to live longer than I should have." Petrov smiled and answered the question that each of us undoubtedly shared. "How much longer? Only the Author knows that. For now, I'm content to serve him as long as he sustains me."

"So, now what? You called us here to help you. What can we do?" I asked eagerly, conveying what I sensed Rob and Trista were feeling at this point too.

Petrov acknowledged my offer with a nod and brought his good fist to his chest. "I thank you for your willingness to help, Hunter. But, in truth, I do not have anything more for you to do. I did not call you here…the Author did. Why all three of you, I'm not sure, but clearly he brought you as an answer to my plea. Because you came, Hunter, I now know the purpose behind Aviad's disappearance—a sacrifice to fulfill the Great Exchange."

"True, true!" Ven agreed. "Why, we've even more reason ta trust the Author's plans t'night than ever before. Thanks ta our good lad Hunter's test'mony." I received a hearty shoulder slap, one I knew I'd be feeling well into tomorrow.

"So, then…we're done here? We go home now?" Trista asked, unsure of how this kind of arrangement worked in Solandria. Truthfully, I wasn't even sure what a typical departure from Solandria to the Veil looked like, but the thought of leaving so soon depressed me.

"Bah! There'll be no talk of leavin' till this weather blows by," Zven replied. "A transport can be arranged the day followin'."

Petrov, aware of my disappointment, added, "All in his good time and place. For now, I'm content to rest tonight, knowing the Author continues to hear and answer."

"Speakin' of rest, Commander," Zven stood slowly, offering a helping hand to Petrov, "we really should be puttin' that arm of yer's back on ice."

Chapter 11

The Calling

Night had descended quickly on our camp. After Petrov had been returned to his room, the Thordin brothers showed us to theirs, which Trista, Rob and I would be dividing between us. The room had been built up a few feet higher than the main hall, with steps leading up.

Trista got Ven's bed and I insisted Rob take Zven's, which left me with the space of floor between them. It was more than comfortable enough after the Thordins spread a few layers of animal pelts out for me.

Despite the comfort of my bedding, it took considerable effort to fall asleep. I was far too excited to be back in Solandria once more. When at last I did sleep, I found it even more difficult to *stay* asleep. No sooner would I doze off then some noise would wake me. Most often it turned out to be one of the Thordins rustling about to throw another log on the fire, or worse, "sawing" logs with their obnoxiously loud snores. Eventually, the noise died down. Even the moaning wind outside our shelter seemed to end. All was quiet.

Determined to return to sleep, I rolled over and pulled the fur coverings tighter around my chin. Gradually, my breathing slowed and I began to drift off.

"Hunter." A low whisper called into the silence.

I bolted upright, eyes darting between Rob and the bedroom doorway; both were still.

"Rob, did you say something?" I asked. No answer. Just slow breathing. I nudged his mound of blankets just to make sure he was still asleep. His breathing skipped a beat, but quickly returned to its rhythmic flow. Unless Rob talked in his sleep, it had not been him.

Wrapping the blankets around my shoulders, I strained to hear the voice again. Nothing came.

Just as I started to lie back down, the whisper repeated its call, "Hunter."

Now fully awake, I was more aware of the voice's tone this time. It was quiet, but not strained; calm and steady, but expectant; urgent, but not demanding.

I threw aside my covers and stepped out into the main hall, wrapping my coat tightly to keep out the cold. The fire was glowing softly now. Against one wall, I could see Ven (or was it Zven?) propped up with a blanket drawn around him. The other brother was conked out on the floor. Neither of them stirred when I walked into the room. They were both sound asleep.

I paused, waiting to hear if the voice would speak again.

"Hunter."

This time I could tell it had come from Petrov's room. Stepping over one slumbering Thordin, I walked over to the hide-covered door and pulled it back a bit, peeking in.

Just like in our room, there was a short hallway, but this one had a few steps leading down. A flickering light danced off the icy surfaces of the room below. *He must be awake*, I thought.

Not wanting to wake anyone, I whispered into the room, "Hello? Petrov?"

No reply.

Slipping inside, I descended the stairs and approached the raised slab of ice that served as Petrov's bed. He was reclined on a pile of fur blankets, his injured arm exposed to the cold air and ice. I spotted his wound and shuddered at the sight of it.

Still keeping to a whisper, I inquired again, "Commander, did you...?"

"Hunter," the ethereal voice called from behind me. The reflected light seemed to swell at the sound of the voice.

Turning around I noticed for the first time that the light was not coming from a lantern or torch as I had expected, but rather from an open flame that rested atop a pedestal made of ice. Somehow, this small flame was not melting the ice or consuming any substance, for that matter. It just was, of its own power.

Carry me.

The utterance clearly emerged from the Flame this time, each syllable emphasized by the pulsing of the firelight. Unsure of how to react to the phenomenon, I stood pondering the sight. *Am I supposed to talk back to it?* I wondered.

Carry me.

The message was repeated calmly, perhaps with a bit more force. It was both soothing and unsettling at the same time.

I cautiously stepped closer and extended a hand to feel for the Flame's heat. Responding in kind, the Flame leaned in towards me till it touched my fingers. The touch was warm, not hot, much like an inviting summer breeze. My hand passed through the fire unscathed, and I watched in wonder as the Flame pooled into my palm, leaving its pedestal behind.

As it reformed its shape in my hand, the gentle Flame spoke again.

Carry me.

"Carry you where?" I asked this time, my voice trembling.

Torpor.

Completely transfixed by the fiery messenger, I was unaware that anyone else had joined me until a hand touched my shoulder.

"I see you found the Flame."

I nearly jumped out of my skin as I whirled around to face Petrov, now standing behind me.

With a questioning look, he eyed my hand holding the Flame and asked, "Or did it find you?"

"I'm sorry. I don't really even know why I came in here," I apologized. "I'll put it back."

"No!" he ordered, taking hold of my arm. "No, that's not necessary." His voice took on an unexpected urgency, "I think I may know why you came. Stay there. There is something you need to read." He walked over to his bedside and lifted a large book off the floor with his good hand. It was his copy of the Author's Writ. I helped steady his hand as he set the heavy volume on the vacant pedestal. Taking out his key, he unlocked it and laid it open. Then speaking to the book itself, he petitioned, "Tell us of the Consuming Fire."

The once lifeless pages sprang into action, rising and falling until at last the requested one was reached. Slowly, the blank surface transformed, drawing its designated passage into focus.

"Read it aloud," Petrov instructed me, pointing to the words that had appeared.

The Consuming Fire

Before the sun rises, darkness must reign;
For seventy times, light's presence will wane;
But no shadow or power can hold back the light
when a new dawn of fire bursts forth from the night.
An eternal flame of consuming power
Will come to the faithful in their most desperate hour.
It starts with a spark—on the first will descend
To empower the chosen to stand 'til the end.
So I, the Author, have written.
A wounded pillar the Fire will take;
A sleeping strength the Fire will wake;
A heart of stone from Fire gains sight;
A precious seed through Fire finds life;
A faithful captive the Fire unchains;
An ember of hope the Fire will claim;
The seventh of seven only Fire can name.
When the seven are marked the Fire will fall,
Not only for seven but on all who are called.

So I, the Author, have written.

When I had finished reading, I looked up at Petrov, expecting him to explain what I'd just read and how it related to the miraculous Flame still cupped in my hand. The Commander only returned my expectant look as he excitedly asked, "Did you feel anything just now as you read the passage?"

Had I felt anything? I wondered. I felt inspired, somewhat hopeful of things to come, but mostly I felt confused. "I'm not sure what you are asking," I replied.

"No?" Petrov's expression dimmed.

"What's wrong?" I asked.

"Nothing, forgive me.... It's just that the passage has posed a mystery to me ever since I discovered it some weeks ago. I thought perhaps I was beginning to understand its meaning more clearly. It seems I was wrong."

He carefully took the Flame from me and held it in his own palm. The moment it left my hand I felt a sudden loss—as if part of me was taken with it. Clearly, this was no ordinary flame. There was power here—real power. Something I didn't want to part with.

"Where did the Flame come from?" I asked, as I gazed into the living light.

Petrov nodded toward the ancient book. "From the Author's Writ. I was studying the prophecies still left unfulfilled when I came across the very passage we just read."

"So, this little Flame...it's the fire that is promised?" I asked in wonder.

"Yes and no. I believe this is only the beginning of the Flame, a spark of what's to come. The seven must still be found. As the prophecy says, 'When the seven are marked the Fire will fall.' There is still more to come."

As he repeated the phrase from the passage, the fire seemed to brighten a bit, pulsing in beat with each word he said.

"So, after the Flame marks these seven things, then the

fire will…"

"Not things, people," Petrov interrupted, "of whom I believe I am the first of the seven."

"How do you know?"

"Because of this," Petrov answered, pulling down the neckline of his cloak to reveal his left shoulder. There, just below his collarbone was a symbol of a three-tongued flame, emblazoned in a golden light. The light pulsed with life on his skin.

"Marked!" I exclaimed. "*You* were marked by the Flame?"

He chuckled, "Yes. Does that surprise you?"

"Well, no… it's just that… I mean, how?"

"As I read the passage aloud, as has been my habit in study, the Flame rose up from the words and I immediately felt a burning in here," he clenched his hand over his heart. "When the mark appeared, it left little doubt that I was now one of the seven."

"Then who are the others?"

Petrov only shook his head. "I'm afraid I do not know that. In fact, I didn't even know exactly how I fit into the passage until I was attacked by the Xin warrior. What I did not tell you earlier was that I had been on my way to carry the news of this prophecy to the other captains and consult with them when the ambush came. The only way I escaped—by the power of the Flame—was when I was somehow spirited away to Galacia. I cannot explain how, as it happened so quickly. My assassin's blade had only a second to graze me before I was miraculously engulfed in light and delivered here."

"It still got enough of you, though." I looked down at the festering wound on his arm.

"So it did, but on the bright side, it did make it painfully clear which of the seven I had been called as." He tapped the open page on the description of the first sign.

A wounded pillar the Fire will take.

There was no doubt about it, Petrov had been wounded and taken away by the Flame. Couple this with the fact that he had been marked and it was easy to figure out that he was the first of the seven.

My mind raced ahead as I read down through the other six signs. "The other signs, could they be referring to the other Resistance leaders? There are seven captains in the Council," I noted.

"The thought had crossed my mind," Petrov agreed. "It was one I wanted to explore. But, so far I have not been allowed to leave this hideout."

"Because of your arm?" I asked.

"In part, yes," he nodded and then lifted the Flame to our eye-level. "More importantly, this is what has prevented me from leaving."

"The Flame?"

He noted my dubious expression and explained, "I have tried to carry it outside my room on several occasions. But every time it returns here. As if it's waiting for something...or someone. Who or what, I cannot say. That's where I've been stumped with my understanding of this prophecy."

"You say you tried to carry it?" I asked, suddenly recalling the whispered command.

"Yes," the surprised Commander answered, eyeing me curiously once again. "Why do you ask?"

As I relayed tonight's extraordinary events, about the voice calling my name and drawing me to the Flame, Petrov's eyes widened. "It *spoke* to you, didn't it?"

I nodded.

"What did it say?"

"It asked me to carry it...to Torpor."

The light of the Flame reformed itself into a long slender shape, which left my palm, raising itself high overhead, encircling us in its blaze. Before I knew what was happening the Flame swooped down and sped toward me, disappearing into the medallion I wore around my neck.

Petrov was awestruck at the sight, breathing a word of thanks to the Author.

I lifted the medallion from my chest to examine it. At the touch of my hand, a sparkle of light flashed across the surface of the Author's mark, assuring me the Flame was safe inside. Then the voice whispered to me once more.

Keep me. Carry me. Follow me.

Placing a firm hand on my shoulder, Petrov stood beside me.

"It seems you have been chosen again."

"Chosen for what?"

"To carry the Flame where I am not meant to go!"

I swallowed hard at the thought of being chosen again. In a funny way, I had been longing for an adventure for months, but now that it was staring me in the face, I felt a bit wary—not because I didn't want to go, but because the memories of how badly my last efforts had turned out reminded me how likely I was to fail. After all, it was my fault the Resistance base in Sanctuary had been compromised; my fault Aviad had gone missing.

"Still doubting are you?" Petrov questioned, reading my thoughts perfectly. "If I remember correctly it was a moment not unlike this one that launched your last quest. You doubted the Author's choice then as well, did you not?"

"It's not the Author I doubt," I clarified. "It's me."

"It is okay to doubt your own strength, so long as you realize the Author's choice in the matter is perfect. You were chosen for a reason. Don't let fear of the Shadow steal your joy in this moment, Hunter. You have a great task in front of you."

His words inspired me, and right then I determined this was my chance to set things right. I had been given a second chance to prove to the Author that I was worthy to be a Codebearer.

"Yes, sir, you're right of course. It is an honor I will proudly bear."

"Good," Petrov stated. "You will carry the spark in search of the remaining six, but you must not let anyone know where it is hidden unless it reveals itself. This may be the last hope of survival for the Resistance. The Flame must not fall into the wrong hands." He looked down at his own wounded arm and back at me. "Understand?"

I nodded and tucked the medallion back into my shirt.

Petrov smiled proudly.

"The Author is with you, my boy; he holds all things together. If you follow the Flame it will never lead you astray."

"I know," I answered, "I'm ready."

Taking me by the shoulder, Petrov lowered his brows, looked me dead in the eye and said, "It seems your next mission in Solandria has just begun."

Chapter 12

Stone-Eyed Sterling

Early the next morning we awoke to find piping hot porridge awaiting us. Trista, Rob and the Thordins listened intently as Petrov recounted the amazing revelation last night had brought. After sending me back to bed for sleep that never came, Petrov had spent the remainder of the night preparing a plan for the mission before us. Seeing significance in the fact that the Author had called Rob, Trista and me into Solandria together, he felt strongly that we should remain "a tightly wound cord not easily broken"—a charge to unity that he passed on to us directly from the Author's Writ. We would carry the Flame to Torpor together.

In order to reach the distant city, we'd have to first fly across the Void—a vast expanse of nothingness that separated the scattered land masses, or "shards" as they were called that collectively made up the world of Solandria. It had been this way ever since Sceleris had attempted to overthrow the Author ages ago, a failed effort that left the world shattered into countless pieces.

The only reliable way off the shard of Galacia was to take a sky ship, which we hoped to find at a nearby port. Apparently these vessels were routinely used to carry cargo and passengers between the shards, though I myself had never seen one. Petrov gave us the name of an innkeeper we were to look for once in town. Stone-Eye Sterling was someone he trusted as a friend of the Resistance, and Petrov believed he could help us negotiate safe passage aboard one of the ships. Once in Torpor, we were to bring the message of the Consuming Fire to Captain Saris. If our hunches were right, he would be the next one marked and could help us on our quest to find the remaining seven before the Resistance crumbled.

The plan was admittedly fragile, but as the stalwart commander reminded us, if the Author was with us we couldn't fail. Armed with this bold confidence, the preparations were made for immediate departure.

By noon, the brothers had graciously tailored some of their warmer clothes and robes closer to our size. We layered the furs over our own clothes and thanked them for their hospitality.

Before we left, we said our final farewells to Petrov. It crossed my mind that this might be the last time I would ever see him in Solandria. Despite the cold, I would have liked to stay longer for that reason alone, another day or two at least, but Petrov would hear none of it. He was anxious to see our appointed journey begin.

"I have a parting gift for each of you," Commander Petrov smiled as he made his announcement. "There is not much more I can give you than what the Author has already given. But what I do have, I pass on freely."

Zven stepped forward, hefting a large bag. Petrov reached his good arm in and jokingly addressed me, "It seems you were in a hurry the last time you left us. You really should keep better track of your things." In a single motion he withdrew a Veritas Sword from the bag and tossed it to me. I caught the gleaming hilt by the handle and immediately recognized it as my own. The weight of it felt good in my hands again, but I hesitated to grip it. The ghost of its past deed rose up to haunt me.

Petrov, recognizing the reason for my less-than-enthusiastic reaction, challenged me. "Fear the Author alone, Hunter, and your blade will not stray."

Reaching once more into the sack, he produced a well-worn copy of the Author's Writ. Zven helped Petrov deliver the weighty book and its accompanying key into Rob's hands. "This once belonged to a good friend and wise teacher, Captain Samyree. If he were among us today, he would challenge you never to take this book for granted. I add to that saying, any mission without its counsel is ill-conceived. The words are faithful. Be faithful to read them, and they will prepare you for every battle."

"Yes, sir," Rob said, receiving the book gratefully.

Finally turning his attention to Trista, he took a moment to choose his words. "You are like a freshly strung bow: young and untested. But I have no doubt in the skill of the Hands which have fashioned you. My challenge to you—when the Author so chooses to pull back your bowstring, do not resist—let the arrow fly." With that he pulled out the last gift, a magnificent bow. The wood was strong and its limbs were graced with flowing scrollwork. In every way it reminded me of the one Hope had carried. Petrov gave me a knowing look before offering it to Trista. "Learn to use it and it will serve you well."

"It's beautiful! Thank you, Commander...sir." This time Trista skipped the curtsy and instead offered her right hand for a handshake. Petrov laughed and Trista blushed, realizing the mistake too late as he took her hand with the backward grip of his uninjured left one.

Pulling himself to full height, the Commander declared in a strong, loud voice, "Never alone!"—a phrase Rob and I echoed before following Ven out the entrance tunnel and on to the adventure awaiting us.

The weather was beautiful, sunny and clear, but the stinging winds made us want to stay inside.

The Thordins led us out to a large shed where they kept their supplies. We wouldn't take much—a small bag of bread and cheese, some spices for soup and a mix of dried fruit. They also entrusted us with a dazzling formation of jagged, blue gemstone they had mined from the shard and saved for such an occasion as this. They figured it would command enough value in trade to get us transport to the Shard of Torpor, where we hoped to recruit Saris' assistance.

"So, how far is it to this port we're going to?" I asked.

"Port Defiance, 'bout eight hours I'd say," said Ven. "Just down this ridge and to the end of the ravine."

"But with high winds like this," said his brother Sven, "why you should be there in no time at all—well before sunset, I'll wager."

"How do you figure that?" Rob inquired as a particularly sharp gust blew past, chilling us to the bone. "Seems like a wind storm isn't the most ideal time to go for a hike."

"A hike?" Ven burst out in heavy, hearty laughter. "Why that's a good one. You hear that brother? They think thar goin' for a hike."

The two boomed with laughter at our apparent ignorance. Ven eventually added, "No, ya won't be doin' any kinda' hikin'. That'd be suicide sure enough."

"Yah sure, anyone goin' out in these conditions without a snow sail would be asking far trouble," said his brother.

"What's a snow sail?" I asked.

"It's what you'll be ridin'. Here, I'll show ya." With that he led us to the opposite end of the shed and threw open the doors. There were two snow sails stored inside, each consisting of a fifteen-foot pole, which was attached at its base to a long ski-like skid.

"These, my friends, are yur snow sails," said Sven, grinning proudly. "They'll get ya down the ravine ta the port in no time."

The two brothers instructed us on how to raise the sails and how to best use the wind to steer. I took to it quickly, having tried my hand at windsurfing on a vacation back home. Since there were only two boards and three of us, Trista shared mine.

"The current should carry you all the way to the port," Ven explained.

"Just don't forget ta slow down before you reach the town, or yur liable ta slip off the edge of the shard. Wouldn't want ya ta fall off into the Void."

Long before we felt ready, we said our goodbyes to the brothers and made our way down the mountainside to the ravine below.

Ven shouted after us, "Trust the Author, my friends. Remember, we're never alone."

If he said anything else we were already too far gone to hear it, riding the wind and speeding into our next adventure. The breeze whipped around us, but we kept pace with it, which seemed to minimize the effects of the cold. We were having so much fun weaving in and out of each other's paths that the hours seemed to slip away with the daylight.

Just as predicted, the sinking northern sun faded behind a small town at the edge of the shard. We slowed to a halt and found a small lean to where we were to leave our snow sails for the night. Gathering our things, we tromped through the snow into town.

"That was fun," Trista said, smiling broadly. "Can we do it again?"

With high spirits and hungry stomachs we entered the town,

hoping to find the inn we had been told about. The air, which was chilly enough by day, had turned to a biting cold, made all the worse by the bitter breeze.

"Not a very big port, is it?" Rob said, looking things over.

"Well, it's not exactly the friendliest climate for visitors up here now is it?" I answered.

Rob shrugged.

"Here it is, Starlight Road," Trista said excitedly. "Not sure how we could miss it, it's practically the only road in town. C'mon, I'll race you to the inn."

Before I could suggest we stick together, she bounded off down the empty snow-covered streets. Despite the fact that it was just approaching evening, only a few figures were out on the roads. It seemed those who knew the town also knew enough to get inside before darkness fell.

When at last we caught up with her, Trista was standing slack jawed in front of a dilapidated old inn that hung, quite literally, out over the Void. A long wooden plankway led out thirty feet to the entry of a shoddy two-story shack on stilts. The ground beneath the lodging had crumbled away years ago, leaving the foundation exposed and reinforced by a series of haphazardly placed beams. It was a wonder the place hadn't fallen off the face of the shard.

A sign was posted at the edge of the ledge that read:

"Well, the name fits, I'll give it that much," Trista said, still amazed that such a place could actually exist.

"You gotta be kidding me. There's no way I'm going in there. It's a death trap." Rob was shaking visibly, partially from the cold, but mostly from the thought of the place.

"Well, it's either that or freeze to death out here," I said, trying to reason with my own better judgment about the place. "We don't have arrangements to stay anywhere else."

"Oh man, I'm going to regret this," Rob gulped, as Trista led him by the hand and I followed from behind, across the rickety wooden plankway.

As we neared the door, a pair of rowdy sailors burst out in front of us, singing a tune and nearly stepping off the ledge a time or two as they wobbled past. They repeated the chorus over and over for the whole town to hear.

Oh, sailing out on the open breeze,
I goes where I wants and I does what I please.
Never a worry and never a care
When I'm sailing out on the open air.

"Catchy tune," Trista hummed as we entered.

Granted, it was not the sort of place kids our age would visit at home, but given the circumstances of our mission, we pushed forward into the precarious establishment. The place was buzzing with activity; all but one of its dozen tables were full of guests drinking, eating and having a grand time.

We stepped up to the counter, which doubled as the front desk for the inn, and tried to catch the attention of the keeper.

"Be right with ya," a giant man with a round belly called out from the other end where he was pouring another round of foamy drinks. When at last he finished his rounds, he stomped heavily across the creaky floorboards and stood directly in front of us.

Rob cringed at the sound of the man's steps, imagining the vast expanse that lay below us. For a moment, I could almost feel the house sway beneath his steps.

"Now, how can I helps you folks?" he asked, dropping a rag on the countertop and leaning heavily on the bar, which also groaned under his weight. He was a strong man, his forearms thick and hairy, colored with ink from years of tattoos. His face was pock-marked and weathered. He had a thick black mustache under his nose, but it was his left eye that most marked his appearance. With a slight scar around the lid, the eyeball itself had been replaced with a rounded grey stone.

"Are you Stone-Eyed Sterling?" I asked.

"Well, I sure ain't Sponge-Eyed Suzie if that's what yer asking. Ho-ho, har-har," the man burst out laughing at his own joke. "Sorry, that one never gets old. Most folks just call me Stoney, but you can call me whatever suits ya. What can I do for you?"

The man seemed jovial and kind-hearted despite his intimidating appearance. Petrov had been right about one thing; he was a likable fellow.

"We're guests of a friend, and we were told you might be interested in this," I said, pulling Hope's necklace out and flashing the Author's mark briefly at the man before tucking it back out of sight.

"Indeed," the man smiled, "I always have room for more friends, but first why don'ts you find yourself a table in the corner and I'll see if I can fix you up with something to eat."

We wound our way across the room to the open table and tried to make ourselves comfortable. The other patrons eyed us warily. We were obviously not the kind of strangers they were used to in these parts.

"He seemed nice enough," Trista remarked.

"I just wish he was a little lighter on his toes," said Rob nervously.

"Shhh, here he comes now," I said.

The room bounced with each heavy step the man took as he strode across the room with a tray full of mugs filled to the brim with some kind of steaming drink. He placed a basket of bread in the middle of the table and a mug in front of each of us.

"This cider's hot so you best mind your lips," he said as he sorted a few plates in front of us.

"Hey Stoney, over here!" a man yelled from across the room.

"KEEP YER SHIRT ON! I'M COMIN'!" said Stoney in a voice loud enough to rattle the rafters. Then he lowered his voice and added to us, "I'm afraid I've got business to tend to, but it'll wind down soon enough, and we can get to talking. I'm anxious to hear what you have to say…mister…uh…"

"Hunter," I answered, "and this is Rob and Trista."

"Pleasure to meet you all," he said with a wink of his good eye.

With that he turned on his heels and stomped away, shaking the entire building as he went. Rob whimpered at the sound of it. Even I began to wonder if it was a good idea to stay inside. After all, there was nothing beneath us but…well…nothing. Still, the rest of the patrons didn't seem to mind the precarious sway of the inn's foundations, so I figured it was safe enough for one night. We ate our fill of the hot bread and washed it down with the cider.

In less than an hour the Cliffhanger Inn had all but cleared out; the last of its guests were gathering their things and heading for the door.

"Thanks for dropping by folks," Stoney called after them. "My door's always open. Come back anytime!"

When at last the door shut behind them, he brought a chair over and sat down beside us.

"Whew! Never a dull moment in this place, I'll tell you that. Keeps me hopping from dawn 'til dusk. But I don't mind it none—keeps me honest. A hard workin' man is an honest man; that much I know. But enough abouts me. What brings you to such a remote part of the world? Not many in the Resistance in these parts, you know."

Stoney was clearly sympathetic to our cause, so I decided to share freely with him.

"We arrived just the day before last," I answered, "from the Veil."

"The Veil you say," came Stoney's reply. "Well, this is a treat; I haven't had a visitor from the Veil in…well…ever! I'll get the burum and we'll drink to it…er…no, no…no! Look at me blabbering like the fool I once was. We don't serve that here anymore. No, just some water for me and some shard-famous cider for you. Dangerous stuff that burum, fills you plenty but dulls the mind, and I needs to stay sharp these days…never know what might happen. There's plenty of trouble afoot, so I'm told."

We drank another round of cider with the man and continued the discussion.

"We're on an important mission for the Resistance, and we're in need of passage to Torpor. You know anyone who would be willing to take us?"

"Torpor, you say," he said stroking his black mustache. "My that is a long way."

"It's an urgent matter, and we're willing to pay."

"How much?"

"This," I answered, confidently showing the sparkling gemstone the Thordins had given us.

Stoney's eyebrows shot up as he observed the impressive piece of blue quartz. "Well now, if you weren't in such a hurry to leave today, this beaut' would buy yer way to most anywhere a man might want to go, but I'm 'fraid to say it's not goin' to do ya much good right now."

"What do you mean?" I asked.

"There hasn't been no sky ships in these parts for nearly a month, least not the kind taking passengers. It's all cargo ships up this way, taking loads of crystals from the mines to the other shards nearby. There's a lot of money in them deliveries. Convincing any of them to fly off-course to Torpor would take a mite bit more than what you've got."

"Oh," I said with marked disappointment.

We had barely even begun this all-important mission and already it was threatening to run aground in failure.

"'Course, I'd take ya there meself if I could, but I've got me hands full with the inn as you can see. But don't worry none, if it's Torpor where the Author needs you to be, there ain't nothing will stop you from getting there. Am I right?"

I nodded, encouraged by the man's honest statement of faith.

"Well, I hate ta say it, but I've got a few errands to run before I can call it a night," Stoney said at last, lifting himself slowly out of his chair to stand. "Come on now. I'll show you to some rooms where you can stay the night, free of charge to me friends, mind you, and I won't take no fer an answer! A good night's rest'll be good fer ya, and we'll have plenty of time to talk more tomorrow, I thinks." He led us upstairs and showed us our sleeping quarters.

"You'll like this room," Stoney boasted, "has a great bay window off the back. Quite the view!"

Rob winced at the thought, "Please no!"

"What's the matter?" asked Stoney, confused.

"He's afraid of heights," Trista explained.

"Ahhhhh, I see. Well, in that case I'd better give you the servant's quarters. 'Course, I haven't had a servant in ages. It's not much to look at, I'm afraid, but that's better than the alternative in your case. I'll put the lady in the larger room next door."

The room Rob and I shared was practically a closet—strictly functional. It fit little more than a wooden bunk bed, the hard kind you expect to sleep in on a traveling quest or college dormitory. But what the mattresses themselves lacked in comfort, the downy quilts that accompanied them more than made up for in warmth. Rob chose the lower of the two bunks and nervously buried himself between the folds of the thick quilt.

"Wake me up when it's time to leave this shack," he mumbled from beneath the safety of the quilt's wrapping. I dropped my backpack down on the floor and a faint yelp emerged, causing both Rob and me to turn our attention to the bag. I opened the top flap to discover Boojum hiding inside.

"Hey, I thought you left us! What are you doing in there?" I asked.

"Boojum back!" he answered simply. "Hungry!"

Rob flopped back down on his bed. "You know, I had a cousin like him once," he pointed out. "Always showed up when he wanted something to eat. Now, I know he's nothing but trouble."

Boojum cocked his head with curiosity at Rob's comment.

"Boojum trouble?" he asked.

"Nah, he's just giving you a hard time," I whispered to the little creature. "Probably jealous that you're mine, right Rob?"

"Oh yeah, that's it," Rob said mid-yawn. "How do you think he knew where to find us?"

"Maybe he never really left, just disappeared," I figured.

"That's so weird," Rob stated. "You know, I bet there's got to be something about him in the Author's Writ somewhere. I'll have to look for it later.... I'm too tired tonight."

"Hungry," Boojum reminded me.

"That's why I don't have pets," Rob laughed, rolling over to get some sleep, leaving me to deal with Boojum alone.

"Hungry, eh? I think I have a little something left over from the fair. It's not much but it might work for tonight."

Rummaging through my backpack, all I could find was a half-eaten snack bar, which Boojum happily accepted. It was enough to keep him occupied for a few minutes while I got ready for bed.

I stared into a small mirror that was hung on the wall. Pulling the medallion off of my chest, I examined it carefully. A faint glow seemed to emanate from within, warming my heart in a way I never imagined possible. The full importance of the Flame still eluded me. All I really knew was that it was mine to carry and protect, and that without it the Resistance would fail. So, protect it I would.

"Carrying the Flame is an important mission, you know. No mistakes this time. The Resistance is counting on me.... I'm going to show everyone how trustworthy I can be."

Boojum finished the snack bar and looked at me with giant bewildered eyes as I handled the medallion. I clutched it tightly in my hands before pulling it back over my neck. Then, I climbed the ladder into my bed.

"Goodnight, Boojum!" I said aloud.

"Nite-nite mine," Boojum whispered back as my eyelids shut.

Chapter 13

Signs of Trouble

A soft winter's snow drifted down on the ruins where the Thordin brothers slept. Petrov alone was awake in the dark, troubled by a vision. He was pouring over his Author's Writ and whispering a silent prayer to the Author.

"Please, not Hunter! Don't let him lose hope," Petrov said under his breath.

There was a short growl outside the door from one of the dogs, but it went deathly silent just as quickly.

Petrov moved for his sword, grabbing it quickly but feeling the ache in his side. The poison was still moving; it wouldn't be long before he'd be joining the Author in another story. This much was certain.

The door flew open but nobody was there. Petrov struggled to his feet, holding his sword with honor in front of him.

"You're too late, Xaul," Petrov said despite the fact he couldn't see anyone yet. "You won't find what you're looking for here."

The raspy half-voice that replied seemed to come from nowhere in particular. "Where is it? Where is the Spark!"

"It's gone, I gave it away," Petrov said boldly.

"Where…is…it!" said Xaul, seething as he spoke.

"Safe" was Petrov's reply. "With the Resistance."

With a long raspy laugh, Xaul stepped out from the shadows, revealing himself at last—first his gleaming eyes then the rest of his form.

"Your Resistance is over," he said at last. "You and your friends have seen the end of your days. Face it, Aviad is dead and with him the lies you tried to spread to the people—my people."

"What is it you are afraid of then, Xaul? Why do you hunt us down if you believe it is all a lie?"

"Some lies should never be tolerated," he hissed. "The fire belongs with us and us alone."

"You are wrong," said Petrov. "The fire belongs to all people, to any the Author will choose."

The last statement angered Xaul most of all.

"Never!" he yelled, igniting the darkened Veritas Sword in his hand. The glow around his blackened sword burned with anger as he lunged at Petrov.

The Commander of the Resistance held his sword firm and closed his eyes, unwilling to fight. With one stroke of Xaul's sword, Petrov's story was finished.

The Thordin brothers heard the commotion and ran into the room, only to find it empty. A black *X* was carved into the rock wall beside the limp body of Petrov, still clinging to his sword.

Without reason, Petrov's body suddenly burst into flames and disappeared in the blaze.

I woke with a jolt from the terrifying dream, to an anxious knock at the door.

"Hunter, get up," an urgent voice called. I stumbled to the door and unlocked the bolt, opening it to find Stoney shifting nervously in the hallway.

"What is it?" I asked, staggering slightly.

"Gather yer things. There's a ship waiting out back. I've decided to take you to Torpor meself, but we've got to leave tonight."

"Tonight? Why tonight?" I asked.

"Because you're being followed."

"How do you…?"

"I went into town to get some supplies, and I saw a man out of the corner of my eye, lurking in the shadows. He was not from around here, and he kept watching me from under his hood. I don't think he knows I saw him, but he followed me back here to the inn. He's watching from across the way, waiting for something."

"Did he have a belt with a red *X* on it?" I asked, fearing the worse.

"Yes," Stoney shot me a look of surprise, "you know him?"

My heart started to pound. Stoney's response could mean only one thing. My dream was real. Petrov was gone and now Xaul had found us. Stoney was right, we had to get out of here… and fast.

"I'll get the others; there's no time to waste," I said.

Stoney could sense the urgency in my voice and followed the plan without hesitation. In no time at all, Rob, Trista and I slipped out the back door, carrying our only possessions—weapons, the gemstone and the Author's Writ. We followed Stoney down the staircase and out the back door onto another long wooden walkway.

Looming before us at the end of the platform was a large wooden structure covered in snow and ice. The doors on the front had already been flung open, revealing what was stored inside—a massive sky ship floating midair beneath the rafters of the shed, protected from the elements. It looked for the most part like a small sailing ship—only in place of the sails a large cloth-sewn balloon floated high over the deck. We quickly boarded the vessel and set down our things.

As Stoney readied the ship for departure, I looked back at the inn with the unnerving feeling I had forgotten something.

"Wait," I whispered, rifling through my backpack. "Where's Boojum?"

"I dunno," Rob replied. "I thought he was with you."

"Wait a minute," Trista said, trying to catch up with the rest of us. "Boojum came back?"

"Yeah, right before we went to sleep, but he wasn't in our room this morning," I explained.

"I thought you said he came back," Rob replied.

"No…I mean he was…but he's not there now. He's…gone… I'll have to go back and look for him."

Stoney seemed nervous, "You think that's wise?"

"No," I answered, "but we can't leave him behind. Get the ship ready for launch. I'll be back in five minutes."

"Be careful," Trista warned.

I lifted my Veritas Sword in response and started back for the inn, making my way carefully toward the main dining room. Even in the darkness I could sense there was someone else there.

Something clattered behind the counter.

"Boojum," I whispered, "is that you?"

There was no response.

Stooping under the countertop, I spotted a trace of movement at the opposite end. Sure enough, Boojum was huddled beside a toppled garbage bin, a leathery strip of dried meat protruding from his mouth. His glowing eyes examined me suspiciously as he munched on the table scrap he had apparently discovered. He was fingering something metal in his hands.

"What are you doing? What do you have there?" I asked as I approached my furry friend.

"Mine," Boojum said disagreeably, holding the metal object out. As he did, a small gold chain hung down from his hands and I recognized it at once—Hope's medallion.

"Hey, how did you…?" I asked, reaching for my neck in grim realization that the Flame was no longer safely with me. "That's my medallion. Give it back, right now!"

I ducked behind the counter to retrieve the medallion from Boojum just as the front door of the inn burst open. A frigid breeze blew through the room before the door shut once more. Huddled on the floor, I knew without looking that we were not alone. Xaul had entered.

The floorboards creaked softly under the light footsteps of the Xin warrior. I caught a sudden lump in my throat at the thought of it and ducked even lower, pressing my chin nearly to the floor. All I could do now was hope the deadly assassin had not seen or heard me when he entered.

Clutching the sword tightly in my fist, I couldn't help but wonder if I would remember how to use the weapon in battle. Not that it mattered now. Even if I did, the likelihood that I would be able to match swords with a skilled Xin warrior was highly unlikely. Besides, the last thing I needed was to get in a sword fight. What I needed was to find a way out of here with Boojum and the medallion—but how?

Before I could come up with a plan, Boojum started to rummage for another piece of food, making far too much noise to stay hidden. Xaul didn't miss it.

The Xin warrior flipped through the air over the counter and landed ten feet from where I lay, his sword raised and ready for battle. The weapon pulsed with an indigo blaze, outlining the darkened blade with an eerie glow. In my dream the man was frightening; in person he was positively terrifying. His silvery eyes hovered in the empty space beneath his hood, freezing the blood in my veins. I felt heavy—unable to move or think.

"What have we here?" he said, spotting the Veritas Sword in my hand. "A code-brat, eh?" His voice was cold as death itself. Xaul stepped forward with a swagger, bringing the tip of his Veritas Sword ever closer.

Boojum dropped his food and darted behind me in fright. I half expected the critter to vanish at the sight of Xaul's sword. Then again, the blade wasn't giving off nearly as bright a light as a pure Veritas did. Still, it was every bit as deadly.

"Stand back...or I'll..." I started.

"You'll what? I could kill you before you even raised your sword, boy. I have no time for games. Now, tell me who has the Flame."

I was running out of options. If I ignited the sword to defend myself, Boojum would likely disappear, taking the medallion with him to who knows where. However, without my sword, I was as good as dead anyway so it hardly mattered.

Suddenly, a thought came to mind. If Boojum could transport things with him when he disappeared, then perhaps...just maybe... he could carry a person as well. It was a long shot and I knew it, but under the circumstances I couldn't think of anything better. Sitting up, I reached behind me and caught a loose hold of Boojum's tail.

"I will never tell you," I said nervously, pointing the hilt of my Veritas Sword toward him.

"Suit yourself," Xaul sneered. "One less Codebearer to deal with."

He surged forward, swinging his blade down in a fit of rage.

"For the Way of Truth and Life," I shouted in defense, igniting my sword at the last possible moment. Our blades collided, blocking his first attack and erupting in a powerful explosion of brilliant light. The moment of truth had come. I shut my eyes, hung tight to Boojum's tail and hoped beyond reason that my plan would work.

With a sudden jolt and an ear piercing scream of pain, everything went hazy and my vision blurred. Boojum had dissipated, pulling me into his altered state of airborne mist. All at once I was being hurled through the air like a rag doll, clinging with desperation to what I perceived to be Boojum's tail. I caught only momentary glimpses of the room whenever my invisible guide shifted directions. The disorienting sensation was unlike any I had ever felt before. The absence of a body left me feeling transparent, thin and ghost-like.

When at last we reappeared, we fell side by side on the long boardwalk behind the Cliffside Inn. Boojum was weaker than he had ever been before—after transporting. He looked exhausted, singed and slightly annoyed at having pulled my weight with him. His hair and skin had already begun to miraculously heal, but his breathing was slower and his eyes full of pain.

"Sorry about that," I said, "but it was the only way to save us both. Come on, we have to hurry!"

I picked up my worn-out pet with care and cradled him under my arm like a football. Racing across the deck toward the sky ship I waved my free arm at the others. The furnace had not yet warmed enough to work the propellers, but Stoney understood my signal and wasted no time in shoving off.

"Quick, grab an oar!" he called out to Rob, pointing to a long pole that hung out over the side. With a great shove of the oar against the dock, the two pushed the vessel away from the inn as I jumped on board. The ship slid silently out into the open expanse known simply as the Void.

We were out no more than fifty feet when Xaul bolted down the dock toward our craft. For a moment I almost believed he might leap out across the gap of nothingness, but he thought better of it at the last moment and held back.

He came to a stop at the edge of the dock and locked his angry silvery eyes with mine. Those eyes, those bright and powerful eyes held more than simply a challenge in them. In that moment I knew he was committed to my destruction. Then, he turned coldly away and entered the inn once more. Seconds later, the inn burst into flames, the fiery tongues lighting the foggy sky.

Poor Boojum was still so exhausted he barely even flinched at the sight of the furious blaze, though I could tell it did bother him. After sheepishly handing over Hope's medallion, he gratefully accepted being put back into the safe, *dark* quarters of my backpack.

"Funny," Stoney said as he watched the Cliffhanger Inn burn away and fall off the ledge. "I always thought the old place would crumble into the Void while I slept. Never thought I'd watch it burn."

Rob, who was standing beside us, looked a bit queasy at the thought of having slept there for any time at all. As much as he was glad to be off the ledge, his new set of circumstances suited him even less. At least at the Cliffhanger there was some sense of solid ground beneath or near you. Out here in the Void, it was nothing but open air.

"Sorry about your inn," Trista said, realizing how much loss the man had suffered for our sake.

"Ah, don't be—the place has been anchoring me down ever since I inherited it years ago. Truth be told, I've always wanted to head back out into the open air."

"You've been so kind to us; I can't thank you enough," I said. Stoney just smiled and waved off the comment.

"It weren't nothing. Captain Stoney at yer service. The Author is calling you on, and I guess I'm going with ya for now," he said.

"We couldn't ask for a better captain," Trista said, assuring him of our approval.

"Well then, welcome aboard the *Bridesmaid*. She's a little unfinished in places, but I can assure you she's as faithful a ship as any. So, let's get going, shall we?" he said, stepping up to the helm and pointing out into the hazy sky. "To Torpor!"

Below deck, the furnace that powered the propellers was blazing hot. With a flick of a lever, the propellers began to whir to life, providing the thrust needed to take us deeper into the Void.

"Who was that back there?" asked Rob, referring to the figure who had chased us away.

"Whoever it was, he'll have a hard time trying to follow us in this weather. We'll chart our course and be out of sight before he can launch a vessel of his own. He'll have no way to know which way we've gone," Stoney boasted loudly.

"It was Xaul, the Xin warrior I told you about," I said softly, holding the medallion out in front of me; the glow was soft and blue now.

"How do you know it was him?" Rob asked.

I explained how I had been having dreams—how I was able to see things, visions of events that were happening in other parts of Solandria. Then, I told them what I had seen of Xaul's encounter with Petrov.

"He was a good man, Petrov. I'll never forget what he done for me. Why I was just an old, drunk sailor when he found me. Didn't care fer no one but me own self."

"So, what happened?" Trista asked, curious as to what had made the change in the man.

"Well, one day when I was a bit…ehem…under the weather, Petrov found me in an alley and took me to Sanctuary, nursed me back to health and fed me proper. He was the one who taught me abouts the Author and Aviad, you know. Even landed me an honest job at the inn with a friend of his. Didn't ask fer nothing in return neither. Never been the same since, I can tell you that much. He'll be missed."

Stoney's good eye seemed to tear over at the thought of the lost Resistance Commander.

"Petrov would have been proud of what you did for us, Stoney," I said at last.

Stoney smiled slightly at the thought. "Maybe so, young Hunter. Maybe so."

There was a moment of silence as we let our remembrances of the man fill the space between us. As we soared off toward Torpor, the *Bridesmaid* swayed back and forth, carried in the currents of the wind.

"Still a bit queasy then, are you, lad?" Stoney asked, watching Rob.

Rob nodded.

"Don't be afraid none; we're in the Author's winds now. Ain't nothing going to happen that we can't handle. You'll see."

He paused for a moment then added.

"Say, that reminds me of a song I likes to sing whenever I'm sailing. You wants to hear it?" he asked. Before we could agree he began bellowing out a tune, similar to the one the sailors had sung earlier that day as they were leaving the Cliffhanger Inn. Only Stoney's version was quite different, both in its lyrics and in its delivery. He was as tone-deaf as a seal and blurted the notes out with such force that it hardly sounded like a song at all:

Oh, sailing out on the Author's breeze,
I goes where he wills for his wind carries me.
Never a worry and never a care
When I'm sailing out in the open air.

Trista and I just laughed at the man as he repeated the chorus a second time, which was unimaginably worse than the first.

"Everybody now," he said at the end of the second chorus. Shrugging my shoulders, I joined the boisterous man and convinced Trista to sing out as well. The two of us joined him in the song, singing at the top of our lungs.

"You know," Stoney said as we finished, "you lot really sounded awful on that last bit."

With that even Rob started to laugh.

Looking back, I watched the shard of Galacia, a floating island of ice and snow, disappear into the hazy atmosphere. When it was gone at last, Stoney offered a suggestion.

"Probably best if you all got some sleep tonight. There are bunks below deck, and I can manage myself for awhile; no use in all of us staying up."

Rob was the first to head below deck, deciding it was better if he were in confined quarters where he couldn't see that we were flying. Despite the bitter cold, Trista and I were far too excited to go back to sleep. Adventure was in the air, and we were on our way at last. We kept watch with Stoney and enjoyed his company. He told tales of his former sky-sailing days and of the dangers of flight: sky serpents, funnel clouds and Void ghosts.

"What's down there in the Void?" Trista had asked at one point.

"Nobody knows for sure," Stoney said. "There are legends of

course, but I don't like to repeat them because there's no telling what's true unless you've been there yerself. Nope, I prefer to leave the mysteries of the Void unsearched."

He could have talked all night, but eventually Trista, obviously troubled by something, wandered away to the railing. I followed, leaving Stoney at the helm alone.

"Something wrong?" I asked carefully.

"No, just thinking," she said. I leaned on the railing beside her and waited.

Just then, the craft broke out of the dense fog and into a grand expanse of sky, scattered with wisps of silvery clouds in a deep midnight blue. Two pale crescent moons, one slightly larger than the other hung overhead, accompanied by an array of stars too numerous to count.

"It's beautiful," Trista gasped. "And to think, all of these years, the stories of Solandria my cousins believed...all of it was true."

"Strange, isn't it," I replied, spotting the silhouette of another shard floating off in the distance. I still wasn't used to the sight.

"Overwhelming actually," she said. "You know, I always had a feeling there was more to life than meets the eye. I just never dreamed there was a world like this."

"I know what you mean. The first time I was called here, I was so full of questions it was infuriating. I thought I had my life all figured out. I was in control and everything revolved around me. And then when things changed I felt so disoriented and lost."

Trista nodded. "So how did you deal with it?"

"Not very well at first," I admitted. "But when I started learning about the Author, things started to get easier to accept."

"That's one of the things I don't understand. How is it that you all are okay with believing there is some great Author at work in our lives?"

"How is it you aren't?" I replied.

There was a long pause.

"Nothing comes from nothing," Trista said at last in a misty voice. "That's what my cousins always used to tell me."

I smiled, "The first truth of the Code of Life. It helps us remember that everything we see owes its existence to something else, something bigger than all of this," I said, spreading my arms out toward the Void around us.

"The Author, huh," Trista answered. It was a statement, not a question.

"Yeah," I replied, "and he brought you here for a reason too, Trista."

"You think?" she asked, searching my eyes with her own.

"Absolutely," I answered, putting my arm around her shoulders and giving them a squeeze.

As the first signs of dawn began to creep into the darkness of the Void, we stood amazed at the sight. A new day had begun and unbeknownst to us, so had an ill-fated journey.

Chapter 14

The Difference of a Mark

"Get your grubby hands off that you little thief!" Rob howled in a fit of rage, throwing a sauce pan at Boojum. It was a good toss too, and would have been right on target had the critter not disappeared at the last possible moment.

Boojum, whose hunger refused to subside, had taken to raiding the galley of the *Bridesmaid* on a regular basis. This time, it was an orange, star-shaped fruit that Rob had intended to cut into equal rations. It was his job to prepare the food, and he was furious that Boojum had interfered yet again.

"Sure, disappear, you lousy rodent," Rob said as he stomped up the steps to the main deck. "But if I catch you stealing from my kitchen again, I swear we'll be having Boojum stew for supper!"

Boojum reappeared and scurried across the deck, hiding behind my leg in hopes of escaping Rob's wrath.

"Take it easy, Rob," I said. "It's not Booj's fault he needs to eat more than the rest of us."

"Fine, I'll remind you of that when we run out of food," he said, stomping back down to the lower level in a huff.

"Wow, someone's in a mood today," Trista said as she passed by with a bucket of soapy water in hand.

"Can't blame him really," I said. "We've been sailing for two days now, and he's spent most of it cooped up below deck. I wish he would lighten up a bit and join the rest of us."

"Cut the guy some slack," Trista replied. "He's afraid of heights, you know."

"I know, it's just that at the fairgrounds he seemed so excited to know there was another Codebearer at school. Honestly, I thought we'd get to know each other better, but here we are on an adventure together in Solandria and I feel like I hardly know that guy. It seems like he just likes to keep to himself."

"Why don't you talk to him about it?" Trista suggested.

"There's nothing to talk about."

Trista rolled her eyes and shook her head.

"Here," she shoved a sponge in my hand, "you can clean those windows on the deckhouse over there, and I'll go keep him company." With that she scooted across the deck and disappeared down the stairs to check on Rob.

With a four-day journey ahead of us, Captain Stoney had suggested we assign duties—the only fair way to ensure each of us carried his own weight. I shared the task of night watch with Stoney (four hours on, four hours off). When not on watch, I was to report to Trista who was in charge of cleaning the ship a bit. It seemed there was always something to be done. Not having seen regular use for quite some time, the *Bridesmaid* was a little worse for the wear.

Rob, on the other hand, preferred to stay below deck and had volunteered for the job of cook. Surprisingly, he wasn't bad at it either. Nevermind the fact that he had a bandage on nearly every fingertip from mishaps with the sharp knives.

At any rate, the galley was decidedly Rob's domain, which of course put him further at odds with Boojum who had a knack for wanting to eat at the most inopportune times.

A loud crunch from over my shoulder near the deck railing caught my attention; the little critter was already happily munching on the stolen starfruit.

"As for you, mister," I threatened, "you're starting to be a bit of a nuisance, you know that?"

His cheeks were fat with juicy pulp, and he wore a puzzled expression. Pointing to his chest, he glanced both ways as if to ask if I meant him.

"Yeah you," I replied.

The creature swallowed a great big gulp of food and spoke. "Boojum good; Boojum help."

"Some help!" I said sarcastically. "So far you've only managed to help yourself."

At this, he dropped his head in shame.

"Sorry," he said, holding the half eaten fruit out toward me in an effort to make amends for his mischief.

"Oh, keep the fruit. Just try and stay out of Rob's way, okay? And no more food without asking, understood?"

"Okee dokee," said Boojum, tossing the pit of the fruit aside and nodding his head eagerly up and down. "No Rob, no foods!"

With that he scurried back to his favorite corner of the deck-house and curled up in a nest of blankets to eat his reward.

I set to work scrubbing the grime off the porthole windows of the deckhouse. Inside, Captain Stoney sat at a broad oak table in the center of the room, studying the navigational maps and stroking his mustache. His normally jovial mood had turned notably sour over the last day, and I wondered what was bothering him. As I finished cleaning the window by the door, I could hear him grumbling to himself inside.

"No, no, no," Stoney said, pounding his fists on the table for effect. "It's all wrong, blast these maps!"

"What's the matter, Stoney?" I asked, wandering in to see if I could be of assistance.

"It's these maps; I can't seem to figure out why we keep getting so far off course. Never had trouble like this before and it's driving me mad."

"How far off course are we?" I asked.

"That's just it, I can't say for sure. We're supposed to be here, near the Shard of Sinos by now," he said, pointing his finger just to the right of the map's center. On the map, his finger was surrounded by a large gathering of shards, the largest of which was named Sinos. I recognized the name, only because it was the part of Solandria my teacher, Samryee, had been from. That was, of course, before he had fallen in the battle of Sanctuary. Like Petrov, he was gone now.

I drove the thought from my mind. As fitting as it was to honor a teacher and mentor, dwelling on the past for too long only robbed the present of its power.

Stoney continued. "As you can see, there should be plenty of land in these skies by now. I was planning on stopping for supplies, but there's nothing out there—nothing but the Void!"

Stoney was frustrated and it showed on his face. Clearly, he prided himself on being an expert airman and was not pleased that his skills were failing him.

"What baffles me the most is that every time I checks our course...our compass here says we're off by a mark one way or the other. It's never spot on when I come back to check it after a bit."

His dirty fingernail pointed to the edge of his compass. The tick marks that surrounded the outer rim were so small and insignificant I couldn't imagine they could make any difference at all.

"Only a mark? That can't be so bad," I said. "We can't be that far off track then, can we?"

"Sure, it don't look like much to you, but one mark can equal a hundred miles or more when you follow it out. Never underestimate the difference of a mark."

"So, are you saying the compass is bad?"

"Nope, this one's as trusty as a snow pup—never failed me before." He set the compass back on top of the maps and slouched back in his chair, putting his face in his hands. Massaging his forehead, he began to think out loud. "Maybe our rudder's out of sorts."

I was no mechanic, but it didn't sound like an easy fix.

"So what do we do?"

He took a deep breath, puffed his cheeks and blew the air slowly from his lips.

"Only one thing *to* do! I'm going to have to go overboard and check it out."

Having made up his mind, Stoney stood up on the spot, letting the chair slide away behind him, and made ready to do what needed to be done.

"You better get Rob. He ain't going to like it none, but I'm going to need his strength as well as yours to hold me while I'm over the rails. I'm not the smallest of men, as you may have noticed," he said, slapping his belly.

With a wink of his good eye he stomped out the door, his mood slightly better now that he had a plan in mind.

Before long, Rob, Trista and I had all gathered around the helm, listening to Stoney's instructions. He had strapped himself into a rope harness and wrapped the slack around several of the rails in a make-shift pulley system that would help hold his weight. A second safety rope was dropped over the opposite side, strung under the ship then back up the near side where it was fastened to Stoney's rope, a few feet up from his harness.

"All I gots to do is get down over the edge for a quick look-see and find out what, if anything, is wrong with the rudder below," he explained. "Once I'm down low enough, Rob, you'll double up the rope on this railing and Hunter will take the other rope over there, to bring me under as close to the rudder as possible. Got it?"

We nodded.

"Trista, I'll need you to relay messages to the lads and to steer the rudder when I tells ya to, okay?"

"Okay," Trista said.

"For obvious reasons, I normally prefer to do this over land. But since that's not an option, the main thing to remember is not to let go of the rope. Otherwise, you'll be flying solo for the remainder of the trip, and old Stoney here will be joining the poor souls of those unfortunate enough to know the mysteries of the deep."

Rob's face whitened at the thought, but honestly, none of us was comfortable with the situation.

"Well, no use putting it off any longer. Here I go."

"Be careful," Trista said as fearless Stoney began his descent to the underside of the ship. Rob and I let the rope out inch by nervous inch until Trista motioned for us to stop.

"So far, so good," Stoney yelled up to Trista in a voice all of us could hear. "Now, send Hunter to pull me in closer." We followed the procedure Stoney had laid out for us with careful precision. With the rope doubled up around the pulley, Rob could easily carry his weight alone. I crossed the deck and pulled Stoney in toward the rudder with the other rope.

When at last he was in place, Trista performed a series of tests. She turned the wheel this way and that following Stoney's commands, but in the end, all it proved was that there was nothing wrong with the rudder after all.

"Bring me up; we're through here," Stoney called out at last. I slowly released my rope, allowing the weight of the man to swing back to Rob's side of the ship once more. But just as I was about to tie off my rope, disaster struck.

Rob shifted to strengthen his stance, taking a short step backward with his left foot. As he set his foot down, his heel landed on the round pit of starfruit Boojum had carelessly tossed away after polishing off the stolen snack. The slimy pit rolled under Rob's foot, dropping him to the ground with a painful twist of his ankle.

Howling in pain, Rob released his end of the rope. The safety rope that held Stoney unwound in an instant and slipped over the edge before anything could be done about it. Suddenly, the rope in my hands became the sole lifeline to Stoney, swinging him under the rudder to the opposite side of the ship. The full weight of the man pulled me to the floor, dragging me closer to the edge.

"Hunter, don't let go!" Trista shouted, racing to my aid.

I plowed painfully into the wooden rails but somehow, against all odds, I managed to keep hold of the rope. Trista and Rob grasped the last few remaining feet of my line before my strength gave out.

With every ounce of strength left in us, we began to pull together, hoisting our captain back up to safety.

"Let's…not do that…again…" Stoney said, looking completely exhausted and frightened as he climbed over the rails and collapsed on the deck. Having come within inches of his death, Stoney's usually enthusiastic voice was much quieter now. It also didn't help to know that he had risked his life for nothing. We were still hopelessly lost in the skies, with no clue as to precisely where we were.

"I'm so sorry," Rob apologized. "I don't know what happened. One minute I was fine and the next, I slipped on something and my ankle twisted…"

"Still, you didn't have to let go of the rope!" I snapped.

"I know, I…"

"You could have killed Stoney! What were you thinking?"

"I guess I wasn't…I just…"

"You were just being clumsy, Rob," I said, feeling the urge to point out his fault for some reason.

Rob gritted his teeth. He already felt responsible for the ordeal; my comment had pushed him over the edge. He hobbled away below deck, sickened by his mistake and unaware that it was actually the pit Boojum had thrown that toppled him.

"Way to go, Hunter," Trista said. "Could you be any more cruel?"

"I wasn't cruel. I just stated the obvious," I pointed out. "Rob has to learn to be more reliable if we're going to trust each other out here. It's not going to get any easier. The Shadow sure aren't going to cut him any slack if he makes a mistake."

Trista shook her head.

"So? What good is it to claim you're different from the Shadow if you're going to act just like them?" Trista pointed out.

There was truth in her words, but I didn't want to hear it. She obviously had no idea what was at stake. The fate of the Resistance depended on us making it safely to Torpor, and clumsy Rob had nearly doomed us to wander the skies alone.

"Fine, I'll talk with him about it when he cools off," I offered. We set to work coiling the ropes and putting away the harness.

"Well that does it then," Stoney said with a tone of defeat. "We're lost."

Hearing the word *lost* come from Stoney was disturbing and final. Suddenly, the air seemed to lose its sweetness.

"We can't be lost. The Author's supposed to be with us...guiding us!"

"Well, it doesn't change the fact that we are. We could be anywhere in the Void," he said, pointing out into the empty skies around us. "It may be too late already."

"What do you mean, 'too late'?" Trista asked nervously.

"Well, I didn't have time to pack a full supply of food or fuel to power the ship's propeller. I figured we'd restock on one of the other shards before continuing on to Torpor. That's not likely to happen now, so we're liable to starve to death before we make landfall anywhere."

"There has to be another way! Can't you fix your compass, or navigate by the stars or something?" I asked.

Stoney sounded more than a little annoyed at my suggestion.

"Look, if I thought I could fix the compass I wouldn't have hung myself off the back of the ship, now would I? It's not like I'm new to sailing the skies, you know. It ain't exactly that easy. Besides, even with a clear view of the stars, I'd only be guessing anyway. On the shards you have a horizon line to work from—out here there ain't nothin' but empty space. The Void is a dizzying place to be lost."

"So, what now?"

"We hope and pray that the Author knows what he's doing. Otherwise, we're goners, I'm afraid. I only have enough fuel left to keep us moving for a week at most. After that we'll be at the mercy of the winds."

That night I lay awake in the crow's nest keeping watch. Rob had managed to stay out of sight the remainder of the evening, probably sulking in his room. I thought it was best to leave him alone, since I was still frustrated with him and his never-ending clumsiness. This last goof-up could have ended with serious consequences, dooming us to wander the Void aimlessly without a captain.

As a result of Rob's absence, no dinner was served but no one was hungry anyway. Considering the severity of our situation, it seemed unwise to eat until we really needed to.

Alone in the darkness, I found myself thinking about our desperate situation. My thoughts shifted from hopelessness to bitterness.

"What's the point?" I wondered aloud. "Why would you bring us all the way out here to die?"

Silence.

I sighed, desperate for an answer. Things were never as easy as I wanted them to be. The Author's ways were mysterious and often confusing. Still, I waited, holding Hope's medallion out from my chest, staring at the simplicity of its design.

I missed her—Hope was always so upbeat and encouraging. She believed in me, even when I didn't believe in myself. I smiled as I recalled how she first gave me the medallion—the night I first flew out over the Void. I promised to return it to her one day.

Who could have known back then that three months later (or years, depending on your count) I would be carrying Hope's medallion across the Void once more? Only this time I was on a ship, not a bird, and we were horribly lost.

You won't be alone out there, you know! Hope's voice seemed to say. It was only a memory yet it seemed so real…and nearby. I looked around, wishing desperately to see my friend once more, but she wasn't there.

What was I thinking? Of course Hope wasn't here, she was dead…and it was all my fault. I was the one who had killed her with my sword. If only I had been more careful that night in Venator's palace. If only I had looked for the face of my enemy before attacking. Then, maybe she would be here with me even now. Instead, I had killed her. Even Rob hadn't made *that* big of a blunder… yet. Now Hope was gone, and nothing could ever change that.

A slow tear dripped down my face, a tear that gave way to more. The tears I had held back for so long finally flowed freely. I sobbed alone in the darkness.

"I'm sorry, Hope," I said, gasping for breath as I cried. "I miss you so much."

Never alone, Hope's voice reminded me.

I knew it was true, but it was hard to believe at times like this. I wept long and hard and finally fell into a deep, fitful sleep, haunted by ominous dreams.

****

Darkness, complete and terrifying.

All was silent, save for the intermittent, staccato dripping of water, echoing mysteriously through the cavernous court of night.

Then light, pure and unrestrained. A spark of fire boldly invaded the domain of darkness, springing to life against overwhelming odds. With the patience of a setting sun, the Flame descended till it came to rest above the face of a sleeping girl. The soft, flickering glow brought the only life to her otherwise statuesque face. Framed by wavy brown hair, her skin was pale, her lips a cold shade of pink.

The light expanded to reveal her full form, a white-robed body floating peacefully above a stone table, a bier, which sat alone on a platform at the top of a rock staircase.

"Release me."

A hushed voice pulsed out from the heart of the Flame. It came from the Flame, but the voice was Hope's. Then, as if it suddenly turned to liquid, the fire poured itself over the lifeless body. The ashen skin, which absorbed the Flames, warmed and now shone brightly from the radiant light within. An awakening power was at work as the gentle rise and fall of her chest welcomed life once more.

Without warning, another face emerged from the light's unreached shadows, drawn by the Flame. The man's features were dark except for a pair of silver eyes. His crouching frame was wrapped in the white garb of a Xin warrior—Xaul had arrived.

Swiftly and silently he stole up the steps, even though no one was around to see him. Sliding up to the bier, he drew himself up to full height, creating a towering silhouette against the girl's luminous glow.

Drawing a black Veritas Sword from his belt, the Xin lifted it high. The blade of negative light flashed angrily out of the hilt. Hope's eyelids fluttered with life, opening wide, but the hardened assassin would not fail in his mission. Turning his sword downward, he plunged it mercilessly into her heart.

With a crack of lightning and a splitting of stone, the room fell into complete darkness once more. Hope's body had disappeared; with it, her light had all but vanished. Only a tiny sliver of a dying flame flickered from between the buckled halves of the stone bier.

His sword replaced, Xaul knelt down to snatch up the Flame. He brought the Flame close to his face, illuminating his silvery eyes and greedy grin before snapping his fist shut around it.

Echoes of an evil laugh peeled across the darkness as two eyes of fire flashed to life where once the silver pair had been.

"Noooooo!"

****

I woke in a full sweat to the sound of my own scream. The night was even darker than before. I climbed down from the crow's nest and stood alone at the ship's helm, staring aimlessly into the sky.

Chapter 15

Snarks and Sparks

Being adrift in the Void was not how we imagined spending our time in Solandria. With each passing day, the mood on the ship became bleaker and bleaker. The food rations were immediately cut to minuscule portions that were hardly enough to keep a rodent alive.

At last, on the fifth day of our journey, Rob stumbled excitedly out of the deckhouse, clutching a book in his hands.

"I've got it!" Rob said triumphantly.

"Got what?" Trista asked.

"The reason we're lost. It's the snark's fault!"

"Snark?" I questioned.

"Yeah, I've been studying the Author's Writ to pass the time lately and I found this passage."

Rob shoved the book under my nose. It was open to a page

with the picture of a small furry creature with giant orbed eyes and a long furry tail.

"Hey, that looks like Boojum," Trista said.

"Yeah, but wait till you read what it says," said Rob, clearly proud of what he had found. I took the book and began to read aloud.

Snarks are small furry creatures with extremely healthy appetites. Their skin is highly sensitive to direct light, which can singe their bodies if exposed even temporarily. Fortunately, a snark's blood carries the extraordinary ability to heal its wounds at an amazing rate. This trait has caused some to hunt snarks and harvest their blood for use in potions and medicines that speed the natural healing process and prolong life.

Snarks can be kept as pets, but only by those whom the snark chooses. These highly adorable creatures have a way of charming most anyone they choose into keeping them. Just remember, if you own a snark, it is only because it chose you as its master. Their sense of curiosity often leads them into trouble. They are fiercely loyal and determined creatures, though not always trustworthy.

A rare breed of snark, sometimes referred to as deviants, possesses an aura of negative energy that can distract or deter its owners. Deviants are physically indiscernible from other snarks—only time will tell if a snark is a deviant.

Snarks are neither good nor bad in and of themselves, so you are advised to carefully consider if a snark is beneficial to your lifestyle before making a decision to keep it. Getting rid of a snark once you have one can be difficult.

"See what I mean?" Rob said proudly.

"Not really," Trista replied. "What does that have to do with us being lost?"

"Watch this," he declared, motioning for us to follow him into the deckhouse where Boojum slept soundly in the corner. Then, quietly picking up the compass from the table, he held it close beside Boojum. As the compass neared the creature, it began to swing wildly in different directions.

"Well, I'll be," Stoney said. "It wasn't broken after all."

Boojum woke up slowly, surprised to see so many of us standing around him. He rubbed his eyes and walked to where I stood. All the way, the compass followed his every move.

Rob was excited. "See, it's Boojum that got us here. His aura has been affecting our compass ever since we got on board. He's the reason we're lost out here—the reason we're starving to death in the middle of nowhere."

Even with the facts plainly before me, I felt a sudden urge to defend my furry friend.

"Quit blaming everything on Boojum. He's done plenty of good things for us too!"

"Like what?" Rob challenged.

"Like retrieving the sword when we needed it in the Sky Cars, or...uh...saving me from Xaul. Doesn't that count for something?"

"Sure, just don't forget he also was the reason you had to lie to your mom about the mess, the reason you were in trouble with Xaul in the first place...and...oh yeah...the reason we're probably all going to die out here," Rob said.

"Hey now," Stoney said, stepping in to break up the argument. "We don't know that for sure...least not until we're dead."

His efforts to sidetrack the argument didn't work—Rob cut right back into it.

"Face it, Hunter. He's a deviant and you know it! You should get rid of him."

"How do you expect me to do that? Throw him overboard?"

"Now that's enough," Stoney interrupted, commanding authority. "This is my ship, and so long as I'm captain there won't be no talk of throwing nobody out nowhere, understand?"

I nodded weakly. Rob just glared back, muttering something under his breath about "pesky rodents" not qualifying for that rule.

"Look," Stoney continued, "even if the compass was working now, it'd do me no good until we knew where we was. And the only way that's going to happen is by a miracle. What we need is a sign—a stroke of mercy from the Author himself."

As he spoke, a soft melody hummed through the air...very low and light. And in my head I thought I heard a voice—a voice not much louder than a whisper.

Hunter. Hunter.

"Yes, I'm here," I answered.

Stoney's good eye shifted from side to side nervously. "I'm sorry, you talking to me?" he said.

"No, not you!"

"Then who did you say it to, lad?"

"The voice," I answered.

"Oh, I see," Stoney nodded. Then, suddenly realizing what I'd said, he asked, "What in the blazes? You're hearing voices?"

Just then a gentle wind began to blow through the deckhouse, accompanied by a steadily growing light. Boojum winced immediately and ran away to a darker part of the ship before it became too bright for him to bear. The medallion lifted itself away from my chest, and the Flame within emerged into the cabin with us. The four of us watched in wide-eyed wonder as the Flame formed itself over the desktop, turning from a low ember to a brilliant yellow.

Let me, the Flame said.

"Let you what?" I asked.

Let me lead the way.

"Of course, why didn't I think of that before?" I said.

"Think of what?" Stoney said. "Is anyone else confused by this, or is it just me?"

"Hunter can hear the Flame speak," Trista replied.

"The Flame?"

"Yeah, it was Petrov's. He told us to protect it and carry it with us."

"A boy that can talks to flames, eh?" Stoney said. "That's a new one."

The Flame floated out into the night sky. It hovered in place for a moment and then curved back to the right side of the ship, leaving a twinkling trail of light in its path.

"Captain Stoney!" I beamed. "We have our bearing…follow the Flame!"

Chapter 16

Torpor

In only two days' time, the Flame led us straight to Torpor. Trista was the first to spot it, though Stoney would claim he had tasted land in the air long before then. It was a glorious sight, and the first time I felt at home seeing a floating land mass hovering in the clouds. I couldn't wait to set foot on solid ground again. We were all so excited that even Rob, who normally would never step near the edge of the ship, pressed himself against the railings at the sight.

"We made it, we're actually here!" Trista said, hugging each of us with excitement.

The first thing we began to talk about was food, what we would eat and how much of it we would have. As Captain Stoney brought the ship level with the shard, I caught my first glimpse of its terrain. I don't know what I was expecting exactly, but the tropical paradise that met my eyes was surely not what I'd thought.

Our journey completed, the Flame returned to the medallion and let Stoney finish the job. We passed through a series of lush mountainous ravines that led to a glittering city nestled in a broad crater. In the center of the crater was a turquoise blue lake with soft golden beaches on every side.

The air was hot and humid, a welcome change from the breezy gusts of the Void. Our senses were pleasantly stirred by the sweet fragrance of flowers.

As we approached the crater's ridge to dock, we all gathered at the deck rails to admire a fleet of significantly larger (and cleaner) sky ships already tethered there. Their regal trimming and brightly polished wood told any common observer that these ships were about important business. Green and blue flags snapped smartly from each sky ship's mast.

Stoney let out a low whistle, being particularly taken with the striking vessels. "What I wouldn't give to take to the skies in one of those beauts!" He studied the fleet with a glint of envy in his good eye. "Not that I'm complainin', old girl," he quickly acknowledged, patting the helm of the *Bridesmaid* tenderly and returning his full attention to navigating his own ship once more.

Easing carefully alongside the other ships, Stoney docked the *Bridesmaid* against the crater's edge. We were met by a couple of bronze, shirtless dock hands with flashing white smiles and eager waves. Stoney tossed them a tether, and they immediately set to work tying off the ship. I helped Stoney lower the ramp from the ship to land once more. Rob was the first across, desperate to get solid ground under his feet. Our first steps on land were welcome ones but also surprisingly dizzying. Trista nearly fell over when Rob leaned into her.

"Ain't got your land legs yet," Stoney said, laughing at our plight. "In time you'll get the hang of it."

"Good rest, my friends!" a man's voice called out from a small hut a few yards away. "Welcome to Ensor, the jewel of Torpor. From where have you traveled?" He was a tall man, dressed in a white poncho shirt that was open on both sides. It looked as if someone had simply taken a square of cloth and cut a hole in the center to poke his head through. Wrapped around his waist, over the shirt, was a red sash. His pants, which extended to just below his knees, were also white.

"From Galacia actually," Stoney said happily. "Didn't think we'd make it, to be honest with you. Bit of a rough go out there, I'm afraid."

"I am sorry to hear that," the man said, bobbing his head as he spoke, "but today is a new day. Can I be of assistance?"

"Yes…er, uh…where to, Hunter?" Stoney muttered out of the side of his mouth to me.

"We're looking for Captain Saris," I said boldly. "Do you know him?"

"Captain? You must speak of the Resistance captain, yes?" he inquired. "I have heard of him, but I don't know where he is. I am sorry. Still, you should try asking for him in the City Circle. His people have been known to mingle there at times. You may have better luck there. Shall I arrange for a transport to meet you at the base of the crater and take you in?"

With nowhere else to go, we accepted the offer and exchanged our blue gemstone for Torporian credits. Stoney balked at my suggestion to pay him anything for the passage he had given us to Torpor; instead, insisting his reward was in simply being along for the ride and seeing how the Author would work next.

We followed one of the dock hands over to the inner ledge of the crater where a wooden cage was suspended from a thick rope, winding down along the crater's slopes through a series of towers and pulleys. It was somewhat like the gondola we had ridden back at the Destiny Fair, only much, much worse for Rob. The primitive design left a lot to be desired for safety, with an ample supply of cracks in the slatted floor for him to "enjoy" the nerve-wracking view. While he curled up in the middle of the "death cage," as he called it, the rest of us took in the sights from the window openings as we were slowly lowered down to the crater floor in a semicircular arc. The white city sprawling out below us was quite plain, yet breathtakingly beautiful in its setting, encircling crystalline waters. It reminded me in some ways of the city of Sanctuary, only not nearly as fortified.

The hub of activity was easy to spot, the City Circle, which boasted the largest building of all. It was a regular palace with bulbous golden domes crowning its halls. Stoney explained that it was where King Zagzabarz lived, the leader of Torpor.

"King?" I asked. "Do you think Captain Saris would be in the palace, then?"

"Not likely," he replied. "The Codebearer captains have little political power these days. He has some interaction with those in the palace, but he wouldn't live there. Most likely they have a meeting house nearby; not sure where, to be honest with ya."

"Oh," I said lamely. For some reason I had imagined each of the captains having more sway with their people. The shift in thinking took some getting used to.

We were met at the base by a man on the back of a massive turtle, large enough to seat us all. Its shell was painted over with advertisements for local merchants. The man was dressed much like the man at the top of the crater, only with a different color for his sash. His tan, pox-eaten face bore a large black beard, which was tied in numerous knots that extended to his stomach.

"Good rest, my friends. You are looking for passage to the City Circle, are you not?"

Eyeing the turtle warily, Stoney answered dismissively, "No thanks, already taken care of. The dockmaster said he'd send word for a transport to meet us here."

The man bobbed his head cheerfully. "Yes! This is why I am here. I take you now, yes?"

Stoney was not impressed. "Eh, don't you have anything snappier? Where's the Uguas?" He was referring, of course, to the large breed of domesticated lizard-like creatures that were quite effective for covering long distances in a short amount of time. I had used one the last time I was in Solandria on another shard.

Indignant at the mention of his obviously superior competition, the driver insisted, "Oh, I can assure you my services are most snappy. She is a snappy turtle, yes." He grinned widely as he rubbed the bulky turtle's sponsor-covered shell affectionately. "You would not be getting Uguas today. The Emissary's visit has used all of them, yes. You ride with me. The walking will take too long for you."

Emissary, huh? I noted to myself. *Guess that explains the fancy fleet we docked next to.*

Confident he had earned our business, he began assertively reaching for our things. "Yes, yes, hop aboard then."

"Hold on, I ain't going on that beast until you tells me what your fare be."

"Of course, of course," the man cast a passing glance over our group and added with a wave of his hand, "only ten credits should suffice. Please, hop aboard."

He extended his hand to Trista who took it without hesitation.

"A turtle, what fun!" she said.

"Wait," said Stoney, before she was up. He narrowed his eyelids at the man. "Is that ten credits each or for the whole lot of us?"

"I am not running a charity, my friend. Ten credits each is more than a fair price for such a journey as this. My family, we are very poor. We need every small amount I can manage to feed ourselves these days. Especially, my aging mother who is not in good health, I'm afraid."

"Right, I think we'll walk then," Stoney said bluntly. "Come along you three." He motioned for us to follow. We collected our things and started to leave when the man hollered out after us.

"Twenty for all. That is half of what I have quoted before, a good price. Please come join me for the ride."

"You'll give us ten or we'll walk."

"Fifteen, then," the man said, "my final offer."

"Please, Stoney," Trista begged. "It looks like fun."

"It is great fun indeed," the man said, jumping at the chance to seal the sale, "and it will help my family. Did I mention my mother is very ill?"

"Yes," Stoney said, knowing a ploy when he heard one. "We'll pay ten credits and not a bit more."

"You drive a hard bargain, my friend. But I will do this for you since you are from out of town. Please, please, hop aboard."

We finally accepted the offer and climbed atop the turtle with our things. Trista brought her bow while I had my backpack with Boojum tucked safely inside. Rob carried the Author's Writ, wrapped in a blanket for safekeeping. I was certainly glad to have Stoney along and marveled at his ability to negotiate such a bargain—he just saved us thirty credits for the ride! But as soon as the driver tapped the shell with his driving stick to kick off our journey, it became painfully clear that this ride was not what we had bargained for. The turtle inched forward at a pace half the speed of a brisk walk—a rip-off at any price.

All the way the man rambled on about the city, how it sat above a dormant volcano, and other useless bits of trivia. I wasn't listening much; instead, I was wondering why there weren't many people on the streets. The entire city seemed to be in a daze. There were plenty of buildings, but it lacked the activity of a normal city its size.

"Where is everyone?" I asked at last.

"Ah, this is one of the hours of Solace, a time for personal reflection and relaxation. Our people are never in a hurry, we believe that life is not to be rushed. You'll find things move at a different pace here in Torpor."

"So I've noticed," Rob muttered loud enough for only us to hear. We all fought back a chuckle as the turtle transport crept along.

An hour later we arrived at the City Circle. The noon hour was near, and we were famished from the journey. We begrudgingly paid the fare and dismounted the turtle. The man counted his money with greedy eyes and watched us as we left.

"Hungry," Boojum said as we walked away, the aroma of food reaching his nose at last.

"I agree," I said to everyone. "Let's eat first, then we can figure out where to go from there."

Everyone agreed.

Aptly named, the City Circle was a circular marketplace that boasted restaurants and vendors of all kinds around its perimeter. Unlike the rest of the city, it was slightly busy. On one side of the circle was a long road that stretched to the palace doors, the other side bordered the lakefront.

Stoney ordered up a meal from one of the merchants, and we indulged our appetites on one of the local delicacies, boiled snails on a stick. At first Trista refused, but after Rob and I had eaten more than our share she gave in and tried them as well. Surprisingly, she said they weren't as bad as she thought, especially with enough sauce.

Boojum was the only one who wouldn't touch the stuff. Whenever I'd pass food into the backpack, he would toss it out. We were just about to finish our third helping of snail-kabobs when a small commotion near the lakefront drew our attention.

"There they are, over there," someone yelled, pointing directly at us. We saw the turtle driver speaking to a tall man dressed in a scarlet uniform and cape. His wrists and ankles were trimmed in yellow, as was his sash, and a golden *Z* was pinned over his heart. On his head was a matching yellow turban, and he was armed with a jagged saber (resembling a somewhat stretched out *Z* with a little imagination.)

"That's them, the ones who cheated me out of my credits!" the driver claimed loudly so that everyone could hear. A small crowd began to gather around us to watch the scene unfold.

"Here now," the scarlet guard said as he approached, "what's this I hear about you paying half what you owe?"

Stoney replied sharply before I could think of a response, "We paid exactly what was agreed upon, and not a credit less."

"He lies," the turtle driver complained. "The fare was for four riders. They had a fifth one hidden inside the boy's pack. If I had known that it would have remained at ten credits each."

The logic made no sense at all. Clearly, the man was trying to weasel his way into more of our money.

"Well then," the guard asked, pointing at me and the backpack beside me. "What do you say to that? Do you or don't you have anyone in the pack?"

The word "pack" was accompanied with a shower of spittle from the guard's lips. I wiped my face on my sleeve and considered my words carefully. As far as I was concerned, we had already been ripped off once by the turtle driver; I wasn't interested in letting it happen a second time.

"Well, speak up!" the guard prodded, showering us again.

"Yes, it's my pet..." I said cautiously, "but he never said..."

"Well, that settles it. Hand it over," the guard said, not waiting to hear the rest of my statement. "Ten credits for each of the five riders is fifty credits. You still owe the man forty for the ride. Settle up...now!"

"We'll do nothing of the sort," Stoney argued, stepping between us. "We're not the thieves, this man is. Clearly, he's trying to line his pockets with our money. I expect any fair man can see it. Or perhaps you stand to make some money on the deal as well, is that it?"

I cringed at Stoney's lack of tact. He had called the guard a thief, a mistake that would likely land us all in jail. The guard was a whole head taller than Stoney, but he was skinny in comparison and much less intimidating.

"Alright, that's going too far!" the guard shouted, locking eyes with Stoney in a silent challenge. "You four...er...FIVE are going to have to come with me."

"Pardon me, Mr. Swift," a new voice emerged from the crowd. "May I make a suggestion?" A young man dressed in a grey hooded cloak stepped forward. As he lowered his hood, the face looked vaguely familiar but I couldn't place it—curly brown hair and dark brown eyes with a look of wonder in them.

The guard, Mr. Swift, answered the boy in a decidedly friendly tone, "Ah, Philan, my friend. Good rest to ya."

Philan. The name brought back memories of a boy in Sanctuary who had bested me in a footrace when I first arrived—a seemingly fearless boy who also led the charge to rescue me from Venator's fortress. Could this really be the same Philan I had encountered before? I examined his features and determined right away it was, but it was no wonder I didn't recognize him at first; he seemed much younger the last time I saw him. Though it had only been three years, Solandrian time, Philan seemed to have grown up almost overnight. He was taller than me now, perhaps seventeen and spoke with an authority well beyond his years.

"Good rest to you as well, Mr. Swift," Philan said with an assuring smile. "I was wondering if the good driver, Mr. Niparret, might allow me to pay the fine in their stead?" As he said this he opened his hand toward the turtle driver with forty credits extended his way.

Mr. Niparret replied suspiciously, "And why would you do that?"

Philan explained, "It just so happens I have some work to do at the old monastery, and I am in desperate need of help. I came to town to see if I could hire some extra hands. Forty credits is exactly what I expected to pay."

"So what?" Niparret asked, not following the logic.

Philan laid it out for him plainly, "So, I'll pay *you* the credits now for the chance to put these four, or five as it may be, to work. It's a fair trade all around...and Mr. Swift won't have to waste any effort on hauling them off to prison."

The unscrupulous driver didn't need any more convincing. "As long as I have my forty credits, I don't care what you do with them."

"Then it's settled," Philan said, quickly handing over the money before the man's mind changed on the matter. "Oh, and I do hope your mother is feeling better, my friend."

Niparret eyed him guardedly, counted the credits and slipped away without an answer. With the trouble over, the crowd began to clear.

Mr. Swift moved to Philan's side and lowered his voice ever so slightly, "You sure you don't need any help rounding them up? These outsiders can't be trusted." He shot a wary look our way as if he expected us to run off at any minute.

Philan smiled, "Thank you, Mr. Swift, but I think I'll take my chances. Good rest to you!"

"And to you," the guard grumbled disapprovingly as he strolled off to attend to his peacekeeping duties. When at last he was gone, Philan spoke first.

"Well, well, if it isn't my old friend, Hunter Brown," Philan said, gripping my hand in a firm handshake and pulling my shoulder into a partial embrace with the other. "It's good to see you again."

"Thanks, Philan," I replied. "Your timing couldn't have been better."

"I seem to have a knack for saving you, don't I?" he smiled jokingly. "You haven't changed a bit."

"No, but you have. You've grown up fast in three years," I noted. "Last I saw you, you hardly seemed ten years old. What happened?"

"I was actually thirteen, but I looked younger. You're not the first to think I was that young. I guess my body just made up for lost time all at once. Actually, I'm *Lieutenant* Philan now, but it's only a title. All Codebearers are equal in the eyes of the Author. Just means that I volunteered to help lead others in battle. But enough about me, what happened to you? Last I'd heard, everyone thought you were dead!"

"I was, but the Author wasn't finished with me yet—it's kind of a long story but well…here I am again," I answered, knowing the explanation was less than clear, but also aware that it was neither the time or place to elaborate on what had happened.

"Indeed, I'm glad you're safe. Who are your friends?"

"Oh, I'm sorry," I said, pointing to each of the others. "This is Stoney, Rob and Trista."

Rob and Stoney nodded in response to my introductions.

"Pleased to meet you," Trista said.

"The pleasure is mine," Philan answered with a bow of his head. Trista seemed somewhat flattered by the gesture, but if Philan noticed he showed no signs of it.

"So then, what brings you to Torpor, my friends?"

"We're looking for Saris actually. We have an urgent matter to bring before him. Do you know where he lives?"

"Know it? Of course, I live there with him. Several of us are working to convert the old monastery into a Resistance training ground of sorts. I'll take you there; after all, you owe me some work if I'm not mistaken."

"Oh right," I answered, not entirely sure if he was kidding or not.

We followed the boy through the tangled web of roads that angled this way and that until we came to the edge of the city and the base of the crater cliff. There, we found a thin ledge of steps carved into the side of the cliff, leading up to a small cave door. Philan didn't break stride, but led us up the steep climb at a quick pace. Stoney brought up the rear in a decidedly slower manner—pushing the limits of both his legs *and* the aged stairs with his expansive waistline. He eventually made it, sweating and wheezing when he finally walked through the door.

Inside, we found ourselves in an expansive hallway lit by what must have been a thousand beams of light shining down from narrow shafts that were carved through the cave wall behind us. They were not visible from the outside because of the sharp angle in which they were drilled, but from within the artistry of the design was breathtaking. The effect was not unlike a giant stained glass window, only without the colors and with more space between each pane. The image it portrayed was of a giant tree consumed in flames.

"Amazing," Rob gawked, staring at the image.

"Isn't it?" Philan replied. "The Xin carved this monastery hundreds of years ago. We were fortunate enough to inhabit the space when they disappeared. I can't imagine a more beautiful place to be hidden."

"The Xin did this?" I asked, pointing up at the tree window.

"Yes, and that's not even the half of it. They were extraordinary artists. You'll find many of our halls are rife with imagery such as this. Come on, there is something I want to show you."

He led us back down a series of passageways. The walls and ceiling sparkled with embedded luminescent blue designs that seemed to glow with surprising vibrancy all their own. The effect was similar to the glow-in-the-dark paint I had used in one of my pranks back home last year.

As we went, a handful of people passed by; all of them wore the Author's mark around their necks and carried Veritas Swords at their sides. Philan explained that men, women and children inhabited the space.

Impressed by the size of the facility, I asked, "How many people can you fit in here?"

"A lot more than we do right now. The meeting hall alone could probably fit close to five hundred, but we're rarely more than fifty strong at any given time. It's been frustrating trying to get much turnout here on Torpor. People just don't want to spend their time studying, training…or identifying with the Codebearers now. They get caught up in doing…well, nothing."

I could hear the discouragement in his voice.

The place he was taking us to was a training room where a lesson in using a Veritas Sword was being given to children by a white-haired woman with her back turned toward us.

The scene, although smaller in numbers, was reminiscent of the

Sanctuary Acadamy where young ones were taught the ways of the Code of Life. I had to chuckle to myself when I saw several slabs of Tempering Stone gathered in the center of the room. The young Codebearers in training were swinging wildly at the stone with no effect—many of them frustrated and dumbfounded at their inability to command the sword.

"This is the Training Round where we practice and teach the ways of the Code of Life. Look familiar?" Philan smiled, remembering how we first met.

"Does it ever—I feel like Sam should be standing right here beside me, shouting out his lecture. He was a great teacher."

Philan nodded in agreement. "His students are now the teachers. Naturally, part of our duty is to train these young ones the best we can in the use of a Veritas Sword. Care to take a shot at it?"

"Well, I don't think I better, you know...interrupt the kids and all...maybe later I can." I began to look for a way out of the situation.

"Nonsense, they'd love a demonstration, I'm sure. Besides, class is almost over for the day," he said. Before I could argue further he called out to the instructor. "Alice, can we interrupt for a moment? You remember Hunter, don't you?"

As it turned out, the instructor was a teenager, not an elder. She was dressed in purple robes and her long, flowing white hair was pulled back in a ponytail. When her silvery eyes caught mine, I remembered right away Philan's friend, Alice.

"Oh, thur thing, Philan," she said with her characteristic lisp. Even though she now resembled a young woman, her voice had hardly changed. "I'll gather the thudenths; come on over."

In a matter of moments we exchanged warm greetings and soon every student's eyes were trained on the three of us.

"Tho claths," Alice said, "Hunter here will be tharing thomthing about the Veritath Thword that he learned when he wath here before. Lithen clothly and give him your attention, okay?"

She gave a gracious bow and backed away, leaving me standing in front of a half-dozen students and one taunting white block of Tempering Stone. With every eye trained on me, I cleared my throat and began to share.

"Well, it wasn't that long ago that I was in your shoes," I said, still unsure of what I was going to say. The pressure of having so many kids hanging on my every word was not something I was comfortable with. Still, I swallowed and continued, allowing Sam's words to speak through me.

"Sam was my instructor back then, and he taught me about the Code of Life. One of the things that helped me the most was to know that we don't fear anything but the Author himself. If Sam were here today, he'd probably say the same thing to you. By fear a man appoints his master," I explained.

"This will come in handy when you are in the heat of battle. I know it did for me." Then turning to the stone, I lifted my Veritas Sword and realized for the first time that as funny as it sounded, I was actually afraid of the Tempering Stone. I was afraid of failing in front of these kids, of not being able to use the Veritas Sword to make a mark in the stone...perhaps even afraid that the Veritas Sword wouldn't work for me this time, or ever again for that matter. I closed my eyes and let the words I had just spoken to the students be a reminder to myself.

By fear a man appoints his master, I thought. *Help me to not be afraid.*

Then, holding the Veritas Sword above my head, I opened my eyes and faced the stone.

"By fear a man appoints his master!" I shouted and lunged at the stone, swinging the sword in a downward slice. To the delight of the students and me, the sword blazed to life in a glowing arc of light, severing the stone down the middle. The gash I made was deeper than any I had managed before. I pulled the glowing blade out and the mark in the stone began to heal itself almost instantly. A smile of satisfaction spread across my face. The truth hadn't let me down. It still worked, even after all this time.

"Well done, Hunter," Alice said, leading her students in a round of applause. "Thank you for tharing what you have learned with uth."

"It was my pleasure," I replied.

Alice gave a wink and a nod of approval and then gathered the attention of her students once again. I turned to face Philan and the others.

"That was fun," I said.

"Good. I'm glad you thought so," Philan replied. "Teaching is one of the most noble things you can aspire to. Every Codebearer needs to invest his or her knowledge into others. I hope you don't forget to pass along what you have learned. Come on, we have some guest rooms prepared down the hallway that you can use. Saris is in council right now; I'll take you to him after you're settled."

As we left, I glanced back over my shoulder at the students who were now swinging their swords in the air and shouting "By fear a man appoints his master" at the top of their lungs. There was a brief flicker of light in the middle of the group, followed by a round of applause. My chest swelled at the sight. I had helped another just as Sam had helped me.

Chapter 17

Saris' Council

Winding through a labyrinth of stone-chiseled hallways, Philan led us toward our rooms. The torch-lined halls eventually ended in a square common area with slightly higher ceilings. In the center of the room was a large stone table and matching benches, all of which appeared to be carved up from the floor. A large spread of fruit, bread and cheese was already waiting for us on the table. It was a welcome sight for everyone, especially Boojum, who had been cautiously watching from my backpack. Having spotted the food, he bounded out of my pack and eagerly helped himself to a red banana before the rest of us had time to claim it.

"Mine, mine," Boojum said, his large eyes sparkling with happiness as he gobbled down the food.

"Boojum," Trista scolded, "where are your manners? You didn't even ask." If he heard her, he didn't show it, still munching away hungrily on the snack.

"It's okay," Philan said. "Help yourself to whatever you find here. I'll let you get settled in while I make arrangements for a meeting with Saris. I'm sure you are exhausted. There are four bedrooms connected to this quad. I'll be back within the half hour." With that he bowed and darted away.

"Well, that was lucky, finding your friends here," Trista said. "And just in time too. Can you image what might have happened if the guard had taken us to prison?"

"Luck had nothing to do with it, Trista," I answered. "The Author is watching over us. The Flame led us here for a reason."

"Oh right," she sighed, "I keep forgetting that!"

"Not to sound like a downer or anything," said Rob, "but what are we hoping to accomplish here anyway? Do you think Saris is one of the seven we are looking for?"

"I don't know for sure; I just know the spark told me to come to Torpor. After that I guess I'm as lost as you," I reasoned.

"So, you think it's safe to tell Saris about the Flame then?" Rob asked.

"Why not? He's one of the captains, isn't he?"

"Yeah, but I just get the feeling that things aren't what they seem here...you know?"

"How so?"

"I don't know, we find them hiding in a Xin temple and our greatest threat just happens to be the rogue Xin assassin who killed Petrov. Think about it, you said yourself he was using a Veritas Sword. Where on earth would he learn to use that unless another Codebearer was training him? Doesn't that concern you or am I the only one who is a little worried about this?"

Until that moment I hadn't considered the fact that we might be treading into a trap. The Veritas Sword connection was a strange one. After all, Codebearers were the only ones who knew how to use the sword.

"Are you saying that Saris and Philan are somehow aligned with Xaul? That they plotted to have Petrov killed?"

"No, what I'm saying is that maybe we should be more careful about what we say…just until we're sure," Rob replied.

I ran my fingers through my hair and held them there, trying to devise a good plan for discovering whether or not Saris was involved with Xaul. Nothing came to mind.

"I know I'm new to this and all," Trista said, "but can't we just assume that if the Author brought us here for a reason he'll give us the sign we need to reveal the Flame to Saris…when the time is right?"

It was a simple statement, but one that carried truth in it.

"She's right, Rob; we do need to be careful, but the Author will make it clear if we should keep the Flame hidden," I said. "Who knows, Saris may already be marked."

"We'll know soon enough," Stoney said. "Here comes that Philan kid."

Sure enough Philan had returned and brought with him the good news that Saris would be ready in a matter of minutes. The four of us (five if you counted Boojum, who rode on my shoulder) were led down the hall to a foyer just outside the council chambers, where he would meet with us. The double doors that opened into the chamber were made of a thick wood, engraved with elaborate markings that resembled the terrain of the Shard of Torpor. A pair of guards flanked both sides of the doors, stoically holding their spears at attention. Even from a distance, it was obvious to me that they were not Codebearers. Their rich robes were striking in that they were distinctly half blue and half green, seamed down the middle vertically with ornate patterns of gold around the trim. The design was unmistakably matched to the flags we had seen flying from the larger sky ships up at the dock.

"So, who are they?" I asked Philan as we made our way up the corridor.

"The Emissary's guards," Philan answered, though with marked annoyance. Slowing his steps, he explained in a hushed tone, "She claims to act as a neutral party between governments, the Resistance and Shadow alike. Each time she visits it is for promoting some new treaty or deal. I can only imagine what it's about this time. Between you and me, I can't wait for them to leave."

As we reached the waiting area outside the council chamber, I recognized the slow, drawn-out speech of Captain Saris rolling out through the open doors.

"...Of course I want peace. The Resistance is as tired of war as anyone, but...peace at what cost? Negotiating to give the Shadow an embassy here in Torpor just seems...dangerous. Perhaps we can find another way..."

"There *is* no other way," a deep-throated man groaned impatiently. "Captain, haven't you been listening to me? King Zagzabarz has *already* signed his name to the Embassy Treaty. As his ambassador, I am authorized to inform you that if you do not sign it as well, the Codebearers will, at best, be viewed as an intolerant threat within the Torporian kingdom and at worst..."

"If you please, Ambassador Narcole," a commanding woman's voice interrupted. Assuming control, she continued in a soothing manner, "Captain Saris, I appreciate the weight of your decision. Serving in my unique position, however, I have already helped the Codebearers on many of the other shards to negotiate similar agreements, and I am pleased to report they are now enjoying the fruits of newfound peace today. Think of it: seven years of peace between Shadow and Codebearer across all of Solandria. Torpor can be next.

Zagzabarz wants to bring this gift to his people. You only have to ask yourself if you are willing to be part of the movement."

I couldn't believe what we were hearing. *Had* others in the Resistance already embraced this treaty with the Shadow? Looking over at Philan, I could see he was especially concerned for his captain's resolve.

Letting out a long sigh, the beleaguered Captain Saris finally replied, "I don't know. This would go against the core of our principles. We simply cannot ally with the Shadow. How can I ignore what has been clearly defined in our teachings for ages?"

"I understand," she replied sympathetically. "But is it not also wise to question our beliefs from time to time, to take a fresh look at them in light of our present circumstances? Often when we do, we are rewarded with a... *fresh... perspective.*" It was unnerving how the Emissary's tone had changed during the careful delivery of those final words. Continuing in the deliberate, low intonations she cooed, "Don't you agree?"

"Yes," Saris answered slowly after a brief pause. He almost sounded dreamy as he said, "I will...sleep on it...and...I will give my answer to the King in...the morning. And perhaps if nothing else comes to me, I will sign...the treaty...with him."

"Excellent! Then we have an understanding. I believe you will be making a very wise choice, Captain," the woman said in closing.

We all stood in stunned silence. Could Saris seriously be considering this treaty?

There was a rustling in the room as each of them rose to gather his things. Startled by the screeching noise of one of the chairs scraping across the floor, a wide-eyed Boojum dropped down into my arms for safety. The guard escorts took their cue to turn and receive the exiting leaders.

A decidedly short man in an obnoxious yellow tunic strutted out first. The silver sash embroidered with the Torporian kingdom's crowned *Z* insignia made it obvious that he was the ambassador, though it was hard to imagine the deep voice we'd heard coming from a man so small. The extra-large turban balanced on top of his head was his best attempt at achieving any stature, but honestly, it really only gave him a bigger head. With his chest puffed up and chin lifted high, he intentionally ignored us as he spun around to wait for his companion. Obviously, he had not let his size keep him from trying to look down on the rest of the world.

A rapid clacking of tiny, but forceful steps followed closely behind, marking the emergence of the second dignitary, the Emissary, as they had addressed her. Unlike the self-important ambassador, the commanding presence of this woman was clearly backed by *real* power. Her profile revealed a determined expression smothered under a heavy covering of makeup, its deep hues complimenting the translucent blues and greens of the long, almost wing-like sleeves of her flowing black gown. In her far hand, she carried something covered by a cloth. With a simple wave of her free hand, she signaled the guards who immediately fell in line behind her and marched away from us down the hall.

Anxious to take up the matter of this newly revealed treaty with the captain himself, Philan hurriedly motioned for us to follow him into the council chambers. I followed behind the others, but as soon as we reached the doors, something caused Boojum to scramble wildly up my arm, pinching me in his frantic climb.

"Ow! Let go, Boojum. What's your problem?"

As my eyes followed to where he was so excitedly pointing, I immediately saw what he was so worked up about. A pair of round, yellowish-green eyes blinked back at us from the face of a snow-white snark riding away on the Emissary's shoulder. Its powdery white tail whipped playfully back and forth upon seeing Boojum, whisking the protective cloth right off of the object in the Emissary's hand and down onto Ambassador Narcole's head. The blinded man struggled to fight off the cloth and couldn't see when the Emissary abruptly stopped in front of him. Crashing into her, he fell helplessly to the ground. She only glared down at him and yanked the cloth off, quickly re-covering the exposed object. As she resumed her march down the hall, I saw what she had been hiding: a glass ball—a harmless item in and of itself—but what I saw inside it made my skin crawl. Staring lifelessly out at me from within the orb was a bodiless, gray-bearded head.

"You comin' or not?" I heard Stoney call to me from inside. Shaking off the unsettling image of the face, I ignored Boojum's pleas to follow the other snark and turned back to the important meeting at hand. If we were right, Saris would be the next one marked.

Ten columns formed a ring around the outer edges of the circular, domed room. Each column held out a golden torch toward the center, casting a soft light over an aged, but beautiful, tiled floor, patterned to form a large crimson *X*. Captivating paintings decorated the ceiling above us, no doubt brimming with artistic significance to the Xin's history, but Philan was not in tour guide mode right now. He marched us quickly across the room to where Captain Saris was waiting in his ornate, high-backed chair. A slow, red glow pulsed out from the Author's mark on his armor's chestplate.

I barely knew Saris from my last visit, but I immediately recognized the older, roundish man's face as soon as we drew nearer… not because of my previous experience, but for the chilling reason that I had just seen it being carried off in the Emissary's glass ball!

Was I just imagining things?

"He's dead," Trista gasped as the captain's head suddenly

slumped forward into his bushy gray beard. His half-closed eyes stared lifelessly at the floor, just like I'd seen in the ball. My head was spinning so fast with possibilities, I couldn't find any words.

"It's alright...really," Philan calmly explained to the group. "He's only dozed off again. He does that sometimes," he added in a somewhat embarrassed tone.

As if on cue, the captain began snoring in confirmation of Philan's diagnosis.

Rob eyed the old, gray-bearded man in amazement. "But didn't he just finish the other meeting a minute ago?"

Philan just shrugged and approached Saris, touching him gently on the arm. "Excuse me, sir."

The old man jolted awake and, much to Boojum's delight, knocked a bowl of shelled nuts from the small table set next to him. My snack-happy snark leaped at the opportunity to clean up the scattered treats, stuffing his cheeks full of them before realizing he would have to open them first.

"Wha...who...oh, it's just you, Philan," the captain said, blinking in shock at the sudden awakening. "I was just... thinking. Yes... ahem. Well, what is it you wanted, Lieutenant?"

Undoubtedly, what Philan wanted most was to engage his captain on matters of the newly proposed treaty, but he graciously deferred to our requested meeting first. "Captain, there are some friends here who wanted to see you. They bring an urgent message."

"Oh?" Saris turned his head toward us and raised his bushy silver brows in curiosity, awaiting our explanation.

As the adult among us, Stoney took it upon himself to step forward and introduce our group, offering his best Codebearer salute by pounding his fist to his chest. "Stone... er, I mean Chester Sterling, sir. At your service. It's an honor fer us to be with you t'day."

He started to introduce Trista next, but Saris had already become distracted, blinking his beady black eyes at me instead as he tried to focus on my face.

"You look familiar, boy," he said, interrupting Stoney to point a shaky finger at me. "I know you, don't I?"

"Yes, sir," I replied, feeling a little uneasy talking to the head from the ball. "I'm Hunter Brown. Maybe you remember me from the Feast of Unitus three years ago. The Council met with me after…"

"Ah, yes!" he exclaimed, his face brightening at the memory. "The last of our feasts, I remember…it was splendid, wasn't it? We have not enjoyed such a peaceful gathering as that since Sanctuary fell to the Shadow. Terrible times. Terrible.... Actually, nothing has quite been the same since then. More fighting, greater losses, divisions within the Resistance…." His words trailed off into a great sadness.

His pained expression reminded me that the rest of the Resistance had yet to learn the truth of Aviad's disappearance. I was unsure if this would be the best time to mention the Flame, but I knew I at least needed to offer this man and his Torporian Codebearers the hope we had.

"Captain Saris," I began, "perhaps you also remember how I met with Aviad about the Bloodston…"

"What's that?" he perked up. "Aviad, you say?"

"Yes, sir."

"You say you just met with him? He's back?" Saris became so caught up in the prospect of the missing leader's return that he didn't give me the chance to correct him. Excitedly standing to his feet, he began talking nonstop. "Nobody has seen or heard from him in quite some time, and now you say he's returned! Fantastic! Lieutenant Philan, my boy, we must double—no, triple—our repair efforts on the monastery to make it ready in case he chooses to visit here next. Splendid! What a day! Ha, ha!" The captain was bursting with so much newfound energy, he didn't know what to do with himself. "But oh! I am getting ahead of myself. First... first let us hear the message this fine young man has brought to us from Aviad."

The old captain finally settled down enough to take his seat once more, beaming at me expectantly with a wide grin that seemed to erase years from his wrinkled face. I felt horrible in saying it now, but the truth needed to be told.

"Aviad is dead, sir."

"What?!"

"I'm sorry. I didn't mean to confuse you," I apologized. "The truth is that after Aviad gave me the mission to recover the Bloodstone halves, he came and united them himself.... The curse was completed in him."

This news did not seem to encourage Saris as it had Petrov and the Thordins. Instead he slumped deeper into his chair; his face drifted further into despair than ever before. "Then we are worse off than I thought," he moaned.

"But sir," Philan spoke up, not quite understanding his logic, "if it's true that the Bloodstone has been destoyed, then..."

"Then we should not still be in the mess we are in today," the captain said tersely. "Think about it.... Supposing Aviad did attempt to destroy the Bloodstone, then according to the prophecy, the curse of death should be lifted. We should be free of the Shadow."

He made a valid point; one we could not readily argue.

"Well, as it stands now," Saris continued, "three years later he's still gone and, Bloodstone or not, the Shadow have only grown stronger every day. With Aviad dead, I fear our cause is hopeless. I had such faith in the man too. He was so young, so strong, so full of life. I thought for sure he was the one to lead us into victory..."

Young? Had I heard Saris right? The Aviad I knew was not young by any stretch of the imagination. Instead, I remembered last seeing him as a frail old man, and somewhat absentminded at that. I had often wondered what everyone saw in him until he proved his power to me in the end. Clearly Saris must be getting delusional with age.

"Well then, that settles it," Captain Saris concluded, slapping his hands down onto his knees with finality. "Without a word from the Author, we must move forward with the Emissary's proposal for peace with the Shadow. I see no other way to survive. Tomorrow I plan to sign the treaty with Zagzabarz. We have waited long enough."

Philan looked devastated at his captain's sudden decision, but that didn't stop him from speaking up. "Sir, with all due respect, we cannot sign this treaty," he said boldly. "It's dangerous ground; I heard you say so yourself. The Code of Life clearly states we are to resist the Shadow, not shake hands with them! Give this more time…the Author will make another way if we only hold on a little longer."

"No, Philan, my mind is made up. We have no other options. Maybe with time something will come, but time is not our friend unless we sign the treaty, I'm afraid. We'll be evicted from this place in short order if we don't concede. And where would we go then?" He sighed, "I only wish there were something else that could be done."

"Hunter," Trista whispered, elbowing me, "tell him about the Flame."

Rob shot a worried glance at us, shaking his head nervously.

"What?" Trista replied, "I think we've heard enough to know

that Saris isn't some kind of enemy spy. He just needs encouragement. Tell him, already!"

"Tell me what?" Saris asked disinterestedly.

I didn't know exactly where to begin until I remembered the approach Petrov had taken with me back on Galacia. "Well," I began slowly, "I think maybe I should show you something first."

Following my lead, Rob hesitantly carried his copy of the Author's Writ over to the small table next to Saris and unlocked it.

"Tell us of the Consuming Fire," I appealed.

Boojum, thinking more treats were being served at the table, had just climbed up when the book began moving on its own in response to my request. Spooked, he darted into Trista's arms as the pages flipped open to the passage I had first read with Petrov. The words etched themselves into existence even as the last page fell into place.

"Saris, would you honor us by reading this passage aloud?" I asked.

"I don't see as well anymore," Saris said squinting at the page, "but I will be happy to try." After finding the right distance from which to read, Saris cleared his throat and began:

The Consuming Fire

Before the sun rises, darkness must reign;
For seventy times, light's presence will wane;
But no shadow or power can hold back the light
when a new dawn of fire bursts forth from the night.
An eternal flame of consuming power
Will come to the faithful in their most desperate hour.
It starts with a spark—on the first will descend

To empower the chosen to stand til the end.
So I, the Author, have written.
A wounded pillar the Fire will take;
A sleeping strength the Fire will wake;
A heart of stone from Fire gains sight;
A precious seed through Fire finds life;
A faithful captive the Fire unchains;
An ember of hope the Fire will claim;
The seventh of seven only Fire can name.
When the seven are marked the Fire will fall,
Not only for seven but on all who are called.
So I, the Author, have written.

When he finished he looked up and blinked.

"So now, what exactly was it you wanted to tell me about this passage?"

"Well, it may sound strange but, did you happen to feel anything when you read it?"

"Feel something?"

"Yes…like a burning or anything?"

"A burning? No, I can't say I felt any burning…why?"

His answer was disappointing to say the least. It seemed we had come all this way for nothing.

"I don't get it," I said in frustration. "The Flame clearly told me to come to Torpor. And Petrov seemed sure that the passage was referring to the Captains…and…"

"Slow down there, boy, what Flame? What are you talking about?" Saris asked.

"You know, the Flame…the one that marked Petrov!" I said, as if they already knew. The room went silent. Apparently, Petrov had never shared the news with anyone else.

"Petrov was marked?" Saris asked somewhat dreamily, his eyes glazing over in thought. "By a flame?"

"Yes, on his left collarbone, just above his heart. I saw it myself!"

"But we received word just yesterday that he passed away unexpectedly."

"It's true," I acknowledged, saddened by the reminder. Before I knew what I was saying I found myself adding, "But he passed on the task of carrying the Flame to me. Actually, the Flame told me to carry it to Torpor. It didn't exactly say why, but Petrov and I figured it would be to find another of the seven to mark."

I cringed, realizing too late that I had said too much. Hadn't Petrov warned me to keep the Flame's location a secret from everyone unless it chose to reveal itself to them? Rob had even reminded me less than an hour ago. I looked over at him for help, but he had his head buried in his hands. There was no way to take anything back now.

"You mean the Flame is here…with you…now?" Saris asked, leaning forward and fixing his gaze on me once more.

I squirmed, not wanting to say anything more, but he knew the answer without my ever saying a word; my face had said it all.

"There! You see, Captain?" Philan said with a contagious joy that quickly spread to the down-trodden captain. "You can't deny it's the Author's hand at work."

"Yes," Saris said, beaming. "Yes! This is great news indeed…. Perhaps there *is* hope for us yet!"

"Not ta damper things here," Stoney interjected in a serious tone, "but if we can't find the other six ta mark, there isn't much ta get excited 'bout…. You see, we were expectin' you'd be the second of the seven, what with being the 'sleeping strength' part."

"Indeed," Saris chuckled, "I've been called worse, I'm sure. But the seven you're after couldn't be captains."

"Why not?" Trista asked.

"Well, to begin with, there are only five captains left now, four if you don't count Petrov who you say was already marked. Sam is gone and Faldyn was removed, gone missing now, as I understand it. We've never really replaced either of them."

I pondered this for awhile, kicking myself for not having thought that part through before.

"Then who should we look for?" Rob finally asked, having given up on being the sole survivor in the blown secrecy pact.

"Who indeed? It is a question that many will ponder," Saris replied; "however, we may not need to find the other six to be saved by it, considering the Flame's hidden power!"

"Hidden power?" Stoney said with curiosity.

"You mean, you don't know about the other prophecy?" Saris asked, somewhat surprised. "Petrov didn't tell you about it, did he?"

I shook my head, confused by what he was implying.

"I suppose he believed it was better that way," he finally said. "Still, I don't know why he didn't keep the Flame for himself; he surely would be alive today if he had."

"What do you mean?" I asked.

"Elsewhere in the Writ is another prophecy. It tells that the Flame holds the key to eternity. Anyone who carries the Flame can never die; the power of eternal life is his. Naturally, this is a power that even the Shadow desire, and not for good reasons, mind you. You said you carried the Flame with you, is that right?"

I nodded nervously, now keenly aware of its inestimable value. Would I really live forever as long as I held the Flame?

"Where is it now? May I see it?" he asked eagerly.

I started to reach for the medallion around my neck, but suddenly, the weight of it seemed to grow heavier. I felt like a child on his birthday, not wanting to share the toy he had just been given. Petrov obviously wanted me to have it, and the Flame had chosen me as well. How could I ever let someone else have it now that I knew the power it possessed?

"I…I…don't know," I said guardedly.

"You don't know? What do you mean, you don't know?" Saris said. His tone switched from friendly to slightly irritated. "If it told you to carry it to Torpor, don't you think it meant for us to see it?"

"Sorry, it's just that…well," I fumbled for words.

"Spit it out, boy, what is it?"

I let out a sigh.

"How can I trust you won't take it from me…for yourself?" I said at last with a somber tone.

Saris sat stunned for a moment. His face reddened in the silence as if he was offended by the question. Then for no apparent reason at all he broke the tension with a burst of laughter so loud and contagious the rest of the group soon found themselves joining in. When at last he settled himself down, he wiped a tear from the corner of his eye.

"Trust me, indeed. Oh, that is a good one, son! You had me going there for a moment. My dear boy, it's not me you have to worry about, I can assure you. I only want to help you in fulfilling your quest."

"How?"

"Well, considering that Petrov is dead, I think it is safe to assume that we are not the only ones who know about the Flame, right?"

I nodded.

"Then you will also be in need of protection—protection I can offer you. Pardon my saying so, but your small company is not the most adequate for the job of keeping such a great treasure safe."

"We can manage ourselves," Rob said in a challenge, holding his Veritas Sword in front of him with pride.

Saris lifted his hands to calm him. "Now, now! I meant no harm by it, boy! I'm sure you'll all do your best. But are you prepared to be tested beyond all possible imagination? Are you prepared to fend off the whole of the Shadow armies if that is what it comes down to? No doubt about it, Petrov knew what he was doing when he gave the Flame away. As long as he held the Flame, he would never be able to live a normal life. Someone knew he had it, and they would not rest until it was theirs. Giving it away was the only way to protect the Flame and himself. He was frightened by the thought of it, I suspect."

"He was not!" I shouted back, once again forgetting to think before I spoke. "He was a braver man than any of you know. Even in death he showed no fear! I watched it myself."

"In death?" Saris asked accusingly. "And how would you know that boy? Did you kill him yourself to take the Flame?"

Stoney's temper flared up at the wild accusation, and he spit out his defense. "How dare you suggest that sort of thing of these kids! They were stayin' at me inn when Hunter here saw a vision of it—a good full day's journey from wherever Petrov holed up, mind you. Why, we barely even escaped with our own lives from Galacia that night."

"So you say," Saris countered. "But how do I know I can trust what you're saying is true? If it wasn't Hunter who killed him, then who was it? What is it you know; what are you not telling me?"

"Stop it, all of you!" Trista shouted. "Bickering is getting us nowhere! You're all acting like a bunch of children!"

Boojum jumped from her arms and ran off to some darkened

corner. I figured he'd been scared off by all the shouting until I felt the warmth on my chest. Looking down, I saw that the medallion had begun to pulse with a blue light, now even lifting itself gently away from my chest. I knew what the Flame was calling me to do.

Amidst the ongoing argument, I pulled the medallion over my head and held it out in my open hand. The Author's marked pulsed with blue light at the touch of my skin. Then, slowly it awakened and hovered over the medallion, burning brightly in my palm for all to see. A hushed quiet washed over the others as they each became aware of the miraculous light.

The flaming glow was no bigger than a fist to start with, but then…slowly and gradually it began to intensify, both in its brilliance and size.

Saris immediately fell to his knees in reverent awe of the Flame.

"Beautiful," he said, his eyes widening in amazement. "Like Life itself."

Philan and the others knelt as well, honoring the Flame I held in my hand. I wanted to let go, to release the Flame and kneel too, but I found myself unable to move; the power at work in this moment held my body frozen in place as the fire continued to grow. Then, an extraordinary thing happened. I lost all control of my senses; even time seemed irrelevant. Words began forming in my mouth, but I neither knew what I said or that it was in fact me that said them.

"Forgive me, Author," Saris replied to the message I had unknowingly delivered. "I have doubted you, and I would have led us into a trap. May it be as you say."

In a flash the fire was gone. I blinked, recovering from the trance to find the medallion still set in my palm. It glistened ever so briefly, indicating the fire had safely returned to its place. Saris was lying on his back, his eyes gazing into an unseen distance. Philan knelt nearby, grasping his own chest as Trista, Stoney and Rob tended to Saris.

"Wh-what happened?" I asked, still shaking from the experience.

"You mean you don't know?" Trista answered, looking up at me.

I glanced around at the others; they were all staring at me now as well.

"No, I don't."

"You just anointed Philan as the next captain of Torpor!" Trista said aloud.

"It wasn't Hunter," Rob said boldly. "It was the Author who did it. He was speaking through Hunter."

"And it was the Flame that marked me," Philan said, pulling his tunic's collar lower so all could see. There on his left collarbone was the three-tongued mark of the Flame. The same mark Petrov had been given.

"Well, I'll be," Stoney said in amazement. "We were in the right place after all!"

There was a moment of quiet reflection as the significance of what just happened sank in for each of us. The second of seven had been found!

Saris moaned something unintelligible, prompting Trista to place her hand to his forehead. "He feels hot," she said. "We need to get him to a bed."

As we lifted him up to a standing position, the captain seemed to come to, looking about and mumbling, "No…no. There is no time…no time for rest now…"

"Sir?" Philan reached in and caught the frail man before he tipped over. "It's going to be alright."

Saris shook his head and reached weakly for the straps on his armor. "Take this," he said in a hoarse voice. Coming to his assistance, Trista helped undo the buckles and removed the breastplate with its captain's cape still attached, hoping it would make him more comfortable. But Saris took hold of the breastplate in Trista's hands and pushed it toward his young lieutenant saying, "You…you must…be ready…"

"Be ready? For what?"

"They're coming…for the Flame. You will lead now…"

"Sir?" Philan was confused. "Sir, who is coming for the Flame? What am I supposed to do?"

Saris simply looked Philan in the eyes and said, "Lead." Then, all at once, the gray-bearded man's eyes fluttered, his knees buckled and he fell limp. Stoney and I were able to move quickly enough to catch him before he hit the ground, but the captain had once again fallen into speaking indiscernibly with a far-off look in his eyes. Philan summoned a pair of Codebearer guards who tended to Saris right away. They carried him off to receive care in his room.

Looking down at the caped armor in his hands, Philan tried to make sense of what Saris had said. "How am I expected to prepare our battalion for a threat when I don't even know who or what it is?"

Swallowing the lump that had built in my throat ever since Saris gave his warning, I started to share what I knew of the man hunting us and the Flame.

"His name is Xaul," I said. "He is the one I saw kill Petrov in my vision before leaving Galacia. He carried a kind of dark Veritas Sword I've never seen before. Petrov believed he was Xin."

"What made him think that?" Philan asked, his eyes a mix of both shock and concern.

"The way he fought," I replied, "or dressed. He wears a red *X* on his belt."

Philan nodded gravely. "Then you are already in more trouble than you can possibly know. If he is truly Xin, he will have extraordinary tracking skills. But the Xin warrior is only one threat, the Shadow will certainly be after you as well."

"You know," Stoney said, "I've been thinking abouts them ships we seen...a whole fleet of 'em with the Emissary's."

"What about them?" Philan asked.

"Well, seems a bit much for peace negotiations. Like something's afoot. I wonder if it ain't best for me to stay with the sky ship and keep a close eye on their activities. Has all the makings of a Shadow attack if you ask me. Might help to have a spy out in those parts, if you know what I mean." Stoney winked at us with his good eye.

"I think that's a great idea," Philan replied.

Stoney wasted no time heading back to the ship, leaving us behind with Philan and the small gathering of Codebearers.

"So what happens to us?" I asked.

"Well, you're going to have a dangerous and uncertain road ahead of you. At least we know that much," Philan answered light-heartedly.

"No kidding," I replied. "I hardly know where to start looking for the next of the seven."

"I imagine the Flame might offer help there, when the time is right. It hasn't steered you wrong this far. Trust the Flame and your path will be true," Philan reassured us.

Looking at Philan now, I was impressed at how he was rising to the incredible appointment of captain. He was still young, but he was not untested. He spoke with confidence in the truths he had been taught and I knew I could trust his words. *A sleeping strength the Fire will wake*, I couldn't help but think to myself.

"But what do we do until then?" Trista asked.

"You train," Philan said, and it was not a suggestion.

"Hang on," Rob answered, "I already know how to use the Veritas Sword."

Trista and I just raised our eyebrows at him.

"What?" he said. Clearly, he had forgotten how clumsy he was with the weapon. If you asked us, he could use all the help he could get.

"You know the basics, yes," Philan replied kindly, "but there is always more to learn from the Code of Life. The Shadow have many techniques they will try to employ to catch you off-guard and weaken your defenses. Once word gets out that the Flame is in your possession there is no telling what evils will come searching for you. It is best to be as prepared as possible. So what do you say, are you ready to commit yourselves to our instruction?"

We all agreed.

"Good, then there's no time to waste. We start now!"

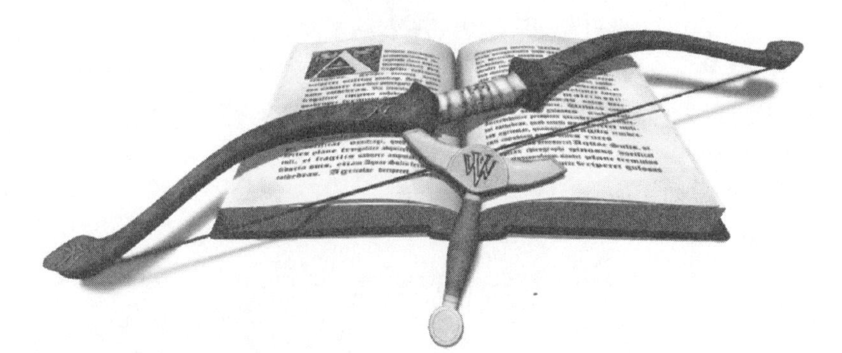

Chapter 18

The Way of the Codebearer

In the Training Round, Philan began instructing Rob and me on the deeper knowledge of the Code of Life, while Trista sat across the room getting basic training on the use of her bow from Alice.

"Remember," Philan taught, "the battle is more than what you see alone. It is a battle for your mind that is either won or lost from within. The Shadow know this well, and they will try to distract you with lies during battle. Only by embedding truth in your mind can you hope to counteract the enemy's temptations and deceptions with the words of the Writ."

"Memorize the truth, got it," I said grabbing my sword. "Let's get to it then."

"Hold on. We won't be training with the sword quite yet. A deeper knowledge of the Code comes by meditating on the words of the Writ first. The Veritas Sword is a powerful weapon, but it is only one in the arsenal of a true Codebearer."

"I thought it was the only weapon able to kill Shadow."

"It is, but where does it get its power?"

"From the Code of Life," I replied.

"And that same Code is what can empower you to do more than swing a sword in battle. It will provide you with a ready defense for all kinds of attacks."

"Like what?" I asked.

Philan smiled and stood.

"Swiftness," he said, speeding across the room and then back again in a silvery streak of light. "To flee an encounter you are not called to engage in."

"Agility," he continued, arching back onto his hands and springing high into the air in an amazing display of acrobatics, "to dodge your opponent's attacks."

"Discernment," with a wave of Philan's hand Rob's sword flew out of his hand and into Philan's own, "to disarm your enemy before damage can be done."

"And resistance, to force your enemy away!" Rob said boldly, hoping to beat Philan to the punch. As he quoted the phrase he jolted his right palm forcefully out in the direction of Philan's chest, apparently hoping to thrust him backward. Instead, the invisible force of his movement backfired and he ended up launching himself backward instead.

"Yes, that's right, Rob," Philan chuckled, "but I think your approach needs a little polishing up…wouldn't you say?"

Rob tried to smile as he picked himself up off the floor.

"Maybe just a bit."

"Good. The main thing to remember in all of this is that these disciplines will come from one source alone. The Author grants them to us through our meditation on the Code of Life. So, let's get to work, shall we? There are many passages we must learn to arm ourselves well."

As Philan led us through a series of passages and truths from the Author's Writ, I couldn't help but steal a glance over at Trista once in awhile. She had been working so hard all day to produce an arrow for the bow, but had not been successful. I could tell she was getting frustrated with herself and the whole lesson.

By mid-afternoon, Rob and I were starting to get better at our swiftness and agility exercises. But poor Trista was still at square one with Alice. Finally, she threw her bow to the floor and stormed out of the room in a mess of emotion.

Stepping away from my training, I raced after her to see what the matter was. When at last I found her she was sitting on the floor in the corner of her bedroom, her knees pulled up to her chest and her head pressed back against the wall.

"Can I come in?" I inquired.

"No," Trista said somewhat forcefully, "just leave me alone."

"Why? What happened in there?" I asked, ignoring her answer.

"Nothing happened, absolutely nothing. That's the problem," she sulked. "I feel like an idiot out there. You guys are doing all kinds of cool stuff, and I can't make even a single arrow for my bow. I'm obviously wasting everyone's time. Maybe I'm not even supposed to be here in the first place."

I couldn't believe what I was hearing. Trista was always so upbeat and happy. I had never seen her so angry before in my life. Something had hit a nerve.

"You're not a waste of time, and you wouldn't be here if the Author didn't have a purpose for you too," I explained.

"Yeah, well, I don't see it. You're the one with all the visions, and you carry the Flame, and Rob—well, he saved us from the Treptors and helped us figure out that Boojum was making the compass go wrong. But, what's my purpose? Why am I even here?"

Her question was real and heartfelt. I knew whatever I said would possibly define how she saw herself. I didn't want to give a trite response so I replied as truthfully as possible.

"I hate to disappoint you, but I can't answer that. I have no clue why the Author brought you here."

Trista looked shocked. It wasn't the answer she expected.

"Exactly! I want to be someone who does something important. But right now I feel completely useless. I'm just the girl who gets in the way. What if we're called away tonight? I'm not going to be ready to be a part of the mission."

"Yes, you will, it just takes time," I said, sitting down beside her and putting my arm on her shoulder.

"Easy for you to say; you can actually use your sword already. I haven't produced even the slightest glimpse of an arrow, let alone shot one. I'm no good at anything."

Her words were obviously an echo of something deeper, a wound in her heart from some past failure. I knew the feelings well.

"Who told you that?"

"Nobody *told* me, I just know," she said, followed shortly by, "I wish I could just go home."

"No, you can't go home. If you give up now, you'll never know what your purpose is here. You have to keep trying, Trista. Don't give up, please!" I was practically begging.

"Calm down, Hunter! I'm just frustrated with myself; you don't have to overreact like that."

"Sorry, it's just that my friend Stretch came to Solandria with me last time. He had a really bad experience here too, but instead of trying to find the purpose in it all, he chose to leave. When he did, it was like the whole trip never happened for him."

"I didn't know Stretch had been here."

"Neither does he. Now that you have seen that Solandria is real, I don't want you to give up either. I don't want you to forget what you're learning here. I can't lose another friend."

It was the first time I had called her my friend. Until that moment, Trista had always been Emily's friend. Now we had been through so much together, I had started to feel she was becoming more than just my sister's friend...she was mine as well.

"Don't worry. I don't really want to leave, Hunter. It's just that I'm not sure I'm going to be ready to fight the Shadow with you guys. I have so much to learn and even though I think I understand things, it feels like I'm not making any progress."

"It's like that at first," I recalled. "It's going to take time; I must have swung my Veritas Sword a million times before I got it to light the first time. The more I focused on doing it myself, the more it frustrated me. But when I realized the power didn't come from me, but from the Author, I didn't mind so much when I made mistakes. I was just waiting on him to help me get it right."

"I know; Alice explained that already. It's just frustrating, that's all. I swear if I have to look at that stupid bow again, I'll break it in two."

"Yeah, I know the feeling," I smiled. "But before you break it there's something else you should know about that stupid bow."

"What's that?" Trista said, sounding completely uninterested in what I was about to say.

"Do you remember Hope—the girl who gave me this medallion?"

Trista nodded.

"Well, the bow used to be hers," I said.

Her expression softened immediately as she realized the hidden value of the weapon she had once called stupid.

"Wow, I didn't know that. Did Petrov tell you?"

"Not exactly, but I know that it is. He intentionally caught my eye when he gave it to you, and I recognized it right away. Hope was the one who saved me from drowning when I first came to Solandria. She was the first person I met here and one of my biggest encouragers when I wanted to give up. You would have liked her."

Trista ran her fingers gently across the bow's gilded etchings as she considered the significance of all I had just told her. "Why do you think Petrov wanted me to have it?" she asked softly.

"I don't know, but I had a vision of her last night."

"Wait a minute…you had another vision and you didn't tell us? What did you see?"

"Hope was lying on a stone table. She looked like she was in some kind of a coma…. I'm beginning to wonder if she is the 'ember of hope' waiting for the Fire to revive her."

I decided to leave the last part about Xaul killing her out of my description for the moment. That part of the vision had been disturbing enough for me to watch, and I didn't want the others to be discouraged by it.

"So, Hope could be alive?"

"Possibly. When I saw you using her bow it reminded me of the vision and how she could be alive out there somewhere—maybe even waiting for us to come save her. Maybe you will be the one to help save her, Trista."

"Okay, you win…I'll keep practicing," Trista said, appearing encouraged by the thought that she just might have a part to play in this mission after all. "But there's one thing we have to get clear before I do."

"What's that?"

"Since we're officially friends now…you'll have to call

me Triss."

"Deal," I chuckled and helped her to her feet. "Come on! I'll race you to the Training Round, *Triss*!"

"No way. I've seen you guys practicing. It's not a fair race!"

The rest of the day Triss worked tirelessly in both studying the Writ and putting its words to use with her bow. By supper, she had been able to produce the tiniest spark of light between her bow. It wasn't a full arrow yet, merely a modest swirl of blue energy in the space between the string and the bow. Rob and I walked up to watch as she finished her training for the day. Trista didn't seem to notice; she was concentrating on the Code of Life and trying hard not to blink.

"True power does not come from the things of man, but from the palm of the Author's hand," she whispered to herself.

"Thath right, Trithta," Alice said. "Dwell on the code. Believe it! For now, keep quoting the Code out loud. Eventhually, you will be able to arm your weapon with only your thought."

The energy swirl was beginning to elongate and thin out on either side into an arrow. Rob and I smiled as we watched Trista's belief grow before our eyes.

"Good," Alice said. "Exthellent! Keep focuthing on the Code—don't think about the arrow!"

Suddenly, the swirling ball that could have become a flaming arrow reverted back to a glowing ball and faded away in a burst of light. I expected to see disappointment in Trista's eyes, but in fact she was excited.

"Did you see that? I almost had an arrow. That was the closest I've come today."

We encouraged her for her discipline and perseverance. Philan announced the end of our training for the night.

"You all should be very proud of yourselves. You've made

extraordinary progress tonight. Let's pick up where we left off tomorrow morning, but now it's time for supper. I believe Stoney has requested a private supper with you tonight, back in your quad. He has something to tell you. So, we'll see you bright and early tomorrow for more training. Good rest to you!"

Chapter 19

The Interpreter

That night, I was too excited to fall asleep right away. I couldn't stop thinking about all that had happened that day: the Emissary's visit, the prophecy of the Flame's hidden power, the marking of Philan and, of course, speculating who the remaining five might be. My mind settled on my growing suspicions that Hope might be one of the seven, the ember of hope. It made sense, didn't it? The thought inspired me. I was anxious now, more than ever, to complete my quest—if only to see her once more.

When at last I did drift off, I found myself dreaming of Hope again.

* * * * * * *

Like incoming waves washing onto the shore, a blurry green glow gradually pulsed its way into the vast expanse of blackness. As it pulled into focus, an identifiable symbol emerged as the source of light. Circular and marked with three interlocking *V's*, the Author's mark belonged to a slowly spinning gold medallion.

The sparkling light that emanated from the medallion's center suddenly blossomed into a flame. Having parted with the Author's mark, the fiery guide began to float away, leading down a winding staircase into complete darkness. At the base of the stairwell, it passed through a massive wooden door and into a rugged terrain, surrounded on all sides by towering rock walls. In the center of the cave a great dragon lay slumbering. The spark passed by the sleeping beast without arousing it and continued on until it came to a crack in the rock wall.

At that moment, I became aware of my own presence in this surreal scene. Gliding effortlessly forward, I followed the Flame into the rift in the rock and down through a winding fissure until the descent stopped at a black stone door. As we approached, the door slid open, accompanied by the sound of grinding rock. The open door revealed our final destination, a massive underground garden.

The garden cavern was rich and fragrant. The rock walls were covered with climbing vines and flowering plants. Despite the darkness of this place, life was here. The Flame rushed off alone into the shadows until it reached a particular spot at the chamber's ceiling. Then lowering itself slowly, it began to reveal the hovering form of a girl at rest on a stone table.

I had seen this vision before. Each time that my dreams had taken me back to revisit Hope, more of the scene was revealed. But this was the only time I felt as though I was actually there.

Climbing the stairs that led to the stone bier, I watched as the Flame once again spilled as liquid light over her body. Her pale skin began to shine just like before. Standing in the glow of her luminescence, I could sense the miracle of life returning and watched with wonder as her lungs began to take in breath anew.

As I reached out to touch her shoulder, Hope's hand suddenly twitched, clasping my wrist in a stiff grip. Startled, I tried to pull away, but then froze when I heard two words sigh quietly past her lips, "*Release me.*"

"R-release y-you?" I stammered in shock. "How?"

Hope's grip loosened and her arm began to fall limply away, but I caught it before it did, pleading again, "How? Please tell me!"

I waited in vain for a response, until an unsettling feeling caused me to turn around. Watching me from the shadows below were two silver eyes.

"Stay back!" I shouted, stepping between Hope and the silently approaching Xin assassin. "You cannot have her!"

Without a word, Xaul leaped over me. I swung a fist at the twisting form as it passed over my head, but my defense was futile; his quick and powerful move took only a second to deliver. The next thing I knew, I was falling down the staircase into a bottomless well of shadows below. As I fell away from the scene, I saw Xaul turn, raise his sword and plunge its dark blade into Hope with finality once again.

The heat of his blade seemed to sear into my own chest as I watched him snuff the last spark of life from Hope. The burning on my chest intensified until I could stand it no longer.

****

Jolting awake, I sat up and fell out of my hammock to the stone floor. I was alone in my room in Torpor, but the strange burning sensation still lingered on my chest as if the fire of Xaul's sword had left its mark on my heart.

Instinctively, I reached up to feel my chest and found the warmth was coming from the medallion itself. The Author's mark had begun to glow with the heat of the Flame within it. Lifting the medallion away from my chest, I watched as the Flame emerged, floating overhead in the shape of a ball.

Take hold, a voice in the Flame whispered.

Though its message was unclear, somehow I instinctively knew it wanted me to touch it. The moment my hand entered the Flame I felt myself being pulled by it into a tunnel of light. My body was fluid and compressed, like toothpaste being squeezed from a tube. The sensation only lasted a few moments, but was disorienting to say the least. When at last it was over, I found I was no longer in Solandria at all.

I was standing on a cement sidewalk, in an unfamiliar city, at the end of a long row of skinny two-story houses crammed tightly together. I didn't know for sure where I was, but things looked and felt a lot like Destiny. For all I knew, it was.

All was quiet except for the tinkling of a windchime somewhere nearby and the howl of a train in the distance. A gentle breeze blew past, swinging a squeaky chain-link gate slowly open a few paces from where I stood. Then, all was still.

The gate belonged to the only house whose porch light was still turned on. Was it a sign for me to come in?

I hesitated to enter at first, still wary of my surroundings, but the medallion warmed on my chest, then lifted slightly away seeming to draw me toward the open gate. Following its lead, I started down the narrow walkway toward the front door of a stranger's house. With every step, I had the eerie feeling that I was being watched by something. There wasn't enough light from the dim porch light to know for sure, but the shadows in the small yard were deep enough to hide a variety of dangerous things.

After three steps up the path, a second gust of wind blew past, slamming the gate shut behind me. I tried not to let it scare me, but a low, guttural growl from a creature in the yard confirmed my foremost fear…I was not alone.

The growling seemed to surround me, first coming from the right side…then from the left. With nowhere to go, I froze in place as the menacing growls grew more intense and irritated with my presence. My imagination ran wild with the possibilities of what it could be. The suspense of not being able to see the threat was killing me. I needed light and protection.

My sword still hung at my side, latched to my belt by a leather clasp. If I moved quickly enough, perhaps I could grab and ignite it before the creature attacked. It was my only shot at protection.

Counting down from three in my mind, I executed the plan perfectly. My sword flashed to light with the will of the Code, revealing the beast that was rushing at me from the right. A large black dog was barreling toward me now, angered at the light and my intrusion on its property. I would have cut it apart to save myself except that a second identical dog began rushing at me from the opposite side of the path. Two dogs, teeth bared, hair raised on their backs, were racing toward me with vicious intentions. I would have time to catch only one with the sword before the other tackled me. Which would I choose, left or right? Before I could decide, their advances came to an abrupt and painful stop as each dog fell back only inches from the pathway I stood on. They continued growling at me from either side, but did not come an inch closer.

"It's all right," a woman's voice called out from the front door, waving me forward. "They can't get you as long as you stay on the path. The invisible fence keeps them in place. Come on in. No use chatting outside this time of night."

From where I stood I couldn't make out the features of the silhouetted figure that had just beckoned me into her house. Even though I normally would never enter a stranger's home alone, I figured it was safe to make an exception this time. It was certainly better than staying in the yard.

As I stepped toward the porch, the dogs moved along beside me all the way to the base of the stairs. Once I took my first step on the staircase, the dogs backed away, unable to follow me further.

At the top of the stairs I discovered the figure was not, in fact, a stranger as I had first expected. Her short white hair, round brown eyes, rosy complexion and friendly, wrinkled smile was one I used to dread, but had come to love.

"Gabby?"

"Yes, it's me, Hunter. Surprised?"

"A little. What are you doing here?"

"It's my home, Hunter; I live in Destiny."

"You didn't tell me that!"

"You sure? I could have sworn I did at the feast when we first met. Of course, I say a lot of things to a lot of people. Not everyone hears everything I say, and I suppose I say more than I should at times too."

This was, in fact, a true statement. Gabby had the gift of... well...gab. She could talk for hours on end if you let her. To some, it might have been annoying, but her joy and passion for life was so contagious you couldn't help but grow to like her.

"Please, come in. I've been expecting you for quite some time, you know."

She was a small woman, but she packed more spunk per square inch than anyone else I knew. I followed her into a cluttered living space highlighted by olive green couches and two orange oversized chairs. The space was not very big, more like an apartment than a home, but it seemed to suit Gabby's needs. The smell of lavender floated in the air from candles burning on the mantle of the fireplace across the room. For the most part the place was tidy, though the small end table beside the couch was piled with past-due bills.

"I have some hot tea on the stove; would you like some?"

"Sure, I guess," I said, still trying to work out why and how I was even here in the first place. At first glance, the décor was definitely that of an older person: white lace doilies, porcelain statuettes, inspirational plaques and, of course, a scattering of family pictures proudly displayed throughout the room. Several of the photographs were of her and her late husband, Gerwyn, who had died trying to save me from a dragon in Solandria. Each golden frame was neatly arranged and dust-free.

But as I examined things closer, I discovered there was also an assortment of items that just seemed out of place. On the coat rack a black hooded sweatshirt hung limply, complete with a trendy skull design on its sleeve. Below it, a backpack and pair of dirty tennis shoes (much too big for Gabby's feet) were slung against the base of the entryway wall. Set up beneath the television was a video game console and a basket of recent game titles, hardly the kind of entertainment I expected a lady like her to show interest in.

"So you live alone?" I asked, curious to hear her response.

"I do now, but I haven't always," she answered as the tray of teacups and saucers she carried clattered across the room. "Those video games belonged to my grandson, if that's what you mean. I have his picture up on the mantle there in the corner. Of course that's three years old…he stopped getting school pictures after the seventh grade."

She handed a cup of hot tea to me in a fragile china cup as I spotted the picture of her grandson. The boy in the 4 x 6 school photo was all smiles, grinning widely despite an obvious gap between his front teeth. His eyes were squinted mostly shut, which drew more attention to his freckled nose and thick brown eyebrows.

"Looks like a funny…er, I mean fun kid," I said, absent-mindedly, hoping she hadn't taken offense to my poor choice of words. She seemed not to notice, so I took a casual sip of tea and nearly burnt my tongue in the process. *This is why I don't like hot drinks,* I reminded myself.

"Yes, Cranton always was a hoot to have around, especially when he was younger."

"Cranton!" I said in shock, nearly spitting what little tea I had sipped into the air. I forced myself to swallow it, and it burned all the way down my throat. That was him. Of course, he was much younger in the picture, and I rarely saw him smile in a friendly manner anymore, but sure enough it was Cranton.

"Did you say Cranton is your grandson?!"

"Well, yes! Why? Do you know him?"

"Yeah, he's been in a few classes with me, but we've never really hung out much. We're not really what you'd call friends, I guess. He's just…uh…well…"

"A bully, I know," Gabby added bluntly.

Her response surprised me; I wasn't used to hearing grandparents talk about their grandkids like that—after all, it was the grandparents' job to gush over how good and sweet they were, not state the obvious.

"Don't get me wrong," Gabby continued, eyeing the look of shock on my face. "I loved the boy dearly. But he chose to make life miserable for himself and everyone around him after his parents died…"

"I didn't know his parents died."

"Yes, it was almost seven years ago now, a car accident. He was in fifth grade at the time, never really recovered from it either. He kept to himself at first but once he hit seventh grade he started finding trouble." I noticed her eyes begin to gloss over as she fought back tears. She wiped one from the corner of her eye and began to choke up as she recalled the choices her grandson had made.

"I had hoped Gerwyn and I could offer him a safe place to grow up—that he'd find some stability with us. But then Gerwyn died and Cranton really took a turn for the worse. I tried my best to explain it to him, but he never listened to me. We'll never know for sure, but I think all of his pent-up anger is what led to the fire."

"Fire?" I asked.

"Yes, the school fire, remember? It was a year ago today."

"There was a fire at school last year?"

"Sure, burned the whole school down too! I have the article right here."

She shuffled through a pile of papers that rested beside the sofa and selected a newspaper clipping to hand to me. The headline of the *Destiny Times*' front cover story read:

Troubled Teen Killed in School Blaze

The picture on the front was of Destiny High engulfed in a fierce fire. A picture of Cranton was also displayed. Below his name a question was printed: Victim OR Arson? Shockingly enough, the date of the fire was the same night we had gone to the fairgrounds.

"How is this possible?" I asked. "The fire would have happened the same night as the fair. That was the night we came back to Solandria. I can't have been gone for a whole year already, can I?"

"Anything is possible, Hunter. As you know, the story of Solandria is not connected directly to our own timeline. The Author can do what he likes between worlds."

"I guess," I said nervously, "I just never expected we'd be gone this long." My thoughts turned from the present to my mom and how awful she would be feeling to have lost me over a year ago. She must think I was dead too.

"Don't worry yourself, Hunter," Gabby said. "Just because you're here now, doesn't mean you'll be here later."

"What do you mean?"

"When you return to Solandria to finish what you have been called to do, a new way home will be made. You likely will return to the precise moment you left the Veil. There have only been a few instances where it has happened otherwise."

The thought comforted me, but only a little.

"But enough of that, I'm guessing you didn't come here to talk about my troubles," Gabby said. "So what is it, hmm?"

"Honestly, I don't know why I'm here."

"That's good," she said sipping her tea. "I'd be worried if you thought you did. Why don't you start by telling me about these visions you've been having?"

"How did you know about my visions?" I asked.

"Do you really have to ask?"

"I guess not," I said, realizing that if she was already expecting me, she probably had been given instructions on how to help me. I started by explaining our mission to carry the Flame to the seven. As I shared the prophecy of the Consuming Fire with her and my visions of Hope asking me to release her, Gabby's face lit up.

"So what do you think it means? Is Hope still alive?"

There was a long pause as Gabby thought about the vision. It was an odd thing to see her pass up an immediate opportunity to speak. When at last she did speak, the tone in her voice was different. Distant and focused.

"It wouldn't surprise me at all. She is frail, of that I am sure. But as long as the Resistance is still around—no matter how weak, we can be sure she is alive. You are familiar with what happened the night the Resistance tried to move Hope to a safe location, right?"

"Yeah, Petrov told me," I answered. "Faldyn stole her."

"Or so we think," Gabby corrected. "We have not seen her or him ever since. One thing is clear, whoever has her must know how important she is to the success of the Codebearers' survival. There would be no other reason to abduct her."

"What do you mean?"

"Hope isn't like the rest of us, Hunter. She's a virtuess."

"Virtuess?"

"Yes, a gift from the Author. She came with the promise that one day she would become something more, something wonderful. An eternal flame in the hearts of all who are called."

"So do you think she's one of the seven? The ember of hope?"

"Yes, I do."

This was good news. If Hope was one of the seven, I would see her again soon.

"But there is something more to your visions."

"How so?"

"In any of your dreams have you ever been able to save her?"

"No, I haven't," I said, suddenly losing my excitement. I wasn't sure where she was going with this, but I didn't like to think about it.

"I see," she said after a long pause. "What happens if you *don't* try and save her?"

"Are you serious?" I blurted out the moment she said it. "If Hope's alive, I have to find a way to save her!"

"That's exactly my point! You are letting your emotions get in the way of doing what is right."

"Huh?" I said, bewildered.

"Let me put it this way, what is it that you *feel* for Hope?"

She couldn't have posed a more difficult question. My feelings for Hope were a tangled mess of complicated emotions. It seemed impossible to unravel one feeling from another—she was all of them combined, and all mixed up.

"I really like her," I started to say, knowing all the words fell short of my true emotions. There was more to it than just that so I continued. "For starters, she always encouraged and inspired me to want to be a better person. When she was with me, I felt like I had a true friend, someone I could really trust."

"Hope has a way of doing that," Gabby said.

"Yeah, and I feel like it is my fault that she's gone, you know? If she really is alive somewhere, I want to set things right, to bring her back."

"Did you ever consider that your desire to bring her back might be for your own selfish reasons? That maybe you could be keeping her from becoming something more—something that is greater than we can possibly imagine."

"Why do you say that?"

"In your visions, Hope keeps asking you to release her. She loved you, Hunter, even more than you love her. But until you allow her to go, her purpose will not be complete. You will have to choose between saving her for your own selfish motives or releasing her into the Author's hands."

"But I can't just stand by and watch her die! What good could possibly come of it? I don't understand."

"When the time is right, you will," Gabby chuckled and added, "soon enough."

Her words were like an irritating riddle. How was I supposed to watch Hope be killed at the hands of a madman like Xaul? It wasn't fair, it wasn't right. I was angry that Gabby had even suggested it would be okay. Furthermore, if Hope was one of the seven as I believed she was, I would have to save her.

"Oh, I almost forgot," Gabby said, "I have something for you before you go."

She motioned for me to follow her, which I did. She led me down a narrow hallway to a small closet door. Opening it, she produced a wooden box from the top shelf, which she dusted off and held in front of her.

"When Gerwyn died," she said, opening the box and looking me straight in the eyes, "I decided to share a token of his life with as many people as I could. Of course, you left before I could give you something to remember him by. But I kept it, just in case we met again."

The wooden lid lifted open on hinges, revealing a lining of green felt inside. She reached into the box and removed a small, square silver trinket, which she handed to me. I turned the flattened piece of metal over in my hand. On one side, a dragon was etched into the metal, and on the other a series of strange markings.

"What is it?"

"Just a trinket, really. It was a cipher for one of the training rooms in Sanctuary. Not much use now—but Gerwyn had a collection of them he used to give out as awards for his students. He and Captain Sam used to teach the young ones together, you know."

"No, I didn't," I replied.

"Yes. They were quite the pair. Anyway, I thought you might like that one because of the dragon on it. Gerwyn would have wanted you to have it, considering the battle you shared before he died."

"It's perfect, thank you," I said, keenly aware of the significance it held. "He was a brave man."

"Yes, he was. My knight in shining armor," she chuckled. "But he wasn't always that way, you know. The Author changed him into the man you knew."

"How so?"

"Well, you knew Gerwyn as a quiet hero. He served without

wanting much in return and I loved him for it. But he wasn't always that way. There was a time when all he cared about was himself and his addictions. You see, a dragon had deceived him into believing that leech blood would make him more powerful than any other person in the world."

"Leeches?" I said, thinking immediately of Belac, the troll who had held us captive on my last trip to Solandria. He made Stretch and me leech bait because of his hunger for the leeches.

"Yes. Well, anyway, as the blood began to course through his veins, he did grow stronger and more powerful, but also more dependent on the blood to sustain his very life. To make a long story short, eventually his power turned him into a monster. One day, a group of Codebearers were passing by, and he attacked them with great fury. They managed to capture Gerwyn in his altered state.

"What did they do with him?" I asked.

"They took him to the cleansing pools of Corinin and bathed him in the healing waters, which quenched his thirst and helped to remove the poison from his body once more. When at last he was sane again, they began to teach him the truths of the Code and he committed his life to becoming a Codebearer. When they brought him back to Sanctuary, I met him, and we quickly fell in love. He was the joy of my life from that day forward."

"Wow, that's a cool story," I said. "I never knew he had been through so much."

"Yes, well, he was a good man," she added. There was a soft smile on her face, one that was meant for Gerwyn to see. "It just goes to show, you never know who the Author will choose. You may see a monster, but there is often much more than eyes alone can see. But, enough of this; I mustn't keep you any longer. Your friends will be needing you to return right away."

"Oh, right," I said, "but how do I go back?"

"Why, the Flame of course!" she answered.

Instantly, the medallion glowed again and the Flame separated from it. The golden spark floated before me, pulsing in rhythm with my heartbeat. I tucked Gerwyn's dragon cipher into my pocket and prepared to leave, pausing slightly before taking hold of the glowing ball of light.

"Thank you, Gabby," I said. "You've been so kind!"

She nodded in return.

With that I faced the Flame and reached out to take hold. Just before I grasped the Flame, Gabby called out.

"Remember, Hunter. No matter what happens when you return, no matter how bad things seem, you are never alone!"

Chapter 20

A Battle and a Betrayal

Arriving back at the monastery, I found things were not at all as I had left them. What few items had once been in my room were now strewn about or knocked over. My backpack was emptied and Boojum was gone. Somebody was searching for something.

Xaul, I thought to myself.

Fearing the worst, I threw on my backpack and slipped out into the common room, searching the other rooms as well. Each one told a similar story. Items thrown around and the beds empty. Signs of a struggle were everywhere…something had happened. Something not good.

Where is everyone?

Just then, a wooden bowl clattered to the floor from the table in the common room.

"Who goes there!" I demanded, expecting to see Xaul appear out of the shadows. Instead, a furry head and pointy blue ears popped out from beneath the bowl. It was Boojum.

"Master safe?" he shouted excitedly.

He leaped up onto my shoulder and grabbed my neck in a soft hug.

"What happened here? Where are the others?" I asked him.

"Bad things," Boojum squealed. "Go home!"

"I can't go home, I need to find the others. Where are they?"

"Gone, away! Not safe."

"How long ago did this happen, Boojum? Are they still nearby?"

He nodded emphatically.

"Come on, we need to find them and we have to hurry."

Grabbing the hilt of my sword, I ran down the maze of hallways in search of the others with Boojum following closely behind. Rounding a bend, I found myself face to face with a half dozen Dispirits. There was no doubt about it; the Shadow were here and in numbers. I never got over how ugly Dispirits were. Their skin a slimy brown, they stood on two gangly legs and walked with hunched backs. They each had six arms, sharp claws and a long deadly tongue that could lash out of their mouths with the speed of a whip.

"There'ssss another one!" the first Dispirit hissed. "Don't let him esssssscape!"

Immediately, the multi-limbed creatures lunged forward all at once, coming at me like a pack of hungry wolves. The sight was fearsome, but I was not afraid.

By fear a man appoints his master.

My sword ignited and I slashed through the first two with a quick spin, dissolving them into a black mist. Alarmed at the brilliance of the weapon, Boojum quickly vanished and squealed loudly.

"Liiiiiiiight!"

It was a horrific sound, but one I was prepared to ignore at least for the moment. The tongues of the remaining four Dispirits shot down the hall, spewing vile comments as they came.

"Clumssssy..."

"Worthlessss..."

"Misssguided..."

"Fool!"

Before I knew what I was doing, my training in agility kicked in. *Avoid the words of lying tongues.* Flipping backward, I dodged the first barrage of tongue lashings without effort. As their tongues retreated into their mouths and readied for another attack, I remembered another truth of the Code.

True power does not come from the things of man, but from the palm of the Author's hand.

Pressing my palm forward, I watched the Dispirits fall back a step or two from the unseen force of energy the Author sent ahead of me. The effect wasn't nearly as powerful as I had hoped, but it was more than enough to cause a small disturbance. In the split second after they felt the blast, I raised my sword and ran through their ranks, swinging wildly as I sped past.

Looking back, I saw four wisps of black mist slip away through the halls. My training had worked.

"Cool."

The moment the sword disappeared, Boojum reappeared, looking a little worse for the wear.

"Light bad!" he said grumpily.

"I didn't have a choice, come on, let's go," I said, holding my backpack open on the floor.

Boojum ran across the room and dove into the backpack where

the light couldn't bother him as much. Slinging the pack on my back once more, I ran through the halls in search of my friends, taking alternate routes or ducking into rooms whenever another group of Dispirits blocked my path. I had decided to try my best to avoid needless conflict with the Shadow, partially because I didn't want Boojum to make too much noise, but mainly because it would only delay my quest to find where the others had gone.

As I neared the Training Round, I heard the sound of voices engaged in a heated exchange. I found a safe position just beyond one of the smaller doors that entered the Training Round and cracked it open an inch to get a better view and listened in. A large Gorewing, dressed in black armor and bearing a cruel black sword, stood in the center of the room, his wings folded back behind him. At his disposal more than a dozen Dispirits and two dozen goblins stood behind him. The Codebearers, less than twenty (and most of them children) including Rob and Trista, were gathered in front of him, disarmed and bound. It was less than half of our number. Where were the rest?

A fat goblin stumbled across the floor on his peg leg to deliver a message. I recognized him at once—Zeeb, Venator's chief aide.

"General Kane, the monastery has been searched; there is no one else, no sign of the boy or the Flame."

"Then search again, you idiot! He can't be far."

"Yes, my lord," Zeeb said with a bow and scurried off.

The report angered the Gorewing, who roared with rage at the captives in front of him.

"Where…is he!"

"I already told you, we don't know," Philan responded with boldness. "And King Zagzabarz won't be too happy when he hears what has been done here tonight: trespassing, destruction of property and attempted kidnapping, are all serious crimes in Torpor, with or without a signed treaty."

Kane's laugh was deep and frightening.

"We are here on Zagzabarz's orders!" Kane said. "He has learned of a boy harbored in this place, who carries an illegal weapon of forbidden power. He is fearful that you intend to use it on his people to take control."

"The boy you are looking for is not here, I've already told you. But as for the weapon you speak of, it is real and more powerful than you can imagine. You would be right to be afraid."

"I've heard enough!"

The high chamber ceiling echoed with the power of his voice.

"Take them to Zagzabarz and tell him we have evidence of dissent among them. They will pay for their crimes."

"You are making a grave mistake, Kane!"

"No, it is you who are mistaken, boy. The Resistance has seen its end. Now, stand down, or I will rip you apart."

Philan didn't move; he stood with courage before the Gorewing, and even though his hands were bound he looked as though he were at peace.

"You will not leave here alive this day, Kane. Of that you can be certain."

"Enough! You have spoken you last, CodeBREAKER!"

He raised his black sword behind him and started to bring it down toward Philan's head. But before the fatal blow could be struck, Philan leaped backward, flipping end over end. The black sword passed just below where Philan spun in the air and miraculously severed the ties that bound his hands.

Philan landed squarely on both feet; with his hands now free he could move even quicker.

Kane, not thrilled at having been shown up in front of his men, swung angrily at the young man who had just evaded his blow.

With each attack, Philan managed to sidestep and tumble out of the way, much to the delight of the Codebearer faithful.

"Kane, Kane, Kane, Kane!" the Shadow warriors began to chant, spurring on their champion to finish the unarmed man. The scene had suddenly turned into a sport.

Despite Philan's heroic efforts, I knew that without a weapon the young captain could never win the battle. Scanning the room, I noticed a table in the corner where the Veritas Swords had been collected. A lone Dispirit kept guard beside it, but he looked to be paying more attention to the commotion in the center of the room than to his assignment.

"You stay out here," I whispered to Boojum, "and don't make a sound!"

"Okee-dokee!" he said, as I slipped out into the Round.

Once inside, I kept to my hands and knees, crawling around the circumference of the room until at last I was directly under the weapon's table. The Dispirit's spindly legs were in front of me, and before he knew what happened, my sword had diminished him to a puff of smoke. Thankfully, in the midst of the ongoing struggle and loud chanting nobody saw or heard him disappear.

Working silently, I reached over the edge of the table and removed the confiscated swords one by one, stuffing my bag full with as many of them as I could fit, all the while keeping an eye out for Philan's own sword. It wasn't too hard to identify; it was the one inscribed with his favorite quote from the Writ: "*Never look down on the young.*"

As soon as I had it in hand, I stuffed another two swords into my bulging bag and crawled back out from the table. Slinging Trista's bow over my shoulder, I carefully circled around into position to deliver Philan's sword.

"Tired yet, Kane?" Philan asked with a smile.

"Never," the Gorewing seethed, "you are but a pesky fly I will crush." He delivered an earth-shaking blow to the ground with his deadly blade. Philan leaped back, now standing less than twenty feet from where I crouched.

Not wanting to waste the opportunity, I slid the Veritas Sword across the floor where it settled between Philan and Kane. Then, I darted back to the door I had entered and disappeared behind it before anyone knew I was there.

Philan spotted the sword hilt right away and leaped forward, grabbing the sword from the ground, rolling across the floor and back to his feet in a single smooth motion. The Gorewing was furious things were not going his way. He looked like he might even call his men to seize the prisoner, but the chant of his name caused him to swell with pride. His eyes burned with fury and he attacked Philan despite his better judgment.

The two went at it, matching each other's blows in mirrored attacks of expert skill. Clearly, this was not an easy challenge for either of them. The crowds backed away from the conflict as the two began to use more and more room in their duel to the death.

I slipped back out of my hiding place a second time and began untying the remaining Codebearers. I whispered to them and handed them their swords, which they held behind their backs in hopes the Shadow would not know they were unbound.

"Where have you been?" Trista asked in a whisper, when I arrived behind her at last, cutting the ropes and handing her the bow.

"Shhh, I'll tell you later; just stay still and wait for my word!"

Philan somersaulted over the brute with his sword flashing brightly in one hand. He landed on his feet and plunged the sword behind himself without looking, wounding the Gorewing in his back. He fell to his knees in pain and anger. Silence fell over the

Shadow as they watched their general fall.

"It's over Kane, I won. Surrender and leave this place...and I will let you live," Philan said.

"You haven't won," Kane scoffed. "You've only sealed your doom, young one."

Pressing a hand to the fresh wound on his back he stood up, now even more determined to rid himself of his adversary once and for all. Only this time, he didn't do it with the power of his blade, but the power of his command.

"Kill him," Kane shouted. "Kill them all!"

The horde of Shadow howled with glee and surrounded Philan, who was grossly outnumbered and now quite tired as well.

"For the Way of Truth and Life!" I shouted the Codebearer mantra.

"For the Way of Truth and Life!" the Codebearers cheered in response. A dozen swords blazed to life and the battle was begun. Trista, who was still unable to use her bow, kept safely behind me. At first, the element of surprise gave us an edge. It seemed as though we would easily win the battle. But just as the Shadow's numbers seemed to diminish, a second round of reinforcements flooded the room from other parts of the monastery.

"You three, get out of here now!" Philan shouted over the chaos. "You can't let them find you!"

What once was a rescue quickly turned to an escape as Rob and I cut a path toward the door I had left Boojum behind. We opened the door to a frightened Boojum who saw our blades and raced away in the opposite direction, screaming at the top of his lungs.

"Boojum, wait up!" I shouted, but if he heard me he didn't show it, running as quickly as he could away from our flaming blades.

"Put your sword away, Rob," I commanded, "or else every Shadow will hear we're out here." Rob reluctantly complied and we caught up to Boojum who was trembling from the commotion.

"Poor guy," Trista said, picking him up and cuddling him close.

"Poor guy? What about poor us? We almost got ourselves killed back there," Rob said. "We need to get out, now!"

"Yeah, but I'm willing to bet the front doors are guarded as well. How are we going to get past them?" Trista asked.

"There has to be another exit," I said.

"What does it matter? Even if we do escape, we don't have a plan. I mean, where are we going to hide in this city if everyone is looking for us?" Rob wondered.

"*The Bridesmaid!*" I exclaimed. "Stoney would still be up there at the ship!"

"At least we hope," Rob replied grimly. We all instinctively knew what he meant by that. Who was to say where the Shadow might have landed first and what might have happened up at the docks before the attack on the monastery.

"I say it's worth a try," said Trista, "but we still have to get out. That won't be easy."

At this, Boojum seemed to light up with an idea.

"Out, out! Follow me!" He leaped out of Trista's arms and scurried down the hallway ahead. We followed. Every so often, Boojum would pause at an intersection of hallways and look both ways, scratching his head as if trying to remember which way to go. Then, with some level of certainty, he would set off in one direction or another.

"This is no good; we're just going in circles," Rob complained. "He's obviously lost."

"No, he's not; look at that!" Trista shouted, pointing to a spiral staircase at the end of the hallway. The stairs led both up to a second level and down to a lower level as well.

"Come, come! Out!" Boojum declared, heading down into the

darkened bowels of the monastery. Only three steps down, I found the medallion on my neck begin to warm, glowing softly beneath my shirt. I immediately stopped my descent and the others following behind crashed into me, unable to slow their momentum in time.

"A little warning would be nice," Rob suggested from the rear.

"No kidding," Trista added. "Why did you do that?"

"Shhh," I said, "the Flame...I think its trying to..."

Up.

The instructions were clear; we were heading the wrong way.

"Well, what's it saying?" Trista asked.

"It wants us to go up," I answered.

"Well, that's good to know; let's hurry," Rob said, leading the way back up.

"Wait," Trista said. "Boojum's still ahead of us. We have to let him know." We tried calling out from where we stood, but Boojum was already too far gone to hear us.

"I'll go get him," I offered. "You guys wait here."

Rob shook his head. "Bad idea, we shouldn't split up."

"We're not splitting up; I'm coming right back."

"I just don't think you should go alone," Rob suggested. "We are trying to protect the Flame, after all."

"I'll go," Trista said. "Boojum likes me better anyway. Maybe we can coax him back quicker."

Rob reluctantly agreed to keep watch from the top of the stairs while Trista and I recovered our furry friend. With each step downward, the medallion seemed to glow brighter, either to light our way, or to warn us of danger. The feeling in my gut told me which it was, but I pushed it aside and continued down anyway.

"Booooojum!" Trista called, her voice echoing through a massive chamber of darkness. There was no response, but a slight scampering sound somewhere across the room. The glow of the medallion only lit a path ten feet in front of us with its golden light.

"This place smells awful," Trista said, covering her nose with her shirt, "like something rotten...or dead."

As we progressed further into the room, we discovered it was filled with a variety of strange and horrible devices that looked like they belonged in a dungeon.

On one wall, an inscription was inscribed in the stone. It read:

PURIFY THROUGH PAIN

"I don't like this at all," I said. "This place gives me the creeps."

"Me too," Trista agreed. "Let's go back."

I was about to agree with her, when I caught the sound of crying somewhere up ahead.

"Boojum, is that you?" I said, hurrying my step. Sure enough, in a corner Boojum was sobbing quietly. "Hey buddy, what's wrong?"

"Bad things," Boojum said. "Boojum wrong way."

Trista picked up the little guy and cradled him in her arms. "It's okay, little fella. You're safe now, let's go back..."

SLAM!

The door at the base of the stairs swung shut and a voice that sounded half-alive echoed out of the darkness of the room.

"Hold it right there. You're not going anywhere. Not until I get what I came for."

Xaul stepped out of the shadows to block our exit; it was the perfect trap. How he had come to find us I couldn't begin to imagine. His blackened blade surged to life, visible only by a faint outlining glow.

"Well...where is it, boy? Where is the Flame?" Xaul pressed. "Tell me or prepare to fight."

"I'll never tell!" I said boldly, igniting my own blade in defiance, ready to defend the Flame at all cost. Boojum disappeared into thin air at the brilliance of my lighted Veritas. There would be no escaping with him this time...I had to face my pursuer...I had to fight Xaul.

"So be it," Xaul said. "Prepare to die." Without another word, Xaul lunged into his first attack. It was a simple forward thrust, which I deflected easily with my own Veritas Sword. His next two attacks came in sequence, a low angled slice followed by an upward stroke. I stepped away from his blows and redirected his sword with my own, leading him away from where Trista and I had been cornered.

He was feeling me out, testing my technique. Then, with a hint of a smile Xaul launched into a full sequence of wild aggressive blows, snaps and thrusts designed to set me off balance. It was all I could do to deflect his attacks.

When the path was clear, Trista ran for the stairs in hopes of alerting Rob of the danger, but the door was locked. All she could do was watch and pray for the best as Xaul and I fought in the center of the room. Blow by blow, my Veritas seemed to guide me, helping me match Xaul's every move so long as I focused on the words of the Writ. But Xaul was better than me and I knew it. Doubts began to creep into my mind, separating me from the words of truth.

Don't lose concentration, Hunter. Stay focused, I encouraged myself. The Code of Life empowered me through the words of the Writ.

"You're slowing down," Xaul chided, trying to distract me. "You are growing weak...just like Petrov...just like your father."

My father? His words shattered what little focus I had left and pulled my mind entirely off of the battle. What did he know about my father? It was only for a moment, but it was all he needed.

I tried to dodge his next lunge, but it came too quickly. His sword caught the side of my left arm and left a stinging black wound below my shoulder before I slipped away.

Howling in pain, I evaded his following blows only by fleeing the fight and hiding in the darkness. I retracted my sword and pressed myself behind one of the gruesome devices that were stored in the Xin temple. My first instinct was to try and repair the wound on my arm with the healing powers of the Veritas…but it wouldn't work.

The wounds of a Veritas can only be healed by the Author himself, I remembered Petrov saying. I winced, remembering what had happened to Petrov's arm. I was in trouble…we needed to escape and now.

"Petrov was a fool to leave the Flame with a child," Xaul sneered as he searched the room for where I hid. "Why don't you make this easy on yourself and give me what I want. You can't hide forever."

Xaul was getting closer, and I began frantically eyeing the room, looking for a window or exit of any kind. Surely there must be some way out. Then, I spotted it. Across the room there was an open door, that led into an even darker room. Trista was only a few feet away from it. With the Author's help I might be able to lead her through it before Xaul could block our escape.

When the moment presented itself, I raced across the room and executed my plan with flawless precision, grabbing Trista by the arm and pulling her into the darkness beyond the yawning doorway. But Xaul was hot on my tail.

Together Trista and I huddled in the darkness behind a stone wall. Xaul entered the room with determined steps and laughed at our futile attempt to escape. His silver eyes hovered in the darkness gazing directly at us, maybe even through us.

"The darkness can't hide you, Hunter! I can still see. Now for the last time, give me the Flame!"

"No," I shouted, stepping back and holding Trista behind me. "It doesn't belong to you."

"Oh, but it does."

"Hunter, stop…I…" Trista started to say, but her warning ended in a heart pounding scream. Falling backward, she grabbed hold of my backpack and yanked us both over a ledge and into a dark pit.

My initial fall was cut short as Xaul reached out and grasped the medallion around my neck. For a split second the chain dug painfully into my neck. I was caught between Trista's weight and Xaul's strength which held tightly to the medallion.

"You should have given it to me!" Xaul said, watching as the chain began to choke life from me. He raised his sword to stab my heart. Suddenly, the Flame in the Author's mark exploded in a flash of blinding light, singeing Xaul's hand and forcing him to let go of the medallion. He groaned in horrid agony from the searing heat of the Flame, letting us fall into the inky black abyss below.

The fall lasted what seemed like an eternity before ending in a painful splash. We submerged several feet deep into a cistern of tepid black water. When at last we resurfaced I was desperate for breath.

"Help….me…" I panted frantically, as Trista and I both came up for air. "I can't swim…." Back under I went, trying desperately not to swallow the water around me. Trista's arm plunged down and grabbed hold of my collar, pulling me to the surface once more. She swam with me to the side of the cistern where we both grabbed hold of a chain and hoisted ourselves up onto a thin ledge, coughing and spitting out the putrid water.

"Thanks," I said, when at last I found breath.

"Don't mention it."

My neck was sore from where Xaul had pulled on the medallion, and my arm throbbed from the Veritas wound. I reached up with my good arm to my neck and discovered something was wrong. The medallion was gone.

"Oh no," I gasped, "I've lost it!"

"Lost what?"

"The medallion, it must have fallen off in the water somewhere."

Without a moment's hesitation, Trista dove back into the cistern in search of the medallion. She resurfaced a moment later, with her bow and my sword, but no medallion.

"I reached the bottom," she explained, "but I didn't see the medallion. I'll have to go under again."

She dove back under the water, but this time did not resurface as quickly as before. I waited as the water surface slowed. After a minute had passed I began to worry. She had been under far too long, I didn't know what to do. Then, at last, the surface broke and with a large gasp for air, Trista was back.

"Good news…and bad news…" she panted. "I found the medallion, but it's stuck beneath a grate in the floor."

"A grate?"

"Yeah, it has a lock on it too. I think there's a drain of some kind underneath; the water's so murky it's hard to tell. The light of the medallion was all I had to go by! I could try again, but…I'll need your help."

"Are you crazy? I can't swim!"

"You don't have to; I'm a good enough swimmer for the both of us. Just use your sword to break open the grate and retrieve the medallion. Then I'll bring us both up for air."

"You make it sound so simple."

"Trust me," she waved me back into the water.

"Oh man, I'm going to regret this," I muttered as I plunged

back into the pool. It went against every ounce of sense in me. I had done something like this only once before in Solandria, when I was emboldened by a false sense that the Bloodstone was hidden under the water. Even then, I had tied a rope around my waist as a lifeline to safety. This time, Trista was my lifeline and as much as I trusted her, I would still be plunging myself underwater. The thought of it made me uneasy.

She wrapped her arms around me in an underwater hug. Then, with powerful kicks she pulled me down to the bottom of the cistern. Twenty feet below the surface, we arrived at the grate she had discovered. Beneath the grate lay a valve where the medallion was resting, its light glimmering ever so slightly through the murky water.

Igniting my sword underwater, I severed the lock on the grate as planned. But I needed more air before we could recover the medallion.

Trista brought me up for air and dove back down again, this time bringing the medallion back up.

"Got it!" she said, holding it overhead.

"Great, but how do we get out of here? Xaul's going to find a way down eventually," I replied.

"I have an idea," Trista whispered to me, "but you have to trust me again!"

"Okay," I said, hoping it didn't involve more swimming, but knowing it would.

"Grab your things and hold on tight!"

I did as she said, allowing myself to be submerged for the third time. Trista pulled us both down with our weapons to the metal grate again. This time, she took us down into the well the grate had covered and even pulled the grate closed over the top of us. *Had she gone mad? She's imprisoning us in a watery tomb.*

I wanted to scream, but then when I saw what she intended to do it made me wish I hadn't trusted her after all. Turning the lock valve on the drain, she began to pull it open, letting huge bubbles of air gulp into the cistern.

Before I could scream a watery "Don't," the hatch flew wide open, creating an instant whirlpool, sucking us down into its gaping throat. I grabbed wildly about, but found nothing to grasp, nothing to keep us from being swallowed whole, pulled down by the unstoppable swirling vortex.

Trista succumbed easily, disappearing into the dark hole first. The downard pull quickly claimed me next, turning into a rushing stream of water, twisting and turning in dramatic fashion through a pathway of pipe. No light was there to warn of the many turns blindly tossing us from side to side, even spinning us upside down at times in the raging current that propelled us ever-downward through its watery exit.

In one last mighty surge, the ride came to its climactic end, plunging us ten feet into a canal of blackened water that quickly pulled me under. Flailing about in the river, I managed to struggle toward the surface, grasping for anything to keep me afloat before I went under again. As my head dipped beneath the water, a hand caught mine and pulled me back up. With great effort, Trista managed to pull me near the shore, where we both collapsed, gasping for breath and glad to be alive.

"Don't ever...do that...again!" I said, panting. "We could have been killed! That drain could have dumped us out into the Void for all you knew! What were you thinking?"

"What I was thinking," Trista replied indignantly, "was that we needed to get out of there fast! Besides, when I saw the medallion on the drain valve, I figured it was a kind of sign...you know...from the Author."

As we lay on our backs catching our breath, we found ourselves suddenly laughing hilariously at how utterly insane that idea sounded, while at the same time marveling at its truth. The Author certainly had been with us.

Still, this was no time to rest. Once Xaul discovered what we'd done, he wouldn't be far behind. Sobered by that realization, we pulled ourselves together and set out toward what we hoped was the sky ship docks. It wasn't much of a plan but reaching Stoney was our only chance of escape. To our relief, the place we had been dumped was actually much closer to the bottom of the elevator than we'd first guessed, allowing us to reach it in only a matter of minutes.

As the elevator pulley hoisted us up the crater, we were thrilled to see the darkened silhouette of the *Bridesmaid* rising up from behind the ridge overhead. Stoney was still here; we weren't too late.

"I hope Rob's still okay," Trista thought aloud as she looked back down into the shadowed streets of the city.

"He's got a good head on his shoulders," I reasoned. "He should be fine. We'll go back to pick him up as soon as we catch up with Stoney."

A few tense minutes later we reached the landing dock and spotted a large man pacing nervously on the deck of the ship.

"Stoney!" Trista yelled, waving her arms as we ran to reach the safety of the ship. "It's us!"

The look Stoney returned, however, was not a happy one. Instead of a friendly smile, he looked almost sorry to see us. His eyebrows were furrowed and full of concern, and he shook his head slightly. Something was wrong.

"Halt!" a commanding voice ordered from behind the stack of crates Stoney was standing next to. Before I knew what was happening, a half-dozen of Zagzabarz's guards scurried out to surround us.

Each of them was armed with curved sabers, which they pointed dangerously close to our chests.

"Are these the ones?" one of the guards asked.

"Yup, that's them," Stoney answered matter-of-factly. My jaw nearly hit the floor. *What was he doing?*

"Okay, that's it, men. Take these troublemakers into custody!"

"Is this some kind of joke? Stoney, what's going on?"

He didn't answer. Chains were snapped onto both of our legs, and our arms were bound forcefully behind our bodies.

"Ouch, my arm…watch it," I said as the guards carelessly gripped the black wound.

"Stoney, please, why won't you help us?" Trista cried.

He turned his back, pretending not to know us as he continued loading the *Bridesmaid* with cartons of supplies.

"How can you do this to us? I thought you were one of us!"

At this, Stoney paused in his work and glanced up at the guards who eyed him with uncertainty. For a moment, nobody said a word.

Then, lumbering forward, the one-eyed man I had once considered a friend came up beside us and said, "You got it wrong, kid!"

He took hold of the Author's mark medallion and jerked it off of my neck. Then he turned around and marched back to his ship alone.

"Okay that's it then," the guard said, forcing us away once more. "You two, take the prisoners away."

"What should we do with their weapons?" one asked, holding up Trista's bow and my sword.

"Send them with the prisoners; they'll be useless anyway. The Shadow have big plans for them on Dolor!"

As we were marched away, I overheard the commanding guard shout another order to the remainder of his men. "Put a hole in that balloon."

"Hey," Stoney argued, "we had a deal! If I gave you the boy you'd let me leave! You didn't say nothin' about tearing up my ship or sending them to Dolor!"

"Zagzabarz's orders. The Shadow don't want to be followed. By the time you repair it, the prisoners will be long gone, a little insurance in case you change your mind."

Chapter 21

Descent into Dolor

If ever a mission could be labeled a failure, the one I had just nose-dived into the ground was textbook. I was supposed to carry the Flame to preserve it until it reached the seven. Instead, my poor judgment had led us right into the enemy's trap.

My legs ached. Their muscles burned. By cruel design, the cramped quarters of the prison boxes we had been forced into made it impossible to sit, requiring me to stand, hands chained behind my back, for the grueling length of the trip.

A day passed with no food, no water, no light and no relief. For me, time had been marked by how many times I could rehash my fateful decision to chase after Boojum instead of following the spark's leading.

To make matters worse, the air had begun to turn uncomfortably warm and humid, a sign I took to mean that land was nearby.

The Shadow guards' commotion outside confirmed my hunch: our descent into the Shard of Dolor had begun, a destination that set even the guards on edge.

"Never alone," I whispered to myself as a calming reminder. It typically helped, but the usual heartening effect did not take this time. Not that I doubted the words…I think it was that I *feared* them now. Any comfort that should have come from knowing I was not alone in this wretched situation had long been soured by the implications: a friend suffered this fate with me. Knowing Trista was here only made my suffering worse. From my darkened cell I had no way to see or speak to her, but she was somewhere nearby, and I hated it.

Our journey came to a jarring halt when the transport ship made ground. The hull echoed ominously from the impact. Guards shouted commands angrily above the din until their voices were drowned out by a dreadful grinding and ratcheting of chains. The arrival of a faint light, now seeping into my pod through its vents, revealed that a door was opening.

Moments later, my container was abruptly yanked to one side, and I felt it being dragged behind the unpleasant grunts of a guard. Metal grated against metal as my prison pod joined the others being hauled off the transport ship. The squealing gave way to a scratching rumble as the container bumped across a more uneven surface. We scraped a few yards over what I guessed to be rock until I was finally dropped carelessly to the ground.

My box landed on its side, but with all the jostling, I landed face down. *That is going to leave a mark,* I thought as I felt a bump already rising from the throbbing spot on my forehead where it had struck.

Now what? I wondered in suspense as I listened to the last few pods being roughly unloaded around me.

"What's the hold-up? Don't just stand there! Start the Descender line," rasped an authoritative, distant voice. It added with nervous impatience, "Quickly!"

The whimpering reply came from somewhere close by, "Sir, it's jammed again, down-line. Sh-sh-shall we signal the Scourge?"

"Imbecile! Didn't I command you not to *speak* of them!" Clearly, the transport crew's fear of Dolor centered on whoever the "Scourge" were.

"But...sir, what should we do with the pods? We have to deliver them to the compound."

Angry footsteps, accompanied by muttered curses, stomped nearer and nearer until they passed me by. When they stopped, the commanding voice finally spoke again, this time with sinister calm. "We *send them down*, of course."

"Sir?"

I heard the scraping sound of one pod being shoved across the rocks until it suddenly rushed down and away, carrying the screams of its unfortunate occupant with it.

"There, delivered." After a dreadful pause, the leader urged his guards on. "Let the devils below sort out whatever's left of them.... What should they care what parts they get to *play* with."

The guards laughed in appreciation of their leader's solution and didn't hesitate to follow his example. In the horrifying commotion that followed, I found myself caught in the tide of fear that was carrying each unfortunate prisoner down to an unseen doom. My heart beat frantically as I twisted and pressed my body hard against the prison pod walls, as if I could somehow dig in and hold back, but there was no stopping this ride. For a brief, terrifying moment, I felt my pod teeter momentarily over an edge. My stomach tightened with anticipation before the final shove sent me racing down a steep and deadly incline.

Shudda-shudda-shudda-BAM!

Shudda-CLANG!

The beating was incessant, both on the pod and on me. Stones clattered off the outside, my body rattled off the inside. The sound was deafening as the metal container drummed down a steep slope. Deeper and deeper, I slid into what seemed like an endless pit.

Please let it stop! Let it stop! Make it–CRUMP!

In an instant, everything stopped, at least as far as I was concerned. The pod might well have still been moving, but I had blacked out.

****

A chorus of distant bells beckoned me from beyond. The sound swelled louder and louder until at last I forced open my eyes. The first thing I realized was that I was no longer in my pod. I no longer felt the cool touch of the metal walls boxing me in; my body was free to move (except for my hands which were still chained behind my back). My ears rang loudly as I struggled to sit up. Painfully, I learned just how many nicks and bruises my tumble had earned me. There was also the matter of my wounded arm, which already felt and looked to have worsened considerably. In time, the black infection would spread and take over my body; without help I was a dead man.

Shaking my throbbing head, I tried to focus on my surroundings. I quickly discovered that I had been ejected onto a rocky hillside, which angled sharply up and down from where I sat.

Just a few yards down the hill, I could make out the battered shape of my former "death ride," the pod door wrenched open. Outside of this immediate area, a shifting grey haze obscured everything else. Its effect was eerie, hanging like thick, dusty cobwebs all around me, leaving me to only imagine what possible secrets it might be masking. At least where I sat now was relatively safe, for the moment.

Content to stay put, I took advantage of my freedom to move and maneuvered my chained hands down and around my feet so they could be in front of me. For some reason the guards had decided to leave my Veritas Sword in my possession. I didn't understand their reasoning, but I was grateful to have my sword at my side.

When at last my ears finally cleared of the ringing bells, I became aware of the faint sound of crying nearby. I held still, trying to discern what direction it came from, and from whom. The more I listened, the more I recognized the cry as human, a girl.

Trista? I first thought, before calling out into the gloom. "Trista? Are you out there?"

The crying stopped almost immediately. A muffled reply swirled back through the mist, "H-hunter? HUNTER?"

"Triss! Thank the Author you're alive! Where are you?"

"Over here! I'm over here," she broke off in tears again, this time tears of relief that she wasn't alone.

Her voice seemed to be coming from somewhere above me, to the right. I gingerly stood up and started carefully picking my way across the rock-strewn hill in the general direction.

"Great! Just stay there. I'll come to you!"

Trista sniffed, then laughed, "Kinda not really a choice; I'm locked in a box. Wait…are…are you out?"

"Yes. Just keep talking. I can't really see anything through the fog out here. I need to follow your voice."

"Okay," she sniffed again. "I'll keep talking…I…oh, Hunter, I'm so scared. When I stopped falling, everything was so quiet and I kept thinking I would be abandoned here to…Whoa! What is that?"

A deep rumble shook the hillside. I felt a rolling tremor pass by, almost as if something had just carved a path directly under my feet, heading up in the direction I had imagined Trista to be. A shiver went up my spine.

"*Keep quiet!*" I whispered loudly to Trista.

"What's going on out there, Hunter?" I could hear the panic rising in her voice. "I can't see anything...Hunter?!"

Suddenly, the hill shook from a powerful eruption above, knocking me to the ground. A desperate scream knifed its way through the gloom as blasted rock tumbled down through the haze only a few yards to my right.

The scream quickly disappeared behind a throaty, monstrous hiss, "Fwwheeeeeh!"

Leaping back to my feet, I retrieved my Veritas from my belt, searching wildly for any sign of what had just emerged. The curtain of haze was drawn in too tight around me to spot anything.

"Trista! Where are you? I can't see..."

BOOM!

A powerful force pounded the earth, ringing loudly against metal. More stones tumbled down. I braced myself as the force struck a second time, and a third.

"Fhehhhh!" the hidden creature spat angrily.

For a brief second, I could hear Trista above it all, shouting hysterically, "Hunter! Help me!

Gripping my sword tightly, I charged up the hill and quickly broke through the grey barrier to discover a hideous creature, gnawing hungrily at Trista's pod. Its mouth was lined with two rows of gruesomely sharp teeth.

Not wasting the opportunity to attack the monster's long, exposed neck, I rushed forward with my sword overhead. When at last I was within range I slashed down in a frontal attack, but my weapon never met its target. For some reason, the blade barely flickered an inch beyond the handle, crackling weakly before it extinguished. The misfire caught me by surprise and I tumbled to the ground.

What had just happened? I wondered.

There was no time to tell. Having heard my approach, the creature shoved Trista's mangled pod away and swooped its head down in search of a softer meal. Rolling to my left, I scurried up the hill and took position behind a boulder. For the first time, I could see the beast in its entirety. It was all neck and no body, or rather it was all one long, wet, snake-like body rising up from a tunneled hole in the ground. There were no eyes that I could see…just a giant worm-like creature with horrid teeth and a ravenous appetite.

Unnerved by the sudden silence, Trista whimpered, "Is-is it dead? Did you kill it?"

I didn't dare answer, but tried to keep calm…

By fear a man appoints his master, I silently recited passages from the Code of Life, hoping to ignite my blade. Each time the blade simply choked out. The creature was swaying closer now, still blind, but somehow honing in on my position. My heart beat louder and my attempts became more frantic, until the Veritas no longer produced a blade of any kind.

Oh man, I'm dead meat! I thought in panic.

As if drawn by that thought, the monster immediately whipped its head around to face me, saliva spraying as it gave its throaty yell, "Fwwheeeeeh!"

"Hunter? Hunter!" Trista shrieked, expecting the worst from what she couldn't see.

I turned to run, but the creature was too fast. Its jaws caught hold of my shirt, flinging me across the hillside and roaring angrily in frustration that it had missed its prey by so little. When at last I rolled to a stop, I turned to face what I feared would be another attack, but instead was amazed to see the once stagnant haze begin to whip up into a whirlwind around us. I squinted to shield my eyes from the sudden rush of wind and watched the monster writhe, retreating back down its hole.

As quickly as it had started, the storm was over, the threat was gone. The swirling haze settled back into place. I had no clue why the fog had stirred, or why the monster had fled. All that mattered to me was to find Trista and find a way out of this place.

Picking myself up again, I half stumbled, half slid down to where Trista was trapped inside the prison pod. She was sobbing with fright.

"It's okay now," I tried to comfort her. "We're okay; that *thing* is gone. I'm going to get you out of there!"

Trista acknowledged my presence with heavy sobs. Her mangled pod was lying on one side, its frame bent so that the door was partly cracked open.

"It's still locked," I groaned, pulling hard on the door with all my might. It was no use, the door wouldn't budge. Looking around, I located and retrieved the largest rock I could lift and brought it back to the pod.

"Scoot back, I'm going to break the lock!" I said.

Trista did her best to back away. I lifted the heavy stone high overhead, but before I could bring it down something whisked it from my hands and tossed it aside.

"Allow usss," moaned a low, wheezy voice.

I wanted to turn, or run, or both… but couldn't do either; something held my body in place. An icy chill passed over me as a dense wave of mist streamed around my arms, legs, neck and shoulders, collecting in front of me like a column. The spilling shape fluidly morphed till it resembled the twisted frame of a man, though no face could be seen.

"We welcome you to Dolor," it breathed hoarsely. *"We hope your stay is long."*

It stretched out its hand in a winding flow till it touched Trista's pod lock. Something clinked inside, allowing the door to fall open. Trista lay motionless inside the container, frozen like me, her face streaked with tears.

"What's h-happening? I can't move!" Trista asked helplessly.

I had no answer, but simply watched wide-eyed as the grey form drained out through both arms until it assumed the bodiless shapes of two massive hands. Both hands wrapped their fingers around our waists and lifted us. With no ability to resist, we were effortlessly carried off in the floating grips, like leaves caught in a stream's current.

The spirit navigated us down through the gloom where we soon approached a knee-high wall of loosely stacked stones, hardly a deterrent of any kind. *"You must stay within these borders,"* the spirit droned, gliding over them untouched, *"unless you prefer the Fangworm's hospitality over ours."*

It was obvious what the Fangworm was, but I couldn't help but wonder who the form was that now carried us.

"We are Scourge, gods of Dolor," came the chilling reply to my unspoken question. *"We are your masters."* The spirit's grip tightened as it said this, momentarily choking Trista and me for emphasis.

Something of a song echoed through the fog, growing louder and louder as we descended deeper into the depths of Dolor. Soon it became hauntingly clear what it was. This was no song, but rather a chorus of moaning and weeping voices rising from the heart of the fog. The sound was accompanied by a sickening smell, the air rife with the sweat and tears of oppressed prisoners.

"Hunter," Trista gasped, her eyes welling with tears, "I can hardly breathe."

At last, the suffocating mist thinned enough that we spotted our first signs of human life, if you could even classify the other prisoners that way. The hunched figures were dirty; their clothes tattered.

Even though they moved, each laboring to carry a large stone off to some unseen destination, each looked more dead than alive. None of them even bothered to look up at us as we passed by.

"This is your new home," our host announced as its hand-forms evaporated, dropping us helplessly to the ground next to a large black stone column. The Scourge reformed as two men-shapes and stooped low to unshackle our wrists. The twin voices of the Scourge spoke in turn.

"These will no longer be necessary."

"You are family now."

It felt good to be freed from the iron restraints, but their cruel play on words was hardly comforting. They had no intention of treating us kindly, of that I was sure.

"Leave us alone!" I shouted, reaching for my sword in an attempt to fend the spirits off, but the bladeless hilt was once again cold and unresponsive in my hands. The Scourge didn't flinch, but taunted me in turn.

"Don't be so hard on yourself."

"It's the same for the others."

"Our climate is just not conducive to your little toys."

"But don't worry; there's no time to play."

Wrestling us up from the ground, the Scourge-men forced both of our backs up against the black pillar, restraining our arms tightly behind us. More haze began pooling in front of us, boiling up from the ground until a third shape emerged, the menacing form of a giant scorpion.

Trista screamed as the scorpion cloud drifted closer, flicking its tail. I tried to turn away, but the Scourge-man behind me forced my head up, holding it there with its paralyzing touch. I was forced to watch, wide-eyed, as the stinger's tip began to steam and hiss, its color glowing red like the tip of a hot poker.

The stinger lowered slowly to hover just inches between my eyes before a crackling voice ominously said, "*Now, we shall give you your new names.*"

Chapter 22

Prisoner 4126

"Leave me alone!" the woman prisoner's voice shouted angrily. "Save your Code-trash for yourself.... IT...DOESN'T... HELP!"

The other party involved in the dispute spoke too softly for me to hear more than a murmur from where I stood, waiting in line. Just like the other prisoners, Trista and I had been forced into mindless slave labor, moving rocks by hand from the lower boundaries of Compound 6 (as we had learned this one of ten was identified) to the upper borders. This was where the Scourge had most recently dictated a pyramid-type structure to be built.

However, the message now being passed down the line was that the self-proclaimed "gods" of Dolor had just ordered the nearly finished project dismantled and the stones redistributed back down to where they had come from. This was not indecision, but a deliberate form of torture. It was a disheartening feeling, even for someone like me who had only spent a few days on the line, compared to the years that some prisoners appeared to have endured.

No wonder someone cracked, I thought in regards to the shouting up ahead.

"I can't take it anymore!" the screaming escalated. "I just… CAN'T…TAKE IT!"

"No! That isn't the way!" a deeper voice shouted.

Through the haze, I saw the murky outline of a woman sprinting away from the line. She scrambled wildly off toward where I knew the upper boundary wall to be and disappeared. No one gave chase for fear of punishment if they left the line—the Scourge were always watching and would know. Their punishment would be swift, severe and unavoidable. There was only one way to escape such a fate—never return.

"I'm free! Free! Aha-ha-ha!"

The entire line stood hushed as the crazed shouts of the escapee faded away into the fog. In only a matter of seconds, I felt a subtle tremor in the hillside and heard the distant, muffled scream as a fangworm collected its meal.

There was an awful silence before the moans and tears of those left behind returned.

I would have thrown up if my stomach had anything in it. As it was, prisoners of Dolor were only fed once at the end of each labor, days didn't count here. Our cruel masters determined when we started and when we stopped, regardless of any prescribed measure of time.

Chains rattled as everyone turned in place to begin slowly filing back down the hill to return our stones, until our cruel masters would most certainly recall the decision.

"Prisoner Seven-two-six-seven," a Scourge form groaned harshly

from behind. *"Come with us!"*

"Ya can't silence me, if that's what yer intendin' ta do. You should know that by now," came the prisoner's husky reply. The voice sounded familiar, the same one that had shouted out after the fugitive woman. "I speak truth! *Your* kind can't touch that sort," the prisoner challenged.

"Move! Your insolence wears us thinnn."

"And that's sorta the point, isn't it?"

This brazen remark triggered a scuffle up behind me that ended with a large prisoner tumbling and skidding down alongside our line. He pulled his broad frame up off the ground and turned to confront the descending Scourge. As his long, unkempt hair fell away from his heavily bearded face, my memories all came crashing together.

Deep accent. Broad frame. Ruddy face.

"Sam?" I blurted out, breaking the foremost rule of silence on the line. "Captain Samyree?!"

Surprised, he squinted back at me, before breaking into a wide smile, "Hunter, what are you doing here?"

WHACK!

An ogre-sized Scourge bashed Sam with a wooden club. Another joined in with a length of chain that it flung over Sam's neck, using it like a leash to drag him down the hill. Despite the brutality, Sam managed to flash me one more smile as they led him away.

"YOU!"

I looked over to see the spindly finger of the Scourge-man thrust angrily at me, dragging itself across the burn scars on my brow. *"Prisoner Four-eight-six-eight. Former names are strictly forbidden."*

"I'm sorry... I didn't..."

A cold slap from its hand silenced my explanation. The shock of it caused me to lose grip of the rock I was carrying, dropping it painfully onto my left foot. Grabbing me by the ear, the spirit twisted it cruelly. *"Oh, you'll learn. Suffering is a good teacher,"* it breathed maliciously. *"Come with us!"*

Trista, who had been a few prisoners down the line from me, shot me a terrified look as I was forcefully led away. She started to take a step out of line, but wisely didn't follow through. I watched her face disappear behind the gloom, her despairing expression marked painfully by four identifying marks branded across her forehead: 8747.

Having taken the form of a winged creature, the Scourge had snatched me up in its large talons and carried me off. With their powerful strokes, the wings brought me quickly down to where the sloping hills of Dolor completely dropped off into a wide-mouthed pit. Taking a wide turn, the Scourge announced our destination, *"Behold, the Crux of Dolor."*

With terrifying speed, we took a spiraled dive into the ominous depths. Pulling up just short of my becoming a splattered mess at the bottom, the Scourge hovered momentarily and then dissolved into a man-shape, letting me fall the last few feet onto the rocky floor.

"This is what awaits every fool who dares resist our rules," the cruel spirit hissed as it took an intimidating turn around me. Sweeping its arms out across the pit, the haze cleared long enough for me to get an unobstructed view of what this place held.

The courtyard, if the bottom of a pit could be called that, was rough, but flat and encircled by a series of stair-stepped rock ledges. Each ledge housed another row of rusty, iron-barred doors, creating cells out of the caves. The walls were riddled with them, too many to count. Each cell framed the face of a cheerless prisoner pressed against the bars.

Rising up from the center of the Crux was a towering rock formation. A spiral staircase wrapped around the enormous spire chiseled into its sides to provide access to the top. But this was one rock you wouldn't want to summit, for fixed atop the spire was a giant sculpture of a vicious serpent head. The jaws of the snake yawned open, bearing its fangs for all to see. Three curled horns angled forward around its head, one on top and one on each side of the jaw. It was no masterpiece, but the crudely hammered metal, perhaps iron, still adequately portrayed the fierce features of its honored subject: Sceleris, the evil spirit and supreme master of the Shadow.

I shuddered, remembering what the real face of Sceleris looked like when I had faced him emerging from the Bloodstone.

Even though it was expansive, everything about the Crux made me feel claustrophobic, especially as the grey fog settled back in. I just wanted out.

"I get it. Your rules are important," I stammered nervously. "I won't...you know, talk in line again."

The spirit chuckled cruelly, *"It's not that easy. To leave the Crux, you must be prepared to give what we require."*

I gulped, sensing there was a steep price to pay for my freedom. "W-what are you asking for?"

It held a twisting hand out to me, *"Your sword."*

"My sword?"

"As a token of your renouncement of the Author and the pathetic Resistance; only then can you return to the upper regions of Dolor," it breathed evilly in my face, causing me to cough.

I had heard this demand from the Shadow before. Venator had wanted the same thing before I, or rather Aviad, defeated him. No matter the circumstance, I couldn't deny the truth I knew.

Aviad is dead. He will not save you this time. Your sword does not even work here—the Code of Life is powerless in Dolor. Like a suffocating smoke, the doubts swirled up in my thinking, clouding my confidence. It was true—I was powerless here. If Sam had been held here for three years, if the Author had not found a way to rescue him or any of the other Codebearer prisoners from this place, then what hope did I have? What hope did I have of surviving, let alone finding freedom, if not by their rules?

"That's right. Our rules are the only way in Dolor," the Scourge coaxed me on as if finishing my thoughts. Somehow, without me realizing it was happening, a smoky arm had draped itself around my shoulder, enveloping me in its clinging cloak. My mind became muddled, my will weak and my body all but frozen.

The voice now whispered gently, lulling me under its persuasion. *"You desire peace. You want to give up the sword and abandon the Resistance."* As it spoke, every counter-thought began to fall. Slowly, under the Scourge's direction, my hand reached toward my sword to remove it.

Suddenly, a high-pitched scream broke the spell of the moment as something swooped down to land next to me. The arrival of another winged Scourge with prisoner in tow shook me out of my stupor.

"Get your claw thingy's off me!" the feisty girl shouted as she struggled to free herself.

The defiant words resonated like a clapper against the bell that traps it. I immediately recognized what had been happening to me and ducked out from under the Scourge's smothering folds.

"Never! I will never give over to the Shadow!" My voice sounded more confident than I felt as I stood my ground.

"Ahhhh!" my guard growled angrily at its foiled efforts. Raising itself to tower menacingly above us, the spirit screamed, *"Then you will die here! Lock these two Resistance rats up!"*

Instantly, the two Scourge figures whipped up into their fist-shaped forms, snatched and hauled us away up the ramps to a vacant prison cave door three ledges up. The door slammed shut with the Scourge's parting threat, "*We will squeeze the Code of Life out of your pathetic bodies yet.*"

Spreading their shapes out to become winged creatures once again, the Scourge guards launched out into the grey void above, laughing cruelly as they disappeared.

"What were you thinking coming down here?" I tried scolding Trista, but it was hard to mask my true feelings. I was glad not to be left alone.

Trista gave her head a sassy turn and snapped back, "As far as I'm concerned *you* dragged me into this mess, so you're stuck with me until you get us out. Besides, *never alone*, right? I figure we were sent here together, we may as well stick it out together." She gave me a reassuring smile, like everything would be okay somehow.

I almost laughed, marveling at what it would take to ever keep this girl down. But this was no time for laughter; the grave reality of our situation quickly set back in.

"Listen," I began, "it's great to have you here, but the truth is, up there we were slaves. Down here…" I hesitated to say it, "they only mean to kill us…or worse. Besides, look at my arm…the wound is spreading already. How long do you think I have before it takes the rest of me?"

Trista's wistful smile faded away as we both took a moment to let that reality sink in. The hollow silence of the Crux's depth took over.

Trista finally broke the silence to ask, "Who was that man you saw up in line? He was a Codebearer captain?"

"More than that…he's my friend," I explained. "Sam was there to teach me and train me from the first day I set foot in Solandria. He was the one who first taught me to use a Veritas. We all believed he had died when he was overcome by the Shadow's attack on Sanctuary. But he's really been alive all this time in Dolor."

"Since the attack on Sanctuary? So he's been held here for three years?"

I nodded with a far-off look, caught up in imagining what it must be like to have survived in Dolor for that long.

"Then," Trista perked up a bit, "that means there's some hope for us, right? I mean, if he's stuck it out that long, then there must be a way."

The seeds of doubt once again began to spread their ugly roots through my beliefs. "That's just it," I sighed. "Sam knows the Code of Life better than anyone. If there was a way to fight this place or escape, he would be the best equipped. But all he's managed to do is survive. He hasn't escaped, he hasn't even been rescued. He's been left here to…" I intentionally let that thought trail off.

My depressing outlook was apparently contagious. Trista didn't give any fight to that argument, but only looked down at her feet and nervously fingered one of the bracelets on her wrist.

I continued, "That's the part that bugs me. Why has he been abandoned? If there had ever been leaders courageous enough to mount a rescue mission to Dolor, it would have been Petrov or Aviad, but they never did and now they're both gone. If Sam's not worth rescuing then how can we expect something more?"

"You certainly know how to cheer a man up," a mysterious voice interjected from the back shadows of our cell. Until now, I had not realized that anyone else was in the tight quarters with us.

"Where…who are you?" I challenged, trying to discover more about our apparent cellmate.

The face of a long-haired, long-bearded man leaned forward into a faint patch of light. "You could call me by my name, but as you may have noticed, it's somewhat taboo in these parts. It's best you know me as Four-one-two-six for now."

Though there were obvious outward signs that he had done significant time here in Dolor, he still looked to have taken care of himself. His hair, though long, was neatly pulled back and held by a strip of torn cloth. Underneath the inescapable grime and the scarred numbers across his forehead, his face looked strong, young, handsome and full of life, his green eyes a particularly striking feature.

"Pleased to make your acquaintance," the man held out an undernourished but able hand in friendship, shaking my hand vigorously. "It's not every day I am fortunate enough to have a visitor; in fact, you're the first!"

"I'm Hun…uh, I mean I'm..." I instinctively looked up at my forehead as I tried to remember my given number.

"New, I see," the man chuckled, taking Trista's hand in greeting as well with a graceful nod.

"Tell me," Four-one-two-six's eyes sparkled as they danced between Trista and me, "what news do you have of the Resistance?"

There was an awkward pause as Trista and I struggled to sort out a bit of "good" we could share from what news we had. From my perspective, all of it kept returning to the same dead end named "failure."

"That bad, is it?"

I couldn't look at him when I answered. "It's all falling apart, the whole Resistance."

Trista added, "We had hoped our mission would change that but…well, here we are."

Four-one-two-six nodded his head solemnly as he walked over to the cell's door and gazed out into the endless grey. I felt awful. People like him (like us now, for that matter) needed hope, but I had nothing to give.

Turning around, Four-one-two-six invited us to join him at the door. "Look out there. Tell me what you see."

I hardly gave a glance before answering, "Nothing."

Trista squinted into the fog, but only shrugged her shoulders. "It's all grey to me."

"Interesting. You didn't see what I could see."

"What's that?" I asked, my curiosity piqued.

"The way out," he stated plainly.

"Way out? Where?" Trista and I both exclaimed in unison.

"There." He pointed to some indiscernible patch of fog, then over to another. "And there. And…here." He gestured broadly to the cell itself and smiled.

My first thought was how the years had not been kind to his mental stability. The next was to quickly gauge what kind of danger this certifiably crazy cellmate might pose to us.

Trista's response was a tad bit kinder. "I'm not sure I understand what you're saying," she said. "Maybe you can explain."

Following a soft chuckle, he obliged. "I am simply pointing out that *where* you look makes all the difference. When you limit your vision to what you see down here, I agree this place is quite dismal. But stop looking in the mud and turn your eyes skyward to the stars and I guarantee your view will improve."

I stole another look out the bars, this time looking up. "Uh… still looks the same to me."

"Hunter," Trista elbowed me, "I think he's talking about our attitudes."

"Partly," Four-one-two-six clarified. "Your attitude will follow where you set your sights. Right now, your greatest enemy in Dolor is not the Scourge, but your own hearts. Now, tell me more about this mission of yours."

"It hardly matters now; the mission is over…. I failed."

"Why are you so sure of that?"

"Well, we're here, aren't we?" I said, sarcastically. "I was supposed to protect the eternal Flame, to keep it from the Shadow's hands until it marked the seven. The Flame would have restored hope to the Resistance."

"I see," the man said, hiding a smile.

"It's hardly funny."

"No, I don't suppose it is. It's just that you said you were supposed to protect the eternal Flame."

"So?"

"Well, you can't protect the Flame, son. The Flame protects you! The Flame is the essence of life—a spark of the Author himself! Make no mistake about it; it was not the Flame that needed protecting."

"Even so, we still failed. We trusted the wrong people, first a devious snark, and then Stoney, a friend." I said "friend" but even as the word slipped off my tongue the wound of his betrayal was reopened. No, Stoney was not a friend; he was a traitor. A seed of bitterness planted firmly in my heart; I would never call him friend again.

At this, the man's smile faded, though his eyes still sparkled with unnatural joy.

"Beware the company you keep. It is a lesson from the Author's Writ itself. There are some in life who, although they may seem good and nice, will only distract you from your purpose and calling. Keep them, and your focus will be divided."

"But that's just it," Trista explained. "Stoney always seemed so genuine in his belief. I never would have thought he would betray us."

"It's true, people don't always do what we expect them to. Even our dearest friends can let us down. But the company I was referring to was the snark you chose to carry with you. Surely you knew that many snarks can be trouble."

"Yeah, I guess I just didn't want to admit it. He was mine, you know?"

"Snarks never belong to anyone. You belong to them."

His words cut to the heart of our problem. If we hadn't kept Boojum, we wouldn't have been in this mess to begin with. We might even have avoided the confrontation with Stoney and escaped with the Flame in our possession. This wasn't the first time Boojum had led us astray. Rob had been right about him from the beginning.

"Well, I sure made a mess of things this time," I said. "The Flame is lost, maybe even in the hands of the Shadow, and now we'll never get out of here to find it."

"But I've already told you…I know a way out."

We both looked at the man, waiting for him to share his escape plan.

"Purpose," Four-one-two-six emphasized. "That is the way out."

"Purpose?" I laughed cynically. "No secret tunnel? No rescue… just purpose?"

He didn't take offense, but nodded calmly.

Trista took a little more time to deliberate her response, reflecting on what he might be saying. "So…do you mean 'purpose' like in 'Nothing comes from nothing' sort of purpose?"

Four-one-two-six smiled broadly and expounded on her insight. "Yes! The Code brings life to all who take it to heart. If we believe that all things were created by the Author, then by extension, everyone and *everything* has a purpose, even our circumstances, even suffering."

"Dolor? You're telling me that three years of persecution and torture—that you can find purpose in all of those wasted years?" I asked incredulously.

"Ah. So are you proposing some things to be untouchable by the Author? Perhaps here in Dolor we are too far for him to reach?" he gently challenged.

How could I argue that point? Of course I believed the Author was still in control. Didn't I? Either way, it didn't make it any easier to reconcile all the pain around us. "But I don't understand. How does purpose…?"

"It gives hope," Trista excitedly chimed in. "Think about it, Hun…er, I mean Four-eight-six-whatever. If we're here on purpose, then that means we are *still* in the Author's plan! He knows where we are, and even *planned* for us to be…here…even me."

"Well said," Four-one-two-six praised Trista's conclusion. "There are no loose ends, no forgotten pieces. You have an important part yet to play or you wouldn't be here."

As I wrestled that concept of "purpose" across my own rough landscape of recent failures, I began slowly to see a clear, connected path through all of its twists and turns, a way of truth and life. Suddenly, our present circumstances didn't seem so overwhelming. The revealing light of this truth chased off the shadows and caused my whole perspective to change.

We have never gone beyond the Author's reach. He is with us, even here. Never alone!

"Remember this truth, *always*," our wise cellmate instructed us, "and it will set you free."

From beyond our prison bars, a deep horn blared loudly, filling the fog-laden courtyard with the thrum of its foreboding echoes. Trista quickly followed me to the door and we pressed ourselves against the bars in an effort to see what was happening.

In swirling patterns, the fog outside began to separate and compress, clearing the center as it supplied bodies to the hundreds of Scourge spirits now amassing around the perimeter ledges. One stationed itself just outside our cell. Something big was happening. I couldn't help but feel like the curtains were being drawn back, the lights dimming, the suspense building at the start of a show—only we were chained to our seats and forced to wait and watch the horror unfold.

"What's happening?" Trista said anxiously, turning back to Four-one-two-six for an explanation. He didn't answer.

"He's gone!" she gasped. A quick search to the back wall turned up empty, but there was no time to contemplate his disappearance. A second horn blared and the nearby Scourge guard turned on cue to face our jail door.

"It's time," it wheezed. The door lock clattered loose and the Scourge spilled in to flush us out from behind. "Move!" it commanded, shoving Trista into me and out through the open door.

Chapter 23

Taking a Stand

We joined in a streaming line of some few hundred captives being led from their cells down the ramped ledges to gather around the foot of the monolithic statue of Sceleris, the serpent lord of the Shadow. Trista, not having seen it before now, looked worriedly my way. We both felt it.... There was something far more sinister to this sculpture than just a tribute to the Shadow's feared master.

"Prisonerss of Dolor! Captivesss of the Cruxxx!" a cold, penetrating voice hissed as a new wave of fog wound through the crowded courtyard, passing through our legs and chilling us to the bone. The winding fog collected beside the center tower and began to rise, forming a much larger Scourge shape than any we'd seen yet. There was also something very different about this form that loomed above us—it had eyes of fire, and its body seemed more defined and

thick, curling around the tower like a snake. When at last the new Scourge took full form, there was little doubt what or who it was. Side by side, the stone tower and the larger fog-born serpent looked identical, down to the three horns protruding from their vicious heads. They each were the embodiment of Sceleris!

Now fully formed, the Shadow lord began to speak again, though its mouth did not move.

"Until now, each of you have foolishly resissted my lordship. You have been brought here to the lowest point of Dolor, the final level, to receive the death that you deserve for your inssssolence. But," Sceleris paused, turning his head to look over each of the prisoners, *"I am a gracccious master, willing to forgive your offenssses. I offer one lassst chance to choose whom you will sssserve. Those who are brave enough to admit their errorsss and come into my serviccce will be rewarded with a chance to be set free. All you must do is agree to shed the liesss you have believed in following the Resissstance, swear your allegianccce to the Shadow and serve me, your true lord, Scelerissss."*

"Don't believe a word of that lying snake!" a booming voice called out from somewhere within the metal sculpture.

The fog-born Sceleris whirled around to face the hidden challenger, spitting viscously, *"Bring out the condemned!"*

A hooded prisoner fell forward from the head of the snake onto the opened metal jaw. Two Scourge guards followed him and quickly fastened his chains to loops inside the mouth, holding him upright in a bent position as he was too tall to stand.

Some of the women among the prisoners began to weep, while men, who apparently knew what was about to come, turned their heads away.

"Look upon the faccce of he who would deccieve you!" Sceleris hissed, prompting the guards to remove his hood. A cry went up from the crowd. When I saw the beaten face and recognized my

friend, my stomach dropped an inch and I wanted to cry.

"Who is it?" Trista whispered anxiously.

"Sam," I choked out, though I could barely breathe. "They're going to kill Sam!" Everything within me wanted to run but there was nowhere to go; I had to stay and witness his torture and likely death.

"I bring thissss prisoner here to you today as a warning to all who still cling to falssse notions that your loyalty to the Resistanccce will ever be rewarded," Sceleris lowered his head over the crowd. *"Death is the only reward that awaitssss you!"*

As Sam looked out over the crowd, I thought I spotted a tear in the corner of his eye. He had suffered so much already, why this? Why couldn't the Author save him from this humiliation?

"You only have one choiccce—to bow now, willingly, or bow in death! By his witnessss, this fool believed he could save othersss. I now grant him that wish. His death will mark the freedom for all who recant the failed power of the Code of Life and come to serve me."

Turning skyward, the phantom snake exclaimed, *"Behold! Your passage to freedom awaitssss!"*

Somewhere high overhead, I heard the ratcheting mechanics of something being lowered by chain from above. Breaking through the canopy of fog overhead, a large metal pallet big enough to hold four cars lowered until it came to hover just behind the back of the giant metal head.

I had not paid attention to it until now, but the sculpted Sceleris had another horn. Its jaw winged upwards and back from around the head to join together some length behind as a longer fourth horn. With the help of three winged Scourge, the suspension chain was lifted and its large center ring hooked onto the back horn's upturned tip. As they let go, the weight of the pallet caused the back horn to lever down and the opened, slack jaw of the metal Sceleris to creak closer shut, tightening its grip on Sam in the process.

"Now is the time!" Sceleris pressed. *"Those ready for a new masssster, step forward and claim your placcce in freedom."*

No one breathed while the great snake bent low over the crowd, searching for any among the ranks who had lost their will to endure. Then, from out of the middle of the throng, a first taker emerged. The man, avoiding the other prisoners' eyes, hurriedly climbed the winding flight of stairs to the awaiting pallet. As he stepped aboard, the jaws pinched tighter under the added load. Sam grunted but remained standing.

"Wise choiccce," Sceleris hissed soothingly to the lone defector. *"Today, you will be free...free to serve me."*

Emboldened by the first man's example, three, then five more desperate prisoners trickled their way out of the crowd, against the pleas of their peers, and began the one-way climb to freedom. Their added weight brought the mighty captain crumpling to his knees, squeezing his breath out of him.

Sceleris' eyes flashed wickedly at the sight of the fallen Codebearer.

"Oh! It's horrible!" Trista cried, burying her head in my shoulder.

It was too much for me to watch as well. I turned my head away and tried to shut out the horrific scene.

"Aha!" I heard Sceleris revel in victory. *"See how he bows to me now? So shall you! Submit now and you will live; wait and this pain of death will be yoursss. When his life expiresss, so will my offer. Do not wait!"*

"NO!" Sam's voice yelled, echoing across the stone walls. I looked up and saw him labor to say, "Re...sist."

Sceleris glowered at the man's attempt to defy him.

With a show of great strength, Sam managed to fight his way

back up to stand, and between panting breaths called out, "Decide fer yourself, who you'll serve…but as for me, I still stand fer the truth. I stand with the Author!"

Trista shook my shoulder, "Hunter, look!"

"No…I can't watch; it's too much!" I cried, pulling away from her.

"No! It's him! I see him!"

Looking up through blurry eyes, I strained to see what Trista was talking about. "Who?"

"That prisoner…Four-one-two-six."

Our vanishing cell mate had made his way up the spiraling staircase and was standing beside Sam, helping him to pry the jaws open again. Together, despite the crushing weight, they lifted the scales upward. I would have expected the Scourge and Sceleris to forbid this bold act, but for some reason they seemed oblivious to his presence there. Sam stood strong, empowered and strengthened by the second man's company. He began to shout.

"I am not alone! The Author is here even now in my moment of trial," Sam shouted loudly. "A new deal is made. He offers freedom—the Author grants freedom for all who come to the scales."

"*Silence,*" Sceleris seethed, "*I make the rules here, I give freedom… I alone!*"

"Don't listen to him!" Sam urged. "If you deny the serpent, come to the scales. By the power of the Author your weight will be held."

Even from where I stood, I could see traces of blood begin to trickle down the prisoner's back and sides. Four-one-two-six was more than carrying his share of the load.

"Poor fool," one of the prisoners beside me began to mutter. "He must be going mad. There's no one up there."

"Good riddance," another said bluntly. "Who does he think he is anyway? Offering to buy our freedom with his blood..."

"Please listen!" Sam cried out. "It is true...you must believe. Look to the man beside me. Freedom is ours."

Inspired by Sam's words, a woman stepped forward out of the crowd. "It's true! There is someone up there, I can see him! He isn't alone!" In a rush of excitement she accepted the offer and raced up the stairs to the scale. Her example became the first of a flood of others who also saw the man beside Sam. Each one stepped to the scales until nearly fifty had added to the number. Surprisingly, with each added person the weight did not seem to crush the men on the stand...their strength held.

When Four-one-two-six looked my way, our eyes met and I knew at once that he meant for us to come too.

"I want to go," Trista said, stealing the words from my mouth.

I took her hand and side by side we climbed the stone steps and added our weight to the scales. There was a buzz of excitement among those who were already there.

Sceleris was still unaware of the other man's presence but he could sense things were getting out of hand. Watching the scene unfold this way was more than he could tolerate.

"*Enough!*" Sceleris shouted as he floated around the device, hoping to regain control of the situation. His serpentine body arced through the air to face his own graven image head on. "*What trickery is this! Why are you not dead? Kneel before your master or I will have you killed!*"

"I will not kneel!" Sam said. "I cannot kneel. The Author's strength is with me. I...will...stand."

The mention of the Author's strength made Sceleris' fiery eyes burn even brighter with anger.

"*Finish him!*" Sceleris commanded.

With a nod of allegiance, the Scourge guards who had placed

Sam in the device slipped into the stone mouth, arming themselves with red hot spears which they formed from the mist. They raised their weapons to put an end to Sam and his courageous act but before the fatal blow could be struck, there was a loud crack. With a powerful rumble the jaws of the stone snake statue began to break in two.

"No more!" Four-one-two-six shouted, and with a final shove the device crumbled from the strength of his power. The scales fell to the ground as it broke apart. The collision sent a shockwave through the floor of the Crux. All who had gathered there fell to the ground with the force of the quake. When the dust finally settled, the head of the stone serpent was no more than a heap of rubble. On top of it all, Sam and Four-one-two-six stood triumphantly, their arms raised in glorious victory. The Scourge that had been sent to kill Sam were nowhere to be seen.

The Codebearer captives began to cheer their approval for the rebellious demonstration toward Sceleris and the Scourge; however, the celebration was short lived.

"Ssso be it," the form of Sceleris spoke. *"You will pay for this treachery."* With that he dissipated into the fog. *"Snuff them out... all of them!"*

No sooner had he left than a multitude of phantom Scourge took form out of the fog. Like ghosts they flew through the air, diving down and passing through many of the captives around the outer rim. Each time a Scourge slipped through a prisoner, their bodies went limp and fell lifelessly to the ground. The Scourge worked their way quickly inward, leaving a trail of bodies in their wake.

Some of the prisoners swung haplessly at the Scourge with their Veritas Swords, but it was futile. The weapons were useless and the victim's souls were collected with a final gasp of breath.

"Never alone!" Sam shouted over the cries of the prisoners. "You must believe it!"

One of the Scourge heard his plea and set out to silence the man. As it approached, Sam held his sword in front of him and shouted the battle cry of the Codebearers, "For the Way of Truth and Life!"

Inexplicably, his Veritas Sword suddenly ignited. It wasn't supposed to but somehow it did! The attacking Scourge had no time to react. Sam held the blade vertically before him and the Scourge collided with it, severing in two. The mist that once formed the Scourge spread out and sank to the floor, coating the ground in a black sooty dust. It was the first time any had seen a Scourge defeated.

The remaining Codebearer prisoners each glanced at their weapons, wondering as I did if theirs might work too.

"You must believe," Sam repeated. "The Author is here and he is with us now!"

The words were more than simply inspiration. Prisoner Four-one-two-six stood beside Sam and to any who saw him—to those who looked on him—belief became easy. Our weapons ignited, giving hope to our cause.

The battle was no longer one-sided. Invigorated by our ability to divide the Scourge, those who truly believed attacked the enemy with reckless abandon. The Scourge were no match for the light of truth, even here in the darkest part of Dolor.

Out of the mist, Sceleris took form once more, his eyes blazing with a wild fury as he watched the scene unfold. Maddened by the newfound strength of the Resistance, Sceleris decided to end the fight himself. His form began to twist and spin until it appeared more like a tornado than a serpent. Only the flaming eyes remained stationary as the clouds around him billowed and added to his violent form.

One by one, the remaining Scourge were pulled into the power of Sceleris, causing the Shadow lord to grow in stature with each added spirit. The remaining captives gathered together near the rubble of the tower. The horrid winds of Sceleris' power whipped around us and blew dust and debris in every direction.

"This is not over," he said at last. *"Dolor is mine. Everything here submits to me."*

Without another word, he dove into the ground, leaving a deep pit where he descended. For a brief moment all was silent, the wind died, the stormy clouds subsided. It didn't last long. The earth began to quake beneath our feet, a rumbling that cracked the ground around us. Something was burrowing below ground, raising a trail across the surface of the crater. Then, out of the dirt a giant, black fangworm, twice the size of any we had previously encountered, erupted from the ground only a few feet from where we gathered. Sceleris himself had become the worm.

"Fwwheeeeeh!" the gruesome creature squealed. It lunged forward, swallowing a captive whose blade was still unlit. Those with weapons began to attack the worm at its middle. Unfortunately, with each cut the Veritas Swords made, the worm's skin began to reform within seconds. The damage was never permanent, and it certainly didn't stop the worm from continuing its attacks.

The fangworm slithered across the ground in search of another helpless victim. With nowhere to run and the Veritas Swords deemed useless, the scene quickly dissolved into chaos. Codebearers were running every which way to escape the giant fangworm and its razor sharp teeth.

"Trista, take out your bow," Four-one-two-six called out.

"But I've never shot it before," she said, pulling it off her back.

"It's time you did," he said, explaining his plan. "It will take only one shot. One well-aimed arrow from Hope's bow will finish that beast…and I want you to take it."

Up until now, Trista had not even been able to generate a single arrow from her bow, let alone target it with any precision. Clearly, the situation was more than she could handle.

"You want me to kill *that* thing?" she said, pointing at the giant fangworm which was in the process of swallowing another swordless victim. "But I can't! I don't even know how to fire an arrow."

"Nonsense," he replied, "it's not about what you *can* do, but what you are *willing* to do when you are asked. The arrow will fly true if you are willing to be used. Are you willing, Trista?"

At first, I thought Trista would say no, she looked so frightened and unprepared for this moment. Four-one-two-six locked his calming gaze on her, and her fears gave way as she became more confident. She looked to me for advice.

"You have to believe, Triss," I said. "Have faith."

"I do," she said at last.

"I knew you would," Four-one-two-six smiled. "Now, aim for its hearts, the sixth segment down from its head."

"Hearts?" Trista said in surprise.

"Yes…five of them. You will only have one shot before the beast comes at you. One arrow alone, but its light should be enough to burn through all five hearts."

Trista looked more than a little concerned.

"But what if I fail?" she asked.

"Just let your arrow fly," he encouraged her.

Trista nodded and set her sights on the worm, pulling back the bow and targeting the neck of the beast to the best of her ability. The difficult task was made even more challenging by the erratic movements of the squirming creature. The chilling screams of another victim were cut horribly short by the crunching jaws of the carnivorous worm. Then, out of nowhere, the tail of the beast whipped around and crossed through our small gathering in the center of the Crux. The tail knocked Trista and me apart and scattered the others. Falling to the ground, I hit my head on a stone and blacked out for a moment.

When at last I was able to pick myself up from the floor, I looked back in hopes of spotting Trista. She was nowhere to be seen. All I saw was a towering shadow fall over me and the heart-wrenching sound of the fangworm's roar from behind my shoulder.

"Fwwheeeeeh," it roared, spewing a shower of sticky slime all over me.

I turned slowly around to find I was face to face with a hundred razor sharp teeth, each easily as large as my body.

"Did you have to do that?" I pleaded, trying not to be nervous.

The beast roared a second time, coating my front side as well.

"Guess so."

Having found its next meal, the fangworm lunged at me with a ravenous appetite. Somehow, I managed to spring aside just fast enough to avoid being swallowed. The worm's face plowed into the ground where I once stood.

I tried to run away, but the slime on the ground caused me to slip and I fell once more. Before I had time to stand again, the worm recoiled and was already looming overhead. That's when I caught a glimpse of Trista to my left, trying her best to arm her weapon.

"Please help her," I whispered in prayer to the Author.

A glowing orb of light began to form in the space between the bow as Trista focused her thoughts on the Code of Life. "Everything for a purpose!" she repeated as the orb stretched out to form a gleaming arrow of light. Then, holding her breath she released the bowstring and let it fly.

Thwoosh!

The arrow soared high, far and terribly off mark. Trista looked away, disappointed in herself. With a shot like that the only damage the arrow would make would be to alert the beast of her new weapon. But something extraordinary happened to change the course of events that would have ended in failure. As the arrow streaked across the sky, the giant fangworm flipped back on itself and twisted its ugly head to let out a victorious roar. Unknowingly, the beast's haphazard move had put it directly in line with Trista's stray arrow, which pierced the sixth segment at a perfect angle.

The arrow of light lodged in its chest like a splinter beneath its flesh, burning into the hearts of the beast. The fangworm fell down with a loud crash and curled around itself in pain. A few moments later the once frightening beast ceased to move, falling limp in a pool of its own blood. Against all odds, Trista's arrow had found its mark.

Four-one-two-six's plan had been executed with flawless precision. It was as if he had known all along that Trista's arrow would stray and that the beast would move at the last second. But how could he have known it? How could anyone have known where Trista's shot would go or how the fangworm would move, for that matter?

The corpse of the fangworm melted into a pool of black tar as a hundred tiny Scourge escaped from its form. Knowing they had lost, the phantom-like Scourge retreated up and out of the Crux.

"That's right," one of the Codebearers shouted. "And don't come back!"

There was a joyous uproar as the surviving prisoners gathered around Four-one-two-six to celebrate the impossible victory. Never before had the walls of Dolor faced defeat. Clearly, the tides had turned.

I hurried to Trista's side to congratulate her on shooting her first arrow and to thank her for saving my life. Before I could speak a word, another man's voice shouted out.

"We've got company. Lots and lots of company."

Sure enough, appearing over the ridge of the Crux and up the steep incline of Dolor's slopes, a thick oppressive fog began sliding down the hill like an avalanche. The ashen fog was swirling with a horde of countless Scourge. Even with the use of our blades, the sheer number of the Scourge that approached would easily overpower us. It would take an army to defeat them all and our number was less than fifty.

With the blanket of death-fog rolling in on all sides, I turned to Trista and offered a word of encouragement.

"Whatever happens, you did good, Triss!"

"Thanks," she nodded back. "It feels good to believe."

She took my hand and squeezed tightly as the horde of Scourge poured into the Crux, rushing toward our small band of Codebearers.

Part 3

Chapter 24

The Rescue

As the raging horde closed in on our position, I focused my attention on the one who had led us into this battle. Four-one-two-six stood unfazed by the approaching storm, his eyes fixed upward, a trace of a smile on his rugged face.

Who is this man? I wondered. *So calm under pressure, so free of fear and worry. A master of faith, the very model of a true Codebearer.*

In his eyes I noticed a spark of fire begin to grow. It was small at first, but it quickly brightened, a reflection of something overhead. I followed his gaze skyward and watched a blazing beam of light rip through the oppressive cloud cover, barreling down upon us. The pillar of fire touched down twenty feet in front of us, then drew a line of flames around our small gathering like one might circle something important on a page.

Looking back over my shoulder, I discovered Four-one-two-six had vanished once more. Where to, I couldn't imagine.

As the first of the Scourge approached the firewall, they attempted to cross the flame but were immediately and completely devoured in its light. A plume of black smoke rose skyward from the battle line.

"Looks like you could use a little help!" a familiar voice shouted from above. I looked up in time to spot Philan flying low on the *Bridesmaid*. Behind him a dozen more Sky Ships followed—each ship filled with Torporian Codebearer warriors. He had done it. The remnant of Torpor had been roused at last by Philan's leadership and they had come to our rescue.

The fleet began its assault on the Scourge, launching a barrage of arrows into the swirling mass of fog. Immediately, the fog thinned out from the onslaught, disintegrating into black dust. Lines were lowered from the Sky Ships and a new squadron of warriors dropped to the ground to join our number. Rushing headlong into the fray, they chased the Scourge out of the Crux and up the incline of Dolor.

The ground assault was reinforced by the ships overhead, which continued to follow the Scourge with a rainfall of arrows. Only one ship remained, lowering itself into the circle of flames. It was the *Bridesmaid*. A gangplank was lowered and we watched as Philan and Rob marched down to greet us.

"Rob?" I said in disbelief. "Is that really you?"

"Surprised?" he asked.

"Yes, I thought you would never fly again."

"Well, I had to make an exception. My friends were in trouble," he said, cracking a smile.

"Wait a minute. How did you know where to find us?" Trista asked.

"It was easy, really. Just had to follow the Flame!" He opened his hand and held Hope's medallion out toward me. I couldn't believe my eyes; Stoney had stolen the medallion from me the night we were betrayed. If he was a Shadow spy as I had suspected, how could it be here now?

Excited, I took back the medallion and immediately, the wall of flames that once surrounded us on the ground rose into the air, gathered together into a small powerful spark and returned to the medallion.

"Where was it?" I said, looking Rob in the eyes and trying to figure out what had happened.

Rob stepped aside. Behind him, standing at the top of the gangplank was a tearful Stoney, who looked worse for the wear.

"Hello, Hunter," Stoney said quietly. His usual boisterous personality had been dampened considerably.

I eyed the man suspiciously, unsure what to make of his presence here. He had betrayed us to the Shadow; because of him we had been sent to suffer on Dolor. How could I possibly trust someone who denied even being a Codebearer only a few days ago? He was a traitor.

"Now, before you say anything," Stoney began, "I just want you to know how sorry I am for what I done to both of ya. I never meant to hurt you guys...honestly."

"Then why did you do it?" I replied coldly, still unwilling to trust the man or even consider forgiveness.

Stoney started to choke up as he answered.

"There is no good reason for it. I was a coward. I didn't know it was the Shadow behind it all. I thought it was only Zagzabarz who was after ya. When I got back to me ship, Zagzabarz's men were already waiting to interrogate me about what I knew of the the three of you. They claimed you were a threat to the safety of the kingdom—plotting to overthrow the king's power. I tried to set them right, but they wouldn't listen. They gave me a choice. I could either help them identify you and be rewarded for it or else they would burn my ship and take me prisoner."

"You traded our friendship for freedom," I said angrily. "How could you when you knew how important our mission was?"

"I didn't mean to turn you in; I wanted to find you first and warn you of the danger, but when you showed up at the docks I knew they were still watching me. At that point I knew you was as good as gone; they had their eyes on ya already. As crazy as it sounds it seemed like turning you in was the only way to protect the Flame. I thought that maybe I could find some way to save ya, or that maybe I'd be the one to continue the mission for you...that I would carry the Flame in your place."

As his story unfolded, Stoney explained how, after he learned we would be taken away to Dolor, he felt unbearable remorse over what he had done. In his moment of weakness, he had betrayed his closest friends to a torturous fate and denied his own faith in the process. Driven by the grief, he tried desperately to gain an audience with King Zagzabarz for help, but his frantic story never got past the palace guardpost. No doubt, Stoney's temper didn't help avoid the scuffle that followed. Provoked to use force, the Torporian guards dragged Stoney outside town and left him severely beaten as punishment for his public insubordination. But more than his body, his spirit was wounded the deepest.

"Who had I been foolin'?" Stoney's voice trembled. "What with sayin' I was a Codebearer, but actin' like a low-life scum—the way I was living when Petrov found me. I mean, it got me thinkin' what good was I really to the Author? If there was one thing I'd proved to myself, it was that it didn't take much for me to fall back to me old ways. It shames me now to say that all I could think of was somehow draggin' my sorry self back into town and leavin' it all in a bottle of burum…that is, until Rob here found me."

Rob placed a comforting hand on the humbled man's shoulders and softly offered, "There's not one of us who could ever go too far from the Author's reach."

The rest of the story revealed how Rob had been anxiously searching the back alleys of the town for any sign of Trista or me, when he happened across the guilt-ridden Stoney. Eventually, Stoney made his way back to the Codebearer's hideout. There, with Philan's help, Rob nursed Stoney back to his senses and helped restore him to the fellowship.

There was only restoration left to be made. I found it hard to look at Stoney when he finally spoke into the awkward silence that had momentarily settled over our group. "I'm sorry for the things I've done to ya. I let you all down, I let the Author down and I even let me own self down. Can you…can you ever find it in your heart to forgive me?"

Trista didn't hesitate to step forward, climbing the gangplank that separated Stoney from the rest of us, to embrace the humbled man in a hug.

"If the Author can forgive me for my doubts, I can forgive you for yours," she said.

In that moment, I saw a glimmer of the forgiveness I had felt in the very presence of the Author when he rewrote my life. This truly was the way of truth and life. Climbing the gangplank, I left my grievances behind and joyously joined her in restoring Stoney as our friend.

"Thank you both," the big man sniffed, drying his wet cheeks with his shirt sleeve. "I was so worried about you guys. I thought you'd be goners for sure."

"As it turns out," Philan said, "your being sent here was exactly what the Resistance of Torpor needed to reunite in our fight against the Shadow. When they heard of your mission and your faith in the Flame, they committed themselves to getting you back whatever the cost. The raid on Dolor has given us new strength in both heart and numbers. I wouldn't be surprised if by the end of this day, we will have doubled the number of Resistance faithful."

It was one of those rare moments when a glimpse of the Author's hand could be seen clearly. By coming to Dolor not only had our fate helped to awaken the Codebearers in Torpor, but it had also provided a way of escape for those who had been held prisoner in Dolor for far too long.

"All things for a purpose," Trista smiled at me, recognizing the truth in the words now.

The clouds of Dolor had all but vanished, revealing the full view of the sky for the first time since we had arrived. The sun was setting in a magnificent display of fiery reds and oranges throughout the atmosphere. The prisoners were freed, the Scourge were no more. It was a place of celebration.

Sam joined Trista and me aboard the *Bridesmaid* to share a meal of joyful fellowship with our reunited friends. We were famished from our stay in Dolor and the deckhouse table held a stack of thickly cut bread, strangely shaped potatoes and a variety of vegetables. There was also a portion of freshly caught sky serpent that was leftover from a previous meal. We ate it all without question, savoring every bite.

The other Codebearers had all been safely taken aboard other ships to be transported back to their home shards. Soon they would be strengthened and reunited with grateful family and friends. Only two ships remained: the *Bridesmaid* and the *Koinos,* a transport returning to Torpor. After supper Philan intended to head back home and finish his job of leading the faithful of Torpor in their new struggle against the Shadow. We would leave on the *Bridesmaid* and finish the quest before us.

Philan was especially pleased to see that Sam was alive and well. We both had been trained under Sam's watchful eye and having him with us was like having a father figure in my life again—at least what I imagined a father to be like…strong, good, encouraging and selfless.

"What did I tell ya, Philan?" Sam boasted, "I always knew you'd be a leader one day. Look at you, all grown up now and a lot stronger, I might add."

"Thanks," Philan replied. "You were always a great teacher. From what I've heard you never stopped teaching others, even here on Dolor. There's even some crazy rumor about you breaking Sceleris' tower?"

At this Sam shook his head, "Bah, I didn't do nothing, there was another man," he explained. "I don't know where he came from or where he went, but he was the one who inspired us to fight back."

"I wish he were here now so we could all thank him," Philan said with amazement. "He should be rewarded for his bravery."

Suddenly stepping into the light, Four-one-two-six appeared before us. "I am here," he said simply.

Somehow, in the time since his disappearance, he had managed to clean up. His face was no longer dirty, his clothes were unblemished and his beard neatly trimmed.

"There is no reward you can give. I did what I came to do," he said mysteriously. "Only one thing remains yet to be done."

No one said a word or even questioned what he meant. The man commanded both respect and awe as he stood before the table. The medallion on my neck began to warm and rise from my chest on its own. The spark within emerged once more and glided over to the mysterious prisoner, who held it in his outstretched palm.

"Two marks have been revealed in your quest for the seven," he said, stating plainly our mission as if it were known fully to him. "Three more will be marked this night."

A hush fell over the table.

"A heart of stone..." the man said casting his gaze over the gathering, pausing for a moment as he glanced at me. Was he talking about me? Something within his brilliant blue eyes reminded me of someone from my past...but who exactly it was I could not decide.

His gaze shifted away and fell on Stoney, who was sitting near the end of the table. "Stone-Eye Sterling."

"Aye," the large man answered reservedly.

"You have been given much by the Codebearers, but have not taken it to heart. Your actions have been noble at times, but your intentions do not always match your words. Do not let your sight be limited to the eyes of this world. You must look at life through the Author's eyes."

Stoney looked away from the man, ashamed of his own lack of vision when confronted with danger. Even as the words were said, I felt a twinge of shame. I had been guilty of the same crime on many occasions. The words easily could have been said of me.

"A precious seed..." he continued after a brief pause. "Trista Nicole Golden."

At the sound of her name, Trista looked up with wide-eyed wonder.

"Today true faith was born in you. The seed is small, but growing strong. Keep the faith. Nourish it, and it will grow. Keep the memory of this day in your mind; let it anchor you for the trials ahead."

"I'll try to," she said, respectfully bowing her head for good measure, unsure if the man was royalty. He nodded back with a smile, took a deep breath and looked over the gathering once more, capturing each of us in his gaze as it circled the table. At last his sight landed on Sam.

"A faithful captive..." he said at last. "Samryee Thordin."

Rob, Trista and I all exchanged surprised looks upon hearing Sam's familiar last name for the first time. Certainly, we all wanted to know if Sam was related to the brothers back on Galacia, but this solemn moment was not the time to ask.

"Sir?" Sam responded to his name, almost questioning the validity of the statement.

Four-one-two-six continued, "The trials you have endured have proven your faith to be true. Your strength amidst the suffering has inspired others to hold on when they might have otherwise given up. Even in the jaws of death itself, you showed no fear. Well done, my friend."

Sam said nothing; he just looked at the man, hanging on his every word with eager anticipation of what was to come.

"The three of you are very different from each other in many ways, but in the most important of ways you are the same. You are part of the seven. You must go to Sanctuary, restore Hope and tell the Resistance that I...Aviad...am alive."

As he spoke the last word, the Flame in his hand began to stir and grow. It became brighter and brighter, until the entire room was enveloped in a sea of light too bright for my eyes. I shut them tightly to shield them from the searing glare. Even with my eyes closed, the light of the blaze glowed through my eyelids with a pinkish hue. The voice of the Flame echoed the commission we had been given.

Go to Sanctuary. Restore Hope!

In an instant, it was over. When at last I could bear to open my eyes, I found the table and deckhouse to be exactly as they once were. But Aviad, Prisoner Four-one-two-six, was nowhere to be seen and our prisoner numbers had been erased.

"I've been marked," Trista said excitedly, her right arm pressed against her left collarbone. Sure enough, at the base of her neck was a golden symbol, the gleaming mark of a three-tongued flame. Sam and Stoney had also received a mark and were examining theirs as well.

As exciting as the news of the marks was, however, the bigger news was the appearance of Aviad himself.

"I still can't believe it was really him!" I said. "To think, all this time we were fighting beside Aviad and we didn't even know it."

"I should have known it was him," Sam pointed out. "My heart was burning when he spoke."

"Mine too," Rob added.

"But he's so young!" I blurted out. "The last time I met him, he looked old and frail. How is it possible?"

Sam explained, "You see him as he intends for you to see him. Aviad is no ordinary man."

"True," Philan added, "and even though he may appear in different forms to you and me, he is the same, of that you can be sure. His character never changes."

We reveled in the joy of the moment. We had seen him with our own eyes. This was a great day for the Resistance.

"So, when do we leave?" I asked.

"At once," Philan said. "I will go back to Torpor and spread the word about Aviad's arrival among the Resistance. The five of you can finish the quest together."

With that Philan shook our hands and waved goodbye as he carried the amazing news of Aviad to the other ship. In all of the excitement I hardly realized a change had come over me as well. Trista was the first to notice.

"Hunter, your arm!" she said. I looked down, half expecting

to find the wound from Xaul's sword had spread even further, but instead the blackened cut was gone. Not only was it healed, it was gone completely as if it never happened. I was amazed.

"Only the Author can heal the wound of a Veritas," I recalled aloud. Aviad had healed me. The only question that remained was, would he choose to heal Hope as well?

"Well then, what are we waiting for? Let's fly!" Rob shouted, surprising us all with his eagerness to take to the air.

"Rob?" Trista questioned. "I thought you were afraid of flying."

"Oh yeah, terrified. But I figure, what's the worst that could happen? I'm with my friends and we have the Flame to lead us. What could be better?"

"So then," Stoney said chuckling, "shall I be getting out the barf-bags for ya before we shove off?"

Rob jokingly put his hand over his mouth and puffed his cheeks out in reply, giving us all a good laugh.

"Well then," Sam shouted at last, "we're off to Sanctuary!"

Chapter 25

Return to Sanctuary

The *Bridesmaid* was buzzing with excitement as we sailed on course to Sanctuary in search of Hope. There was a lot to catch up on with Sam. We learned that he was, indeed, related to the Thordin brothers (second cousins once removed). While it was news to him that they were now settled on the shard of Galacia instead of his home Shard of Sinos where they had all grown up, he was not at all surprised that they had chosen the severe climate conditions.

"We Thordins are a hearty breed," he boasted. "It's me mum's snake stew that's the secret to our strength, eh, Hunter?" He nudged me with his elbow in jest, knowing full well I'd had difficulty stomaching the bitter, stringy concoction the last (and only) time he was allowed to cook for me.

The conversation eventually steered to more important topics, with Sam trying to catch up on all he had missed during his years in captivity. Surprisingly, he had been able to piece together most of what happened from various tidbits of news that arrived with each new prisoner, but the complete story was never fully known. He was still anxious to hear a full telling of it first-hand for a change.

"Sounds like ya had quite an adventure there, Hunter!" Sam beamed after hearing of my fight with Venator. His dark skin and flashing white smile were a welcome sight. "I jus' wish I coulda been with you fer it."

"You were, Sam!" I explained. "The lessons you taught me never left my mind!"

"Then I musta done somethin' right. So, let me get this straight now. We're going to Sanctuary to find Hope?"

"Yeah, something like that. I've had visions of her lately, and I think Faldyn may have hid her in one of the Revealing Room environments."

"Well, that's no good," Sam said with a groan.

"Why?" Trista asked.

"Well, assuming the Revealing Room even still exists after the siege, there must be at least a hundred-thousand different environments for ya to dial up. It's a clever hiding place, to be sure—probably too clever. How are we going ta guess which one she's in?"

"We don't have to guess!" I announced, digging in my pocket and producing the small metal cipher that Gabby had given me. I tossed it to Sam who caught it midair. "Look familiar?"

"Why, sure, it's a cipher for the Revealing Room dials," he replied. "Where did you get it?"

"It used to be Gerwyn's. Gabby gave it to me as a gift, as a sort of tribute to his life and the sacrifice he made for me."

"That's pretty special then...but how exactly do you know this'll be the room Hope's been hidden in?" Sam asked.

"Because in my visions, there was a dragon guarding the entrance. And if memory serves me right, you, Hope and I visited there once before by accident, remember?"

"Oh yeah, the final exam," he said ominously. "But uh…there's something I should tell you about that one."

"What?"

"Nobody's exactly ever passed it before. That dragon, she's… uh…different! Now, I'm not one to say the Author makes mistakes but she's as close to one as he could have made. Why he created her, I'll never know. Impenetrable scales, thicker than the armor of any known to man, covered in razor sharp spikes that can pierce your heart by just looking at 'em. Why, if her fiery breath doesn't roast you, the spikes on her tail or snout will certainly stab you to death. She's a killer that one. No, we never took any of our students to see her, least not on purpose that is! Especially after we lost one kid in there…what was his name again? Brady, no…Barty…that's not it either…uh…"

"Bobby," Rob said confidently.

"Yes, that's right, Bobby. He wasn't supposed to be in there in the first place. 'Course some of the kids called him Bobby Bungle because he was so clumsy. He…uh…oh, my…" Sam stopped his thought midsentence and glanced over at Rob. "What did you say your name was again?"

"Rob…but you can call me Bobby, if you'd like."

"Well, I'll be," Sam said happily. "You're him alright, the boy we lost in the final exam. I guess I never lost a student after all! You were my only exception, me boy! How did you make it out of there anyway?"

Rob shared his side of the story, a riveting tale of his youthful desire to impress his friends. Even back then, he was as awkward with a Veritas Sword as he was today. He explained how one evening, while everyone else was leaving the Academy for the day, he entered the Revealing Room alone, determined to prove that he wasn't a klutz.

The first room he dialed ended up being the final exam, and he quickly found himself in more trouble than he bargained for. Rob tried to escape but the dials wouldn't turn back. Soon, he was running through the cavern, dodging the attacks of the massive beast and scared out of his wits. Just then, Sam entered the Revealing Room in hopes of retrieving a book he had left behind. When he saw the final exam already dialed up and Bobby Bungle in trouble, he raced in to save him, catching the beast's attention and drawing it away from the boy.

He shouted for Rob to get back to the atrium where the pedestal stood, as it was the only place that could move between the environments. Sam managed to land a boulder on top of the dragon's tail and fled for the dial as well. As he turned the last numbers into sequence and readied to press the dial, Rob had motioned with his sword that the dragon was getting free. His sword slipped from his grasp and flew across the room. Sam pressed the button just as Rob leaped to retrieve his sword, leaving him behind. Rob picked up his sword in desperation and ran for a small crack in the wall, where he hoped to hide from the dragon. Scooting back into the darkness, he found himself suddenly and inexplicably transported back home to the Veil.

"So that's what happened to ya!" Sam said. "I musta come back only a minute or two later and when I couldn't find ya we figured the worst had happened! We never took anyone back after that day for fear it was too difficult a challenge. Like I said, you were the only student I ever lost."

"Well, technically, I really never was lost so I guess your slate is clean."

"Still, I think it's a terrible mistake going back in there. Nobody ever completes that challenge."

"Well, we're going to have to be the first," I said boldly. "Hope's life depends on it; we think she's the sixth mark of the Flame. If the Resistance ever hopes to be strong again, we need her."

"I don't like it none, but I'm with you to the end," Sam offered.

"Me too!" Trista added.

All eyes turned to Rob, who sat silently beside us. He obviously didn't want to go back either. "I'll come too," he said at last, "but I'm not sure how much help I'll be."

The memory of his former mistakes had dampened his spirits a bit.

"Hey now," Sam said, "assurance comes from the Author, not from yourself. I, for one, am looking forward to fighting along side ya again. Only this time not as your teacher, but as your friend!"

Rob smiled.

"Aye and don't be forgettin' about me none," Stoney boasted. "I may not have found me sword yet but I can put up quite a fight. Why, I'll even sit on the beastie if that's what it takes!"

A round of laughter burst into the air as we all enjoyed a moment of common purpose. Our spirits were high with anticipation of what the Author would do. I hoped the feeling would never end.

We arrived at Sanctuary three days later, though it felt like half the time now that our purpose was clear. Our first glimpse of the fallen city brought a sobering feeling.

The once great white wall was toppled to the ground, nothing more than a heap of rubble. Fire had ravaged what remained of the city and many of the buildings looked to be only ghosts of their former selves. The Academy grounds were a desolate, deserted field of overgrown grass and toppled statues.

"Can't say I like what they've done with the place since I've been gone," Sam said.

"It must have been beautiful," Trista imagined.

"It was," I remembered, as Stoney dropped anchor outside the Academy and lowered the gangplank. After disembarking the ship we agreed Stoney would keep watch, in case anyone or anything had followed us.

Stepping up the cracked, battle-scarred steps and through the lopsided doors, we followed Sam to the long staircase that descended to the Revealing Room far below. Along the way, we brushed huge cobwebs away and had to step over piles of crumbling rocks where the walls had started to give in. After a long hike down the winding staircase, the four of us were standing at the foot of an enormous wooden door without any handles or hinges.

"Well, here it is..." Sam said, blowing dust off the brass plaque that was embedded in the floor. *Only the humble of heart shall pass,* the words read. "Guess I'll go first then," Sam said, walking straight for the door without slowing his pace.

Effortlessly, he passed through the door as if it didn't exist. Rob was next and did the same with little effort. Next up was Trista.

"Just remember," I explained, "you have to have a spirit of humility to pass through the door."

"Right," she said in her usual bubbly tone. "Just walk forward with a teachable spirit. Got it," she claimed. She started to take a step when I interrupted her with another instruction.

"And, don't go too fast or it will think you're cocky!"

"Okay, not too fast," she said, starting forward again.

"But not too slow," I interrupted again, "because it might think you don't trust what we're saying!"

"Not too slow, thanks," she said, resetting her position and taking a deep breath. She was about to start again when I offered another round of advice.

"Oh, and don't worry if it doesn't work the first time. It took me awhile to get it right. Just try and do your best."

"Anything else you want to say?" she asked, a little annoyed that I had interrupted her approach more than once.

"No...sorry...just stay calm and lead with your head, because if you go nose first it might...you know, hurt a little more."

"You're nervous, aren't you?" she said in response.

"Me? No...Okay, yes. Maybe just a little!"

When at last I promised not to say another word, she approached the door and stood in front of it. Then, closing her eyes she stepped through without any trouble at all.

"Beginners luck," I grumbled, marching toward it full speed.

Smack! It was the nose again!

Two minutes later, I made it through the door at last, a sufficiently humbled man with four bumps and countless bruises on my forehead to prove it. The stone walkway that led up to the podium seemed like the longest walk of shame I had ever taken.

As I stepped up the atrium steps, I could tell Trista was trying not to laugh.

"Well then," Sam said loudly, clearing his throat and pretending not to notice my face. "Now that we're all here, let's take a moment to ready ourselves for the final exam. The Code of Life, as revealed in the Writ, tells us that all things come from the Author alone—even big ugly dragons like this one! There is no doubt in my mind that the challenge ahead will be difficult, but he has brought this team together for this purpose."

The plan was for Rob and Sam to work together on distracting the dragon, while Trista and I looked for the crag in the walls that led to Hope's chamber. When at last nothing else was to be said, I handed the cipher to Sam, who dialed up the sequence on the rotating pedestal and pressed the button in the center of the device.

The darkness lit up all around us like the lights suddenly flicked back on after a midnight power outage. All at once, we found ourselves standing in the dead center of a massive cavern, the throat of the dragon's cave.

Chapter 26

Finding Hope

The cave floor was littered with the remains of fallen creatures who had met their end as a tasty meal within the walls of this cavern. Though there was no sign of the beast itself, it was clear we were in the right place, though I doubt there is ever a right time to find yourself in the middle of a dragon's lair.

High overhead, the ceiling of the cavern was open to the outside world. The sky was an inky midnight blue crossed with streaks of silver clouds reflecting the moonlight. The wind howled across the top of the dragon's lair, whistling a low and eerie tone.

The medallion glowed brightly in the cave, its light pulsing like a heartbeat outside of my body. I took it as a good sign.

"We're getting close," I said, excitedly. "Hope is nearby!" I started for the atrium steps but Sam cut me off.

"Hold tight a minute, Hunter. Let us go first."

He motioned to Rob who nervously followed Sam down the steps and around the perimeter of the room. Each footstep seemed to echo off the sides of the cavern. Nobody said a word, but it was clear we were all thinking the same thing. *Could it be that we had entered the dragon's lair while she was away?*

"Too easy," Sam whispered to Rob. "Something is not right here!"

"Over there!" Rob said, a little louder than he intended. "That's the fissure I hid in."

Sam wandered over to the entrance to check it out. The way seemed clear, and the path through the rock took a sharp turn at the end. Satisfied with the results of their scouting, Sam turned around and motioned with a large wave toward us.

"It's all clear, come on down!"

Only then did I notice the rocks above the crack begin to shift in unnatural movements, lowering themselves toward Sam. Two fiercely red eyes shot open amidst the stone and I realized that we had just found the dragon. It's camouflage was perfect, the scales blending with the rock on which it perched.

"Sam, behind you!" I yelled.

He spun around with his sword blazing and gasped at the sight of the creature. "Clever!"

A blast of flames accompanied the deafening roar of the once slumbering beast that we had awakened. Raising his sword, Sam quoted a passage from the Writ that I did not yet know.

"My sword and my shield!"

The fire seemed to divide around Sam, surrounding him in flames but protecting him under its invisible cocoon. This angered the creature even more and she lunged at Sam with deadly speed. Sam rolled forward under the creature's attack and out from beneath her. Now in the clearing, we could make out her form completely. She was more frightening than even I had remembered from my brief encounter before, a massive creature nearly fifty feet high, riddled with clusters of spikes along her spine, wings and tail. The tip of her nose was crowned with a large protruding horn like that of a rhinoceros.

Sam scurried to his feet and raised his sword again as the creature spun around in search of the lost meal. Rob picked up a rock and threw it at the creature, hitting one of its glaring red eyes. The dragon winced momentarily, then whipped its massive tail across the room and plastered the wall above Rob's head.

A cascade of rubble fell from the side of the cave, forcing Rob to run away to avoid being buried. He tripped on a rock and fell to the ground. This delighted the dragon who prowled over and ignited the air with its fury.

"I can't watch!" Trista said, ducking close to me behind one of the atrium's pillars.

Sam sped to the rescue and blocked the blast of fire intended for Rob. Then, after helping him to his feet, the two of them fled to the opposite side of the cave, luring the dragon away with them.

Sam yelled at me as he ran, "Now's yer chance, Hunter. Run for the cleft while you have a clear shot!"

"But I can't leave you!" I shouted.

"Don't worry about us. Just stick to the plan, finish what we came for!"

Following orders, I pulled Trista to her feet. We raced for the fissure and the hidden room I hoped to find behind it. The path was tight, the way narrow enough in places that we had to turn sideways to pass through it. But eventually, it widened and separated into three pathways.

"Where to now?" Trista asked.

The medallion tugged slightly to the right.

"This way," I said, choosing the rightmost of the passageways.

With each familiar footstep I ventured further into the depths of the cave. Each curve in the trail triggered my senses to believe I might only be dreaming, but I wasn't dreaming—not this time. We were here to find Hope.

The passage lowered into a steep decline and ended in a small cavern, a dead end. Spinning around, I searched the walls for an entrance into another room. There was none.

"What's wrong?" Trista asked, sensing my concern.

"I don't recognize this place. In my dream there was a black door and behind it a massive cavern."

"How do you know you can trust your dreams?"

"They haven't been wrong yet. Besides, the Flame led me here; I'm sure it's the place."

"Well, there's no black door."

"I can see that!"

"Maybe you just took a wrong turn or something? We can go back and try another tunnel."

"No," I said. "It's here somewhere. I just…can't…"

Before I could finish the thought, a trail of footprints on the dusty floor caught my eye. The prints led straight toward a tiny fracture in the red rock wall. The crack shot straight up, then turned overhead and came back down a few feet to the left of where it started—the perfect shape for a door.

Placing my palms flatly against the cool stone between the cracks, I shoved forcefully against it. The stone slid slightly forward, but only an inch. Still, it was enough to prove my suspicions had been correct. Inspired by my discovery, Trista joined in helping push the stone further. The hidden door opened on unseen hinges, revealing a space behind the wall.

Stepping inside, I led Trista into the open chamber…Hope's

chamber. The room glistened with an aura of light, which seemed to be coming from everywhere at once. No natural origin or source could be given; it just was. A sparkling pool of fresh water gathered in the center of the room, fed by a small stream that trickled down the sloped path in front of us. Flowers and plants bloomed all around, somehow taking root in the stone and finding enough nourishment to grow. Even the air smelled sweet and full of life, which was surprising, considering how far below ground we must be by now.

"It's like an oasis underground!" Trista said, marveling at the beauty of the place.

Near the center of the room, a twenty-foot boulder that looked like a stone tower stretched up and out of the pool, commanding our attention and drawing our gaze to the flattened ledge at the top. A steep rock staircase was carved into the side of the boulder, which led to a stone altar at the top.

The medallion warmed on my chest and pulled gently toward the stone tower in the center of the room. Even from where we stood, I could tell there was a figure hovering over the table. It was Hope. It had to be Hope.

As we reached the base of the stairs, I stopped short of climbing them. After all this time, I wasn't sure if I was ready to see her once more. My mind became an instant breeding ground for doubt. What if I was only dreaming? Or worse yet, what if my worst dreams came true? Would the Flame save her? Could I bear to lose Hope again?

My heart pounded in perfect rhythm with the pulse of the Flame, which swelled in the medallion.

Trista sensed something was bothering me and stepped up beside me, grasping my left arm gently in her hands.

"You should go alone," she said, encouraging me to continue

up the stairs in spite of my doubts. "I'll wait for you here until you need me."

I thanked her with a nod and stepped forward to ascend the staircase, treading gently on the solemnity of the moment. When at last I reached the table's edge, I gazed down on the one I had been searching for.

There, lying still, as if in a peaceful slumber was Hope, floating a good six inches above the stone table. She was dressed in a simple white gown with a squared neckline and long flowing folds. Her face was peaceful, eyes closed, lips sealed and her skin perfect, without any blemish whatsoever. Her hair was longer than I remembered, tied up in a golden ribbon to keep it from floating wildly out of place.

I recalled what Gabby had said about Hope being sent from the Author himself. A virtuess she had called her—whatever that was. I studied her features for a moment longer, looking for any sign of life behind her tranquility.

Release me, a voice whispered. It was only a memory from past visions.

"How?" I wondered aloud, answering my memories.

The Flame, Hope's voice replied. This time, it sounded real and nearby. Her lips didn't move, but I knew she was speaking to me.

The medallion lifted gently away from my chest, wanting to return to Hope. Removing it from my neck, I placed it over hers and let the Author's mark insignia fall on her skin, just above the neckline of the dress. The medallion began to glow, pulsing with the beat of her heart. A moment later, the golden mark of the three-tongued flame etched itself on her shoulder, just below her collarbone. The mark confirmed what I hoped to be true; she was the sixth. The ember of Hope.

The fire's mark sparked life in her and in a moment of pure

radiance, her eyes opened, searching the room and finding my face.

"Hunter?" she whispered, her voice still weak.

"Yes, I'm here," I answered.

"You came."

"Of course I came," I said, finding a tear building in the corner of my eye—a tear of joy. Knowing Hope was alive birthed a swell of emotion within me that I couldn't fight or ignore. For the first time I could remember, I wasn't trying to impress her or act cool. I just wanted to be near her. It was enough.

She reached out her hand and took mine. The warmth of her skin filled me with peace.

"Hey now," I said jokingly, "the last time I tried to hold hands you freaked out on me."

"Oh stop it," she said, fighting back a small chuckle and sounding a little more like herself.

"You're laughing, that's a good sign." I breathed a sigh of relief. Everything was going to be right now; I had Hope again. She was going to be okay.

"I'm glad you came. I have something important to tell you…"

Suddenly, her eyes shut in pain and she tightened her grip on my hand.

"Not now, we can talk later," I said, wanting to keep her from exerting herself too much, too soon. "We'll get help."

"No, Hunter. You don't understand. Something difficult is going to happen. You have to let me go."

"Let you go? What do you mean let you go? I just came all this way to find you. I'm not leaving you…or letting go…or whatever… I'm here to save you!"

"No, you can't, Hunter. The Author's plan for me is not yet complete; you have to trust him."

"I do."

"Then promise that you will release me. Say it."

"I…I'll release you," I forced myself to say. I didn't fully understand what it meant but I hated the sound of it just the same.

She smiled softly. "You're just saying that aren't you?"

"I just don't like the idea of losing you again."

"Nobody said you had to," she replied, squeezing my hand tightly in understanding. "When it's over…when I'm gone…you must still believe. The Author gives new hope when we need it most."

Just hearing her say the words "when I'm gone" caused tears to well in my eyes. I couldn't stand to hear it again.

"But I don't want a new hope; I want you. Why do you have to go? I need you…the Resistance needs you. They're falling apart and you're…"

"You don't need me. You must believe, Hunter," she said again. Her grip on my hand began to weaken, her eyes closing and her voice softer. "Go back to the Veil, and save him…from the fire."

"Save who?" I asked.

Before Hope could explain, Trista started to scream something, but her voice was cut short. I spun around to see what was happening. Xaul's hand smothered Trista's mouth, and the blackened blade of his Veritas Sword was pressed across her neck.

"Put down your weapon," said Xaul, "or your friend will die!" I looked at Trista, her eyes frightened and apologetic.

"Do it!" Xaul demanded, pressing the sword even closer to Trista's neck. I released my grip on the sword. The metal hilt of my Veritas fell to the floor, clattering loudly on the stone and echoing off the chamber walls.

"Now, step down from the altar," Xaul commanded.

I glanced back toward Hope one last time. She nodded knowingly as a tear slipped from the corner of her eye. Torn, I forced myself to turn away and began descending the stairs one horrid step at a time. As I walked down, Xaul stepped up, keeping Trista with him all the way to the top platform, passing me on the way. Once our places had been exchanged, he tossed Trista carelessly aside, letting her tumble painfully down the stairs. Her head hit the last step with a loud thump and her body fell limp. I rushed to her side. She was alive, but unconscious and would be dealing with a powerful headache when she awoke.

Xaul circled the stone table, eyeing the weak form of Hope with wicked intentions.

"Well, what have we here? So this is it, huh? The Codebearer's last hope. If she dies, everything you believe dies with her."

"Leave her alone, Xaul," I pleaded, knowing full well my words fell on deaf ears.

"Why should I?" he replied coldly, "The Codebearers didn't leave the Xin alone. They deceived my tribe into believing in a false hope as well—an Author who doesn't exist. Someone so great and powerful that certainly nothing bad could happen to us if we trusted him…LIES!" He shouted the last word.

"It's not that simple."

"Of course it's not simple. My people were annihilated by the very enemy the Author claimed to save us from."

He raised his sword and pointed it at me from a distance.

"And it would never have happened if we had kept to our Old Ways. We used to believe in an Author of fire and strength who lived within us…the Xin were the Authors and the Author was the Xin. We made our own destiny. We wrote our own story; we controlled our fate through power and strength."

His words were a series of twisted truths from the pages of the Writ. The Author was with us and at work in all things, but that didn't make us part of the Author. That was what Sceleris had wanted to be, the Author of this world.

Xaul turned his attention toward Hope once more. The Flame within the medallion she wore held everything he thought he wanted.

"At last, the power of the eternal Flame will belong to the Xin again."

Raising his blackened Veritas Sword in a slow purposeful movement, Xaul held it over Hope's heart for a moment. I wanted to freeze time and stop Xaul from killing Hope, but I was helpless.

There was nothing I could do as he took in a breath and plunged the sword deep into her chest, through her back and into the stone table below her. As weak as she was, her body still lurched forward from the pain of it.

I turned away. Seeing Hope die a second time was far too painful to watch. I wanted to cry but the horror of the moment stole all other emotion.

When at last I looked back, Hope's body lay lifeless on the stone table. No longer was she hovering over it. Her limp arm hung over the side.

Then, even her body faded away, disappearing into nothingness as I had when the Author took my heart. All that remained on the table was the golden medallion and the Flame within it.

The light of the room faded away to only a fraction of what it once was. Even the flowers folded into themselves and drooped low. It was as if Hope herself was what brought life to this place.

Hope was gone.

Chapter 27

Playing with Fire

With a wicked grin Xaul snatched up the medallion and eagerly pulled it over his head. The Author's mark began to steadily glow on his chest, as it once had on mine. Xaul closed his eyes and breathed deeply, relishing the sense of invincibility that accompanied the Flame.

"At long last, the moment I have waited for has come to pass. The power of the eternal Flame has returned to my people. The Xin will rise again."

Seeing Hope's killer wearing her medallion made my stomach turn. It wasn't right. It wasn't fair! Every instinct told me to rush up the stairs and fight to take it, but something else held me back—the realization that Hope had known about this all along. She died willingly, as if it was part of some plan.

I knelt in stunned silence beside Trista, unsure of what to

do next. Without the Flame I was helplessly lost and confused. I had failed the Codebearer Resistance—the Flame belonged to Xaul now.

Xaul sauntered back around the altar and kicked my Veritas Sword down the staircase. It clattered near the edge of the pool not far from where I knelt.

"Pick it up!" Xaul demanded.

The weapon was well within my grasp, but I didn't reach for it. I knew it wouldn't matter. Even with the sword in hand, I was unlikely to win this fight.

"I won't fight," I said, turning my gaze back toward the still unconscious Trista. She showed no signs of movement; only the slow rise and fall of her breathing assured me she was even still alive.

"Oh you will fight all right," Xaul hissed, eyeing Trista. "Fight, or she will be the first to die."

"Leave her out of this!" I shouted back in desperation. I had already lost Hope; I couldn't bear to lose Trista as well.

"Then, FIGHT!" shouted Xaul, lunging forward with his altered sword raised in a lethal attack. I tumbled to the side, recovering my Veritas only a moment before Xaul's blade collided with the ground where I once knelt.

A moment later we were engaged in full combat. For the most part, I managed to match each lunge and swipe of his blade with exceptional precision. But just as before, he was quickly gaining ground. I needed to take another approach.

Relying on my swiftness training, I darted across the room in search of a better place to hide. Crouching behind the safety of a stone boulder, I waited for any sign of his approach. I needed an edge...I needed the element of surprise.

A moment passed without any sign of Xaul. I began to wonder if I had actually given him the slip. Then he appeared again.

"You'll have to be quicker than that, boy," Xaul said, dropping from somewhere overhead and swinging his sword at my face. I ducked just in time to avoid the edge of his blade across my neck as it singed the stone behind me.

Igniting my Veritas, I stood up and blocked his next two blows, one high, another low. His third attack, however, caught me entirely by surprise because it didn't come from his sword at all.

Thrusting his palm forward, a blazing stream of fire shot out, knocking me square in the chest and sending me tumbling headlong into the shallow pool behind me.

What was that? I wondered as I lay in pain.

"Behold the true power of the Flame," Xaul boasted, as if he had heard my thoughts. "The power of the eternal Flame is mine to hold—mine to control."

"No power is given that does not come from the Author," I replied, citing the words of the Writ.

"Then let's see whom the Author has chosen," he said with a sneer before sending three more painful shots of fire into my body, pushing me back toward the chamber wall with each consecutive blast.

The bursts were hot and painful though they didn't burn like true fire. Traces trailed down my limbs and off my fingertips like an electrical current. I couldn't move—the shock of the blasts had numbed my ability to react.

"Hurts, doesn't it?" Xaul asked, stomping toward me. "But you'll get used to it. Who knows, you may even grow to like it before I'm through with you."

He made his way to where I lay and grabbed hold of my hair. Jerking my head up from the ground, he forced me to look into his face. His hood was pulled back now, revealing the extent of his blackened features for the first time.

"Look at me! Tell me, what do you see?" Xaul said.

His entire head was a dark charcoal, burned and gruesomely scarred beyond healing. It looked like the head of a match after it had been struck and consumed by its flame. His eyes, brilliant silver, seemed to be the only unscathed parts of his body.

"I see a murderer and a thief," I said weakly, too afraid to ask what had happened to him—to his face.

"Wrong! What you see are the scars of perfection, the skin of sacrifice. Something I wouldn't expect Codebearers to know anything about."

He released his grip on my hair and let my head drop to the stone floor. The impact was sharp and sudden, but the pain didn't come all at once; it came a moment later. A trace of warm blood ran down my forehead, accompanied by a throbbing headache.

"Purify through Pain…" I muttered to myself, recalling the inscription I had seen in the lower levels of the Xin monastery. His people, the Xin, must have subjected themselves to horrible torture in their misunderstanding of the Author and his ways. The prophecy of the Consuming Fire was clearly one of the centerpieces of their beliefs. Only, they had taken it to unimaginable extremes.

"That's right," Xaul smiled. "Pain is the only way to achieve perfection. We must earn the right to receive the fire. That is why you could never keep it. It belongs to one who is worthy of its power."

"No one is ever worthy to be chosen by the Author, Xaul," I said, applying pressure to my wound, "not on your own anyway. No amount of pain—nothing you do—can ever make you perfect. Only the Author can do that."

My words angered Xaul even more. After all, if what I said was true it would mean his entire life, all of his sacrifice, was a worthless cause.

"Keep your Codebearer lies to yourself. You call me a thief, but actually the Codebearers are the real thieves. You took what was rightfully ours. The Xin were once the keepers of the Flame long before your people found us. It was only after the Codebearers came that the eternal Flame and its power disappeared from our people completely. And THAT is why I will not rest until every Codebearer is dead."

Without warning, another steady stream of flames extended from Xaul's hand. This time, the flames lifted me off my feet and pinned me firmly against a wall, a full twelve inches above the ground. The pressure on my chest threatened to choke the life from me. I wanted to give in, to be taken into the Author's presence as I had been once before. Unable to move, I stared at the medallion on Xaul's chest. The three *V's* of the Author's mark seemed so meaningless now.

The Way of Truth and Life? What did it matter? The Author's Flame itself had granted unimaginable power to Xaul, the Codebearer's enemy. How could the Author allow it? Was it possible that Xaul had been right about the prophecy of the Flame? Was it really for the Xin all along and not for us?

With no sword, no energy and no hope, I was at the mercy of Xaul. No, I was at the mercy of the Author.

"Help me," I whispered, feeling a trail of blood slip warmly down my face.

Xaul released the Flame and let me fall to the rocky floor. I collapsed on the ground.

"Help you?" Xaul sneered as he approached with his ignited Veritas Sword. "Who's going to help you down here? Look around, Hunter, your Author doesn't care what happens. There's nothing left for you to believe in."

Believe. It was what Hope said to do. It was her last word before she died.

"You're wrong. I can still believe....I choose to hope," I said boldly.

As Xaul raised his sword to deal another blow, a sharp flash of light crossed the room, piercing his right arm and forcing him to drop his sword. Trista had apparently recovered consciousness and found her bow. Her arrow had found its mark.

Howling in pain, Xaul turned to confront his new threat. He started toward her, but the Flame in the medallion emerged once more and began to circle around Xaul. At first he was unsure, maybe even slightly amused at the ordeal, but as the Flame quickened its cycle it grew into a glowing inferno. Xaul's confidence quickly faded and he realized that something was wrong. He was trapped in the center of the whirlwind of fire.

Xaul covered his face and fell to his knees. When he looked up at me his eyes were burning with a fiery blaze.

"What's happening to me? It's not supposed to be this way. My eyes...my eyes...I can't see!" he shouted, but the Flame did not slow.

Trista ran quickly to my side, carrying my Veritas Sword with her.

"What did you do?" she asked.

"Nothing...I didn't do anything."

The flaming cyclone increased in brilliance until it was almost too bright to look at. Then a voice, or rather a series of voices all speaking as one, called out from the fire itself with final authority.

"Behold the fire that consumes!"

Xaul screamed as the fire engulfed him in its flames. When at last the whirlwind of fire thinned into only a sliver of light and disappeared completely, Xaul was gone with it.

Immediately, we scoured the place where Xaul had been, in search of Hope's medallion. I spotted it first, but it wasn't the same—the Flame that once lived within it was gone. The metal was cold and lifeless. As I pulled it back over my head, Trista discovered Xaul's Veritas on the ground.

"Hunter, look," she gasped, pointing to the base of the hilt where an etching of a name was engraved. "Caleb Brown. Isn't that your...?"

"My dad?" I questioned aloud.

"But if the sword was your father's, how did Xaul get it?"

"I...I don't know," I replied, confounded by the new revelation, but in my mind I couldn't shake the thought that Xaul had likely killed him.

I took the sword in my hands and held it close. It was the second item of importance I had recovered of my father's in Solandria. The mystery of his involvement with Xaul sparked new interest in what had become of him.

A woman's voice interrupted the silence.

"Well done, Hunter. You've made excellent progress today." It was the Emissary. She stepped out of the shadows and into the open, carrying the glass ball in front of her, covered by a silk cloth. "I've been observing you for quite some time and I must say, you're doing great. I like how you're wrestling with your ideas."

"What are *you* doing here? How do you know my name?" I asked, noticing for the first time that Boojum was perched on her shoulder. "And why do you have Boojum?"

Boojum waved back at the mention of his name; he was sitting beside another white snark, both of them munching on some kind of treat the woman had given him.

"The question isn't why am I here, or Boojum, or Trista for that matter. The question is why do you want us to be here?" she answered.

"I don't want you here at all," I challenged, igniting my sword in defense and holding it out in front of me.

"Oh, but you do," she said soothingly, "you really do."

As she spoke my mind grew clouded and fuzzy. I couldn't think straight.

"You see, Hunter," she continued, "Solandria IS you.... There is no one else here. No Author, no Shadow, no Flame...only you."

As she spoke, my vision began to blur and the walls of the room swayed back and forth as if we were underwater.

Trista grabbed my arm and started shaking it wildly to catch my attention. "Snap out of it, Hunter! What's happening to you?"

I wanted to "snap out of it" but I couldn't figure out how to.

"Don't listen to her," the Emissary added. "She's not real anyway. When all of this is over none of your friends will remember what happened. They are only here because you want them to be. You make the rules here, Hunter. This is your world; you are in control."

The Emissary pulled the sheet off of her glass ball, revealing what was hidden beneath it. I heard Trista scream but all I could do was stare at the head that inhabited the ball. This time, it wasn't Saris, but my own disembodied head staring back at me. Everything around the ball melted away into blackness. All that remained was the glass ball that held my head; then, with the drop of a cloth that too disappeared.

"Well, what do you think?" the Emissary asked, her voice still soothing but much more excited.

I opened my eyes and found myself reclined in a plush chair in the middle of Ms. Sheppard's Serenity Center. I had no idea how I had come to be there, or why I was there at all.

"I'm sorry," I said, "what did you just say?"

Ms. Sheppard scribbled some notes on her pad and repeated the question. "I was just asking if you agreed. I thought this time went pretty well. We made some great breakthroughs for our first session, don't you think?"

This time? What did she mean by this time? Was I dreaming now, or was I dreaming before?

Centered on the table between us was the glass ball, uncovered and empty.

"I...how come I'm here?" I asked.

"I wanted to meet with you, remember?" Ms. Sheppard said. "Your second vision really is extraordinary though, I must say. Many of the others I've worked with aren't able to let me in for quite some time. You, on the other hand, have excellent control over your vision."

"Second vision?" I said, sheepishly.

"Yes...well, you've had enough for one day. We'll pick up where we left off another time. You really should be getting home; I wouldn't want your parents to worry about you."

Ms. Sheppard stood promptly and motioned with her hand toward the green door that led out of her office. I stood as well, still uncertain of what was happening. Was everything I had done, everything I had seen, just a part of my so-called second vision?

"Wait a minute, did you say my parents are waiting for me?" I asked.

"Yes, they're waiting right outside the door. Go see for yourself."

I turned to face the door and wondered if it could really be true. Were my parents really together again? It didn't make sense, but I longed for it to be true. I started toward the door, but a voice in my mind stopped me before I reached it.

Don't believe it, Hunter, the voice whispered from somewhere distant. *You cannot trust your vision....* The voice was familiar—the voice of the Flame—the voice of Hope. My heart quickened at the sound.

Suddenly, I noticed a coat rack in the corner of the room. Hanging on the rack was a black robe, a cloak that looked every bit like the one my stalker had worn at school. All at once it hit me. Ms. Sheppard was the stalker and the Emissary—she wasn't a peacekeeper—she was Shadow.

I turned slowly back toward Ms. Sheppard, now keenly aware of the true danger she posed.

"What's wrong, Hunter?" she asked. "Is there something else I can do for you?"

I said nothing in return; instead, my eyes fell on the glass ball. All at once it made sense. The ball…that was how she was controlling me; it was how she had controlled Saris and Mr. Strickland as well. I clinched my fists tightly at the thought of her deception. My hand felt as if I had just gripped my Veritas Sword but looking down, I saw that my grip was empty. I couldn't see the hilt, but it felt as if it were there. The trouble was…which was true?

Believe, Hunter. You know which is true.

I squeezed the sword even tighter and stared into the glass ball.

"None of this is real, is it?" I questioned aloud, not letting my vision leave the ball.

"What do you mean it's not real? Of course it's real. Don't let your second vision control you. It's all in your mind…"

Looking closer, I noticed the reflection in the ball was not of this room…it was of a cave.

"No more doubts, no more lies," I said firmly as I raised the unseen sword overhead.

"Hunter, STOP!" Ms. Sheppard pleaded, but I didn't listen. I knew what I needed to do.

"*Via, Veritas, Vita*!" I shouted as I brought the sword down to crush the glass ball.

"Nooooooooooo!" Ms. Sheppard howled, but there was nothing she could do. The ball cracked and all at once the sword was visible in my hand once more. I looked up at Ms. Sheppard and surprisingly, her face began to crack with the ball. As pieces of the ball fell apart, so did Ms. Sheppard, revealing another face behind hers—the true enemy in all of it. Venator.

"You are still mine; you are still Shadow!" Venator burned with anger. "Forever Shadow..."

The room fell to pieces as the last edges of the glass ball dropped to the ground, leaving a faint sphere of scarlet light in its place. Then a powerful explosion of light hurled me and Venator through the shattered walls of the Serenity Center into the empty blackness beyond.

Chapter 28

To the Other Side of the Page

Darkness gave way to light and movement. My vision was still blurry, but the shapes of people began to form around me. There were voices calling my name.

"Hunter, are you okay?" one said.

"Talk to us, Hunter…can you hear us?"

When at last I could see again, I found I was surrounded by Trista, Sam and Rob in the garden chamber where Hope had once been.

"You're not dead!" Trista shouted, wrapping me in a hug.

I returned the embrace and then took Sam's hand as he helped lift me back to my feet.

"What happened to Ms. Shep….er…I mean the Emissary?"

"She was controlling you with that ball," Trista said, "trying to get you to walk through a green door that appeared out of nowhere.

I kept trying to call to you but you couldn't hear me. When you smashed the glass ball there was an explosion and she vanished."

I explained what I had seen and how the Emissary was Ms. Sheppard, who was really the stalker, and Venator, in disguise.

"What about you guys?" I asked, looking to Rob and Sam. "What happened with the dragon?"

"I killed it," Rob said proudly. "Expert swordsman Rob at your service."

"That he did," Sam added. "I would have never known there were a weak spot in her armor if he hadn't thrown his Veritas right at it. Come to think of it, how did ya know about that?"

Rob looked slightly embarrassed, "Actually, I didn't mean to throw the sword. It slipped, on accident."

"Well, it's a good thing," Sam explained. "I would have been a gonner fer sure. That dragon was right on top of me when you caught it in the back of the head like that."

Rob smiled at the compliment.

"Good job, Rob," I said. "I only wish I could have saved Hope. She's gone and so is the Flame.... We failed."

"Nonsense," Sam said. "We didn't fail 'cause it wasn't up ta us to begin with. It's up ta the Author to work things together. Whatever his plan is, you can be sure it's still unchanged."

"What do we do now?" I asked.

"Only one thing to do," Sam answered. "Wait and trust the Author will reveal what his purpose was in all of it. Come on, we better head back and share the news with Stoney. He'll be waiting."

We gathered our things and headed for the door. Before we stepped out into the tunnels, I looked back once more at the stone tower and the table where Hope had been kept. It was so cold and dark in here now...so hauntingly lifeless. I was going to miss her.

"Yours?" a scrawny voice called up from the ground. It was Boojum and his white snark friend. The two had apparently been abandoned when I defeated the Emissary.

"Yours, yours?" the other creature squeaked.

"No, not this time, Boojum," I answered. "I can't keep you.... I have to stay focused and...you wouldn't be good for me."

Boojum cocked his head with curiosity and stared back at me with his glowing blue eyes.

"No Boojum come?" he asked, pointing to my backpack.

"No," I said firmly. "Goodbye, Boojum."

I started to walk away and heard him in a weak voice say, "Bye-bye, Mine." There was a puff of smoke and he was gone, followed by the white snark as well.

When at last I stepped into the corridor beyond the room, the others were waiting. Together we retraced our path back toward the dragon's cave. When the exit was within site, Rob stopped in his tracks and held up his hand.

"Wait, do you hear that?" Rob asked.

"No, what is it?" Trista said.

"I don't know. It sounds like music coming from somewhere back there."

He turned around and pointed down an alternate tunnel that veered left when we had gone right before. It was a skinny tunnel that appeared to lead to a room lit by firelight.

"Maybe it's the Flame," I decided. "We should go check it out!"

"Fine by me," Sam said, "but that tunnel looks a might bit small fer my frame.... I'll have to wait here."

"We'll just take a quick look and be right back," I said.

The three of us stumbled through the tunnel and spotted the source of the light and noise. A ray of light poured in through a large crack in the stone wall, providing a window into the other side of the wall. Rob was the first to walk up and peek through to the other side.

"Do you see that? It's the Fair…in Destiny!" he shouted excitedly. "Amazing, I can even see the Sky Car ride right over there." He leaned against the stone wall as he said it and vanished in an instant, leaving Trista and me to speculate what had happened to him.

"Where did he go?" Trista wondered.

"No clue," I replied, "but I'm guessing it was the fair. Maybe this is the portal Rob found by accident years ago. That wall must be a rift between our worlds—a gateway back to the Veil."

"How can you be sure?" Trista asked a little nervously.

"I can't, but I don't think it's the work of the Shadow; let's go take a closer look."

We stepped up to where Rob had disappeared and took a look for ourselves. What we saw through the crack was clearly not what Rob had seen. There was no fair, no Sky Car of any kind. Instead, the gleaming rift displayed an image from outside our high school.

"School? What happened to the fair?" Trista asked.

"Maybe the Author has another place for us to be," I answered. "You ready to go through the gateway?"

"Wait, shouldn't we test it first?"

"How?"

"Throw something through and see if it makes it to the other side, okay?"

I conceded and retrieved a small rock, which I tossed through the rift. As soon as it hit the wall the rock disappeared and landed on the pavement of the school parking lot.

"Good enough for you?" I asked.

"I guess," she replied. "We have to go back sometime; I just didn't expect it to be now."

I took her by the hand and leaned into the wall. Before we knew it, we were walking across the cracked pavement of the school parking lot under a stormy night sky. We had crossed over to the Veil—back home in Destiny. Trista still carried her bow on her shoulder, and I still held my Veritas Sword in my hand. I was glad to have been able to bring it with me this time.

"I wonder what day it is?" Trista asked.

The school reader board lit up with the answer.

FREE FAIR ENTRY TONIGHT!!! SHOW YOUR ID!

"Wow, it's like we never left," Trista noticed. The reader board lit up again, this time with the time and date.

FRI 9TH-18TH ▪ 10:47 PM

"Okay, I was wrong…two hours late," she said.

"Not bad for a weeklong vacation," I joked.

"THAT was no vacation," she said with a slight chuckle, "but I have to admit, I'm glad I went. I'm just not so sure why we came back here."

She had a point. Why had we come here? I started to think about Hope again. There was something she said about the Veil, something important. What was it?

Bleep.

Trista's cell phone chirped in my backpack. She fished it out of the front pocket and read a text message aloud.

"It's from your sis, like an hour ago. She wants to know where we are. What should I say?"

I wasn't listening; I was staring at the reader board blankly, trying to recall what Hope had said about going back to the Veil and saving him from a fire. It didn't make sense.

The time on the reader board changed to 10:48 P.M. *Why did it sound so familiar?* Suddenly, my mind shot back to the encounter with Gabby. I recalled the newspaper headline.

TEEN BOY KILLED IN SCHOOL BLAZE.

The article had mentioned the school fire was reported at 10:48 tonight—the fire Cranton died in.

"That's it! Go back to the Veil and save him…from the fire!" I said out loud.

"You want me to say what?" Trista asked.

"No, it's what Hope told me to do; Cranton's in the school and he's in trouble. There's going to be a fire. Call 911! Get someone here now!" I started running for the doors as Trista called out after me.

"Where are you going? Are you sure there's a fire? It doesn't look like there's a fire," she replied.

Before I could reply, two of Cranton's friends burst out of the front doors, gasping for air and stumbling down the steps. A trail of black smoke wafted out after them; then cut short as the hall doors shut behind them. Trista started dialing for help.

"Where's Cranton?" I yelled at one of his friends as they ran off, hoping not to be caught.

I pulled on the front doors, but they had locked behind the two as they escaped. Using the hilt of my Veritas Sword, I broke the lower half of the glass door and crawled into the hall.

Smoke was swirling across the ceiling like a cloud overhead, growing thicker by the minute. I covered my mouth with my arm and headed toward what seemed to be the source. The door to the basement was swung wide open and even from the top of the stairs I could see the flickering light of flames reflecting off the walls.

"Cranton!" I yelled down. "Cranton, can you hear me?"

I thought I heard a muffled moan. I darted down the stairs toward the flames, going against every instinct in my body. The flames were coming from several toppled shelves full of cleaning solutions, all of which had spilled, mixing into a deadly concoction of chemical fuel for the fire.

Cranton was trapped under one of the shelves. The fire from the first shelf was already spreading to the base of the one that trapped him. There was a pool of blood under his head and a large gash on his forehead.

"I'm stuck," Cranton cried out, pulling at his leg, trying to get away from the approaching flames.

"Hang on, I'm coming!" I shouted through my sleeve, which now covered my nose.

At first I tried to lift the shelf unit, but it was weighed down by the other shelves that had fallen like dominos on top of each other. It was no use, the shelves were too heavy. I raised my Veritas Sword and decided to cut him free.

"Hold still!" I shouted to Cranton as I ignited the blade and sliced through the shelf on either side of his foot.

"Here, take my hand!" I offered, reaching out to help him up.

"What are you doing here?" he said, shocked to see me and not his friends standing around him.

"I'm here to save you," I answered. "Now take my hand!"

"I don't need your help, I can…do it…myself," Cranton claimed, trying to stand up but finding his ankle couldn't hold his weight.

"Hang on, you're hurt pretty bad. You have to let me help you." I slung his arm over my shoulder and hoisted him to his feet.

"Let's get out of here already!" Cranton said in a panic. Before we could move, the fire reached another mixture of chemicals and erupted in a massive explosion of flames. Bright orange tongues of fire licked the ceiling panels and started to spread through the room. Just like that the path back to the stairs was cut off by a new trail of fire.

We were trapped. The smoke that filled the room had already begun to sting my eyes. With Cranton leaning on my arm, I could no longer cover my nose to keep from inhaling the smoke. If we didn't get out now, it would choke the breath from our lungs and we would die in the blaze.

Then, a miracle…

"Hunter, over here," a girl's voice called out from across the room. I squinted and wiped the sweat from my eyes. When I spotted her at last, I could hardly believe what I saw. She stood in the middle of the flames, unscathed by the fire and entirely unafraid. Her soft face and warm brown eyes calmed my nerves instantly. I was filled with a sudden, unexplainable peace. It was Hope.

"It's you? But how? I thought you were gone?"

"I've been rewritten by the Author. The seven were marked and I've come to rescue you, Hunter," she said.

I could hardly believe it; Hope was alive! Then, to my surprise, she changed form. No longer was she merely standing *in* the flames anymore—Hope *became* the flames. Her flickering form danced across the floor, guiding the fire away. The flames pulled back like a curtain, revealing a narrow path to the base of the stairs.

"Go!" Hope commanded. *"Now!"*

With no time to lose I led the way, pulling Cranton through the flames, up the stairs and down the hall to safety. As we stumbled out the front doors of the school, I turned back to look for Hope but she was gone.

"Never alone," her voice whispered.

Stumbling down the front steps, we were greeted by the distant sound of emergency vehicles heading our way. Help was coming. Cranton and I collapsed on the front lawn, waiting to be rescued.

"Why did you do it?" Cranton asked weakly. His face was pale and he looked as if he might pass out again. "Why did you save me? I've never been nice to you."

"Because it's what the Author would want," I answered. "I believe he has a purpose for everyone, Cranton…even you."

The words were heartfelt and true. My adventure in Solandria had helped me to see something different in Cranton. He wasn't just a boy, he was somebody's grandson. He wasn't just my enemy, he was a person with a troubled past and his own share of pain. And, more importantly, he was in my life for a reason.

"That's what my grandfather used to say," he said quietly, holding back tears. "I just never believed him."

"It's never too late to start believing," I said, putting my arm on his shoulder to comfort him. The next thing I knew, Trista was rushing to our side. She threw her arms around me in a frantic hug.

"You made it!" said Trista. "I'm so glad you're safe. You were gone so long I started to worry that you wouldn't make it."

"We had help," I said excitedly. "We weren't alone in there; Hope is alive!"

I explained what had happened, how Hope had appeared in the flames and how she had led us out safely. Trista took it all in without a word and then began to process out loud what I had just said. "She told you that the seven were marked?" Trista asked.

"Yes, but we never found the seventh mark, did we?" I counted out, "Petrov, Philan, Sam, Stoney, Hope and you. That's only six."

"Right, so who was the seventh?" Trista asked.

I shrugged my shoulders.

"The seventh of seven only Fire can name," I repeated the prophecy aloud.

"Maybe that's the point," she decided. "Maybe we were never

meant to find the seventh person. I think the Author alone knows who it was. He meant for it to be a secret."

Our thoughts were interrupted as a pair of emergency vehicles raced into the school parking lot and a team of medics rushed to our sides. Within moments they began loading Cranton and me onto stretchers and wheeling us into our respective vehicles. Cranton was taken in an ambulance while I was loaded into the back of a white van with flashing red lights. Trista promised to call Emily and meet us at the hospital as soon as she could.

The back doors of the van slammed shut, locking me inside, but I wasn't alone. Two medics hovered over me in the back of the van. One was a man seated beside me, the other a woman, seated near my head. They were both dressed in official looking blue dress shirts and matching blue pants. As the van pulled away, the female medic began checking me over for burns.

"Are you Hunter Brown?" the man prodded, as he placed a mask over my face.

"Yeah," I answered, a bit surprised they already knew my name.

"He's one of them alright," the woman interrupted, pointing to my collarbone, "He's got the mark."

Her words caught me by surprise.

Mark? What mark? I wondered.

"Is everything okay?" I asked.

"Don't worry about it," she assured me. "We know just how to take care of your kind."

"My kind…what do you mean my kind. Ouch! What are you doing?" A sharp sting in my thigh drew my attention to a large needle the man had jabbed in my leg. I wanted to ask him what it was for, but my mind began to wander and my body relaxed. I struggled to focus my vision on the medics seated beside me. As my mind grew hazy, my vision began to change. That's when I saw their eyes were hollow, empty and as black as night.

These were no medics. Something was wrong.

My eyes rolled back and my heavy eyelids began to droop shut. The last thing I heard was the man's voice talking to someone on his cell phone.

"We found another one. Prepare the chamber."